Can't Stop Lovin' You

Also by Lynnette Austin

The Maverick Junction series

Somebody Like You

Nearest Thing to Heaven

Can't Stop Lovin' You

LYNNETTE AUSTIN

New York Boston

This book is a work of fiction. Names, characters, places, and incidents are the product of the author's imagination or are used fictitiously. Any resemblance to actual events, locales, or persons, living or dead, is coincidental.

Forever Yours
Hachette Book Group
237 Park Avenue
New York, NY 10017
hachettebookgroup.com
twitter.com/foreverromance

First published as an ebook and as a print on demand: February 2014

Forever Yours is an imprint of Grand Central Publishing.
The Forever Yours name and logo are trademarks of Hachette Book Group, Inc.

ISBN: 978-1-4555-2839-4 (ebook edition)
ISBN: 978-1-4555-7577-0 (print on demand edition)

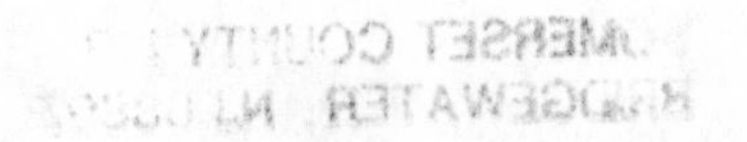

To Deb Kribbs. Thanks for the Dairy Queen trips.

And to Dave—the love and light of my life.

Acknowledgments

Starting a new story is like beginning a trip to somewhere you've never been. It's exciting and just a little scary. Along the way, though, are markers and signposts—yes, and that blessed GPS—to help. I'd like to thank some of those who encouraged me as I found my way from the first sentence to the last of *Can't Stop Lovin' You*.

I want to give a big shout-out to Southwest Florida Romance Writers. This group trumps any and all, and it's through this writers group that I've met some of the most important people in my life, some of my very best friends. Support, education, friendship, and opportunity—you've provided it all.

Thanks to my Waffle Wednesday gals—Jo Hiner, Patti Spicer, and Maria Jones—for keeping me steady and stable. According to Maria, I'm eccentric. What a wonderful euphemism. ☺ We all know I border on crazy—especially near deadline. Patti scours the stores with me, looking for that just-right table covering for a book signing, that perfect trip to Curaçao, and...sigh...she even brings me horseshoes. And Jo—always there for me—no matter how big or small the crisis or celebration. During walks on the beach, she listened as I plotted my very first book. How lucky I am to have you all in my life. I couldn't do any of this without you, friends.

To my critique partners, Diane O'Key and Joyce Henderson, I owe a huge debt of gratitude. We lost Joyce near the beginning of this book, and so our Three Musketeers became two. Not a day goes by that Joyce isn't in my thoughts and in my heart. I miss her friendship and her wisdom beyond words.

To Barbara Bent for traipsing through the garment district in NYC with me as I did research for Maggie and Brawley's story and for so much more.

A huge thank you to my incredible editor, Lauren Plude, for always knowing exactly what is needed to make the story that much better, and to Morgan Doremus, my awesome publicist. The same thanks extends to all the other wonderful, hard-working people at Grand Central Publishing. You make my dreams come true; you make magic happen.

Nicole Resciniti, my agent. How do I thank you enough for giving me this opportunity to share my stories? You always go above and beyond, and it's oh so appreciated.

Then, there's Dave. My other half. The voice of reason. Of sanity. God surely did smile on me the day he brought you into my life.

Last, but certainly not least, a heartfelt thanks to all who pick up my books and read my stories. You are appreciated more than you can know.

Welcome back to Maverick Junction!

Thanks so much for stopping by my small Texas town again, this time for Maggie and Brawley's story. Talk about two people at cross purposes. Their relationship goes back to first grade and is as fiery as Maggie's red hair.

When I started *Somebody Like You*, the first book of this series, I had no idea how real this fictional town would become to me. I swear I've walked that Main Street and can all but taste Bubba's barbecue. I hope once you've shared time with Annie and Cash, Sophie and Ty, and Maggie and Brawley, you'll feel the same.

I've never lived in Texas, but I did live in Wyoming for nearly twenty years, and can I just say there's nothing that beats a cowboy, whether he's from Wyoming, Texas, or parts in between. Cowboys are strong and confident, and they're not afraid of equally strong women. Instead, they celebrate them. Cowboys honor old-fashioned values. They stand for their country and its flag, say yes, ma'am and no, sir, and love their mamas and daddies. They know how to treat their women and aren't afraid of emotion, whether it's anger or passion. They're a throwback to a slower, easier time but with a kick-ass edge, and they're irresistible in worn jeans, cowboy boots, and Stetsons.

So get comfy, pour yourself a big old glass of iced tea or a cup of hot coffee, and saddle up for Maggie and Brawley's story.

I'd love to hear from you!

Lynnette

www.authorlynnetteaustin.com

Can't Stop Lovin' You

Chapter One

Brawley Odell figured his life wouldn't be worth one plug nickel the second he stepped foot inside Maggie's shop. Too damn bad. He hadn't driven the thirty miles from Maverick Junction to back out now. He was goin' in.

After all this time, he'd come home...and she was leaving.

He grasped the brass knob and shoulder-butted the oak door. It flew open, the bell overhead jangling. Maggie Sullivan, all that gorgeous red hair scooped into a jumbled mass, stood dead center in the room. Dressed in a skirt and top the color of a forest at twilight, she held a fuzzy sweater up in front of her like a shield. Those amazing green eyes widened as he stormed in.

"We need to talk." He ignored the woman at the back of the store who flipped through a rack of tops.

"What the—?"

He held up a hand. "Don't speak. Not yet."

Her mouth opened, then closed.

Anger boiled in him, but he needed to find some modicum of control. Taking a deep breath, he held it for the count of ten, then slowly released it. "Did you plan on telling me?"

Her eyes narrowed, but she said nothing.

"You're invited to New York City for a showing of your new line, and you don't share that with me? I have to learn about it second-hand?"

"Last I heard this wasn't about you, Brawley. In fact, my life, my business has absolutely nothing to do with you."

His jaw clenched. "Anything that affects you is my business, Mags."

She snorted. "Get real, Odell. You gave up any and all rights years ago." Her head tilted. "Why are you even interested? You want to attend so you can show off your latest Dallas Cowboy cheerleader? Maybe order her trousseau?"

He shot her a deadly look, one that had made grown men back away.

Not Maggie. She actually took a couple steps toward him. The woman had no survival instincts. Another reason she had no business heading off to New York alone.

She tapped a scarlet-tipped finger on her chin. "Oh, that's right. There'd be no trousseau for your honey, would there? Maybe a weekend-fling outfit for your date *du jour*? A one-night-stand set of lacy lingerie."

"Shut up, Maggie."

"Make me." Her eyes flashed.

This time the look in his eyes must have warned her she'd treaded too close to the edge. She stepped back.

"You challenging me, Maggie?"

When she wet her lips, his gaze dropped to her mouth, followed the tip of her pink tongue as it darted out.

"Only one way I could ever get you quiet," he said.

Her hand shot up. "Don't even think about it."

"No thought required. Been wanting to do this a long time now." He closed the distance between them and dropped his mouth to hers. Fire. Smoke. Hell, a full-out volcanic eruption.

The dressing room door opened. Brawley dragged his lips from Maggie's.

"Maggie, honey, this is fantastic! I'd like— Oh." Her customer stared at the two of them. At the friend who, now sitting on the love seat, waited for her while watching the show he and Maggie had put on. From the expression on her face and the quiet little sounds she made, Brawley assumed she'd enjoyed it a whole hell of a lot.

Maggie pushed him away as if burned.

But if what he'd just felt was mutual—and from the glazed expression on her face, it had been—the kiss had short-circuited more than a few wires for her, too.

Still, that famous temper flared.

"Stella, run and get the sheriff for me. Tell Pete an idiot has come into the shop and I'm being assaulted."

Brawley frowned, then turned his megawatt smile on the women. Two could play this game. "A little lovers' spat here, ladies. Sorry to make you a party to it. I should have waited till Maggie locked up for the day." He tipped his chin toward her. "But, hey, isn't she lovely? Hard to stay away till closing time."

A quiet growl erupted from Maggie.

"As much as I hate to interrupt your shopping spree in Maggie's wonderful little shop," he continued, "how 'bout you take a short break? Run on over to the Cowboy Grill and put your feet up. Tell Ollie that Brawley Odell sent you. Have a coffee or iced tea on me. Maybe a piece of his lemon meringue pie. My treat. Y'all order whatever you like. Give us a few minutes."

"No! Don't go anywhere." Maggie rounded on Brawley. "You can't come in here and chase my customers away."

Instead of answering, Brawley walked to the front door and held it open. Hesitantly, throwing speculative glances at each other, the two women hung their items on the end of a rack and walked out the door, crossing the street to Ollie's.

The door had barely closed behind them when Maggie stamped her foot. "If I had Grandpa's shotgun right now, Brawley Odell, you'd be picking lead out of your useless, no-good hide."

"My lucky day, I guess."

"Ohhh! You think that attitude is going to do what? Make me apologize to you? I don't think so. If that's what you've come for, you might as well follow my customers right out of here."

"You hurt me, Mags." Though he kept his tone flippant, it was the honest-to-God's truth. A truth he hadn't meant to voice out loud. But there it was. "How could you make such an important decision, have something so monumental happen, and not tell me?"

"Hmmm. Could it be because you shut me out of *your* life years ago?"

"I didn't."

"That's a matter of semantics." She shrugged. "Why does it matter to you where I live? You don't live here, either, not in Lone Tree *or* Maverick Junction."

"That's where you're wrong. I rented Dottie Willis's apartment today. Now that Sophie and Ty are married, the place is empty again. In fact, my new landlady is the one who told me you're leaving."

"You're moving back to Maverick Junction?" She looked like a five-year-old who'd just learned there is no Santa Claus. "I don't remember you telling me about this."

"I'm telling you now."

"I see." Her eyes narrowed. "So it's okay for you to make decisions and tell me about them afterward. I, on the other hand, have to report to you when I'm considering a change? Get your approval?"

"I never said that."

"Sure you did. When did you decide all this?"

"I've been kicking it around for a bit now."

"You're taking over Doc Gibson's practice."

He nodded.

"I knew you'd been helping him out, but—" She spread her hands. "Gramps doesn't know yet."

"About your line?"

"Oh, he knows about that, but not..."

"The fact you're moving to New York."

"Yes."

"Don't you think it would be better if he found out from you?"

She wrung her hands. "I can't find the right words. I don't want to hurt him. And I hate to leave him alone."

"Then don't."

"Oh, Brawley, I've wanted this as long as I can remember. This is my dream."

"I thought this shop was." His gaze wandered over the space she'd created from a dilapidated storefront that had seen better days. He knew for a fact she'd been the one to paint that soft pink on the walls, the chocolate brown on the crown molding and chair rail she'd installed. She'd hung the lace curtains at the windows, stenciled her name on the glass. In the middle of this butt-ugly, one-horse town, Maggie had created a veritable oasis.

The place even smelled like her. Feminine. Sexy. Secretive. Made him think of nights spent in a woman's arms. Of long-ago nights in *this* fiery redhead's arms.

"New York's a big city," he said.

"Really?" She pulled an innocent face. "I didn't know that."

He refused to rise to the bait, so he said nothing.

"Dallas isn't?" she asked.

"Isn't what?"

"A big city. Try to stay focused, Brawley."

Brows furrowed, he thumbed back his hat brim. "What does that have to do with anything?"

She crossed to the jewelry counter and leaned against it. "Seems to me you ran off to Dallas and left everything and everyone behind."

"This isn't about you and me, Maggie."

"No?"

"No."

"Good to know. I thought maybe we were in the middle of a repeat performance from ten years ago. You know, the one where you decide my future for me. The one where I have no input whatsoever."

"I handled that night badly. I'll admit it. But everything I did, I did for the right reasons."

"According to you."

"Yes, according to me."

A fleeting expression crossed her face. Not anger. Sorrow? But it was gone so quickly, he couldn't read it.

"So you're moving home," she said. "Are you planning to bring a playmate along? One of your cheerleaders, maybe? Have you found one who'll put up with Maverick Junction's small-town way of life?"

"I've come home to work. To live."

"And I'm going to New York to work…and live," she countered. "Don't let the door hit that cute tush on the way out."

She turned on those sexy-as-sin heels and walked into her back room, leaving him standing there—alone. Maggie didn't intentionally swing those hips, didn't intentionally make a man drool whether she was coming or going. She simply had that effect on men. She was Maggie. It was part of her DNA.

He took two steps to follow. Stopped. A wise man circled the wagons and regrouped before a second attack. He considered himself wise. Damned wise.

The bell over the door tinkled as he left. He supposed Maggie would take it as the white flag of surrender. She could safely come out of hiding.

As long as he was in Lone Tree, he might as well have a late breakfast. At the same time, he could give the ladies an all-clear and send them back to Maggie's.

He'd provided the gossips with plenty of ammunition for one morning.

He grinned. *I have a cute tush?*

* * *

The busybodies were on their feet before Ollie's door had closed behind him. Like vultures, they smelled fresh fodder.

Brawley held the door for them. Doffing his hat as they passed, he said, "Have a nice day, ladies."

"Oh, we will," one of them answered before hustling across the street.

"I see you survived." Ollie, wearing an egg-stained apron, set a steaming mug of black coffee in front of Brawley when he straddled a stool at the counter.

"Depends on your definition of survival. I made it out alive. Didn't gain a thing."

"Trying to talk her out of leaving us?"

Brawley scowled. "Did everybody but me know about this?"

"Not her grandpa. Don't think she's told him yet. Made us all promise to keep it a secret."

"Some secret."

"Humph." Ollie rolled his linebacker shoulders and lifted his chin in the direction the women had taken. "Ladies said you and Maggie were having yourselves a real knock-out, drag-down tussle."

"The woman's got a temper."

"And you don't?"

Brawley ignored Ollie's question and blew on his coffee. Taking a sip, he scalded his tongue and set the cup back on the counter. "It matches all that fierce red hair." Hair he missed running his fingers through. Hair he missed having the right to touch. But then, he'd chosen to give that up years ago.

Did he really want to kick up all these feelings? Had they ever truly gone to sleep? For either of them?

Ollie was watching him closely. "And a mouth to match," he finally said.

"Oh, yeah." Brawley didn't even want to think about her mouth. Those full lips. The luscious taste of her. He readjusted himself on the stool, instantly uncomfortable in his snug jeans.

"How about you throw a big old steak on the grill along with a couple eggs?"

"You got it. Home fries?"

"The works." He might as well satisfy one appetite.

Chapter Two

Maggie stepped out of the back room. Her shop, her lovely shop, was empty. Yet she still felt Brawley's presence. So masculine in this feminine space. So devastatingly handsome in his worn jeans and scuffed boots, that Stetson tipped low.

And lest she forget it—so dangerous. Brawley Odell had single-handedly ended her naïveté, her belief in knights in shining armor and Prince Charmings. At least when it came to *her* love life.

Now, by moving back to Maverick Junction, he threatened her dreams of a new life in the Big Apple. How many nights had she lain awake, praying for him to come home? To come back to her. But now? Fate was, indeed, a cruel mistress.

Her eighteen-year-old self had been putty in his hands. One touch, one kiss, and reason left her. She'd been totally defenseless when it came to him.

But she wasn't eighteen anymore. Once burned, twice learned. And, boy, had she learned. She had to hang tough. Could not give in.

Walking to the stereo system, she hit play and smiled when Luke Bryan's peppy new country song filled the room. Sauntering over to the love seat she'd painstakingly reupholstered in a beautiful floral pattern, she flopped down. Brawley had a way of leaving her feeling as though she'd just weathered a Texas tornado. When the door flew open and he'd thundered in, her heart had stuttered. The man did that to her. Always had, and she was deathly afraid he always would.

But that didn't mean she liked him. She didn't. Not anymore. They shared friends, and because of them she couldn't totally avoid him. But the less time spent near him, the better.

He'd hurt her and would again if she let him get a boot in the door. She wouldn't. Nope, when it came to that cowboy, she'd bolted and padlocked her heart—and thrown away the key.

At fourteen, she'd decided to marry him someday. And at fifteen and sixteen and seventeen and eighteen she stood by that decision. Five years. Long enough for her dreams of Brawley Odell to seriously settle into her heart and take up permanent residence. She'd figured by now they'd have three or four mini-thems tearing around their house. Yeah, she'd pictured the goofy, lovable dog, the white-picket fence. The whole shebang.

Big dreams.

Big heartbreak.

Now she was honest enough to admit she'd set herself up for it. But damn him, he'd helped her.

It had almost killed her when he'd headed off to Texas A&M and left her behind in Maverick Junction to finish high school. But that first semester, he'd burned up the road between college and home.

Then one Thursday morning he'd phoned to tell her to expect him the next evening; they needed to talk. Her mom and dad were in San Antonio on business and would be gone till Monday. She and Brawley would have the house to themselves.

She played hooky Friday and fixed dinner for them, set out candles, and wore her best dress. Her nails shone from a fresh manicure.

When he slipped her engagement ring on her finger, she wanted everything to be perfect. This would be the night he proposed. They'd get married, and she'd live in College Station with him while he finished school.

What a fool.

He hadn't proposed.

The dinner sat uneaten; the candles burned to a nub.

Brawley hadn't stayed more than ten minutes. He hadn't even gone inside with her. His mouth set in the familiar tight line that said he'd made up his mind, he'd ended her fantasies.

There on the front porch, the sun riding low, he told her they needed to concentrate on their futures. He had eight years of school ahead of him, and he wanted her to go to the design school she'd talked about, not wait in Maverick Junction for him.

When he left, he kissed her on the forehead and wished her well. Remembering it now, Maggie's anger rose to the surface. Nothing she'd said could change his decision. They were finished, no longer a couple. Brawley Odell had spoken, and apparently his word was law. How had she missed this autocratic streak in him?

The rest of that night and the next day were a blur. Her world had shattered. She couldn't sleep, couldn't eat. Sprawled on the sofa, she watched the sun set, then rise again. How could she face life without Brawley? She loved him. No. She hated him and would as long as she lived. If only...

And then, Cash Hardeman, friends with both her and Brawley for as long as she could remember, stopped by. Concerned, Brawley had asked him to check on her. Cash had cleared the table of last night's dinner, done the dishes, then held her while she cried.

Absolutely certain life could get no worse, a month later she'd faced the fact that it actually could.

Maggie shook herself and moved across the shop to tidy a display of evening bags. She glanced across the street and wondered if her customers would be back or if they were grilling Ollie about her and Brawley.

She'd been young and foolish because through everything, she'd told herself Brawley would be back. That she'd get a phone call from him telling her how much he missed her. That there'd be a knock on the front door and he'd be standing there, waiting to sweep her off her feet and make that dream of happily-ever-after come true.

Eventually, though, she'd admitted none of that would happen. Reflecting on her relationship with Brawley, she realized there'd never been any promises spoken. They'd all been in her mind. In her heart.

So she'd kicked the lout out of her heart. Had cleaned house and trashed those dreams. She'd moved on, made new plans, and started her own business. A business that now, thanks in large part to Annelise, Cash's wife, had grown beyond her wildest expectations.

Smiling, Maggie settled into one of the upholstered chairs.

Annelise Montjoy Hardeman, wealthy as the legendary King Midas, had worn one of her designs to a fund-raiser and then even more spectacular, Annelise had chosen Maggie to design a wedding gown for her big day, a day covered worldwide by every newspaper, magazine, and TV station. One thing led to another and now, in one short month, she'd show her fall line at a huge, honest-to-God New York City fashion show. They'd opted for an off-season showing rather than wait another half-year for September Fashion Week.

She pinched herself, still unable to believe it was all true.

The door opened and she started, sitting bolt upright.

Stella and her friend. Maggie sighed. Her customers were back, their eyes burning with unanswered questions and the excitement of having been part of the little drama here in her shop. Well, she thought, pushing up her sleeves, she didn't intend to feed the mill.

Retrieving the dress Stella had hung on the rack before she left, Maggie asked, "How'd this fit?"

And it was back to business as usual.

* * *

Maggie stopped by Ollie's at the end of the day to pick up a sweet tea for the ride home. While she waited at the counter, she called her grandfather to see if he wanted anything.

She didn't regret for a minute having left Maverick Junction to move in with her widowed grandpa in Lone Tree. It had been good for both of them. But she missed her folks, missed seeing them every day. She missed her friends. Still, this had been the right thing to do—and in under an hour she could be back with everybody.

"Hey, Pops," she said when he answered. "What's up?"

"You comin' home soon?"

"I'm on my way. Before I leave town, I thought I'd check to see if you need anything."

"Nope. Just you. Your mom called. We're meeting her and your dad at Bubba's Roadhouse for dinner."

"Tonight?"

"Yep."

"Why didn't she call me?"

"Guess you'd need to ask her that."

Maggie sighed. After the morning she'd had, she wanted nothing more than to go home, climb into her pajamas, and veg out. Not gonna happen.

"If we plan to make it on time," her grandfather continued, "you'd better get a move on."

"Are you ready?"

"Yep."

"All right. I'll need two minutes to change, then we can hit the road." She hung up, and Ollie handed her the go-cup of tea. "Thanks, Ollie. Gotta run."

When Ollie didn't remove his hand, she met his eyes.

"You need to tell him."

Maggie's stomach fell. "I know."

"Lots of people are in on the fact you're heading off to New York. It's not a secret anymore. Only a matter of time till somebody lets the horse out of the chute. If your grandpa finds out from one of them, it'll go down a whole lot harder."

She nodded. "It's tough, though, you know? He'll be alone again."

Ollie's dark eyes twinkled. "You might be surprised."

"What's that supposed to mean?"

He swiped at the counter with a white bar cloth. "Just sayin'."

"Do you know something I don't?"

He laughed. "At my age, I'd better. Seriously, though, you need to tell him. The sooner, the better."

"I will."

* * *

Hands on his hips, Stetson pushed back on his head, Brawley stood in the middle of his new home and took in the Tiffany blue walls, the girlie lights, the frou-frou. It had to go. All of it. It might have worked for Annie, then Sophie, but it sure as hell didn't work for him. One more night here and he'd have to have his testosterone levels checked 'cause they were bound to cry uncle and start jumping ship surrounded by all this female nonsense.

He'd slap something neutral on the walls. Bring in his leather sofa, a few pieces of his Native American pottery, a couple of the paintings he'd bought at the arts and craft fairs, and it would do.

He peeked into the bathroom and checked out the huge claw-foot tub. It might be fun to play in—and damned if Maggie's face and curvaceous body didn't jump into his brain—but he needed a shower. He worked too hard to be satisfied with baths. The plumbing in Dottie's hundred-year-old house was bound to be a nightmare, though. Not something he wanted to get into, especially since the small, second-story apartment was a temporary landing pad.

Maybe he could do something about a shower over at the clinic.

His stuff was in storage, ready to head to Maverick Junction as soon as he gave the word. He'd spent last week packing up and meeting with the movers. Damned if he knew whether or not he'd made the right decision, but it felt good, coming home after over a decade away.

Doc Gibson, the only vet within a fifty-mile radius, had finally called it quits, and Brawley had decided to take over his practice. He'd be glad to be back doing the work he'd trained for.

In Dallas he'd worked with pampered pets and their even more pampered owners, never really sure he was making much of a difference. Here he'd be working with ranchers and their livestock, working with the pets of people he knew and cared about.

And there was the rub. The double-edged sword. He'd know everybody who came in to see him. They'd know him. Gone was the anonymity he'd enjoyed. The freedom to come and go as he pleased. To do whatever the hell he wanted.

Despite the fact he'd turned thirty on his last birthday, he'd be back to answering to his parents. Back to the obligatory Sunday dinners with his family.

Back to being able to pick up the phone and get in touch with his best buds over a beer. He smiled. And that's exactly what he intended to do. Right now. Pulling his phone from his hip pocket, he hit Cash's number before he remembered his pal, now married, might not be free to come out and play. Ty had tied the knot, too, a month ago. They'd married cousins. Go figure.

Annie answered. "Hey, Brawley. How's my second-favorite cowboy?"

"Better now that I'm talking to you, beautiful. Is Cash around?"

"He'll be with you in a second. I've got him on a ladder in the closet arranging some purses for me."

Brawley winced. "You think I can borrow him after he finishes? I'd like to meet him at the clinic. Get his take on a couple changes I'm considering."

"Absolutely," she said. "In fact, he's due for a little R-and-R time. Maybe when you're done, the two of you can stop at Bubba's and catch up."

"Annie, darlin', you're as close to perfect as God ever made. Sure you don't want to swap out guys?"

Her laughter came quick and easy. "I love you, Brawley, but I think I'll stay with what I've got."

"Hey, you makin' time with my girl?" Cash, Brawley's friend since first grade, came on the line.

"Figured she might have come to her senses by now," Brawley said. "Never hurts to try."

"Oh, I don't know about that. I've been known to deck men for a lot less."

Brawley laughed. "Yeah, you have. Most of the time, though, I've had to step in and save your sorry ass."

"In your dreams. So, what's up?"

* * *

The two met outside the veterinary clinic that had been Doc Gibson's for the last forty or fifty years. After unlocking the door, Brawley hit the light switch. Barking dogs and howling cats greeted them.

He moved into the side room and visited each one of the overnighters. Then he waved Cash back to where Doc had his office.

"I'd like to gut this whole area. Make a new, up-to-date office space, add some built-in bookcases, and bring the electrical wiring into this century." He opened the door that led into a small, private, and very antiquated bath. "There's a storage closet next to this. Don't need it. Figure if we knock down the wall between, I might be able to add a shower. I'd like to be able to clean up here at the end of the day rather than go home to a bath."

"You don't like the old claw-foot in Dottie's apartment?"

"I do—for lounging. Not for washing away a day's worth of work, though."

"Annie and I had some good times in that—"

Brawley stuck his fingers in his ears. "Too much information, pal."

Cash chuckled. "Shame you don't have somebody to share it with. You might change your mind."

"You're such a newlywed."

"I am that, and I'm enjoying it immensely."

"Bragging SOB."

"Not bragging. Simply telling it like it is." Before Brawley could respond, Cash said, "I think all this is very manageable. Let's run to Bubba's and draw up some plans over a beer. Maybe have Ty meet us there. Since he and I both did most of the work on our houses, we should be able to handle the renovations ourselves. Most of them anyway."

Cash slung an arm around Brawley's shoulder. "Good to have you back."

"Tell Maggie that."

"Different rodeo, buddy."

"You know she's leaving."

"Yep."

"Shit. Everybody but me." He pulled out his cell and called Ty, who took a pass. His triplets were in a play at their preschool.

On the drive to Bubba's, Brawley and Cash tossed around the chances of the Rangers having a good season, the reasons the Cowboys hadn't had one, Cash's ranch, and Brawley's new business.

Just like old times. A night out with his best pal. Finally, he was in the driver's seat, figuratively and literally. Nothing could upset him tonight.

Chapter Three

Hurt Brawley Odell?

What a bunch of bull. How did you hurt a man who had no heart?

For the briefest instant, Maggie's conscience threatened. None too gently, she nudged it away.

Still, her traitorous mind flashed back to that awful night before last Christmas. It had been Brawley who'd decided to stop at Sophie's with a tag for her cat, who'd walked in on her and the creep from Chicago who'd broken into her apartment. While Ty soothed Sophie, Brawley had nailed plywood over her broken window and swept up the glass. Sophie had said that beneath his golden tan, Brawley had been nearly as pale and white-lipped as she had. Still, he'd done what needed doing.

She'd watched him care for Doc Gibson's four-legged patients, his compassion almost heartbreaking at times. He talked quietly to them, soothed them and their worried owners.

So, obviously, somewhere in that tanned, muscled chest there actually was a warm, beating heart. Too bad it turned to stone whenever she was involved.

It hadn't always. Images of them wrapped in each other's arms in the back seat of his dad's Chevy, lying together in a field of bluebonnets under the hot Texas sun, playing down at the swimming hole. They'd been inseparable. Maybe they'd been too intense. Like anything else that hot, the relationship had burned itself out.

For him, anyway.

Mentally rearranging tonight's plans, adjusting from dreams of a quiet evening reading to a boisterous night at Bubba's with the whole family, she pulled into the drive of her grandfather's house and stopped at the mailbox. The usual. A telephone bill, two catalogs—one selling seeds and the other novelty items, a grocery flier advertising the week's must-have deals, and a hearing aid advertisement.

Entering the house, Maggie kicked off her heels and dropped both her purse and the mail on an oak stand in the foyer. She carried the remnants of her iced tea into the living room.

Her grandfather lounged in his recliner, remote in hand, flicking through the channels. He popped an almond into his mouth from the little bowl at his elbow.

Maggie's heart twisted. She hated the thought of leaving him here alone while she flew off in search of her future. She had to tell him. Tonight. Before someone else did. Her stomach tightened in anticipation. He'd be lonely, but he'd be furious if she gave up her big chance to stay here with him. *Damned if you do, damned if you don't.*

She forced a smile. "Fletcher Sullivan, you are one handsome cowboy. I'm going to have to beat off all the women tonight once they catch sight of you."

"Not bad for an old geezer, huh?" Voice gruff, dressed in his best western shirt and a new pair of jeans she'd laundered last night to get rid of the initial stiffness, he grinned. He'd combed his silver-white hair neatly from a side part. "Goin' out with my favorite girl. Got to look good. Don't want to put you to shame."

"That'll never happen, Pops. I'm the luckiest granddaughter on earth."

He pushed himself out of the leather chair, crossed the room, and gave her a hug and a kiss. "We need to talk, honey."

Oh, God, he knew. Her mouth went as dry as week-old cornbread. "Pops—"

He shushed her. "First, though, I understand Brawley came by the shop today. Gave you a bad time. Want me to talk to the boy?"

She smiled, relieved at the reprieve. "No. I can handle him." Sure she could. The way a rabbit would handle a rattler and probably with the same results.

"You sure?"

She nodded.

He didn't look convinced, but he let it drop. "We still have to talk, sugar, but it can wait till we're on our way. Your mother called again to make sure we'd be there. Told her to keep her pants on, that we'd be there when we got there and not a minute sooner."

"I'll bet she loved that. Give me five." She flew upstairs to her room, filled with dread. Since it wasn't Brawley's visit, he either already knew about her move…or something was wrong with him.

Oh, boy. Silly to let her mind leap to that. Pops was healthy as an ox and busier than he'd been in ages. She had a hard time catching him home anymore. It seemed he had plans with the guys almost every night, out doing whatever guys his age did. And that was a good thing. Friends. The staple of life.

Once in her room, she closed the door, leaned against it, and let out a huge sigh. Felt the day slip away. She loved this room. The rest of the house remained locked in a time warp. Nothing had changed in the old two-story since forever.

After Grandma passed away and Maggie moved in, she'd understood his need to keep his wife of nearly fifty years close.

Because of that, she'd resisted any and all urges to redecorate. She had, though, totally redone one of the guest rooms and made it her own.

The Baxters, Grandpa's closest neighbors, had decided to modernize their farmhouse living room. That included tearing out a beautiful old fireplace surround. When Maggie heard they intended to toss it, she'd snapped it up, painted it a soft ivory, and turned it into her headboard.

Both her bedroom walls and a salvaged chandelier were now the color of good champagne. She'd mixed in splashes of midnight blue. She squinted at a throw pillow. The exact color of Brawley's eyes. Oh, God. Why hadn't she realized that before now? It was so not the reason she'd chosen the shade, though. She'd picked it because she liked it. Because it soothed her. Normally.

Well, enough lollygagging. Time was wasting. She unzipped her slacks and stepped out of them, slid the soft sweater over her head. Standing in her closet doorway, she sighed. Smiled. Her private closet looked darned near as pretty as her store. Clothes were the love of her life.

And those clothes, the designs she'd created, had lavished her imagination on, would take her away from her grandpa. Oh, he'd be stoic about it, tell her she had to follow her heart, but still…Maybe he should close up this big old house and move in with her parents.

That wasn't going to happen, and she knew it. He and Gran had moved in here as newlyweds, had brought their baby, her dad, home from the hospital to this house. Had raised him here.

No. Fletcher Sullivan wouldn't leave this house. But anticipating telling him about her plans was definitely taking some of the shine off her dream.

And now there was Brawley.

She pulled out her best pair of cowgirl boots. If she was going to

Bubba's with Pops, boots were almost a requirement. A pair of jeans and a floaty top in shades of green finished her off. She took three minutes to refresh her makeup, then unclipped and shook out her hair.

Bounding down the stairs, she saw Pops in the foyer, hat on. Obviously he was in a hurry to get the show on the road.

He opened the door, and she stepped out into the early spring evening. The temperature had plunged, and she hesitated, wondering if she should run back upstairs for a sweater. Nah. Bubba's would be warm, and she could run the heater on the way home.

Neither of them spoke as she backed the car down the drive and headed toward Maverick Junction. The moon was nearly full, the sky clear, the stars amazing. Maggie considered turning on the radio but realized that would be cowardly.

Before she could find the right words, Pops cleared his throat. He didn't look at her, stared straight ahead. "Maggie, honey, it's time we had a talk. One I've put off too long. Shouldn't have."

A groan welled up in her, but she batted it down. She'd waited too long. Someone else had told him.

"It's as much my fault as yours, Pops." She took one hand from the wheel and gave his a squeeze.

"Your fault?" His head snapped around to study her. "Why in the world would you say that?"

She frowned. "I—"

"No," he said. "Just listen. Time I took this old bull by the horns and had my say."

"Okay." Jeez, the way her stomach was flipping around, she'd never be able to eat a bite if they didn't get this hashed out before they reached Bubba's.

"You're a good girl, Maggie, and I'm proud of you. I understand people look at you and see what you want them to see. You like some bling, like your fun. But you also like the status quo. Despite all the glitz and glamour, at heart, you like nothing better than a rainy Sunday spent in an old pair of pajamas, reading."

"True, but—"

"I loved your grandma with all my heart. Always will."

What the heck? Maggie shot him a glance. What did Grandma have to do with her move? This definitely wasn't the direction she'd expected their conversation to take.

"I know that, Pops. But what does any of this have to do with New York?"

"New York?" He reared back. "Who said anything about New York?"

She inhaled sharply. "I'm confused."

"'Course you are. You keep interrupting me instead of listening."

And she'd been chastised. Sure not the first time. Better to say nothing, simply wait for him to finish.

"Okay, then." As if in a rush to get the words out, he blurted, "Dottie and I are getting married."

"What?" The car swerved into the other lane. She whipped it back. Her eyes fastened on her grandfather briefly. His gaze focused on the passing scenery, he braced his feet on the floor, grabbed the hand rest, and pressed his back into the seat.

"Pops," she snapped. "Look at me. Say that again."

"You'd best watch where you're going before the sheriff's got to send the ambulance out for us."

She turned her attention back to the two-lane highway that stretched ahead for miles and miles.

"I asked Dottie Willis to marry me. She said yes." He swallowed hard.

"Dottie?"

"That's what I said, didn't I?"

"Dottie Willis?"

"Yes, ma'am. Nothin' wrong with your hearing."

Her eyes flicked from the road to him, back to the road. She tried to speak, but no words came. Her grandfather and Dottie Willis? And she'd been clueless.

"I know this probably comes as a surprise to you—"

"A surprise?" she croaked.

"We've been seeing each other on and off since Cash's Fourth of July barbecue."

"That's almost a year."

"Yep."

"All those dinners and nights out with the guys?" She took a sip of her now warm tea.

He had the good grace to look shamefaced. "Some of them actually were guys-nights-out, but I spent a lot of them with Dottie. We took it slow." He gave a nervous little laugh. "Although at our age that's probably kind of risky."

He shrugged. "I love her, Maggie. The woman makes me feel like a man again instead of some old, worthless, worn-out bag of bones."

She rubbed her forehead, not wanting to dig too deeply into what exactly that might entail.

"This doesn't change anything, sweetie. Dottie and I haven't decided if we're going to keep her house or mine, but we'd love to have you live with us."

She laughed. "With a couple of lovesick newlyweds?"

Her grandfather scowled. "It's won't be like that. We're too old to be carrying on." He actually blushed and gave her a sidelong look, his lips curving into a slow smile. "Much."

Maggie was glad she'd swallowed her last drink of tea. Otherwise, sure as the sun rose in the morning, she'd have spurted it across the dashboard. Hot on the heels of that thought came the realization that her grandfather wouldn't be alone when she left for New York.

A heavy weight lifted from her shoulders, and a huge grin broke free.

"First, Pops, let me say congratulations. As soon as I get parked at the roadhouse, I'll give you a big old hug and a kiss. Then, I'm ordering a bottle of Bubba's finest champagne—if he carries any—and which will probably be one step away from rubbing alcohol—to toast your upcoming nuptials."

She paused, let out a huge breath. "There's something else, though. Something *I* need to share. To discuss with you. It's what I thought you were upset about."

"I'm not upset."

"I realize that now. But you said you wanted to talk, and you were acting kind of funny."

"I was nervous."

"Nervous? You?"

"About telling you. Afraid you'd think I was being unfaithful to your grandmother."

"Oh, Pops." Her eyes filled with tears, and she blinked frantically. "Never. Grandma Trudy was a lucky, lucky woman. All anybody had to do was look at the two of you, and they couldn't help seeing the love you shared. You were a great husband; she was a wonderful wife. You set an incredible example of what marriage should be."

Her hands gripped the wheel a little tighter as emotion flooded her. "But Grandma wouldn't want you to live the rest of your life alone." She glanced up through the windshield and waved a hand at the early evening sky. "My guess is that biggest, brightest star up there is her, smiling down on us right now. Giving her blessing."

Maggie heard a muffled sound and swiveled to see her grandpa blowing his nose on the white handkerchief he always carried. Even in the dim light from the dash, she saw his eyes were moist. Her own throat ached with unshed tears.

My news, now. Time to dive in. "You know I signed to do a fall line of clothing."

"Yep. For one of them big labels. I'm so damned proud of you,

Maggie, girl. You put off going away to school to help with Grandma when she got sick, then one thing and another. Turns out you didn't need that piece of paper. You're gonna be a huge success without that degree."

"I think the jury's still out on that."

"You've got a gift, Maggie, and now the world is gonna get to see it."

"The show's in New York."

Dawning realization flashed in his eyes. "How long you gonna be gone?"

"I'm moving there, Pops."

Voice thick, he said, "Should have guessed that. Probably would have if I hadn't been so wrapped up in my own doings."

He patted her shoulder. "You've worked hard to make this happen. Can't say I'm not gonna miss you 'cause I will. Like I'd miss my right arm. But I'm happy for you, sweetheart. You're gonna take that city by storm."

He raised a hip and tucked his hanky into his back pocket. "Looks like we've got ourselves some major celebrating to do tonight."

"Is Dottie coming to dinner?"

"She'll join us a little later, but we figured I should be alone with all of you when I dropped the bombshell. Give you and your folks some time to settle into it. Little bit of chicken in her, maybe. What do you think?"

"I think she's a smart woman. Very smart. And very, very fortunate."

Still more than a little shell-shocked, Maggie parked the car in the Roadhouse's dusty lot. She spotted her dad's big truck under an oak, so they were already here.

After nearly smothering her grandfather in a hug, she and Fletch crossed arm in arm to the ramshackle building. Bubba'd hung a few early plants on the wide, wooden porch. Several Texas redbuds struggled to brighten the sides of the restaurant. But even at that, the place looked a little worse for wear, the siding weathered, the railing in need of stain.

They walked up the stairs, and Pops, ever the gentleman, held the door for her. She stepped inside, half-blinded by the comparative darkness, and straight into Brawley Odell's arms.

"Hello, sweetheart. Didn't expect you here tonight."

She yelped and would have backed away had he not reached out and clasped both her arms.

Pops, who didn't seem to notice her discomfort, nodded at Brawley. "Heard you were in Lone Tree today."

"Yes, sir, I was."

Pops turned his attention to Maggie. "Your mom and dad are already here. I'll go on over while you two chat."

With that, he left her alone with her nemesis.

"Let go, Brawley." She kept her voice low.

He dropped his hands to his sides.

"What are you doing here?" she bit out.

"I might ask you the same."

"I came for dinner. With my folks."

"And I came for a beer. Cash is at the bar. He's gonna help me draw up plans for a few renovations at the clinic. We decided to do it over a cold one."

"Renovations?"

He nodded. "Doc hasn't made a single change to that place in way too many years. It's long overdue for a face-lift."

Even at five-eight, she had to tip her head to meet his eyes. "Why are you doing this, Brawley?"

"I told you. Doc hasn't—"

"No." She shook her head. "I'm not talking about remodeling. Why are you really back here? Why this pretense?"

"Pretense?"

She made a sound low in her throat. "We both know you're not Maverick Junction. Not small-town Texas. You belong in the big city with all its money and nightlife. The social niceties. The socialites. You're at home there. Go back to Dallas, Brawley, and leave us alone."

Us, she thought. She wouldn't use *me*. That would make it too personal, feed his already inflated ego.

She shrugged off his hand but hadn't taken two steps before he was beside her again. He leaned into her, trapping her between the solid wall of his body and the building's rough wooden one.

"Brawley!" She shoved at him. "People are looking."

"Let them."

"My parents are here."

"Yep. Saw them come in."

"What do you want?"

His eyes darkened to the color of midnight. "You."

"Bullshit!" She shoved at him.

"You look good tonight."

"Really? Personally, I prefer seeing the backside of you—while you're walking away. And it is, after all, what you do best."

He shook his head, straightening. "Maggie, sweetheart, God broke the mold after he made you."

"Go to hell, Brawley. And I'm not your sweetheart."

His face took on an edge. "You know, you accuse me of being big city, but who's heading to New York, the biggest of them all? Have you told your grandpa?" His words stopped her. "It's really not much of a secret, you know. Somebody's bound to let it slip tonight."

"I told him. On the way here."

"Good. 'Cause secrets have a way of turning on you."

For one awful second, she wondered if he'd uncovered the secret she'd buried years ago. No. Brawley didn't talk in riddles. He said what he meant and meant what he said. It was that simple.

Without another word, he left to join Cash.

She hadn't been lying. She did enjoy the backside of him. Watching him walk away, she swore the man wore a pair of jeans better than any male alive. The sight was enough to make a grown woman drool.

With her next breath, she cursed the day she'd met him. Every time she figured she'd exorcised him, he showed up again, proving her wrong. Unfortunately, like most things that tempted, Brawley was bad for her.

She was strong, though. She could resist. At some point, he would become yesterday's news. And even though she longed to put him out of her mind, out of her heart, that idea saddened her.

Around her, everyone quickly looked away, pretended they hadn't been indulging in a little harmless voyeurism. They slipped easily back into their own conversations and dinners. Maggie doubted there was a person in the room who didn't know her history with Brawley. That he'd left her high and dry.

Her dad waved from the corner table beneath the Lone Star flag, and she returned his greeting. Pasting a Miss America smile on her face, speaking to friends and neighbors as she passed, she sauntered across the room to join her parents. The entire time, she felt Brawley's gaze follow her.

She would not look back. She'd already spent way too many years doing exactly that.

The chrome Wurlitzer played a song about a man with wandering eyes and a cheating heart. Maybe she should buy a copy of it and play it till it seared itself into her memory bank. She snorted. As if she needed a reminder.

Chapter Four

Steaming mug of coffee in hand, Brawley stepped out onto the second-floor landing of his new apartment. He fought the temptation to leave the door unlocked. Maybe if he was very, very lucky, somebody'd come by and steal all the fussy doodads Annie'd left behind. Annie, then Sophie, he amended.

Both cousins had lived here in Dottie's second-story apartment when they'd come to Maverick Junction. Both planned on a short stay, and each had ended up marrying one of his best friends. Darnedest thing.

He propped his elbows on the railing, drinking in the early morning calm. A couple birds twittered from high in the trees. Below, Dottie's garden was springing to life, bright blooms sprouting in patches.

Dottie Willis. He loved the woman. She... and her cookies... had been a part of his life forever. Her son Wes had been a couple years ahead of him in school. He'd played basketball, a damned good point guard who now lived in Albuquerque, where he had a law practice. Her daughter Lacey, a pretty little dark-haired thing, lived in San Diego.

Too bad. Miss Dottie would make one heck of a hands-on grandma, and both Wes and Lacey had kids. He often wondered why she didn't move close to one of them.

She'd surprised him when she'd shown up at the roadhouse last night. All dolled up in pink silk pants and top and smelling heavenly, she'd given both him and Cash a quick peck on the cheek, then joined Maggie and her family. Old Fletch had a grin the size of Texas on his face and had even kissed Dottie's hand. The man was a true gentleman.

Kisses and hugs had flowed freely at the Sullivan table.

He'd nursed his beer and wondered how long it would take all that to dry up if he moseyed over to say hello. Once welcomed by the family, he'd become a persona non grata.

His fault. His bed to lie in.

Carrying his coffee, Brawley hustled down the stairs. He'd stayed longer at Bubba's than he'd intended last night. He and Cash had planned to grab a single beer and play with ideas for the clinic's renovations. Brawley had hoped it would kill two birds with a single stone—get the plans under way and, at the same time, take his mind off a certain woman he couldn't get out of his head.

Then, he'd walked over to say hello to a friend and the door opened. Maggie waltzed through it, right smack into him.

Damn his luck anyway.

He unlocked the door to his Chevy Tahoe, set his coffee mug in the holder, and slid behind the wheel. Turning the key, the vehicle rumbled to life and he backed down the drive.

All things considered, he supposed last night could have turned out worse. A lot worse, actually. He wasn't really sure who'd come closer to losing it—him or Maggie's dad. Sean Sullivan had considered Brawley a son back in the days when everyone assumed he and Maggie would get married.

Not so now. Man, if looks could kill, his mama would be planning his funeral this morning.

After his initial shock at finding Maggie in his arms, he'd felt more than seen Maggie's dad go on full alert. Then, out of the corner of his eye, he'd watched Sean Sullivan come halfway out of his seat when he'd touched Maggie during their heated conversation.

No doubt about it. He'd walked a thin line.

Maggie's mom, though, had managed with a single touch to Sean's arm and a few quiet words to get him to sit back down. Sean hadn't taken his eyes off him and Maggie, though, and Brawley knew that one wrong move, the man would be all over him.

Pops, who'd been friendly enough when they'd come in, didn't look any too happy, either. Papa bear with his cub, both of them.

Brawley turned onto Main Street. He'd grab breakfast at Sally's. The truth? He deserved anything Maggie's family could throw at him—and more.

The memory of her eyes bothered him most. Those spectacular green eyes had been bruised with hurt as they'd met his. Hurt and anger. The lady wasn't one to pull punches. Nothing about Margaret Emmalee Sullivan came close to lukewarm. If she was involved, she was in it up to her eyeballs. And you never had a lick of doubt about how she felt, because she had no problem telling you.

As spitting mad as she'd been at him, though, she'd worked the room as she crossed to her parents' table, stopping to talk to friends, kiss someone's baby, laugh at a joke. By the time she made it to her folks, her anger seemed to have dissipated.

She'd put him out of her mind.

He'd been working on doing the same with her for over a decade now and still hadn't managed it.

The rest of last night had been hell. Straddling the cowhide bar stool, pretending she wasn't there, pretending she didn't matter.

He'd sipped his beer and half-listened as Cash dissected the Rangers' game that had just ended.

All the while, he watched Mags. She'd leaned down to kiss both her parents, dropped another kiss on her grandfather's cheek, and took her seat—back to him.

Despite the rocky start, the Sullivans appeared to be in a celebratory mood. They'd even broken out the champagne after Dottie arrived—if you could stretch the stuff Bubba stocked to fit the category. No doubt Maggie's parents were proud as hell of their little girl and applauding her achievements.

Little girl, his foot. Hah. Mags was a woman. All woman. Maybe she always had been. Brawley couldn't remember a time when she hadn't gotten him all churned up.

Maggie's mom surprised him, though. He'd have thought she'd be all teary-eyed at the idea of her baby leaving. Instead, Rita Sullivan, her hair a short, curly bubble, the same vivid red as her daughter's, was all smiles. But come time for Maggie to hop on that New York–bound plane, no doubt Rita would turn on the waterworks.

Pain seared his chest.

Good thing he didn't still love her, or he'd sit right down and cry, too.

Heaven on the eyes, hell on the heart. Oh, yeah, that was Ms. Maggie Sullivan. The man who'd written that song must have met her.

Odd. While he hadn't been surprised to see them break out the bubbly, the toasts seemed aimed at Pops. And Dottie. What was he missing?

He'd finally turned his back on their table and gotten down to business with Cash. By the time they'd finished their second beers, they'd come up with a fairly decent plan for the office renovations.

Then Cash had gone home to his wife, and he'd gone back to Dottie's, to his frilly, girly apartment. Not quite what his life had been in Dallas. But then he hadn't wanted all that anymore, had he?

Still, he'd lain awake half the night rehashing things in his mind, hoping he hadn't made the second biggest mistake of his life by moving back to Maverick Junction.

He parked his Chevy outside of Sally's and spied Mel heading into the *Maverick Junction Daily*.

"Hey, Mel."

"Brawley." Mel stopped, key in the newspaper office door. "You're up and around early today."

"I am every day. You had breakfast?" He tipped his head toward the café.

"Yep. Ate at home."

"Want another cup of coffee?"

Mel shook his head. "Too much to do. I'm on deadline."

"Okay," Brawley said. "I'm gonna grab a bite, then I'll come over, talk about what I had in mind for that ad I want to run."

The minute he walked into the restaurant, he knew something big was in the air. The place buzzed with excitement. He'd barely sat down at his usual table by the front window when Sally, her frizzy blond hair pulled into a ponytail, hurried over. Whatever the latest gossip, it brought heightened color to her cheeks.

"You hear about Dottie?" Then she swatted him with the menu in her hand. "'Course you have. You're renting from her now, aren't you?"

Brawley frowned. "Yeah, I am, but no, I haven't. What's going on with her?"

"She and Fletch Sullivan are getting married."

"What?"

"Dottie and—"

He shook his head. "I heard you, Sally. I'm just trying to decide if my brain processed the words correctly."

"Can you believe it?"

Struck mute, he simply stared at her. Guess that accounted for the champagne last night. Maggie's grandpa and Dottie Willis? And nobody'd told him?

And they hadn't called him over, hadn't shared the news, the excitement, with him. Time was they would have. And Dottie. She hadn't told him. Family first. He knew that. Still, it hurt.

Maybe he had stayed away too long.

* * *

After downing an egg-white omelet as penance for yesterday's steak, he loped across the street to the newspaper office and pushed through the door. "Hey, Mel. I've got the copy written for that ad. Time to let the town know I'm taking over for—"

Maggie leaned into the counter, her head close to Mel's blond one. At the sound of his voice, she turned, cocking a hand on that curvy hip. "You do insist on a grand entrance, don't you? This makes two days in a row you've come barging in on me."

He frowned. "Difference is that yesterday I meant to. I didn't expect you'd be here today. Shouldn't you be in Lone Tree?"

A wise man, Mel said nothing. He simply straightened and watched the two, a half-smile on his lips.

Today, fire-engine-red colored Maggie's nails. She tapped one on that full bottom lip, drawing his gaze. "Are you stalking me, Brawley Odell?"

"Hah-hah. Very funny. I was about to ask you the same," he returned easily.

Those perfectly manicured brows rose in disdain. "I was here first."

"Yeah, you were. But I was at Bubba's first last night." He turned to Mel. "Did I or did I not tell you I'd be in after I ate?"

"You did."

Brawley swiveled back to Maggie. "You were outside, heard, and waited for the right moment. So you'd get here before me."

Her mouth dropped open. "You arrogant—"

"Hey, you accused me first."

She glared at him.

"Doesn't matter," Brawley said. "Not in the least. I came to do business."

"Me, too. I'm placing an ad. I need to hire someone to run the shop while I'm gone."

His heart, damn it all to hell, gave a frantic leap of joy. "While you're gone? So this move to the city isn't permanent?"

"Of course it is. But...well, I'd like to keep the boutique open for a while yet."

Crestfallen, his idiot heart stopped its happy frolic and collapsed. Still, his voice sounded steady when he said, "That's probably smart."

Maggie, rather than answer, returned her attention to Mel. "So we're good to go here?" She tipped her chin at the paper between them.

"Yep."

"And it'll run starting this afternoon?"

Mel nodded.

"Okay. Thanks a bunch." She gave him a quick peck on the cheek and swung around to leave.

Brawley caught her arm.

She stared at his hand, then up at him. "This seems to be a habit of yours, so I feel compelled to say it again. You're going to want to let go of me."

He did. When she took another step toward the door, he said, "Wait a minute, Mags. Why didn't you tell me about Fletch and Dottie yesterday?"

"They weren't the subject of our conversation. Besides, when we talked earlier, I didn't know. He told me on the way to Bubba's."

"Seriously?" He whistled softly. "That must have been some chat the two of you had last night. Both of you with big news."

"Yeah." She chuckled. "I almost drove off the road when he dropped his on me."

"Bet you did." He grinned.

"It made my announcement a whole lot easier."

Brawley nodded. "Pops won't be alone. That matters to you."

She met his eyes. "It does."

"I'm pleased for you, Mags. For you, for Fletch, for Dottie. They're great people. They'll be happy together."

"Yes, I think they will. I still haven't had time to really wrap my head around the whole idea of them as a couple. And I don't know how I was so blind." She slapped her forehead. "I never saw it coming."

"Things sneak up on us sometimes."

"They do. Between Maverick Junction and Lone Tree, the Sullivans have about cornered the good-news market." She looked at Mel. "And you can quote me on that, Mr. Newspaper Editor."

"You bet." Mel saluted.

"When do you leave?"

"In two weeks." She reached for the door.

"Have dinner with me tonight," Brawley blurted.

She looked down at the floor. "I can't."

"Can't or won't?"

"Does it matter?" She met his gaze.

"Yes, actually, it does." A muscle worked in his jaw. It did matter to him. A whole hell of a lot.

"I won't."

Those two words, delivered so succinctly, sucker-punched him. Still, he tried. "Maggie, all that was a long time ago."

"Yes. It was. And I need to keep it that way." She closed the door quietly behind her.

Yep, he'd been right. He'd waited too long to come home.

Chapter Five

They want to do what?" Phone to her ear, Maggie dropped the sweater she'd been folding onto the display table and collapsed into a chair. "Mom, that's not possible. Today's Tuesday."

Her mother's sigh made it clear she'd get no argument from her.

"They're dead set on it, Maggie. Come hell or high water, Fletch and Dottie intend to get married this Saturday in her garden. Lacey and Wes are flying in Friday with their families."

"Where will they stay?"

"With Dottie. She insists she's got plenty of room. Can you meet us this afternoon?"

Maggie ran a mental scan of her day's schedule. "Today's tough. Ella McCormack's coming in for an interview at two, and I'm expecting a shipment later this afternoon. I really can't promise to be there before six, Mom."

"That'll work. I'll call Dottie. Plan on dinner here. I'll fix something girlie for us. Your dad can eat at the café or at Bubba's again."

"Sounds good." Maggie took another peek at the clock, trying to decide which of today's have-to-dos could wait till tomorrow.

"When you talk to Dottie, tell her I'll pick her up. No sense both of us driving."

Maggie stomped on the little voice that wondered if Brawley might be hanging around when she stopped at Dottie's. Not wondered, she corrected. Worried. Because she did not want to see him.

"Sophie and Annie would probably love to help," Maggie added.

"Good idea. With both of them recent brides, they'll be up on all the latest, no doubt have some great ideas. Will you check with them?"

"I can do that." She moved behind the counter and picked up a *Town and Country Weddings* magazine a client had left behind. She tucked it into her purse. It might come in handy.

"Good. I'll make extra food—not that either of them eats enough to keep a sparrow alive." After a slight pause, her mom said, "Ella McCormack. Tunney's widow?"

"Yes."

"Fate sure dealt those two a cruel hand. So young."

"I know. She called me first thing this morning to ask if the job was still open. To be honest, and shame on me, I was a little hesitant to even interview her."

"Why?"

"She's a single mom with two kids. And before you nag me about how unfair that is, I'll admit you're right. But it's not like I'm hiring somebody to fill in a few hours once in a while. I'll be halfway across the country, so I need someone I can count on. Every single day."

"I'll be here, honey. I can always take over in a pinch."

"I appreciate that, Mom, but you shouldn't have to. Anyway, I thought about it some more. Both Ella's kids are in school. Her mother-in-law lives in town and has offered to watch Benjy and Sadie after school. The bus will drop them off at her place till Ella closes up, so that part should be okay."

"I hope it works," her mom said. "With two children, I'm sure

Ella can use both the extra money and a little adult socialization. Besides, it'll give the kids some grandma time. That's important. Even though they all live in Lone Tree, I'm sure Tunney's mom worries about losing touch with them now that he's gone."

A few minutes later, Maggie hung up and sent texts to Annie and Sophie. Pops & D 2 marry this wkend. Yikes! Can u help? Tonite @ Mom's. 6:00. Dinner included.

She hoped they could both make it. The extra hands would be welcome. Less than four days to plan and execute a wedding? By itself, nearly impossible. On top of everything else she needed to do before leaving? Oh, boy.

Overwhelming.

Maybe she needed to think of it in terms of the old joke about how to eat an elephant. One bite at a time. Somehow or other, it would all get done.

Standing at her shop's display window, Maggie looked out over Lone Tree's main street. So much was changing so quickly. Fingering her pretty lace curtains, she wondered if she was truly ready. She had a good life here. Was happy.

Would she ever again stand here all alone in her pretty little shop, her family and friends close? Her workroom in the back had provided a haven. She could hide there with her beautiful fabrics, and with pencil, paper, scissors, and sewing machine, bring her ideas to life.

Could she turn all this over to Ella McCormack, or anyone else for that matter?

And home. Once Pops and Dottie got married— Well, she couldn't even begin to imagine it. Maggie and her grandfather enjoyed each other's company. They'd settled into a routine. She liked living with him. Liked the familiarity of the house she'd romped in as a child. That would change after this weekend.

Fleetingly, she wondered where they'd decide to live. Which

house they'd eventually choose. She smiled, imagining Pops living in Dottie's Candy Land–pink house. That should be interesting.

But, then, she wouldn't be here to watch, would she?

It had been her decision to follow her dreams. Her decision to leave all this, all the people she loved, life as she knew it, to go to New York.

And while it was exciting, it loomed over her as more than a little frightening. A dose of the old "be careful what you wish for"?

It felt a little like jumping off a cliff without a parachute. Thrilling? Yes. And more than a little dangerous.

Still holding her phone, she called Pops and filled him in on her mother's plans. "So you're on your own for dinner."

"Think I can manage to feed myself, girl. You have fun and help Dottie. The woman's a nervous wreck over this."

"You two didn't give us much time to pull everything together, Pops."

"Be plenty of time if you females could keep things simple. Don't see why there has to be such a fuss. Be a heck of a lot easier to give Father Tom a call and have him meet us at the house. He pronounces us man and wife, then we all run down to Sally's and grab some lunch."

Maggie laughed. "Boy, aren't you the romantic?"

"I can be. When the situation warrants it. Got the woman to say yes, didn't I?"

"You sure did. I love you, Pops, and it appears Dottie does, too. I still can't believe I missed all the signs."

"It's 'cause you're busy."

"Guess so." Guilt dropped over her. Was she really that wrapped up in herself that she'd missed something so big, so momentous? "However, Pops, as much as we all love you, your plan won't wash."

He harrumphed. "Silly to waste time and money on all this foolishness."

"Dottie wants it."

"So she'll get it," he conceded, his voice softening.

Yes, she would, Maggie thought as she ended the call. Between friends and family, they'd make Saturday's wedding special.

And she could add to it by creating the perfect dress for Dottie. Something light and floaty, something exactly right for a garden wedding.

Ideas chasing each other through her head, she grabbed a pencil and her sketch pad. As the design began to take form, she grinned and lost herself in what she loved to do. The dress would have to be pink, of course. A soft petal pink. Maybe a matching tie for Pops.

Oh, yeah. She could do this.

In between customers, she tweaked the design, then sketched a second to give Dottie a choice. Still, she really hoped Dottie would go with the first.

Fortunately she'd thrown a salad together before she left the house this morning. Digging it out of her small back room fridge, she munched on it while she made lists of all the things she needed to do this week.

Dottie's son would walk her down the aisle, and Maggie's dad had been tapped as best man. Maybe she'd make them matching ties as well. If they survived the pre-wedding madness, Saturday should be fun.

When the bell over the door jangled, she glanced up, her shop-owner's smile on her face.

Ella McCormack walked in, and Maggie knew instinctively she was the one. Casual elegance with an air of competence and self-assurance but without any of the arrogance that sometimes accompanied that demeanor. In slim navy pants and a white top, her blond hair pulled back in a sleek ponytail, Ella looked the consummate professional. Maggie preferred bold color choices for herself, but Ella would serve as the perfect backdrop for the store's merchandise.

The two had met before but they'd never exchanged much more than the polite talk between strangers. Maggie fixed them each a cup of coffee, and they sat in the shop's deep armchairs. *Simpatico*, Maggie realized. Ella was made for this job. At thirty-eight, she brought a certain maturity with her that put to rest Maggie's fears.

Her chest tightened. This was a big step. She would be entrusting everything she'd worked so hard to build to Ella. Putting it all in her hands.

Understanding that, Ella offered to stay for the rest of the afternoon. Kind of a trial-by-fire. "If you don't like the way I interact with customers, just say the word and I leave. No harm, no foul, and no hard feelings," she promised.

"I have no doubt you'll be wonderful with them," Maggie said. "But it would be great if you could stay, since our biggest problem is time. We only have two weeks before I leave, so the sooner you start learning the ropes, the better. There are supplies to order, books to keep. Stock to rotate. So many details. My mom has offered to help in a pinch if you need her."

"So I'm hired?"

"You are."

Ella's eyes closed fleetingly. When she opened them, they were filled with emotion. "Thank you. I won't let you down." She took a deep breath. "You must be so excited."

"I am." Maggie grinned. "And more than a bit nervous. I've never, ever lived anywhere except the Texas hill country. I grew up in Maverick Junction, then moved here to Lone Tree to live with my grandfather."

"After your grandma passed away."

Maggie nodded.

"Trudy was a wonderful woman. She baked the most incredible chocolate pies."

At Maggie's startled expression, Ella laughed softly. "Tunney and

I went to the same church as your grandparents. Once in a while, she'd bring one of her pies for bazaars and such."

While they talked, they folded stock and rearranged racks. They worked well together. When customers came in, Maggie introduced them to Ella, then stepped back, only offering help when needed.

Ella proved a quick study. She'd do well.

Maggie was both relieved and saddened. Today marked an end as well as a beginning.

Locking up that afternoon, she waved good-bye to Ella and stood in the door watching as she headed off to pick up her kids. Maggie decided against running home to change. Her aqua linen slacks and print top would be fine. The shoes would go, though, as soon as she hit her mother's front door. She'd spent a lot of the day on her feet.

Her mind was a disaster. Too much thinking, too much rolling things around in her head, which was beginning to ache. Once in her car, she popped a couple aspirin, slid a country-western CD in the player, and cranked up the volume. She opened the sunroof and relished the play of fresh air over her. Singing along with Tim McGraw, she drove to Maverick Junction in record time.

Turning into Dottie's, she saw the kitchen light on. God, after this weekend, this would be her step-grandmother's house. How strange was that?

An image of Vivi, Cash's twenty-eight-year-old scheming step-grandmother, flashed through her mind, and she thanked God Fletch had more sense than to get mixed up with someone like that.

She walked up to the house, but before she even had time to knock, Dottie called for her to come in. Maggie stepped into the pink-on-pink kitchen and there sat Brawley at the counter, dunking one of Dottie's famous chocolate chip cookies into a big glass of milk.

"Hey, Red."

"Hey, yourself."

"Do us all a favor and pull up a stool. These cookies"—he held up what remained of the one in his hand—"can't be beat. They'll wipe that frown off your face."

"I'm not frowning."

"Yes, you are."

She made an exasperated sound, then decided not to give him the satisfaction of an argument. "I totally agree about the cookies, but I really don't have time. I have somewhere I have to be. Dottie does, too, so you'll need to run along now."

Surprise registered on Dottie's face, and Maggie felt a flush of embarrassment. Yes, she'd been rude, but damned if she'd apologize. Brawley had a way of bringing out the worst in her, and she suspected a lot of it was intentional.

"He has time to finish, honey, while I freshen up and grab my purse."

Maggie threw her a forced smile. "Great."

The instant Dottie rounded the corner, Brawley grabbed her hand and gave it a good tug. She gasped and found herself sitting on the stool beside him.

"No need to get all wound up, Mags." He dunked his cookie again. Instead of popping it into his mouth, he held it up to hers. Surprising herself, she opened her mouth, took a bite, and closed her eyes. Oh, yeah. Dottie baked the best cookies this side of the Mississippi.

"Want more?"

Her eyes flew open. Brawley had moved in, his lips only a few inches from hers.

She swallowed. "Go away, Brawley."

"Not gonna happen, sugar."

"Don't call me that."

"You'd prefer vinegar, maybe? Might actually suit your disposition better."

"I'll tell you what I'd prefer. You—"

"Okay, sweetheart, I'm ready." Dottie bustled into the kitchen, purse strap over her arm. When Brawley started to rise, she waved him back into his seat. "Don't. You're fine. Stay as long as you want and eat as many of those as you'd like." She nodded toward the plate of cookies. "When you're done, just turn the lock and pull the door shut. I have my key."

"Is your porch light on?" he asked.

"Yes, dear." She kissed his cheek. "It's so nice having you here."

"Not everybody agrees with that." He eyed Maggie.

Running a hand over her already immaculate cloud of white hair, Dottie chuckled. "Don't you worry that handsome head of yours. Everything will work out as it's meant to."

She opened the door and stepped outside. Behind her, Maggie turned to Brawley and impishly stuck out her tongue.

When his mouth dropped open, she grinned. Who said you always had to behave like an adult?

But when he stood and took a step toward her, she threw the fight without raising a hand. Hurrying out the door, she tugged it shut.

* * *

Brawley leaned against the kitchen sink and watched her stroll down the drive in those sexy-as-hell shoes. That bluish-green outfit, with her hair and eyes? Incredible.

As good as Dottie's cookies tasted, it was Maggie, always Maggie, who made him salivate. She affected him on some deep-down level.

The woman exuded sex appeal. She didn't dress in overtly sexy clothes. Didn't tease. But oh, boy. Maggie Sullivan was some kind of beautiful.

And his memories didn't help. Not one bit. He remembered the taste of her. The softness of an eighteen-year-old Maggie wrapped around him. How it felt to bury himself deep inside her.

What would this older, even sexier Maggie feel like?

He slapped a hand on the counter. He'd so screwed up. Young and dumb. Then pride had stepped in and kept him from fixing things. Stupid, stupid, stupid.

He'd never meant for their separation to be permanent. Had assumed—what? That she'd be here waiting? He'd told her not to do that. And for once she'd listened to him. Damn it all to hell.

He'd come home to stay—to make a home—with her. And now she wanted to leave.

Well, he couldn't hang out here mooning over her. Dottie said Sophie and Annie were meeting with Maggie and Rita tonight, which meant Ty and Cash would be free to help him get his project started. Ty would have the kids, but that was okay. Jesse, Jonah, and Josh. The Triple Threat.

His friend had done a hell of a good job with the boys. Had to have been a hard road to hoe, what with Julia dying right after the triplets' birth.

Then, this last year he'd met Sophie. She'd embraced the boys the way the parched earth did rain on a hot summer's day. Living on a Texas ranch still posed a big challenge to the city girl, but he gave her credit. No quitter there. She was gaining ground.

Hopefully, Ty could toss the kids into the van, and they could all meet at the clinic for pizza, then start tearing down walls. The kids should get a real kick out of that. Hell, Cash could even bring Staubach, his ugly, loveable mutt. The more, the merrier.

Chapter Six

Brawley flustered her.

As Maggie drove to her parents' house, Dottie chatted happily about food and flowers. When she asked a question, Maggie blinked. "I'm sorry. What?"

"I asked if you knew Ollie offered to provide sweet tea and coffee for the reception."

"No, I didn't. But it sounds like him. He's quite a guy."

Ashamed of herself, Maggie forced her mind back to her grandfather's bride-to-be and swore not to do or say anything to ruin this evening. They'd have fun tonight. That meant pushing the dark, broody veterinarian from her mind.

She tooted the horn when she pulled up to her parents' house.

Her mother, bless her, had a pitcher of sangria chilling in the fridge and poured her a glass the minute she walked in. And sitting at the dining room table? Annie and Sophie. Yes, the night would be fun!

"You beat us," she said.

Annie nodded. "The men decided to go into town, so I rode to

Sophie's with Cash. He hooked a ride from there with her guys in their van."

"What are they up to?"

"Knocking down walls."

Maggie frowned.

"At the clinic," Sophie said. "After tonight I'll probably have to keep anything resembling a hammer out of the boys' reach."

Maggie laughed. "If anyone can keep them from tearing down the ranch, you can. You ride herd on those triplets like no one I've ever seen…and they love it."

Sophie smiled. "So do I. I thank God every day Annie ended up in Maverick Junction when she ran away."

"I didn't run away."

"Sure you did. For a good reason. Still…" She shrugged.

Her mom held up the pitcher. "Ladies?"

"I'm driving, and I've been up since early this morning, so I think I'll pass," Annie said. "Maybe a decaf soda?"

"I'm not driving," Sophie said. "Bring it on."

Drinks in hand, a tray of appetizers within reach, they settled down to business.

Maggie studied the two cousins, their heads bent over a magazine. So very different. Annie, her long dark hair scraped back in a ponytail, wore faded denims and an incredible blue T-shirt that set off those ice-blue eyes. Sophie resembled a fairy straight out of a little girl's storybook, her pale-blond hair a little longer than when she'd come to Maverick Junction, her brown eyes huge.

Both had overflowing idea folders from their weddings. They dug into them, chatting a mile a minute, and pictures and clippings soon littered the table.

Dottie insisted the day be kept easy and informal.

"You don't want to be rushing around on your special day," Annie said. "Delegate as much as possible. Just because it's at your home doesn't mean you have to do everything yourself. And because it *is* at your house, you'll be tempted to try."

She reached across the table. "As part of our wedding gift, Cash and I are hiring a cleaning lady."

When Dottie opened her mouth to object, Annie shook her head. "Not negotiable."

"No use arguing with her." Sophie scooped up a tortilla chip and popped it in her mouth. "I've known her all my life. Believe me, when she gets an idea, there's no stopping her."

"That's right," Annie agreed. "So save your breath."

"What are your thoughts about flowers?" Rita asked.

Maggie watched as sweet, always cheerful Dottie crumpled. Her bottom lip trembled, and tears spilled from her eyes. She quickly swiped them away with the back of her hand.

"Dottie?" Maggie rose and started around the table, but Dottie waved her away.

"Sit down." She sniffed. "I'm fine."

"But you're crying." Sophie sounded horrified.

"I know. Old fool that I am." A little hiccup escaped. "It's just that—oh, I'm getting married." Fresh tears ran unimpeded down her cheeks. "I never expected this. Never even considered it. Harry and I were happy. I spent my life with him, bore his children. Now Fletcher and I—"

She made a fluttering motion with her hand.

"It's not too late to call it off if you're not sure," Annie said.

"Not sure?" Dottie sniffed again. A watery smile lit up her face. "I've never been so sure of anything in my life. I love Fletch." She shook her head. "I never thought to say that again."

Her gaze moved around the table. "And what's truly amazing is he loves me back."

The women stood and moved in for a group hug.

After whispers, hand pats, and exchanged kisses, Dottie cleared her throat. "Okay, girls, I think I've got myself under control. I'm sorry."

"Sorry?" Rita grinned ear to ear. "Honey, you've made my year. I love my man more than the day I married him. You and Fletch are further proof that love isn't only for the young. We're never too old to tumble head-over-heels."

"No, we're not."

Maggie, halfway back in her chair, felt four pairs of eyes on her. "What?"

"It seems to me..." Rita's gaze drifted around the table. "My daughter is the only non-bride here."

"Brawley seems interested," Sophie said.

Maggie snorted.

Annie shook her head. "Whatever happened between the two of you took place a long time ago. It's possible he's changed."

"Oh, yeah," Maggie said. "The leopard lost his spots. Annie, Sophie, you're both romantics. Newlyweds. It's not going to happen. Ever. Besides, in case you've forgotten, I'm leaving in a week and a half."

A traitorous sliver of her brain cried out that her timing stunk. She tried to squash it, but the idea dug in its heels. Would she and Brawley have a chance if she stayed?

No. Absolutely not. She'd end up another notch on his bedpost. But wait. She was already there, wasn't she? Shoot! A big mistake. One she would not repeat.

Dottie interrupted her thoughts. "To get back to the flowers. Maybe we could simply do some bouquets from the garden."

Maggie wagged her finger. "Uh-uh. Leave the blooms there. You want the backyard to look beautiful. Full. We'll call Bitsy at Heaven Scent and hire her to do your flowers."

When Dottie hesitated, Sophie whispered, "You're getting married. Everything should be perfect—without running yourself ragged."

"All right. But I want lily of the valley in my bouquet. They represent happiness."

Sighs escaped around the table.

"You need a photographer," Maggie said.

"Taken care of." Dottie's eyes glinted.

"Excellent."

"Brawley's doing the pictures."

"Brawley?" Her jaw dropped.

"The man's a genius behind the lens."

"Brawley?"

"You're sounding a bit like a broken record," Sophie said.

"I know, but Brawley?"

"Have you seen his work?" Dottie asked.

Mutely, she shook her head.

"You need to. After his things come from Dallas, you need to stop by. Check out some of his photography."

A little off-center, Maggie listened as the discussion drifted to food and seating and candles. As they ate homemade taco salads, Dottie informed them she and Fletch had already made arrangements with Father Tom.

Maggie helped her mom with the flan and coffee. She took a bite of her sweet treat, then said, "One last thing."

Reaching into her luggage-size purse, she withdrew the sketches she'd done earlier.

Tears pooled in Dottie's eyes for the second time that night. "Oh." She covered her mouth with her hand. "These are magnificent, honey."

"Decide which you like best, and that will be your wedding dress. Unless you already have something."

"No, I don't. I thought I'd make a quick trip to Austin, but—"

"No buts. I'm counting on Pops never getting married again. The least I can do is deck out his bride in a Maggie original."

She grinned and watched as the others bent over the drawings, pointing out details.

Her mom shot her a pleased glance. "These are delightful, Maggie. What a great idea." To Dottie, she said, "I don't think you can go wrong with either. They'll both suit you."

"They're spot-on," Dottie agreed. "And pink."

Maggie shrugged. "I can make them any color."

"No, you can't. Not for my wedding. It's pink or nothing."

She grinned. "That's what I figured."

"A little more coverage than you girls needed." Dottie shot a quick glance at Annie and Sophie. "But they're not at all matronly." She shook her head. "Definitely not matronly."

"You should do a line of these," Annie said. "There has to be a huge market for dresses for the more mature bride."

"I agree." Sophie trailed a finger over the first pencil drawing. "These are brilliant."

"Do you have time to do this?" the bride-to-be asked.

"You bet I do. I can work fast when I have to. Right, Annie?" Maggie looked at her friend. She'd made a red carpet–worthy dress for her in less time than she had now. And that dress had started this whole fantastic New York ride. Had earned her national attention.

"Remember the one I wore in Dallas, Dottie, when you attended the fund-raiser with Cash and me?"

"How could I ever forget it...or that night? Pure magic."

"And now you're getting married." Annie wrapped the woman in a hug.

"I am. And I want to do it in this dress." She pointed to Maggie's first choice. "I feel like I've fallen into a fairy tale."

In the sketch, the soft pink silk flowed to the floor. The skirt had a sheer overlay. Silvery beads traced over the delicate jacket. Its asymmetrical hem would trim a few pounds off Dottie's ample figure.

"It's perfect, Maggie. Absolutely perfect." Dottie clasped her hands over her heart.

"When Fletch gets a sight of you in this, he's going to wonder what he did to deserve you."

"Oh, go on." Dottie batted at Sophie, then turned back to Maggie. "How can I ever thank you?"

"You already have. You've given Pops a new lease on life. Made him feel whole again."

"Isn't it wonderful?" Her mom breathed the question.

Dottie wrung her hands. "I was so afraid you'd all be upset about this."

"Upset?" Maggie frowned. "Why would we be upset?"

"I don't know." Dottie toyed with the edge of the tablecloth. "I worried you'd think I was trying to take your grandma's place. I'd never do that."

"We know," Maggie soothed. "How do Wes and Lacey feel about it?"

"They're ecstatic."

"So are we." Maggie took Dottie's hand. "This is the beginning of a new chapter, but it doesn't erase the ones that went before."

"No, it doesn't."

"Okay," Annie said. "We'll all be crying like babies if we don't cut this out."

"You're right. Let's talk jewelry," Maggie said. "Diamonds to be exact. Is Pops buying you one?"

* * *

The rich, pungent smell of pizza mingled with the scent of disinfectant, and the high, shrill laughter of the young bounced off the clinic's walls. Staubach, Cash's homely mutt, roamed from one boy to the next, hoping for a bite of pizza, a slice of pepperoni. Ty had left Trouble, their pup, at home, figuring he'd be underfoot the whole night.

Brawley took a long drink of lukewarm soda. He'd been right to do this tonight. They had no overnighters scheduled, and he'd arranged for alternate boarding in the event of any emergencies. It sure beat the heck out of anything else he could think of to take his mind off Maggie.

He'd already hung plastic over the door openings between the back office area and the front reception and examination rooms. Hopefully, they'd be able to keep the clinic open for emergencies.

And speaking of emergencies. His apartment more than qualified. Doc Gibson had promised to work the clinic tomorrow so Brawley could have the day to pull his place together. Make it his own.

Right now, everything in his life was in upheaval, and he felt more than a little out of kilter because of it. He needed someplace he could relax. That felt like home. A small piece of sanity. His mom had promised to help him with it tomorrow. Go, Mom!

"Where will you board any animals that need to be put up for the next few days?" Ty snagged a piece of pepperoni off the last pizza slice.

"At my cousin Dawn's. She does kenneling along with her dog-grooming business. It would be impossible to make the kind of mess we're going to with animals here."

Cash wiped his hands on a napkin, looked at Ty and the boys. "You guys ready?" He rubbed his hands together in anticipation. "Nothing better than all-out destruction."

"Yeah," three voices chorused.

Ty pulled a face. "Hope we're not creating monsters."

Brawley reached into a bag and passed safety glasses to Cash and Ty, then grabbed a smaller bag off the front counter.

He knelt. "Okay, guys, come over here. Safety first on any job site."

Jesse, Josh, and Jonah crowded around him and nodded solemnly.

A quick stop at Sadler's Store had netted no eyewear small enough to fit the tykes. So, after some head-scratching, Brawley had headed into the sports section and found exactly what he needed. Swim goggles. Then he'd spent five minutes digging through the bin to find three exactly the same to avert any fights over who got which one.

"Here you go. Put these on and leave them on whenever we're working. Sophie'd never forgive me if one of you put out your eye."

"Our eye?" Josh raised a hand to his. "That would hurt."

"Yes, it would. But keep these on, and you'll be safe."

"'Kay." Jonah turned to his brother. "We won't get hurt, Josh." He pulled his goggles over his head.

The other two did the same, looked at each other, and giggled hysterically. Then they all tore off to check themselves out in the bathroom mirror.

"We look funny, Uncle Brawley," Jesse said as they ran back to him. "Are you gonna wear some?"

Brawley pulled his safety glasses from the larger bag and slid them on. He handed each of the kids an upholstery hammer, small enough for them to handle but big enough to produce some results.

Leading them over to an office wall, he drew a big X on it. "This needs to come down, men. Get 'er done."

"You want us to hit the wall?" Josh wanted to be really sure before he did something undoable.

"Yep."

Again, the triplets' heads swiveled as they looked at each other, then at their dad.

"Can we, Daddy?" Jesse asked.

Ty nodded. "You sure can."

With whoops and hollers, the three tore into the wall. Laughing like loons, they watched as little chunks flew.

Ty, hands in the pockets of his jeans, watched them. "Might be the beginning of something here. The boys can run a wrecking business when they get older." He laughed. "Hell, they run one now. At the house. Poor Sophie. I don't think she really understood what she was getting into when she took us on, but I sure am glad she did."

He raised his sledgehammer and took down half a wall. Sheetrock and dust flew.

The boys clapped in delight.

"Wow, Daddy. You're strong."

Ty raised an arm, showing off his muscles.

Working beside the others, Brawley asked, "How long do you think Maggie will stay in New York?"

Cash and Ty exchanged intense looks.

"She's moving there, Brawley," Cash finally said.

"Yeah, but—"

"This is her dream, pal." Ty rested his hammer on his shoulder.

"I know that."

"Do you? You've been gone. You haven't seen how hard she works at her business."

A muscle ticked in Brawley's jaw. "I'm not gonna screw it up for her."

"Good, because she deserves this shot," Cash said.

"Understood." He brought his own tool down hard enough to crash through the wall, boards and all.

* * *

Done for the night, Brawley found himself unable to settle. He grabbed a Lone Star from the fridge and took it downstairs. Sitting in the dark in Dottie's garden, he stared into the vast Texas sky and watched the stars twinkle to life overhead.

Nursing his beer, he thought about Ty and Cash. They'd both driven home to their families. Would be tucked into bed tonight with their sweethearts. Would he ever get there?

He'd kept an eye on Ty and the boys tonight. Brawley wanted kids. Had always figured he'd have some by now. But his plans had gotten derailed somewhere along the way.

Maggie.

The moonlight turned the white flowers in Dottie's garden into shimmery, glowing torches. A place for fantasy. The perfect spot to sit and think about Red.

He'd loved her through junior high and high school, then had made the biggest, boneheaded move of his life. He'd honestly thought he was doing the right thing all those years ago, stepping aside so she'd go to her design school. That after they both finished college, they'd hook up again.

They hadn't.

Maggie being Maggie, she wouldn't forgive him. He'd miscalculated her fiery temper. Her stubbornness.

So he'd moved to Dallas after he graduated, certain he'd stop loving her eventually. He couldn't. So what had he done? Decided to pick up and move home. Woo Maggie. Court her. Storm her walls till she caved.

How had that worked, dumbass?

She was leaving. Moving to New York to follow those very dreams he'd given her space to find.

His timing was off. Way off. Again. But Cash was dead right. He had no business standing in her way.

He glanced again at the sky. Star-crossed lovers? He didn't believe in that shit. Tipping the longneck bottle, he drank. Maybe if he had a couple more of these, he could sleep tonight.

A couple crickets chirped, their voices sounding loud in the quiet. Thinking about heading upstairs to fetch another beer, he heard Maggie's car pull into the drive, watched the swath of light her beams cut through the darkness.

An overhead light went on when she opened her door, and quiet music from her radio spilled into the night. Apparently Rita had cooked more than the girls could eat because Maggie got out and her head disappeared into the back seat. She came out with a plate of goodies.

His stomach rumbled. He'd worked off every bite of that long-ago pizza.

Maggie walked Dottie to her door and saw her safely inside. She still wore those sexy-as-hell shoes, and his engine kicked into overdrive.

When she started back to the car, he called out, "Hey, Red. Got any more food stashed away in that car?"

Her head swiveled around, hand to her heart. "Geez, Brawley, you could give a girl a heart attack."

"Didn't mean to startle you."

"Didn't you guys eat tonight?"

"Yeah, but we busted butt. I'm starving again."

She opened the back door and took out another plate. "You know my mom. She always makes twice as much as we need."

"I was counting on that."

She made to hand him the plate, but he shook his head. "Join me. Hold on a sec." He zipped upstairs and grabbed two more beers.

Coming back down, he saw she'd moved to Dottie's little turquoise table and had unwrapped a taco salad, complete with sour cream and guacamole.

He handed her a beer, then broke off a piece of the shell and used it to scoop up salad. Mouth full, he mumbled, "Mmmm. Your mom's one of the best cooks in the county."

They sat in the moonlight and devoured the salad.

She laughed. "Guess I was hungry, too."

Their fingers touched, and he linked their hands, held tight when she tried to pull away.

"Brawley—"

"No, let's not fight. Not tonight. Give me fifteen minutes under the stars, Maggie. Surely we can manage that." But he wondered if he could. He wanted, desperately, to kiss her.

"You ever go swimming at the hole anymore?" he asked.

When she shook her head, the moonlight glinted off her hair, her earrings. She looked for all the world like a fairy princess.

"Not anymore," she said. "It's been years."

"Wanna go?"

"Now?"

"Yeah."

"You're crazy, Brawley."

"About you."

Her sigh filled the garden. "I really do have to go. I'm a businesswoman, and I have to be up early."

He nodded.

She stood. "This was nice. Thanks."

He took both her hands in his. She swayed toward him, started to kiss his cheek.

"No." He met her lips with his. Hunger, raw and deep, ripped through him. He tasted the same emotion on her lips, in her. One kiss led to another and another.

Breathing hard, she broke away, running her fingers through her hair to push it off her face. "I can't do this. It was never a question of chemistry. We had that in spades."

"We still do." His voice was husky and ragged.

"I can't and won't deny that."

"Come upstairs with me. Stay the night." He trailed kisses along her neck, her collarbone. She shivered, and he knew she was close.

But she put her hands on his arms and pushed away. "I can't."

"I know I handled things badly, but how can you hold it against me so long?"

She didn't answer. Simply turned to walk away.

He grabbed her hand and kissed it before she melted into the night, leaving him standing in the dark, wanting more. So much more.

He wanted to bawl like a baby.

Chapter Seven

A pesky ray of sunlight caught him square in the eyes. Brawley rolled over, taking his pillow with him. Damn. He'd forgotten to close the shades.

There'd been some interesting goings-on in the driveway late last night. But he wouldn't think about that. Not yet.

Maggie would skin him alive if she found out about it and knew he knew but hadn't told her. The old rock and a hard place. He rubbed a hand over his chin. He should shave, but hell with it. He wasn't going into work, so why bother?

With every move, his muscles grumbled and groused, reminding him it had been way too long since he'd indulged in any real physical labor. The punching bag and weights in his fancy Dallas gym kept him in decent shape, but they sure as hell hadn't prepared him for hours wielding that sledgehammer.

By the time they'd destroyed and cleaned up last night, the kids had crashed. Jesse'd curled up on the reception room sofa and fallen fast asleep. Jonah had chosen the armchair next to him. They'd finally found Josh flat on his back behind the reception counter. All three still wore their swim goggles.

What amazed Brawley was that they hadn't so much as stirred when Ty removed the goggles or when the men hefted them up, carried them to the van, and strapped them in. Ty said they'd sleep all the way home, and he'd toss them into their beds, grubby clothes and all. Brawley wondered what Sophie had to say about that.

All in all, it had been an interesting evening.

His mind turned to Maggie. Last night in Dottie's garden, in the dark, he'd hoped. For what? Forgiveness? A turning back of the clock? It wasn't gonna happen. And that was about the most depressing thought he'd ever had.

He'd wanted her. Right here in his bed. Had, instead, stood and watched her drive away to her own.

And speaking of beds. Thank God, this would be his last night in this one. Way too soft. His own should arrive tomorrow. Before that happened, though, he had a lot to accomplish today.

Tossing the pillow aside, he squinted at the little jewel-box alarm clock. Another of Annie's treasures. Why neither she nor Sophie had taken it with them he didn't know. Today, though, it would be out of here, along with the rest of the fluff.

He groaned as he rolled over again. The next few hours were going to be busy. Time he crawled out of bed, got dressed, and threw on a pot of coffee. Cash should be here soon to help him haul away this stuff. Both Annie and Sophie had already assured him there wasn't anything here they needed or wanted.

He and Cash would toss everything in a neighbor's storage shed for now. Later, he hoped to hold a town-wide yard sale. One of the most appalling things about Maverick Junction was their lack of a humane society. He'd use the leftovers here to kick-start the fundraiser.

Maybe he could talk Sophie into spearheading it. When she'd come into the clinic last fall, dragging an unkempt stray cat with her, the options had been limited. At the mere mention of euthanasia, she'd decided to keep Lilybelle. And because of that bedraggled animal, he and Ty had stopped by in time to beat the bloody hell out of the bastard who'd been stalking Sophie.

A knock at the door snapped him out of those unpleasant thoughts, and he unfisted his hands. "Door's open."

Cash walked in, sniffing the air. "That coffee I smell?"

"Sure is. Those donuts I smell?"

"Sure are." Cash grinned and set the bag of fresh-baked donuts on the table. "Stopped by Sadler's. Figured if you were gonna work me like a mule today, I needed my sugar fix first."

"Amen to that." He squinted at his friend. "Annie didn't fix a big farmhouse breakfast for you?"

Cash snorted. "You kidding? When I got up, she threw me a sleepy smile, pulled the covers over her head, and mumbled something about me having a good time with you today."

"Smart woman. I wanted to stay in bed, too. I sure appreciate you coming over to help." Brawley poured two mugs, and they stood, hips against the counter, drinking coffee and eating the dunkers.

Cash glanced around the apartment. "Annie and I had some good times here, but I sure can see why you want a change. Way too girly."

Brawley chuckled. "Girly gone wild. Has she tried to do this to your house?"

"Nope. Thank God." Cash took one last swig of coffee, then rinsed his cup and set it in the sink. "Okay, pal, let's get started. The sooner we do, the sooner we finish."

They hauled and lugged. By their fourth trip, they cursed every one of the stairs up to the second-story apartment.

"Can I give you boys a hand?" Wiping her hands on a tea towel, Dottie opened her kitchen door.

"Thanks, but we've got it covered," Cash said.

"That girl of yours sure ended up with a lot of stuff, didn't she?"

"Yes, ma'am." Cash turned his ball cap backward.

"That your grandpa's sofa?" She nodded at the deep brown couch they'd set in the driveway.

"It is, and it's going home with me. I sure am glad Annie saved it from LeRoy's secondhand shop. I love this thing." Cash ran a hand over the back of it. "I can't wait to watch my next ball game sprawled on it. I think it'll be real happy in our family room."

"I think it will, too. Your grandpa would be pleased you're keeping it."

"Yeah, he would."

They slid the last nightstand into the back of Cash's truck as Brawley's mom pulled up in her snazzy little red convertible.

"Hey, good looking," Brawley called.

"Hey, yourself, handsome. See you two got an early start."

"If we're gonna hit the paint today, it made sense to clear out the place. Empty rooms paint easier. I talked to the moving company in Dallas yesterday, and they promised to deliver my stuff tomorrow."

She nodded toward the truck. "Is that your bed in there?"

"Yep." He scuffed his boot over the drive. "Well, technically, it's Annie's."

"Where will you sleep tonight?"

"I've got a sleeping bag. I'll be fine."

"Oh, honey, that's nonsense. Why don't you stay with your dad and me? It doesn't make sense to bunk on the hard floor."

"I'm good. Honest." He kissed the top of her head. "Don't worry about me, Mom. I'm a big boy. Let me give Cash a hand with this load before we run to Sadler's for the paint."

"Did you pick out your colors?"

"Yes, ma'am, I did." He pulled the paint cards from his pocket and tapped the pale gray. "This is it."

"For the whole apartment?"

"Yep."

"You're going to paint all the walls in every room the same color?"

"I am."

"You are such a guy."

"At the risk of sounding repetitive, I am."

She reached up and ruffled his hair. "Yes, you are."

"Except the ceilings. I'm gonna leave those cream. Annie painted them not even a year ago."

"Hallelujah." His mom raised her eyes to the heavens. "I hate ceilings. No matter how careful I am, I end up with more paint on me than on the Sheetrock."

Cash laughed. "Wish the two of you could have seen Annie when I walked in on her painting this place. What a mess. It seems heiresses aren't expected to slap paint on their own walls, so she'd never lifted a brush in her life. But she was game. Have to give her that."

"She's a good woman, Cash," Karolyn Odell said.

"Don't I know it. The day she rode into Maverick Junction on that big black Harley of hers was the luckiest day of my life."

"Oh, geez." Brawley groaned. "Cut it out, Cash. You're feeding into all of my mom's fairy-tale shit."

"Sorry." The grin on Cash's face belied his words.

"Too bad somebody else can't settle down with one woman." Karolyn's gaze strayed to her son.

"See? See what you've done?"

Cash laughed out loud.

Brawley scrubbed both hands over his face and let out a mammoth sigh. "Maybe you could run to Sadler's, Mom, and pick up the paint while we deal with this." He nodded to the loaded truck.

"I could. And if you think I didn't catch that less than subtle attempt at changing the subject, you'd be wrong."

"No, ma'am, I didn't. I wasn't aiming for subtle." He fished a credit card from his wallet and passed it to her. "We'll need some rollers and—"

"Son of mine, I've done this a thousand times. I know exactly what we need." Her eyes narrowed as she studied the paint chip. "Not sure I'd use this everywhere, but I have to admit it's a good choice. It'll go great with your furniture."

When he nodded, she asked, "You sure you don't want a couple accent walls?"

"I'm sure."

"Okay." She drew out the word. "You're the one living with it."

She stuck her head inside Dottie's open door. "You want to ride to Sadler's with me?"

"Give me two seconds."

True to her word, his new landlady was out the door almost before the words left her mouth. In no time flat, Dottie and his mom were strapped in and headed to the store.

"Wonder what color she'll bring back for your accent walls," Cash said.

"Your guess is as good as mine."

* * *

Brawley's mom straightened, arching her back. "And that's that." She laid her roller in the pan. "Looks wonderful, doesn't it?"

"Yes, it does. Gotta give you credit. You were totally right." And she had been. She'd come back from Sadler's loaded down with paint supplies and his pale gray paint—and another couple gallons of a dark charcoal gray.

Every room had one wall in the deeper color, and darn if she hadn't nailed it. Exactly right. Masculine. Clean. Him.

Now if he only had some furniture.

He wrapped his mom in a big hug, smearing paint on both of them. "We did good, didn't we?"

"Yes, we did." She rested her head on his chest. "I'm so glad you've come home."

"I don't think Dad shares your enthusiasm."

"He'll come around. At the bottom of it all, he's as happy to have you here as I am. He's just not sure it's best for you."

"It is. It's what I want."

"I know. Your dad will get there. Give him time."

Through the open window, Brawley heard the crunch of tires. Glancing out, he saw Maggie's deep-blue, several-years-old Chrysler 300.

"You've got company."

"Don't think so. It'd be a cold day in hell before Maggie came to see me." Drying his hands on a paper towel, he stepped outside.

When the wind caught the door and slammed it behind him, Maggie glanced up. Her smile slipped away, and she reached for her back-door handle.

"Hey, Red. Wait a sec."

"Why?"

"You can't take a minute or two to be neighborly?"

"Last night was nice, but nothing's changed."

"You look tired, sugar."

"Well, there you go, Brawley Odell. All that flattery. Who said you don't know how to sweet-talk a woman?"

"I didn't say you look bad, just tired." Bad? No, sir. Not by a long shot. Dressed in a flame-red, silky top and pencil-thin black pants, the lady gave off enough heat to kindle a prairie fire.

Reaching into the back seat, she drew out a garment bag. "I couldn't sleep, so I ended up in the shop today before the sun topped the horizon."

"That's not fun."

"No. But—" She held up the bag. "I have Dottie's dress almost finished. Thought I'd stop by, do a rough fitting."

"Her dress?"

"For the wedding."

A grin split his face. "You're making her wedding dress?"

Maggie smiled and heat raced through him. "Yes." She sighed. "Dottie and Pops. Can you believe it?"

"Gotta admit they caught me by surprise."

Brawley's mother poked her head around the corner. "Maggie. Hello."

"Hi, Mrs. Odell. I'd ask what you're doing here, but from the gobs of paint on your face and clothes, I can figure that out. Brawley put you to work, did he?"

"I volunteered. His furniture's coming tomorrow."

"That's good. Did you finish painting?"

"Sure did," Brawley said. "Mom's a slave-driver. Come up and take a peek. Looks a little different with all that blue gone."

"I liked the blue."

"You would."

"What's that supposed to mean?"

"Nothing. You like color, that's all."

He watched while she replaced the garment bag in the car. Curiosity ran strong in her. He'd known she wouldn't be able to resist. Especially with his mom here to provide a safety net.

She sauntered across the drive on heels nearly as high as stilts and every bit as red as her top. Oh, yeah. Shoes like that did crazy things to a guy. He swiped a hand over his mouth. Those legs should be registered as a lethal weapon.

When she reached the top of the stairs, he stood aside while his mom carefully kissed Maggie's cheek so as not to get paint on her. He envied his mother when Maggie kissed her back.

The two loved each other. His mom had been beyond sorry when things hadn't worked out between them. She'd welcomed Maggie into the family, considered her the daughter she'd never had.

His dad, on the other hand, had been relieved he'd ended the relationship and made no bones about it. He loved Maggie, but he wanted more for his son and figured she'd hold him back. All these years later, Trace Odell made it clear that Brawley had better have moved back home for the right reasons—and not because of Maggie.

Brawley assured him he'd returned to Maverick Junction because he'd wanted to. Because he missed the simple things. Friends stopping by. Easy evenings over a beer. People who cared. His mom spending the day with him, helping him paint his walls.

Ten years ago, he'd embraced Dallas. Had wanted big city. Now he'd had it and was done with it.

"Don't I get a hug?" he asked.

The look she shot him could have frozen Lake Travis in thirty seconds flat.

Dottie yoo-hooed from below. "Are you showing off your new paint, Brawley Odell, without inviting me?"

He chuckled. "Not a chance, sweetheart. We're waiting on you. Come on up."

He opened the door and held it while the three women filed in.

"Well, would you look at this." Dottie let out a small whistle. "These old walls haven't seen this much paint in the last century. Nice. Very nice. Very different."

"I like it." Maggie turned in circles, taking in the mix of colors. Her eyes fixed on his. "Truth. Did you choose these shades?"

He glanced at his mom. "I picked the pale gray. Mom decided we needed a touch of the dark to go with it."

"Good choice, Mom." Maggie gave her two thumbs up. "I absolutely loved Annie's colors. They fit her. The whole apartment did. It fit Sophie, too, after she put her own little touches on it. But this. This is right for you, Brawley."

She turned another circle. "It's strange to see it empty, though. The light fixtures, the vintage table Annie sanded and refurbished. All the little knickknacks. Gone."

"They weren't me, Maggie."

"No, I don't suppose they were."

"This is temporary, but I might as well be comfortable while I'm here."

"You could have come home, son. You're always welcome."

"I know that." He laid a hand on his mother's shoulder. "As much as I love you and Dad, that's not the best idea. I'm too used to being on my own. And you and Dad are used to living your lives without me there."

"While I'm sorry you don't have him, Karolyn, I'm awfully glad he's here," Dottie said. "For as long as he wants to stay."

"He should be handy to have around." His mom patted his cheek. "Before I go, son, I have something in the car for you." Halfway out the door, she stopped. "You need to promise to tell me if I start suffocating you."

"Oh, believe me, I will."

His mother scurried down the stairs.

Brawley looked at Maggie and Dottie. Both women simply shrugged.

Karolyn was back in a flash, a huge box in her hands.

"What's that?"

She opened the crate and pulled out a huge wreath. "For your door. To celebrate spring."

His mouth dropped open, and he took a step back. "Mom, it's covered in flowers."

She squinted at it. "Oh, my gosh. It is!" Then she laughed at the horror-struck expression on his face.

He shook his head and stuck his hands in his back pockets. "Men don't decorate their doors with flowers. Especially not Texans."

"Sure they do." She gave him a smacking kiss and hung the wreath.

He winced. Shit! He'd have to hide the thing when Cash or Ty came around, then hang it back up before his mom showed up again. He glanced at Maggie and glowered at her grin.

Before he could come up with a legitimate argument against it, a huge truck lumbered down the street. Brawley eyed it speculatively. Then, making out the mover's logo on the side, he fisted his hand in an air-pump. "Yes! My furniture. It's here a day early."

"You want us to help?" Maggie asked.

"No. The movers will haul everything up. Between starting the demo on the clinic last night, clearing Annie's stuff out of the apartment with Cash this morning, then painting the rest of the day, I'm bushed. I'll have them set the furniture in place and just stack the boxes anywhere they can for now."

"But we could—" Dottie started.

"Nope. You've got a big event coming up this weekend, and Maggie's got something special to show you. Why don't the two of you run along downstairs? I'm in no hurry. When it's all put together, I'll have everybody up for drinks. Some snacks."

When his mother started back into the apartment, he shook his head, grabbed her by the waist, and turned her around. "You're leaving, too. I've got a hunch your body's chewing you out nearly as much as mine is me. Go. Get cleaned up and make Dad take you out to dinner."

He gave her a kiss and herded her down the steps, then walked to the end of the drive to meet the movers. Finally. Once he had his things around him again, he'd feel a whole lot better.

Behind him, he heard Dottie's cry of delight.

"My dress!"

"It's not finished yet, but I want to see how it fits."

He turned to see the two disappear inside and remembered

how tired Maggie had looked when she'd pulled in. Looks like the hours had paid off. Her unselfishness had made Dottie one happy woman.

* * *

Brawley fished out his wallet and tipped the two men healthily. Job done. Then again, as he looked around the apartment, maybe he should make that job barely started. What the hell would he do with all this stuff?

Everything had fit nicely in his Dallas place, a condo three times this size. He'd moved quite a bit of his furniture into storage. Still…This should prove interesting.

First things first. Food. As the moving van headed off to Dallas, Maggie stepped out of Dottie's, chatting a mile a minute.

The gods had smiled on him. Had presented the perfect opportunity to grab Maggie for dinner. To take another small step toward making peace.

Halfway downstairs, he called out to her. "Hey, Red, it's dinnertime."

She made a production of checking her watch. "Actually, it's closer to a quarter past."

"Hah-hah. You hungry?" he asked.

"I am. Thought I'd stop by Sally's and pick up a burger to eat on my drive home."

"I have a better idea. I'm on my way out to grab something, too. Let's go together."

"I'm not having dinner with you, Brawley."

"Why not? You're hungry, I'm hungry. Makes sense. It's not like I'm asking you for a date. Loosen up."

"Loosen up?"

He walked down the last few stairs and closed the distance between them. "Look, I'm gonna be living here in Maverick Junction. From now on."

When she opened her mouth, he laid a silencing finger on those luscious lips. "I know you're leaving, but when you come back to visit—and I know you will—I'm gonna be here. Your friends are my friends. We need to learn to coexist. Last night was a good start. Consider tonight a second tutoring session."

She laughed. "Oh, that's rich, Brawley. *You're* going to teach *me* how to play nice?"

"Guess you could say we'll learn from each other."

Her eyes went a deeper shade of green. "I don't know that you and I ever played nice with each other."

"Then maybe it's time we started."

She cursed the timing. If she'd been five minutes sooner, she'd have escaped this little scenario. Since Dottie stood at the kitchen window smiling at them, she probably shouldn't knee Brawley and take him down. Though damned if there weren't still times she dreamed of doing exactly that.

Make him hurt in the most elemental of ways. As she had.

As she still did.

Because of their shared friendships, she couldn't always avoid him. Like now.

She'd rather eat dirt than a burger alone with Brawley, but he'd trapped her. And he would pay.

She narrowed her eyes. "I want it understood this is against my better judgment. I won't enjoy this and neither will you."

"Understood. Let's go have an awful time." He held out his hand.

"I'll meet you there."

* * *

Half an hour later, she had to swallow her words along with the burger. Although she'd spent the better part of the day beating herself up for last night's shared kisses, here she was enjoying herself with him again. She'd forgotten how much fun Brawley could be. Had forgotten that rapier-sharp wit.

He'd led her to a small table at the back of the restaurant, speaking to everybody he passed, poking fun at himself, assuring them the animal clinic would be open again in a few days, and totally ignoring the speculative glances sent their way.

After they sat down, Brawley asked, "Dottie like the dress?"

"She loved it. It's absolutely stunning on her."

"Figured it would be. She's a good-looking woman, and you're one hell of a designer. Winning combination."

Sally brought them sweet teas without needing to ask. They ordered cheeseburgers and greasy fries. He pulled the lettuce off his the instant their waitress set his meal in front of him.

"You're not going to eat that?"

"Nope."

"Lettuce is good for you."

"Not on a hot sandwich," he groused.

Maggie forked the lettuce and added it to her burger. "You have some strange habits, Brawley Odell."

"Possibly," he conceded. "How many will be at this shindig on Saturday?"

Maggie shook her head. "A whole lot more than we'd originally planned. Dottie and Fletch decided on an intimate family wedding. As it turns out, practically the entire town wants to come, and everybody assumes he's invited."

"So small and intimate has shifted to large and complicated."

"Exactly. And that's okay. It's only fitting that all of Maverick Junction and half of Lone Tree celebrate with them." Maggie took a bite of her burger, her tongue sliding out to lick a speck of mayonnaise from the corner of her mouth.

Brawley breathed deeply and wrestled his overactive libido to the ground.

"For the town, it's an opportunity to get dressed up and party. Pops and Dottie aren't exactly your typical bride and groom."

"Because?"

"Well, they're…more mature. They're in love with each other, not in lust like most newlyweds."

"In other words, you don't think they'll be falling all over each other?"

"Brawley! We're talking about my grandfather."

"Yeah?"

"So this isn't young love with all the hearts and flowers. Not that Dottie doesn't deserve the romance."

"Oh, I think they're doing okay in the romance department."

She laid down her sandwich. "What do you mean?"

Oh, boy. Now he'd stepped in it. He sipped his tea, giving himself a minute. "Forget I said anything."

"How am I supposed to do that?"

"Come on, Mags. You're a big girl. You know what goes on between couples."

She grimaced.

He laughed. He couldn't help it. "They're older, not dead, sugar. There's still plenty of heat."

Slowly, she shook her head. "I don't even want to know how you can be so sure."

He popped a fry in his mouth.

"This is a ridiculous conversation," she said.

"Your grandfather stopped by for a booty call after you left last night."

She choked. "Oh, geez."

He made to pat her back, but she elbowed him away.

"I was at the window when he came out, all mussed, shirt half unbuttoned, and barefoot. The two of them shared a real nice kiss before he got in his truck and drove away. Believe me, sweetheart, theirs is not a platonic relationship."

"I never said it was."

"Good." He swirled another fry in ketchup.

"Please tell me they weren't rolling around naked in the garden."

"In the garden? No."

She pressed her fingertips to her eyes as if blocking the visual. After a full minute of silence, she threw him a wobbly smile. "I'm happy for him. For both of them. It's a good thing."

"It is." He crunched his pickle. "Sad state of affairs, though, when an octogenarian is getting more than I am."

"Yeah, isn't it?" She grinned wickedly.

More than ready to leave the topic behind, he asked about Ella. "How's she working out?"

He questioned Maggie about her plans once she hit New York, she asked about his for the clinic. Any trace of awkwardness disappeared.

He finished his fries and started on hers. She slapped his hand away. "Eat your own."

"I did." He pointed at his empty plate. "They're gone. Sally didn't give me as many as she gave you."

"Bull. Order some more."

"Nah, I'm okay." Lightning quick, he grabbed a couple more of hers.

"Okay, so I've heard the company line."

He quirked a brow. "About what?"

"The clinic. I know what you're telling everybody, but will your doors open on time?"

"Yep. I had a crew working today. Cash and Ty are gonna meet me there tomorrow. So's my dad. If we put in a couple long days, we'll make it."

"What all are you doing?"

"Out front, not too much. A little reorganization of the reception area, some sprucing up in the exam rooms. You know, slapping some paint on the walls, new flooring. Most of the changes are in the back. We're doing some work in Doc's office. Knocking out a closet, enlarging the bath, sticking in a shower."

"Whoa! A shower? That sounds pretty major to me."

"Dottie's place is great, and I love the claw-foot for soaking. But a man can't live without his shower. After a day working with animals, I can be pretty grungy. With a tub, I feel like I'm soaking in my own dirt. I need to wash it away, right down the drain, and I'd prefer to do it before I leave the clinic."

"Makes sense."

"Want to stop and take a peek at what we've done so far?"

"I'm dying to, but I need to get home. Tomorrow's another busy day. Between planning this weekend's wedding, training Ella, and getting everything ready before I head to New York, I'm meeting myself coming and going."

They argued over the check.

"It's not a date," she reminded him. "Therefore, I pay for my own meal."

"It's two friends—"

At her raised brows, he backtracked. "It's two *old acquaintances* sharing dinner. If one wants to pick up the other's tab, why not?"

"You're impossible."

"My mom's told me that a time or twelve."

He walked her to her car. Before she could open the door, he snaked an arm around her waist and pulled her to him. When his mouth came down hot and hard on hers, she shocked him by rising on tiptoes to meet him. She melted into his kiss. It had been so long and felt so good. So right.

When he lifted his head and stepped back, Maggie blinked. The world tilted, shook, then resettled.

"Why did you do that?" she whispered.

"I'm a starving man, Maggie Sullivan. I've been aching to taste those lips again. That mouth."

"That's your definition of friendly?" She fought to get her breathing under control.

"Not yours?"

"No."

"Don't guess it was." He tucked his hands in his pockets.

Reaching behind her, she opened the car door and slid in. If her hands shook when she inserted the key into the ignition, it was because she was tired. It had grown late and she'd had a long day.

It had nothing whatsoever to do with the man standing beside her car, watching her like a cat. Nothing to do with that kiss he'd just planted on her.

Nothing to do with the hunger he'd ignited.

Damn him to hell and back.

Chapter Eight

Radio blaring, windows down, and the wind whipping through her hair, Maggie wondered at the wisdom of keeping her shop open. Barely noon and here she was on the road to Maverick Junction again. She'd driven this stretch of highway so many times this past week, her car could probably make the trip without her.

Her mind raced. So many things to think about, decisions to make. The shop and Pops. Even her mare.

Staring out at the open range on either side of the highway, Maggie realized how much she'd missed riding Duchess. She'd taken her out every day when she lived at home. Then she'd moved in with Pops and, even though it had about killed her to be separated from the horse, Maggie had left her with her folks.

Her original plan had been to drive over to her parents' after work several times a week and take Duchess for a run. That hadn't happened. She hadn't counted on the long hours it would take to start up a business. To make it successful.

Now, with the move to New York coming up, her horse would get even less exercise. It wasn't fair to Duchess, one of the best barrel racers in Texas. They'd won medals galore. How long had it been, though, since they'd competed? Six months? A year? Geez.

Maybe she'd ask Ty if he wanted her. She'd make a good ride for Sophie.

Maggie grinned. Sophie. City slicker through and through, she'd started to settle into Texas ranch life. She didn't spook every time a cow lowed or a bull raised its head to drill her with those bloodshot eyes. She still couldn't fish worth a darn, but Maggie figured there were worse crimes.

Spotting the side road to Cash and Annie's, she slowed and made the turn. Annie'd called early this morning, wanting her input on some wedding-centerpiece ideas before she showed them to Dottie.

When Cash's log house came into view, Maggie sighed. She always did—every single time she visited. He'd built it himself on the edge of his grandfather's land. A lake backed up to the house and lent a serene air. Flawless.

Lucky Annie. She'd won not only Cash's heart but got to wake up here every morning as a bonus. And Maggie couldn't be happier for her.

As she slid from behind the wheel, Brawley limped around the corner of the house.

Maggie gawked at him. "You're missing half your pants."

He looked down at the gaping hole in the denims, a sheepish expression on his face. "Had a bull who wanted to get a little too friendly this morning."

"You could have been hurt."

"Would you care?"

"Of course I would." She paused. "I like your mama, and she'd have been brokenhearted."

"You're a hard woman, Maggie Sullivan."

She shrugged. "He didn't really hurt you, did he?"

"Nah. Dinged my pride a little, that's all. I didn't deal with many bulls in Dallas. Got careless."

"So why are you limping?"

"Lot of weight behind him. Left a bruise. No big deal." He waggled his brows. "On the other hand, maybe it does hurt some. Want to kiss it? Make it all better?"

"In your dreams."

"Yeah." He sighed. "Figured that's how you'd feel."

"A customer of mine said to tell you thanks, by the way."

"Oh?"

"Seems you recommended she take her scraggly-looking mutt to Dawn Marie to be groomed. Let me tell you, she did one heck of a job. I barely recognized Farley. He looked ten times better than the last time she brought him to the shop."

"A cocker spaniel?"

"Yes."

"I remember him. Mrs. Wilson needed a miracle, and Dawn's the best."

"She is that." Maggie slid her sunglasses on top of her head. "So what are you doing here? Last I checked, there wasn't any livestock here."

"No. As much as our Annie loves the horses, I don't think she'd stand for them grazing in the front yard."

Maggie wished Brawley would take off his dark shades. They added to his hot, sexy attitude, but they hid his eyes, and that left her uneasy.

"Cash and I rode a couple of his horses over. I'm thinking about buying one now that I'm gonna be here."

"Which one?"

"Black Jack."

She closed her eyes. The huge black stallion. Magnificent animal. "You couldn't make a better choice."

"That's what I'm thinking. Now that I've ridden him—" He spread his hands. "What can I say? Love at first sight."

She nodded. "I'm trying to figure out what to do about Duchess."

"Why?"

"Duh. I'm leaving."

"I wouldn't sell your horse yet. Give yourself time. Take things in steps."

"It doesn't seem fair to her. Even being here, it's been so long since I've taken her out for a ride." She sighed. "There are never enough hours in the day."

"I'll see she gets exercised."

"I can't ask you to do that."

"You didn't. I volunteered. You need to let your dad know, though. He'd love the chance to shoot me and chalk it up to horse thievery."

She rolled her eyes.

"Hey, just saying. Cash and I thought we'd try to sweet-talk Annie out of lunch."

Annie stepped through the open sliders just then. Surprised registered on her face. "Hey, Maggie. Brawley."

"What?" Maggie asked.

"Nothing. Not used to seeing the two of you together without weapons drawn."

"Very funny."

"What happened to you?" Annie stared at Brawley's torn jeans.

"A little accident. I'm fine."

Before Annie could grill him anymore, Cash rounded the corner and leaped onto the deck. "Hey, beautiful." He swept Annie into a lusty kiss.

"In case you've forgotten, we've got an audience," Annie managed when she caught her breath.

"I didn't forget." Cash lifted his head. "Thought I'd give my pal

Brawley some pointers. Figure he must need them."

"That would be the day," Brawley threw back. He sent a sideways glance at Maggie.

"Don't even think about it." She planted a hand on his chest.

"We could show them how it's supposed to be done."

Her tongue flicked out, and she shook her head. "No, we couldn't." She dared a glance at Cash. "Call off your dog."

He frowned. "Staubach?"

"No, this one." She jerked a thumb at Brawley.

At exactly that instant, Staubach came tearing around the corner. He made a flying leap, catching Brawley waist high. One slurping kiss aimed at his face, he did a U-turn and headed toward Annie and Cash.

"Stop," Cash ordered. The dog paid no heed, barreling into them and nearly knocking Annie off her feet.

She laughed and knelt to rub the dog's lopsided head. "You're a good boy, aren't you?"

The dog, in total ecstasy now, rolled over, legs in the air, to have his belly rubbed. Annie succumbed.

"Damn dog gets more attention than I do," Cash muttered.

"Oh, that's so not true." Annie stood and made a pretense of rubbing Cash's belly.

"A little lower, honey."

She leaned in and nipped his neck.

"Ouch."

Annie feigned innocence. "Something wrong?"

"Nope." He nibbled at her lower lip.

She gave him a gentle push. "You're so bad."

Motioning to Brawley and Maggie, she said, "Come on in, guys. Get washed up, and I'll set out some lunch. Afterward Maggie and I have some business to attend to."

"Business?" Brawley frowned at Maggie.

"Wedding business."

"Ah." Brawley took Maggie's hand in his and led her up the walkway. She tried to convince herself the tingles that ran up her arm and made their way through her were simply her imagination. It didn't work.

Immune to Brawley Odell? No way, no how.

But she'd ignore both him and the effect he had on her. Another week and she'd be gone.

* * *

Brawley followed Cash inside. Bringing up the rear wasn't really all that bad. When you had two women like Maggie and Annie in front, the scenery proved pretty darned good. First class, in fact.

He stopped in the foyer. "Damn, Cash. Every time I walk in this place, I'm amazed all over again. You've done yourself proud."

"I have, haven't I?" Hands on hips, Cash swiveled to take in the view. His gaze stopped on his new wife. "House isn't bad either, is it?"

Brawley laughed.

Maggie shook her head. "Oh, you're a smooth one, Cash Hardeman."

"He thinks it'll earn him an extra piece of pie." Annie ran a hand through her hair and grinned. "He might be right."

"Pie? You made pie?" Maggie stared at her as if she'd grown a second head. "From scratch?"

"It's sort of my new hobby. I've been trying out different recipes and playing with the crust. My mom would die if she saw the mess I make. But... my kitchen, my mess."

"My wife." Cash kissed her forehead, then swept off his hat and tossed it on the couch.

Brawley carefully set his on a table in the foyer. He didn't consider himself superstitious, but still. No sense asking for trouble. You set your hat brim up, not only did you keep it in better shape longer, but if a little good luck passed by, rumor had it the hat would catch it.

Right now, he figured he could use all the luck he could get.

Cash, on the other hand, was on a real winning streak. Brawley had never seen his friend happier.

His gaze slid to Maggie dressed in well-worn, skin-tight denims and a silky little top. His mouth watered for more than Annie's pie. So, yeah, he could use some luck.

"Do you mind if Maggie and I look at a couple of these centerpieces before we eat?" Annie called from the study.

"Good with me. While you do that, Brawley can take a peek at the info I have on a couple bulls I'm considering. Give me his opinion." Cash laughed and yanked at the torn denim flap on Brawley's jeans. "He's an expert on bulls."

* * *

"You think I might borrow your horses after lunch?"

Cash's forehead creased. "Sure. Anytime. What are you up to?"

"Nothing. Thought maybe I'd talk Maggie into a quick ride. She told me earlier she hasn't taken one for a while."

"A ride? That's the only thing on your mind?"

Brawley glanced toward where the women sat huddled over sketches of floral arrangements, studying them as though they meant the difference between life and death.

"Yeah," he answered. "A ride."

Cash moved to the fridge, grabbed two Cokes, and tossed one toward Brawley. As he caught it, Cash snapped his own open and took a long drink. His eyes never left Brawley's.

"We've been friends a long time."

Brawley nodded.

"You know I love you like a brother."

"I do."

"Maggie means the world to me, too."

"Understood." Brawley chugged his own soda.

"You can't hurt her again."

"I don't intend to."

"You don't *intend* to," Cash repeated. "That leaves a lot of open ground."

Brawley didn't flinch. "I can tell you what you want to hear. I can stand right here in your kitchen, with the scent of Annie's fresh-baked pie in the air, and promise not to hurt Maggie. Again. But you and I both know life doesn't come with guarantees. None of us can see into the future or know for certain what will happen down the road."

A muscle ticked in Cash's jaw. "You weren't there to see what your leaving did to her, Brawley. You didn't hold her while she cried. For you. For the future you destroyed when you told her you weren't coming back."

"No, I didn't. Was I scum for the way I handled that whole thing? Without a doubt. Even though my intentions were good, I was careless with Maggie, and I hurt her." He rubbed the back of his neck. "If I could go back, do it over, it would never have gone down that way."

"But you can't," Cash said.

"No, I can't. I sure as hell can try to repair what's left between her and me, though. I want to do that."

"She's leaving. Why not just let it be?"

"Because, pal, it's eating a hole in my gut." He set his soda on the counter. "Can I borrow your horses? Easy question. Yes or no."

"Oh, hell. Of course you can. But Brawley?"

"Yeah?"

"Don't make me hunt you down like a coyote on the prowl."

Brawley nodded.

They gave the girls another ten minutes. Geez, how long could it take to decide between pearl white, soft white, or antique white ribbons for the bridal bouquet—and what the hell difference did it make?

"Should we start whining about how hungry we are?" he finally asked.

"I don't know about you, but I wouldn't have to fake it. Thought Annie said a few minutes." Cash raised his voice a little. "I'm famished. My wife sent me off to work without breakfast."

"That's because you had other activities on your mind when you woke up this morning," Annie said from the other room.

"Yeah, I did, didn't I?"

Annie laughed. "You weren't complaining about the lack of food when you headed out the door. In fact, if I remember correctly, you had a mile-wide smile on that smug face of yours."

Brawley grinned, thinking Cash looked pretty damned pleased with himself even now.

Annie stood when they moseyed into the dining room. "Think we should feed these two?"

"Since I'm hungry, too, I'll vote yes." Maggie pushed back her chair, then ran a hand through that glorious mass of red curls.

Brawley found another appetite whetted. "What's for lunch?"

"Sandwiches and pasta salad." As Annie started pulling things from the fridge, she said, "Sorry, guys. Meant to do lunch first, but I showed Maggie one of the pictures, and, well..." She shrugged. "Lunch will be on the table in no time."

Sure enough, inside five minutes, they relaxed on the back patio, the sun warming their backs, eating egg salad sandwiches and pasta salad, and eyeing huge slices of still-warm apple pie.

Staubach sprawled close, tail thumping against the deck, one eye open in case anything remotely edible fell.

Brawley kicked back in his chair and studied the lake with its clear blue water, a few birds skimming its surface. Behind him, pots of geraniums and daisies brightened the log home, Annie's mark, no doubt.

He envied his friend this piece of paradise.

His stretch in Dallas had been like time out of time. He'd lived well there. Sowed more than a few wild oats trying to dislodge Maggie from his mind and heart and never quite succeeding. Now, he was done trying.

This, right here, was what he craved.

Across from him, Maggie's ivory complexion fairly glowed. She slathered blocker on it constantly and stayed out of the sun as much as possible. The bane of a redhead's existence.

That sun glinted off her red curls and created a halo effect. Talk about deceptive. Maggie? An angel?

Not likely. His Maggie was real. As red-blooded as they came.

She popped the last bite of pie into her mouth and licked her lips. "Incredible, Annie." She pointed her fork at her now empty plate. "You ought to enter this in the fair."

"Seriously?"

"Absolutely. You'll win hands down."

"And wouldn't that send Ruby Dunst into a tailspin?" Cash asked.

"She still winning every year?" Brawley asked.

Cash nodded.

"I don't want to make anyone angry," Annie said.

"And there's my opening." Brawley shot to his feet, held a hand toward Maggie. "I'm sure *you* don't want to make anybody mad, either, sugar, so come take a ride with me."

"Excuse me?"

One side of his mouth kicked up in a grin. "Cash says we can borrow his horses. You're dressed for it, so let's see what you've still got."

"I can sit a horse better than you any day, Brawley Odell."

"Prove it."

Maggie stood, started for the door, and stopped. "I need to help clear lunch first."

Annie shooed her away. "I've got this. My helper here..." She tipped her head at Cash. "Works cheap."

"Stay away at least an hour." Cash winked at Brawley. "Give my wife and me some time. I'm awfully tired. Think I might need a nap."

Annie swatted him. "Hands to yourself, big boy."

"Not in this lifetime." He grabbed her around the waist.

"Time for us to skedaddle and give them some privacy." Brawley grabbed Maggie's hand and pulled her behind him.

* * *

Mistake. Big mistake. The words played in a loop in Maggie's mind as she walked beside Brawley. Too close. His hip brushed hers. His thumb rubbed across the back of the hand he held, sending frissons of electricity shooting through her.

She didn't like this man. He was bad for her. He'd cost her more than she could ever admit, even to herself.

And still, she found herself attracted to him.

She needed to keep her distance.

That was out of the question—physically—right now. But she could hold her emotions in check. Could recite all the wrongs he'd done her. They'd carry her through a ride to Dallas and back.

Yet when they reached the horses, she couldn't regret going along with him. It had been so long. She rested her head on the roan's and cooed to her, ran a hand down the horse's flank.

"Aren't you beautiful, Indigo Girl? You and Duchess would like each other. Yes, you would," she soothed. "You going to let me take a ride? Hmm?"

She placed her booted foot in the stirrup and swung herself up into the saddle. Beside her, Brawley mounted Black Jack in one smooth move.

He clucked his tongue, and the stallion took off at a canter. Maggie followed, smiling at the wind on her face, in her hair. Better, far better than in any car, convertible or not. She and Indigo settled into a rhythm beside Brawley and Black Jack.

He'd chosen well. The horse suited him. Both dark and brooding. Both handsome, brilliant specimens.

They rode over the range without speaking. Maggie gave herself up to the moment and simply enjoyed. Brawley finally pulled on the reins, slowing Black Jack to a trot. They rode into a meadow, bluebonnets rioting around them.

He stopped and dismounted. Letting the reins trail, he turned to Maggie and held out his arms. She hesitated.

"You're safe with me, Maggie."

"Said the serpent to Eve."

He had the good grace to laugh. "Seriously. Come on."

"I can get down from a horse without—"

"I know you're a liberated, independent, self-sufficient woman, Red. I know you can dismount. Hell, I've seen you do it a hundred times. Remember all those rides you, Cash, and I took? We rode for hours on end."

"We had fun, didn't we?"

"We did." His hands still reaching for her, he said, "So just this once. Let me help you down. I won't tell a soul."

She punched him on the shoulder but leaned into him. His arms closed around her, lowering her very slowly to the ground, sliding her along the length of his very hot, very hard body.

By the time the toes of her boots touched the earth, she could barely breathe.

"Brawley—"

He shook his head. "Uh-uh. No serious talk." He pulled a blanket from his saddlebag and shook it out. "Lie here with me for a few minutes."

"Won't the horses wander away?"

"Nope. This is a test. Cash insists they're trained for ground tying. Drop the reins, and they'll stay put."

"And if they don't?"

Brawley held up his phone. "We call the cavalry."

Dropping onto the blanket, he took her hand and gave it a tug. "Come here." His voice sounded husky.

"This is a bad idea."

"No. Two friends, beautiful weather, wildflowers blooming. Don't overthink this. Just enjoy. I'm not gonna bite."

"Biting isn't exactly what I'm worried about."

"I didn't bring you out here to seduce you, sugar."

Heat flooded her face.

"I love it when you blush like that."

She threw her hands over her cheeks. "One of the curses of a redhead."

Giving in, she relaxed onto the blanket. She lay back and stared up at the sky. "It is a gorgeous day, isn't it?"

"This is one of the few times we've been totally alone together since—"

"Since you threw me back like a fish that didn't measure up?"

He winced. "That's not what happened."

She raised herself on one elbow. "It's exactly what happened."

"I can explain."

"I don't want you to." She stuck her fingers in her ears. "La, la, la, la, la."

Brawley sat, turning his back on her. He plucked a dandelion, then a second and a third, threading them together to make a dandelion bracelet. He wrapped it around Maggie's wrist.

Tears burned the backs of her eyes. How many times had he done this when they'd been kids, then teens? Damn his sorry hide anyway for ruining something so special.

Before she could stop herself, she leaned into him to buss his cheek. He turned his head at the last second, met her lips instead. The kiss, hot and deep, full of passion and memories, sizzled. Maggie wondered they didn't set the blanket on fire.

Just as suddenly, he pulled back, clearing his throat. "Think we've given Annie and Cash enough time for their afternoon delight?"

Cheeks flaming, she nodded.

His hands touched those cheeks, cooled them. He brushed a wild tendril behind her ear. "I miss you, Maggie."

"I'm sorry, Brawley."

She found Indigo Girl waiting patiently, just as Cash had promised. Catching the reins, she mounted, watched while Brawley did the same. Then, with a light tap of her heels on the mare's flanks, she galloped away, Brawley right behind her.

* * *

They rode back in silence. Her eyes caught on the silly dandelion bracelet Brawley had put on her wrist, and she steeled her heart against the feelings that fought to break free.

She couldn't go back to the time when this man beside her was her world. She'd worked too hard to move past that. Worked too hard on her dreams, which didn't include him. Not any longer.

In a few short days she'd be winging to New York City. She had to stay focused. Forget the kiss that hadn't really been meant as a kiss. It had been more of a fluke. An accident.

Annie, snuggled into her husband on their porch swing, waved when she and Brawley rode into the yard.

Cash stood, settled his Stetson more firmly. "How'd Black Jack do?"

"Since we haven't talked price yet, I should tell you he's okay. Not bad." A grin lit Brawley's face. "But I can't. Black Jack is a creature of beauty, and I've absolutely got to have him."

"You won't do any better, pal."

"I know. This little sweetheart," he pointed at Indigo Girl, "is something else, too. If I hear of anyone looking for a roan, I'll pass it on."

"Appreciate it."

Cash planted one last smoldering kiss on Annie before he and Brawley headed to the stables.

"Wow," Maggie said. "Who knew Cash had all that in him?"

Annie chuckled. "Lucky me, huh?"

"You bet."

"Did you and Brawley have a nice ride?"

"We did."

"And that's all you plan to say about it?"

"It is. How about a glass of iced tea, then we can get back to whittling down Dottie's choices so she's not overwhelmed? Bitsy will need to know today, though, so she can order the flowers."

While they poked through the photos of floral arrangements, an ache started in Maggie's heart. She had to be more careful. She couldn't be alone with Brawley. Her heart couldn't take it. The man was addictive. She couldn't have a single taste, a single crumb, without wanting more.

And more would be bad. More would be a disaster.

More would be her downfall.

Chapter Nine

Brawley'd put in a long day. The temperature had spiked to near eighty, and his shirt stuck to him. First thing tomorrow he'd call and get the AC people to check the unit at the clinic. It was probably as old as doc. How the staff had put up with it all this time was beyond him.

He still had to run out to his parents' before he could go home and put his feet up. His mind on the drive to his folks' place, Brawley strode past the *Maverick Junction Daily* just as the door flew open. Maggie collided with him. He automatically reached out to steady her—and found himself with his arms full of beautiful woman.

Dressed in a flirty little sundress and sandals, her hair hanging loose, she did things to his insides. What the hell? He might as well take advantage of the situation. When opportunity knocked...

His head dropped to her hair, and he sniffed. "You do smell good, sugar. Strawberries and sunshine."

"Let go of me, Brawley."

"In a few seconds."

"Now." She kept her voice low. "We're making a spectacle of ourselves."

"That didn't used to bother you."

"Didn't used to," she repeated. "That was a long time ago. Now let go. *I've* grown up."

He chuckled. "Give me another minute."

"What I'll give you is the count of five." Her right leg moved slightly so that it rested between his.

He grinned, till he realized she'd lined her knee up perfectly with his family jewels. The expression on her face assured him it was no accident.

To passers-by, it would look so innocent. A smile curved one side of her lips. It never wavered as, her voice low, she said, "One one-thousand, two one-thousand, three—" Her knee inched upward with each count, and damned if there wasn't a twinkle in her eye.

The little spitfire would take him down. She had before. But damned if he'd be unmanned right here on Main Street. Out of the corner of his eye, he glimpsed Mel at the window. No doubt he understood exactly what was happening. He was every bit as sure his good *friend* wouldn't lift a finger to help.

Brawley dropped his hands and stepped away.

And didn't the smug she-devil raise her hands above her head like a boxer in the ring who'd scored a knockout.

"You're a mean one, Maggie."

She shrugged. "That's what happens when a girl has two ornery boys for playmates growing up. You're the one who taught me that move, by the way."

"It was for protection," he growled. "In case you found yourself in a bad situation."

"I just did."

"Bull." He scowled, and she tipped her head back and laughed.

Ivy Dickerson and Luanne Edwards stopped across the street. Ivy whispered something to Luanne, and Brawley waved at them. Both women hurried into Sally's Place.

He turned his attention back to Maggie. "Thought you hired Ella for the shop."

"I did, and she's working out great."

"So why are you here again?"

A quick glance toward the window confirmed that Mel had disappeared. The traitor was probably at his computer gleefully composing a story for tomorrow's edition about Maggie taking him down. He'd be disappointed to learn it hadn't happened.

"Checking Mel's progress. He's printing the napkins and place cards for tomorrow's wedding. With Dottie and Gramps in such a rush, we're running right down to the wire."

"Everything coming along okay?"

"You bet. Other than a quick stop at Dottie's, Mel's last on my to-do list."

"Good." He caught her hand. "Ride out to my parents' with me. I need to pick up Dad's sander, and I'd like some company."

"His sander?"

"I found this incredible desk at an antique shop outside Dallas. But it's in desperate need of refinishing."

"You continue to surprise me, Mr. Odell. I would never have guessed you refurbished clinics, let alone furniture."

"I'm a man of many talents, sweetheart."

"Yeah, I'll bet. Tell you the truth, though, I've been running all day and didn't take time for lunch. I'm starving." She laid a hand on her stomach, drawing his eyes to her flat abs, tiny waist, and curvy hips.

"Come with me. It won't take long. On our way home, we'll stop at Bubba's," he drawled. "I'll treat you to a big old steak."

She sighed. "I should probably stick with a salad."

Startled, he lifted his eyes to hers. "A salad? You?" He laid a hand on her forehead, and she knocked it away.

"Cut it out, Brawley."

"Since when do you eat rabbit food?"

"Since I'm moving to New York."

"What the hell?" He stared at her. "Excuse me if I don't see the connection between the two."

"I'm going to be surrounded by model-thin women," she wailed. "I'll stand out like a sore thumb."

Surprise rattled through him. Damned if she didn't mean it. He read a touch of insecurity in those extraordinary green eyes. Wrapping one hand around the back of her neck, he massaged it with his thumb.

"Honey, you're right. You will stick out—the way one of England's crown jewels would stick out in a box of coal."

She dropped her head and studied a weed protruding through a crack in the sidewalk.

Dread pummeled him. She hadn't even left Maverick Junction yet, hadn't made the move to New York, and already it was changing her.

He put a finger beneath her chin and raised her face level with his. "Maggie, sweetheart, don't do this to yourself. Don't let them change you, who you are. You're stronger than that. You're unique, and they're gonna love you because of that."

She pressed her lips together, then nodded. "I don't know about them loving me, but you're right. I am who I am. Let's go get that sander, then I'm going to order the biggest steak Bubba's got."

"Good girl."

"Just a sec." She stuck her head in the newspaper office.

After Mel assured her everything would be ready on time, she walked with Brawley to his SUV. As she slid in, his gut worried that

Maggie hadn't really bought in to what he'd said. That she was only giving lip service to it.

* * *

When his mom opened the door, she gave a happy little cry and wrapped Maggie in a hug. "What a nice surprise. Come on in, honey."

She grinned at her son. "Nice to see you, too, sweetie."

Brawley shook his head and followed the women inside.

The house, quiet and cool, comforted him as always. Torey, his mother's Siamese cat, came around the corner and wound between his legs. He leaned down and scratched her head.

"Dad said you were dropping by. What are you sanding, Brawley?"

"An old desk."

"Do you need help?"

"Nope. I think I've got this."

"Good for you. You'll stay for dinner, won't you? I made plenty. Unless the family's getting together tonight, Maggie."

"No. Dottie's kids and grandkids flew in today, and they're planning a quiet dinner at home, resting up for tomorrow. Dad and Mom went over to Lone Tree to spend a few hours with Gramps."

Brawley met Maggie's eyes, and she nodded. *Bye, bye Bubba's steaks.*

"Sure," he told his mom. "We're both starving. Where's Dad?"

"In his study. Why don't you go get what you need, then drag him in here for dinner. Everything's ready."

Maggie helped Karolyn set the table while Brawley and his dad went out to the barn to find the sander. Dinner smelled heavenly, and Maggie's stomach rumbled.

She laughed. "Sorry about that. I skipped lunch today."

"You have a lot on your plate right now, don't you?"

"Sure do."

"You could have knocked me over with a feather when I heard about Dottie and your grandpa." Karolyn fished some crackers from the pantry and arranged them on a small platter. She added some sliced cheese. "Here you go. Nibble on this while we wait for the guys."

"Thanks." The cheese took the edge off her hunger.

Karolyn's cheerful yellow and blue kitchen hadn't changed much since Maggie'd last been here. It felt almost as much like home as her own did.

She wandered to a wall covered with photos. Karolyn and Trace's wedding picture, Brawley as a baby, then on his first horse. Him and his dad fishing. Christmases, Thanksgivings, birthdays. A proud mama's wall. A strong family.

Maggie studied Brawley's high school graduation picture. So young and handsome in his cap and gown. It had galled her that she'd be back in high school the following year while Brawley and Cash went off to college. But she'd been confident, certain she and Brawley would always be together.

Then everything had changed.

"Iced tea or water for dinner, Maggie?"

"I'll have iced tea, please, if you have it made."

"I do."

She heard ice rattling in a glass as she looked at the last photo. Julia had taken it. Maggie stood between Cash and Brawley at their favorite swimming hole. The guys, bare-chested, had seemed so sexy, so hot. But since then? They'd both filled out nicely. They'd matured. Morphed from boys to men.

She wore the two-piece suit she'd pleaded for on a shopping trip to Austin. The mint green showed off both her hair and her figure. *Good choice, Maggie.*

Karolyn came up behind her. "The three of you were so close." She sighed and wrapped an arm around Maggie's waist. "We never could figure out what happened between you and Brawley. He wouldn't talk about it. Not then and not now. And I'm not going to pry. It's your business. But we've missed you."

"I've missed you, too." Maggie laid her head on Karolyn's shoulder.

The screen door opened, and the women drew apart. Brawley's mom moved to the oven and took out a pan of green chili enchiladas, the cheese bubbling on top. Maggie's taste buds did their own little happy dance. Nobody made enchiladas like Karolyn Odell.

"Maggie, do you want to get the salad out of the fridge? It's already dressed."

"Sure."

"Oh, and there's a bowl of sour cream in there, too."

She set the bowls on the table as the men came in through the mudroom. Trace's suntanned, leathered face lost its smile when he spotted her.

"Maggie." He nodded her way. "Good to see you. Been a while."

Brawley's mom said, "I told you if we gave things enough time—"

"Now, Karo, don't start that. The kids are here for the sander and dinner. They didn't come so you'd start poking your nose in their business."

"I'm not poking—except at you." She pointed a long wooden spoon at her husband and son. "You two wash up. You've been out in that barn digging around, and heaven only knows what kind of dirt you've picked up."

When Trace opened his mouth, she said, "Uh-uh-uh. No sass from either of you. Get in the washroom and clean up. Maggie's hungry."

She loved it. Loved this family and their dynamics. They were so easy with each other. And she'd told Karolyn the truth. She had missed them terribly—well, all of them except Brawley.

Okay, so maybe she'd missed him a bit. But only because—because she'd loved him. A long time ago.

They ate in the kitchen, the conversation light and relaxed.

"Everything's ready for the wedding?" Karolyn asked.

"I think so—or almost."

"How's your grandpa holding up?"

"Amazingly well," Maggie answered. "He's happy again."

The years melted away, back to when she'd eaten nearly every Sunday dinner right here at this table. The best time, though, had been when she and Brawley had been able to sneak away alone. She'd lived for that. How many nights had they parked in the dark on one of the back roads?

Remembering those nights, she squirmed in her chair. Brawley slid a hand on her leg, under the cover of the tablecloth. He squeezed lightly.

"You okay?" he mouthed.

She nodded, not trusting her voice, as his warm hand trailed up and down her leg, setting off sparks when he flirted with the hem of her sundress, traced a pattern on her bare skin.

She wanted to pull away. Needed to pull away. Couldn't.

"Could you pass the salad, son?" Trace asked.

And with that, their contact ended. The heat and the storm passed. She waited for her heartbeat to slow and reminded herself again why this was dangerous. Every minute spent with Brawley was like playing with fire. The only result of that? You got burned.

They declined dessert.

"Maggie's got a long drive back to Lone Tree, Mom."

Karolyn insisted on wrapping a plate of leftovers for her.

Brawley's parents stood together in the front yard, the porch light behind them, waving good-bye. The temperature had dropped off, and Maggie hugged herself as she hurried to the SUV.

Neither of them spoke on the way home. Brawley navigated effortlessly through the dark, and she closed her eyes. As wonderful as tonight had been, it had stirred up some powerful memories. A Chris Young song spilled out of the vehicle's sound system, and Maggie hummed along with it.

On the outskirts of town, she remembered she needed to stop by Dottie's. She wanted to use the buttons from her first wedding gown on this new one. A piece of her past carrying her into her future.

"Before you drop me at my car, would you mind terribly stopping by Dottie's? It's getting late, and…"

"No problem."

"I'll only be two seconds."

"Fine."

A few minutes later, he pulled into the drive. Maggie hopped out and ran to the door. Brawley got out, too, and sat on the stairs to wait.

Dottie came to the door, a quizzical expression on her face. "Hey, Maggie. Brawley. Did you two come together?"

"We've been running errands," Maggie said quickly. Here was the trouble with small towns. Your business became everyone's business. "I thought I'd pick up the buttons while I was in town."

"Let me grab them." Dottie stepped inside, and Maggie heard a drawer open and close. "Here you go." She handed Maggie a baggie.

"Thanks, Dottie. This is a great idea." She nodded toward the living room where light flickered from the TV and a battle cry rang out. "Everybody got in okay today?"

"Yep. They're all in the living room watching an old Star Wars movie Wes left behind." She grinned. "Sure is nice having them all here."

"Enjoy them. Maggie hugged her tightly. "Night."

"Night. Night, Brawley."

"Night, Dottie," Brawley called out.

Maggie started to the SUV, but he crooked a finger at her. "Come upstairs with me."

"No."

"Geez, don't get all prickly. Thought you might want to see the apartment now that my furniture is moved in."

"Maybe another day."

"Aren't you the least bit curious?"

Damn him. She was. He knew her too well. Knew which bells to ring. "Just a quick peek, then I have to go."

He hustled up the stairs, and she followed more slowly. By the time she reached the landing, he had the door unlocked and the kitchen light on.

She stepped inside. Wow. She wouldn't have recognized it. Annie had turned the place into a very eclectic Tiffany blue jewel box. Very feminine, fun, and colorful.

Brawley had gone sleek and modern. White leather and dark fabrics. Masculine and sophisticated against the gray walls.

She turned to tell him she loved it and found him all but plastered to her. Her hand came up to rest on his chest. "Back up, Brawley. Give me space."

"Can't we talk?"

"Not now. Not tonight."

"When?"

"Talking won't change anything." She stopped. "What's this?" Crossing the room, she picked up a battered copy of *Where the Red Fern Grows*. Opening it to the title page, she read the message her sixteen-year-old self had written.

To love, deep and true.

Yours forever,

Maggie

"I couldn't throw it away," Brawley said.

"Do you keep trophies from all your girls?"

"That's both unfair and out of line." Anger rang in his voice.

"You didn't answer the question."

His jaw tightened. "No, Maggie, I don't. Just one." He pulled her to him and backed her into the wall.

Before she could utter a sound, he was kissing her. He took her breath away. Her legs went rubbery, but he held her in place. Oh, God.

When he finally lifted his head, he said, "I won't apologize for that."

"Good. Then I won't apologize for this." She wrapped a hand around his neck and drew him close for another…and another.

Breaking contact, she found herself more shaken than she'd imagined possible.

"Stay tonight, Maggie."

"I can't."

"What are you doing? You run hot and cold."

She pressed fingers to her forehead. "I know! And I *will* apologize for that. I'm trying like hell to avoid you, but you won't let me. This physical thing between us—it just takes over. Makes me forget what I want, what I don't. But it's chemistry, Brawley, pure and simple."

"It's more than that and you know it," he growled.

"Maybe."

"Maybe?"

Oh, he was pissed. Time to call it a night.

"Do you want to drive me to my car, or should I ask Dottie for a ride?"

"I'll take you." He grabbed his keys from the counter and jerked the door open with so much force she was amazed it didn't come off the hinges.

The silence took on a hard edge as they drove through Maverick Junction. When he pulled up to her car, she hopped out before he could move around to get her door.

Without a word, she slid into her Chrysler and started the engine. Brawley idled in his black SUV as she drove off. His headlights shone in her rearview mirror, almost daring her to outrun them.

She'd come so close to giving in—to him, to herself.

What had she been thinking?

Chapter Ten

Saturday morning dawned bright and clear. Down the hall, Maggie heard the shower start. Good. Pops was awake. She hoped he'd slept well last night. Today was his wedding day.

Slipping out of bed, she padded to the window. She fingered the drape aside, raised her eyes to the sky, and imagined Grandma Trudy on one of the clouds in the sea of blue.

"Grandma, I hope this is okay with you," she whispered. "Pops still loves you, and he always will. We all will. But he's lonely. Dottie will take care of him for you."

A single tear plopped onto her hand. Sniffling, she swiped at her eyes. Enough. The only tears allowed today were happy ones. They had a wedding to celebrate.

She rested her forehead against the glass pane. White pickets fenced in the yard below, and a rabbit nibbled at tender new shoots of grass along the driveway. A weathered picnic table huddled in the shade of an oak.

As a child she'd played for hours in this yard. Pops and Grandma taught her to ride her bike without training wheels on the paved drive. She and her parents had picnicked at that table many Sundays after church. Her grandmother's potato salad couldn't be matched.

Today marked a beginning…and an end. A realist, she understood nothing would ever be quite the same. Come tonight, Dottie would be part of the family, the Sullivans and the Willises joined.

Maggie tried to imagine how Pops must be feeling, what he was thinking this morning. He'd loved his Trudy with all his heart. But he also loved Dottie Willis, and this afternoon, in her lovely garden, surrounded by friends and family, he would take her as his bride.

Was he looking forward or back? Maggie guessed a little of both. He couldn't help comparing this day to a long-ago day when, as a young man with his entire life in front of him, he'd taken another woman to wife.

She turned from the window to the picture on her dresser of a very young Trudy and Fletcher Sullivan. Her father sat on Grandma's lap. Maggie missed her grandmother. Missed her gentle touch, her often acidic remarks. Her down-to-earth practicality. Most of all, she missed her unconditional love.

Okay. She blinked rapidly. Hadn't she promised not to cry?

Grabbing her robe, she tossed it on. Running fingers through her disheveled hair, she hurried down the hall and knocked at the bathroom door. "Pops?"

"Yeah?"

"Want some coffee?"

"Love some, honey."

"It's a big day, Grandpa."

"Yes, it is." He cleared his throat. "Been thinking about your grandma."

"Me, too."

"I'm not making a mistake, am I?"

"No."

The medicine chest door opened. "I'd like to think Trudy's happy for me."

She swallowed the lump in her throat. "I'm sure she is, Pops. She wouldn't want you to spend the rest of your life alone."

When he didn't respond, she said, "I'll start that coffee and put together some breakfast. I picked up a nice ham steak at Sadler's. You'll need the protein today."

"And then some," he mumbled.

Coffee. Priority number one. Once she had it brewing, she started the ham and eggs, then opened a jar of Rosie's jam for their English muffins.

Rosie and her husband Hank would be at the wedding this afternoon. Hank had worked for Cash's grandpa and had been foreman at the Whispering Pines Ranch for years. Inside the house, though, nobody questioned Rosie's authority. Together, the older couple practically ran Cash's ranch.

Because Hank was getting on in years, Cash had decided to hire a new hand, and that's when he met Annie. That had been an interesting series of events.

Although Cupid's arrow had wobbled a bit, it had finally hit home, and Cash and his Annie had tied the knot.

And today, her grandfather was tying that knot. Deciding the day called for more than English muffins, Maggie mixed up some pancake batter. Upstairs, Pops's electric razor buzzed. She poured batter on the old cast-iron griddle and watched the edges bubble.

Her mind bounced to Brawley and last night's disastrous dinner with him and his parents. That wasn't fair. The dinner itself hadn't been disastrous. In fact, she'd enjoyed her time with Karolyn and Trace. But afterward. Geez, talk about an avalanche. One kiss, and she'd lost her mind. Almost. Fortunately she'd come to her senses in time. Best to put it—and him—out of her mind.

And she'd done that—sort of. So why was she thinking about it now? Disgusted, she flipped the pancake.

This last week had sped by. Between training Ella, stocking the shop, and taking care of the thousand details for Pops and Dottie's wedding, there hadn't been enough hours in the days. And packing for New York? She hadn't even started.

From all accounts, Brawley, too, had his hands full, scrambling to deal with the contractors, plumbers, and Sheetrockers he'd hired to finish the renovation job at the clinic.

And in between hanging doors and laying floors, he'd made emergency trips to care for sick horses and cows. Maggie refused to admit she'd held out the teeniest hope one of those calls would have him close enough to Lone Tree that he'd stop in.

Whatever else he might be, Maggie had no doubt he was one hell of a vet. He cared too much to be less.

Her grandfather came up behind her and laid his hands on her shoulders. "How do I look, Maggie, honey?"

She turned and took his gnarled hands in hers. "Oh, Pops, I've never seen a more handsome groom in my life." Then she squinted at him. "You're not wearing those old jeans, though, are you?"

He chuckled. "No, sirree. My tux is safely zipped in my garment bag. I'll change at your folks' place."

"Okay. You have a shirt?"

"Yep."

"Shoes and socks?"

"I've got everything I need, including my cuff links. And before you ask, my suitcase for this coming week is already at Dottie's." His voice grew gruff. "The woman insisted I take dress clothes along. Don't know why we need to fuss."

"She wants her new husband to look dapper when he takes her out on the town."

Pops's ears turned red. "You gonna stand there yapping or you gonna feed me?"

She kissed his cheek. "Sit. I'll wait on you this morning."

Her grandfather might have been nervous, but it didn't interfere with his appetite. When he reached for a third pancake, she said, "There will be food at the reception."

"I know that. Heard you gals talking about the menu enough, didn't I? Can't a fellow be hungry?"

"Yes, a fellow can." She tucked into her own pancake, savoring the pure maple syrup and wondering why she didn't make them more often.

Breakfast finished, the dishwasher loaded, and the car packed, they headed to Maverick Junction.

Forty minutes later they arrived at her parents'. "One step closer, Pops."

"Yep."

When her phone chirped, she checked the message. Brawley.

Looking 4ward 2 wedding. C U soon, beautiful.

What the heck?

Not if I C U 1st, she texted back.

She hit send, leaned her head against the seat, and closed her eyes. What was she? Ten? Why did she let him get to her? They were too old for games.

"Everything okay?" Pops asked.

She plastered a smile on her face. "Sure is. You ready?"

"As I'll ever be."

They'd hadn't even stepped inside the door before all hell broke loose.

"Maggie, I'm so glad you're here." Her mother met her with a quick cheek kiss. "The caterer had trouble with his van. I called Ty, and he's making a run in his to pick up Emerson and the food."

"So it's under control." Maggie switched the dress bag she carried to her right hand and handed Pops the garment bag with his tux. "Why don't you take this upstairs? You might want to start getting ready."

Her mother remained in the doorway.

"Mom, you're going to have to move so we can get inside."

"You can't stay."

"What do you mean I can't stay?" Maggie shifted her weight to her other foot. "I have to get dressed."

"They need you at Dottie's."

"Why?"

"Seems our unflappable bride is having a meltdown over her shoes."

"Her shoes?" Both Maggie and Pops echoed the words.

Rita nodded and waved a hand at Maggie. "Go. Reassure her. Do whatever you can. Take your dress with you and get ready there."

"But her son and daughter are with her."

"Wes is the one who phoned."

Maggie threw her grandfather a pained look. "Pops, you sure you want to go through with this? Not too late to back out."

"Margaret Emmalee, bite your tongue," her mother shot back. "Now go. Fix this." She trained her gaze on Pops. "And you. Go upstairs and make yourself even more handsome."

Maggie gave her grandfather a big hug. "See you at the wedding!"

He grunted.

* * *

When Maggie arrived, she found Dottie sitting on her bed, surrounded by shoes. It turned out she'd bought a second and then a third pair and couldn't decide which to wear. On any other day, it would have been a trifling matter. But this was not just any day. This was her wedding day, and the problem had grown to gargantuan proportions in her mind.

"You'll look beautiful regardless of which shoes you wear."

More tears welled in Dottie's eyes.

"Oh, Dottie." Maggie sat beside her and wrapped her arms

around her soon-to-be step-grandma. She glanced up in time to catch Dottie's son and daughter deserting ship. The rats.

She picked up one shoe, then another. "They're all beautiful."

"Yes, they are." Dottie sniffled.

"If you don't wear them today, you can take them on your honeymoon. Surprise Pops with them."

Dottie smiled tremulously. "I can."

Maggie walked over to Dottie's dress and held up the shoes one at a time. "Any of them stand out?"

"I love them all."

Maggie smiled. "Then you can't make a bad choice, can you?"

Dottie shook her head.

"Here's my thought. Try on each pair, walk into the kitchen and back, and you'll know which is right."

"Walk to the kitchen?"

Maggie nodded.

"Okay. I don't see how that will help, but…" She slid on a pair and left the room. When she came back, she changed to the second pair, then the third.

Stepping back inside the bedroom, she pointed at the second pair. "Those."

"The most comfortable?"

Dottie grinned. "Yes. And I'm going to be on my feet a lot today." She hugged Maggie. "You're a smart woman."

Maggie grinned. "Yes, I am." She let out a relieved breath. Peace reigned once again. "And now, I'm going to slip into the bathroom and change."

When she stepped out, Dottie said, "The caterer's here. He and Ty have everything unloaded."

"Then all's well."

Standing at the kitchen door, Maggie found herself amazed. The backyard and gardens had been transformed into a fairyland of twinkling lights, tables, and flowers. A pole tent placed on one side would hold the luncheon spread. An arch draped in fresh flowers waited at the far end for the bride and groom. Bitsy, from Heaven Scents, flitted from table to table, fussing with the centerpieces.

Car doors opened and closed, and the seats began filling. Relief spilled through her when she heard her mother's voice, followed by Pop's.

"Dottie, Fletch is here. As much as I hate sending you to your room, that's what I'm doing. He can't see you before the wedding. We want to cut him off at the knees when you walk down that aisle to him."

"You're right, dear." With a small giggle, Dottie scooted off, her daughter and granddaughter hurrying behind her.

When her grandfather walked in, Maggie sighed. "Oh, Pops, you're gorgeous."

"Men aren't gorgeous," he grumbled.

"Sure they are. I like your tie."

"Pink." He fingered the silk.

"You'd better get used to it if you're going to be living with Dottie." Maggie's father turned to her. "Where's Wes?"

"In the living room."

"Think I'll join him." Over his shoulder, he said, "Don't waste your breath arguing with her, Dad. She's stubborn as the day is long."

"I am not."

"You are." Fletch disappeared around the corner behind his son.

"Where're the others?" Rita asked.

"Lacey and her daughter are with Dottie. Both her husband and Wes's wife are outside with the boys."

Rita nodded, then she and Maggie followed the men into the living room. Maggie stopped in the doorway. Her grandfather walked the length of the room, then back. He made another trip.

"Pops, if you don't quit pacing, you'll have to buy Dottie a new carpet."

"You're right. Can't seem to sit still."

When the men started to talk baseball, she decided it was time to escape to the kitchen. The back door opened, and a flash exploded. She scowled at Brawley who stood, expensive camera in hand.

"You really are doing the photos?"

"Yeah."

"You any good?"

"Sugar, I'm good at everything I do." He shot her a sexy smile.

She rolled her eyes. "I'd think Dottie would want a professional for a day as important as this."

"I am a professional."

She rolled her eyes. "A professional vet. I meant a professional photographer."

"I'm that, too."

"Right. And I'm Miss America."

"Maggie, Maggie. Always the cynic."

"Much as I hate to stick up for this scoundrel," her grandfather said, sneaking up behind her, "the boy does good work. Ought to take a peek at his website some time."

"You have a website?"

"I have unplumbed depths, Maggie," Brawley teased. "Like an iceberg, only the tip of my many talents is visible to the casual observer."

"Oh, spare me."

"Think I will. I want to catch a mix of casual and posed shots of the bride primping for her wedding." He took off down the hall.

Maggie marveled at the way the expensive suit pants hugged his derrière. Whoever his tailor was, the man knew his job. The fit was impeccable, the material expensive.

Beside her, Pops tugged at the neck of his shirt, then his tie. "These are too tight."

"No, they're not. They fit you perfectly," her mother said. "It's nerves."

"You'd think I'd never done this before," Pops groused.

"You haven't," Maggie said. "Not with Dottie. You're starting a whole new chapter of your life."

"Hmmph."

Annie, radiant in a one-shouldered red dress, stuck her head in the back door. "It's time, Mr. Sullivan. We need you and your son up front with Father Tom."

Fletch wiped the palms of his hands over his tux trousers and blew out a tornado-force breath. "Still think we should have eloped. Taken a quick trip to Vegas."

Annie grimaced. "Cash's grandpa tried that with Vivi. Considering the way it turned out…Not sure I'd go there."

Fletch threw back his head and let out a loud laugh. "No, guess not. My Dottie's got more class in her little finger than that money-grabbing woman has in her whole body." His smile faded. "Sorry Leo got involved with her. Vivi hurt a lot of good people, including you, Annie."

"It's water under the bridge."

Pops patted Annie's cheek. "And you're one hell of a woman. Cash is a lucky man." He glanced sideways at Maggie. "Too bad somebody else doesn't follow your lead and find herself a decent, hardworking husband."

Maggie stuck out her tongue.

His lips tilted in a smile. "Young people these days have no respect for their elders." One hand on the door, he looked toward his son. "Let's get this show on the road."

Sean joined him, and a camera flashed as they walked out the door.

It had barely closed when Brawley sidled near.

"Smile for the camera."

"I'm not the one you should be taking pictures of."

"You don't think your grandfather will want a photo of you looking like this?" He gestured toward her. "Maggie, honey, you look good enough to eat."

She raised a brow, and he laughed.

"You're blushing, sweetheart."

"I'm not your sweetheart."

"You could be."

She decided to ignore that.

"Come on, Mags. Smile for the camera."

Thinking about her grandfather and Dottie, their newly found love, she smiled.

Click. Click. Click.

She frowned. "Enough."

He shot her a lopsided grin, and she about swallowed her tongue. Too damn bad the man was such a jerk because he sure was easy on the eyes, and he cleaned up so well. No doubt he'd often traded his worn, torn jeans for suits in Dallas, but it wasn't a sight she saw often.

Again, she gave silent kudos to his tailor. The cut was flawless. His fancy, go-to-church cowboy boots shone like a mirror and went perfectly with the suit. With him.

He held out a hand. "You really do look incredible."

She willed her heart to behave and dipped her chin. "Thank you."

"That one of your designs?"

"Yes." The pastel, flower-printed material had been a dream to work with. She ran a hand down the form-fitting silk skirt. She'd paired it with a sweetheart neckline and set it off with her new hot-pink stilettos—in honor of Dottie and her penchant for the color.

He whistled low. "If this is what you're gonna hit them with in the Big Apple, you'll have everybody sitting up, begging for more."

"From your lips to God's ears."

He toyed with the cocktail ring on her finger. "Thought I'd walk you to your seat. I'm guessing you have some real mixed emotions rolling around in that brain of yours today."

"Oh, Brawley." Her eyes misted.

"Don't you start crying on me now." He thumbed away the single tear that spilled over. "I'm no good with that."

She tipped her head. "You know, I think I have to disagree. The night Nathan showed up, you were great with Sophie."

"I was there. I did what needed to be done."

"No. You did more, far more."

He shrugged, obviously uncomfortable. *Interesting.*

That night had affected her deeply. After Brawley'd gone home, he'd called her, bit out what had happened. Later, when Sophie had filled her in on the details, the ice around Maggie's heart had cracked, gone into full glacial meltdown. Later, she'd worked hard to shore it up again. There were times like today, though, when thin fissures reappeared.

"Give me a second to check Dottie one last time."

"Okay, but make it quick. I need to be in place when she walks out."

"Will do."

"While you're doing that, I'll hustle outside and take some shots of Fletch and Sean waiting for the bride. I'll be back by the time you are."

"Deal." She scurried down the hallway and tapped lightly on the bedroom door.

Lacey opened it a crack, then swung it wide when she saw Maggie. Stepping aside, she swept a hand toward her mother. "Isn't she gorgeous?"

"Oh, Dottie." Maggie crossed the room and gathered the wonderful woman in her arms. Then she stepped back to study her. "Lacey's right. You look marvelous."

"A wonderful young lady I know designed this especially for me." Dottie ran a hand over the soft pink beaded jacket, the flowing skirt.

"That young lady might have a future in the business," Maggie parried. "What do you think?"

"Not a doubt in my mind. And these buttons are perfect." She fingered the dyed-pink buttons on the jacket's cuff and sobered. "I love your grandfather, Margaret Emmalee. I hope I can make him happy."

"I wouldn't worry about that for a single second. He loves you right back. I fought with myself about leaving for New York because I didn't want Pops to be alone. And now he won't be. He'll have you."

"And I'll have him."

"Yes." Maggie's chest tightened with emotion, and she took Dottie's hands in her own. "Now. It's time the bride takes her walk down the aisle. Fletch and Dad are waiting with Father Tom—for you."

"Oh, my." Dottie laid a hand over her stomach. "If I had any more butterflies, I wouldn't need feet—or shoes. They'd float me right down that aisle."

Maggie grinned. "That would make a great scene in a Disney movie, wouldn't it? And speaking of fairy tales. Your garden is fairy-tale beautiful."

"I know." The soon-to-be bride let out a happy sigh. "I've been peeking out the window. Everything is perfect. It's like a dream." She put a hand to her mouth. "Lots of people showed up, didn't they?"

Lacey came up from behind and slipped a hand into her mother's. "Did you think for even a second they wouldn't, Mom?"

"I don't know what I thought, except that I'd never be doing this again."

"Life sometimes surprises us." Maggie thought of the man who stood in the kitchen waiting for her. Some surprises were good ones. Others? Well, you dealt with what you were given.

She handed Dottie the bouquet of pink lilies, white hydrangeas, lily of the valley, and soft pink roses tied with a simple antique-white satin bow.

Dottie buried her nose in them. "Bitsy outdid herself. Heavenly, aren't they?"

"So is the hat," Lacey said. A beaded, pink pillbox perched atop Dottie's blue-gray curls. A birdcage veil finished the look beautifully. "You're absolutely ravishing. You'll knock Fletch right out of that new pair of boots."

Mother and daughter embraced.

"You ready?" Maggie asked.

Dottie nodded.

"I'll let them know."

She walked to the kitchen and found Brawley snitching olives from one of the trays. "Get out of there."

"Just taste-testing."

"Olives?"

"You never know." He held out his hand. "Come on, sugar. Let me escort the most gorgeous gal in Texas to her seat for her grandpa's big day."

She smiled. It felt right. For today. When she put her hand in his, electricity sizzled between them. She nearly tripped.

"You okay?" His breath tickled her neck as he leaned down.

"Absolutely."

Outside, she nodded at the DJ, then took a seat on the far side of her mother. Brawley plunked down in the empty chair beside Maggie.

"I can only stay a minute. Then I have to play shutter-bug."

The chairs were close, and the heat from his thigh practically branded her through the thin silk of her dress.

Not willing to go there, she directed her attention to her grandfather and her dad. Both men looked incredibly handsome, the white of their shirts deepening their tanned faces. Her dad's hair still had as much pepper as salt, but Pops's hair was pure white. His mustache, trimmed neatly, gave him a dignified air. Sullivan men were lookers.

Strains of "A Time for Us," the theme from Romeo and Juliet, drifted over the garden. Brawley jumped up and positioned himself with his camera as everyone turned.

Dottie stepped into the sunlight on her son's arm, her smile nearly blinding. When Maggie glanced toward her grandfather, the expression on his weathered face made the breath catch in her throat. To love and be loved like that. What a gift. And these extraordinary people had found this not once, but twice.

A tiny voice inside Maggie cried out for someone for herself, someone like the man who'd been sitting beside her seconds ago. She ignored it. Refused to think about it today.

When Wes and Dottie reached the preacher, Wes gave his mom a quick kiss and man-hugged Fletch. Then he joined his family in the front row.

The ceremony, brief and touching, had more than one woman dabbing at tears. Before them stood two people eager to commit to one another.

After Father Tom pronounced them man and wife, Fletch kissed his new bride soundly. A blushing Dottie grinned and wiped a smudge of lipstick from her new husband's mouth.

Together, they strolled down the rose-strewn path to the Beatles' "In My Life," the song both a fond remembrance of those who had been such a part of their lives and were now gone, and a nod to the future and their new love.

* * *

Brawley, taking a break from shooting pictures, leaned against the rough bark of one of Dottie's magnificent shade trees. The girls may have had less than a week to pull this wedding together, but they'd done one heck of a job. He'd been to some pretty elaborate weddings but couldn't remember ever seeing a happier bride and groom.

When Dottie had walked across the yard to where Fletch waited for her, Brawley swore she'd nearly floated. And wasn't he waxing poetic?

If so, it was Maggie's fault. The woman was a vision. Her dress made him think of peppermint ice cream. She made him hungry.

An arm slipped through his. Rita Sullivan.

He sniffed the air. "You smell great."

"Thank you. I have to say, Brawley, you're looking awfully handsome today, all spiffed up. Nice suit. What happened to your tie?"

He grinned and pulled the rolled-up silk from his pocket. "A man can only wear one of these for so long before he starts to get itchy."

"Guess so." Her gaze roamed the garden. "Not many ties in this group."

"Nope."

"I couldn't help noticing you watching my Maggie."

He cringed. Had he been that obvious?

"You still love my little girl, Brawley Odell?"

Responses to that flew in and out of his head. He rubbed his jaw but could come up with no good answer. Kind of like a woman asking if her outfit made her butt look big. Damned if you do, damned if you don't.

So he settled on the truth.

"Yes, ma'am, I do. Always have. And I'm afraid I always will."

"You planning on doing something about it?"

He hesitated again, then shook his head. "I can't, Rita. I can't hold her back. She's following her dream, and that's the way it has to be."

When Rita opened her mouth to argue, he said, "I think we've all recognized right from the start Maggie was something special. She has a gift, and she's been given a chance to fly with it. I couldn't stand in the way of that—before or now."

Her brow furrowed in question.

"So where do Pops and Dottie plan to spend their honeymoon?"

"Aren't you the clever one?" She patted his cheek. "Don't think for one minute I don't know what you're doing, but I'll let you get away with it this time. Austin. They're going to Austin for a few days."

Thankful she'd allowed him to change the subject, he chatted with her another few minutes before someone called her away to see about cutting the cake.

Time for *him* to cut his losses. But damned if he could.

Chapter Eleven

Maggie sat on the front porch steps, staring up into the night sky, enjoying a moment of peace and quiet. The day had been long—and oh, so special.

She slid off her shoes and wiggled her toes. Ohhh, that felt good. Pops and Dottie had driven away in a flurry of birdseed. A full moon shone, forming lace patterns across the lawn as it filtered through the large trees in front.

Voices drifted from the back of the house where a few guests lingered. Soft music floated on the night air and mixed with the scent of flowers, both from Dottie's gardens and the impressive centerpieces Bitsy had created.

All was well with the world.

Footsteps sounded on the walk, and she turned to see Brawley coming toward her.

"Mind if I share your stoop?"

Maggie's heart stuttered. The man was movie-star handsome. Rugged. Moonlight glinted off his thick, dark hair. Her fingers itched to bury themselves in it, and she had to fight to keep both hands in her lap.

He stood, waiting for permission to sit. Always the gentleman.

No. Not true. He hadn't been a gentleman when he'd dumped her all those years ago.

"Not at all. Sit." She swept the skirt of her dress beneath her.

Their shoulders bumped as he dropped onto the step.

"Tired?" he asked.

"Exhausted."

"It went well, Red. Everything was top-notch."

She smiled. "It was, wasn't it?"

When he reached for her hand, she drew it back. Without a word, he tucked his own into his jacket pocket.

"Can we ever be friends again, Maggie?"

"I don't know."

"I thought we took a step in the right direction last night."

"Brawley, I enjoyed dinner with your family. But one good night doesn't outweigh the past."

"I understand that."

"And what happened after dinner—"

"We kissed," he said.

She swallowed. "Yes, we kissed. That shouldn't have happened."

"I'm gonna beg to disagree on that."

"Whatever. That's your prerogative. The thing is, it's not possible to wipe the slate clean. To pick up and go on as if the past never happened."

"Why?"

She met his eyes. "You have to ask?"

"Yeah, I do."

"Okay. Truth? I'm not sure I can trust you."

He flinched. "I'm sorry."

"Me, too."

He looked skyward, his eyes moving as he studied the stars. "It would take a miracle to make up for everything I've done wrong. I understand that. I made a stupid decision, then compounded it by not admitting it. My only defense is that I was nineteen and foolish."

If he only knew. For about five seconds, an overwhelming urge to tell him everything battled inside Maggie. She pushed it back. The time for that had long passed.

"Brawley, you've been doing what you want."

"I've been missing you."

She couldn't squelch the laugh that forced its way out.

"You think that's funny?" He sounded offended, actually looked hurt.

"Come on, Brawley. I saw the pictures of you at that fund-raiser with Annie and Cash...and Ms. Dallas Cowboy Cheerleader, who was spilling out of her dress and all but crawling down your throat."

"Rachel? No, she wasn't."

"Yes, she was. Annie had pictures of you two dancing. And Rachel was only one of many."

The flicker in his eyes warned her she'd said too much.

He leaned back, resting on one elbow. "You been following my social life, Mags?"

Exasperated, she sighed. "Hardly. I'm just saying that, to be honest, you really didn't look like you were suffering all that much."

"One evening. A public one."

She snorted.

"What? You want me to wear a hair shirt and shave my head?"

"No." Before she could stop herself, her fingers ran through his thick, dark hair. "I love your hair."

He grabbed her hand, brought her arm to his lips, and kissed the inside of her wrist. She was really, really glad she was sitting down, not at all certain her legs would have supported her right then.

She'd been watching him, thinking about him these last few days. She hated what he'd done to her. The way he'd done it. She'd convinced herself she hated him. But despite that, she wanted him, and that really pissed her off. This week, that want had grown to gargantuan proportions. She could barely think, couldn't sleep.

Maybe she should give in to those needs one more time. Maybe she'd built him up in her mind, fantasized what they'd had. Reality couldn't possibly come close, and once she proved that to herself, she could shut the door on that part of her past.

On Brawley.

Then, again, giving in might prove fatal.

When he reached to tuck a strand of hair behind her ear, she caught his hand in hers.

"What are you doing?" he asked.

"I want to see what a country boy turned city slicker's hand looks like."

"City slicker?"

He started to pull his hand away, but she grabbed it back. "What's this?"

"A scratch."

"Scratch my eye. Brawley, this is a nasty cut."

"It happened while we were tearing down a wall at the clinic. One of the triplets took a good whack, and my hand was where it shouldn't have been. I tore it on a nail snatching it away."

"You ought to see a doctor."

"Maggie, I am a doctor."

"An animal doctor."

"Doesn't matter. A cut's a cut. I'm fine."

Without thinking, she carried his hand to her lips. Kissed it. Then she dropped it like it was on fire. "Sorry. I didn't mean to do that."

"Oh, yeah?" He jerked her to him. "Well, sugar, I do mean this."

He'd have kissed her socks off if she'd been wearing any.

She worked a hand between them. "You're dangerous to me, Brawley. My Kryptonite."

"I've changed."

Her lips curved downward.

"I have," he insisted.

"Again, I'm remembering that bosomy brunette on your arm in Dallas."

"I've never claimed to be a saint." He ran the toe of his boot over the stair.

She laughed. She simply couldn't help it.

He scowled at her, and she sobered. "I can't be around you, Brawley."

"Why?"

"Because you make me want more. Too much more." She stood. "I'm joining the others."

"Uh-uh. No way. You can't tell me something like that, then walk away."

She shrugged.

"Let's declare a cease-fire for this weekend, Maggie. I don't want to spoil what's left of the wedding."

"The bride and groom are gone."

He lifted his brows.

"Fine. A temporary truce."

"Absolutely." He dared to grin.

The music changed from a fast song to Michael Bublé's "The Way You Look Tonight."

Brawley stood and took Maggie's hand in his. "Dance with me here in the moonlight."

"I don't think—"

"Good. Don't think. Just dance with me."

She let him lead her into the grass. "I'm barefoot. Don't you dare step on my toes."

"Have I ever?"

"No." She sighed when he pulled her into his arms. She laid

her head on his chest and listened to the slow, steady beat of his heart.

The music, the moonlight, the soft night air wrapped around them. For this short moment in time, she'd let herself enjoy.

One dance led to another.

His head dipped, but she turned, and his lips grazed her cheek.

"Everything's under control here," he whispered into her ear. "Can you leave?"

"Brawley—"

"It's okay. I'm not stealing you away to ravage you."

"Darn."

His head whipped around so fast, she thought he'd surely need a chiropractor. "What?" He stared into her face.

Her tongue shot out to lick suddenly dry lips. Leaving with him had bad idea written all over it. "I was kidding, Brawley. Joking around."

"Oh. Okay. You sure? Because if you want to ravage or be ravaged—"

"I'm positive."

"If you change your mind—"

Her chest tightened, but she gave him a small poke in the arm. "I won't."

"Gee, don't try to let me down easy or anything." He held out his hands, palm up. "Seriously, though, I want to show you my office, the clinic. We've finished all but the last few details. A crew's coming in tomorrow to take care of those."

"On a Sunday?"

"Yep. Overtime pay."

"So you'll be able to open Monday?"

"Right on schedule."

"I'm glad."

"Me, too. Here's the thing." He caught her hand in his before she could pull it away again. His thumb circled over the back of it, and she closed her eyes.

"You're going to be leaving, Red, starting a new business of your own. You, above all, understand how much this means to me."

Still, she hesitated.

"Come on. Take a ride with me and look at the place, for Pete's sake. No monkey business." He paused, tilted his head. "Unless, of course, you change your mind and insist."

That beautiful, unrestrained laugh he loved bubbled up and out of her, spilled through those lips.

How could he stand to watch her walk away? How would he bear being here without Maggie? Again he wondered if coming home had been a mistake. Maverick Junction without Maggie Sullivan would not be the same place.

But then, he'd left her, hadn't he, all those years ago? He'd expected her to go to design school, though, so it was different, wasn't it? He'd thought they'd end up together again.

"Let me get my purse."

When she disappeared inside, he prayed she wouldn't change her mind.

Sean Sullivan chose that exact moment to walk around the front of the house. "You seen my daughter?"

Oh, boy. "She went in the house for her purse."

"Why?"

"We're gonna take a ride."

Sean's hands curled at his side. "You think that's a good idea?"

"I want to show her what we've done at the clinic."

"Uh-huh." He seemed to be fighting with himself. "Rita tells me I need to mind my own business. That the two of you will either work things out or you won't. That Maggie's a big girl now."

Brawley waited.

Sean shook a finger at him. "I don't care how old she is. She's my little girl. Always has been, always will be. You hurt her before. Don't do it again. I'm keeping my eye on you."

With that, he headed back to the festivities.

Brawley leaned against the porch railing, chewing on Sean's words. He'd been warned.

In no time flat Maggie sailed out the door, purse slung over her shoulder.

Brawley, hand on her back, walked her to his Tahoe and held the door for her. He didn't have a clue why she'd decided to go with him. Curiosity? Nostalgia? Whatever. He didn't care. All that mattered was Maggie sitting beside him in his vehicle for the first time in way too long.

As he drove down Main Street, one hand on the wheel, the other arm propped on his open window, he hoped someone, anyone, saw them. He'd won the lottery. He and Maggie together again on a Saturday night.

Every store along the street was locked tight, windows dark. The good people of Maverick Junction not still at the wedding were home, doing whatever they did on Saturday nights to unwind from a long week's work and activities.

As he turned onto the side street that led to the clinic, he reminded himself he'd be a fool to assume her agreeing to come with him meant she'd had even the slightest change of heart. Most likely, it signified absolutely nothing. On the other hand, there was the slightest chance it meant she hadn't totally closed the door on him.

She had agreed to a truce, after all.

One thing he did know. He was alone with Maggie. The SUV's interior smelled of her. Feminine and sensual. Sexy.

Maggie, Maggie, you make it hard on a fellow.

* * *

The second Brawley pulled into the parking lot, Maggie saw the new sign, an oval of dark wood, the carved name painted white. DR. BRAWLEY ODELL'S ANIMAL CLINIC.

A surge of pride swelled in her.

"It's what I've always wanted."

"You surprise me." She undid her seat belt. "I honestly thought you liked the big city."

"I did. For a while. But this—" He swept his arm to encompass the building, the grounds.

"Why didn't you come back sooner?"

"I didn't want to get in Doc Gibson's way. Didn't want to compete with him. He had a good practice and made a good living. I'm not sure there's room for two vets in town."

"So the timing's right."

"Yeah." His gaze burned into her. "Except you're leaving."

She hopped out rather than answer. "You've given the old building a fresh coat of paint."

"Inside and out." He unlocked the front door and ushered her ahead of him, then flicked on the overheads.

Maggie stood for a minute, taking it in. "You've made more than a couple changes. Wow." She ran the toe of her shoe over the flooring. "That ghastly green linoleum is gone."

"Yeah, one of the first things I ripped out. Had to have been the ugliest ever made. Sure hope Doc got it cheap."

She grinned. "And new countertops. You moved the reception over a bit."

"It'll keep Bobby Sue out of the direct path of the door. Before, anytime somebody came in or left, she got blasted either by the heat or the cold."

"Good for you for caring."

"When the help's happy..." He shrugged. "The biggest changes are in the back."

As she started down the hallway, Maggie let out a happy squeal. "You arched the opening into the office."

He nodded.

"Oh, and look at these." Like a lover, she ran a hand over the massive double doors, curved to match the arch. "They're spectacular."

"Had them made in Dallas. Once I decided to go ahead with the move, the renovations, I knew I wanted to change the office doorway."

He opened them and hit the wall switch. An impressive antler chandelier lit the room. Maggie stilled, her hand going to her mouth.

"Oh, my gosh, Brawley. How did you manage to do all this?"

"Ty and Cash busted their butts beside me this week. I owe them."

"I used to help out here." Maggie shook her head. "Doc Gibson's office was a cluttered, dark little hole. What a change."

"If I'm gonna be spending a lot of time here, I might as well be comfortable."

She walked across the room to run a hand over the impressive oak desk. "This is the one you refinished?"

"Yep."

"Wow again." She gave a half laugh. "I don't know what to say." Bending down, she traced the lone star carved into the front, noticed another had been etched near the top of a floor-to-ceiling bookcase. "Did you do that, too?"

"No. My dad did."

A cowhide rug covered the deep wood floor in front of his desk. He'd placed a leather chair by it and moved a love seat in the corner. Comfortable and welcoming.

Everything in the room was Texas-themed, from the lamps to the coat tree. The walls, painted in textured browns and coppers, had the look of leather.

"You're staying," she whispered.

"I am."

"You'll be happy here, Brawley."

"I'll miss you."

"You've lived without me for a long time."

"But I always knew you'd be here. That I could get my Maggie fix whenever I needed it with a couple hours' drive."

"Brawley—"

"I know." He held up a hand. "Not fair. I won't ask you to stay. I know better than that. This is something you have to do."

"It is."

"Once you're in New York, though, if you don't like it, I'll be here."

"That's not going to happen."

"Red, if there's one thing I've learned, it's never say never."

"Fine." Her heart hammered in her chest. She moved to the leather love seat, her hand stroking it. "This is yummy."

"So are you." The thought tumbled out before he could stop it.

She turned, so close he could feel her breath on his face.

He hadn't meant for it to happen. He hadn't brought her here to make a move. But damn if he could keep his hands, his mouth, off her.

He'd watched her all day, that gorgeous red hair done up in a tumbled mass, curls escaping and trailing down her neck. He'd itched to pull out whatever pins held it and spill the fiery strands around her. Wanted to run his hands through it, feel the silky softness.

More, he wanted to unzip that swath of silk and let it slide to the floor. Wanted to touch the creamy white skin beneath. Needed to taste her. Her lips, the back of her knees, her stomach.

Needed to know if she still wore the little silver ring through her belly button.

Needed almost more than his next breath to hear her quiet little sighs, her cries of delight as they made love.

His gaze drifted to her red, red lips when her tongue peeked out between them.

"Maggie—"

"Brawley?"

"Yeah?" He raised his eyes back to hers. They always reminded him of a Texas meadow right after a spring rainstorm. What man could resist? Sure as hell not him. He caved. Pulled her to him. Felt her heat.

The first kiss was tentative. After that initial foray, though, he lost sight of his good intentions, of right and wrong.

Soft. So very soft.

His hand moved to the back of her neck, drawing her closer still. Inching into that silken mass of hair, he removed the pins one at a time, sighed when the strands spilled loose over his fingers, his hand, his arm.

His mouth left hers, traced a path along her chin, over her cheek. He buried his face in her hair and breathed deeply. God, she smelled good.

Maggie gave him those little sighs, those moans he'd been craving.

His lips trailed back to hers. When they parted, he slid his tongue inside to dance with hers. He backed her up till she was against the sofa.

Sliding a hand beneath her knees, he scooped her up and laid her on the soft leather, then followed her down. His hands ran the length of her, his fingers trailing beneath the hem of her dress.

He felt her cool hands on his heated flesh. Somehow she had his shirt out of his pants and half unbuttoned. Her head lowered, and she trailed a line of kisses across his bare chest. She stopped at the small scar just above his navel, flicked her tongue over it.

Brawley sucked in his breath. Maggie had been the one to mark him there with a stick when they'd been eight-year-old pirates fighting it out with pretend swords. He put a finger beneath her chin and raised her head to taste her lips again.

She had matured, ripened. Was everything the eighteen-year-old Maggie had been and more. Much more.

"Oh, Mags," he whispered into her ear. "You're killing me."

She answered with a long, deep kiss.

He groaned. "I want you so badly it hurts."

"Shut up and kiss me, cowboy."

Somewhere in the back of her mind, even as those words slipped out, Maggie's conscience started throwing a tantrum. *Wrong*, it screamed. *This is wrong.*

She didn't care. It had been so long. Too long.

Brawley had changed, his body now that of a man rather than a teenager. He had muscles on top of muscles. Ripped abs. Oh, Lordy, what this man hid under his black T-shirts and this crisp, white dress shirt.

His mouth roamed over her face, her neck. His fingers tunneled through her hair, and she cried out.

Aware she'd no doubt hate herself in the morning, Maggie threw caution to the wind and simply stopped thinking. His hands on her felt so good.

The zipper to her dress slid down, and Brawley slipped it over her shoulders. It whispered over her body, his mouth following. He tossed it to the floor.

The wisp of lace covering her breasts followed. He drew back, his eyes hot. A fingertip toyed with the emerald and silver ring piercing her navel. He sucked in his breath.

"Panties and stilettos. What a combination. You're beautiful, Red. So beautiful."

Tangled together on that wonderfully soft leather sofa, his fingers moved to the edge of her panties. His lips inches from her skin, he whispered, "Are you on birth control?"

He might as well have dumped a bucket of cold water on her.

An ache tore through her, and she stiffened as reason returned. Now? He thought to ask her that now? Too bad he hadn't kept that in mind years ago. But then, their hormones had raged so violently, had been so uncontrollable, neither of them really cared.

"No, Brawley, I'm not." She pulled away, tried to sit. "I don't make a habit of falling into bed with guys nor had I planned on it tonight. Let me up."

"What?"

She ran a hand through her hair and gave him a small push.

It was like running into a concrete wall.

"This isn't right."

"Why?"

"Because…because…argh. There are a thousand reasons." Realizing what had almost happened, what *had* happened, her heart kicked into racing mode. "We never finished things properly. You had your say, but I never really had mine. I couldn't think straight that night, and I let you go without telling you how I felt. But this won't help."

Hurt darkened his eyes. "How do you know that, Maggie?"

"Because I'm leaving. You're staying. Last time around, I stayed and you left. There's no future for us."

An arm over her breasts, she sat up and reached for her bra, draped over the back of the sofa.

Brawley tugged at her arm, and she jerked it away. "Quit."

"You're gorgeous, Maggie. You were incredible at seventeen, at eighteen. Now—I don't have the words." He rose on an elbow to kiss her.

She turned her face away.

"I think it's time to have that talk, Red. For both of us to share."

"Not now. Not tonight. It won't do any good, Brawley. We waited too long. A few words can't erase years of pain."

"No, I don't suppose they can, but we could make a start."

She shook her head, slipping her bra straps up her arms. "We already did that. Years ago. You and I made a start, a beginning. Then we ended. Your choice." Her voice trembled. "Tonight was a huge mistake."

"How can you say that?"

"Easy. I move my lips—"

"You don't want me? Is that it?" He sat on the edge of the love seat.

"I did. I wanted you more than I wanted my next breath. But too much has happened, too much has changed."

God forgive her. She was lying through her teeth. She wanted this more than she'd ever wanted anything. Maybe she was making an even bigger mistake by not grabbing this night with Brawley.

But the moment for that had passed.

He was on his feet, stabbing his arms into his shirtsleeves, his jaw set, that sensual mouth compressed tightly. No doubt about it. He was good and pissed.

Well, too bad. So was she, mostly at herself for letting things go so far, get so out of hand.

She picked her dress up off the floor and shook it out. Scattered hairpins dusted the cowhide rug. There'd be no fixing her hair. She'd run her fingers through the tousled mass and hope no one noticed.

"I need to go, Brawley. I left my car at Dottie's. My folks will be worried."

"No, they won't. When you ran in to grab your purse, I told your dad I was bringing you here."

"You what?" She drew back.

"I told your dad—"

"I heard you," she hissed. God, she sounded like a fishwife. Rubbing her hands over her face, she said, "I can't believe you did that."

"Why? He was looking for you. I didn't want them worrying."

"He'll know."

"So?"

"So?" Flabbergasted, she stared at him. "So I don't want my dad knowing I'm off making out with you."

"See, there you go with your snap judgments, Margaret Emmalee. How did I know you had that in mind?"

Her mouth dropped open. Guilt made her angrier still. "Of all the arrogant—"

"Don't." He laid a finger over her lips. "Don't say something you'll regret."

She brushed his hand aside. "Take me back to Dottie's."

They finished dressing in silence.

Feeling like dirt, she walked to his SUV while he locked up and set the security system. She couldn't blame Brawley for what had just happened. No. She'd been right there with him. What they'd shared on that couch tonight had been magic. So had dancing in his arms under the stars.

But, then, reality struck. Magic didn't really exist, did it? Smoke and mirrors. That's what the two of them had always been.

She'd simply been too naïve to realize it their first go-around.

She'd been wrong, though, thinking she'd exaggerated the chemistry between them. No one affected her like he did. She doubted anyone ever would, more's the pity.

Neither spoke on their way through the small town. When they reached Dottie's, Brawley strolled around the front of the vehicle to open her door. Everything was quiet, the house and grounds dark.

"There you go, Cinderella. Home before your fancy dress turns into rags and your chauffeur into a rat." He removed his hat and bowed low.

"I wouldn't be too sure about that last part."

"Low blow, darlin'."

"Sorry. Brawley, tonight was..." She raked fingers through her tangled hair. "You've done a beautiful job with the clinic, and I wish you well in your new venture."

She dug out her keys and started toward her car.

He snagged her arm. "Wait a minute. That's it?"

"No." She jangled the keys in her hand. She had to do this and do it now before she lost her courage. The truth wouldn't set either of them free, would only complicate things and cause more hurt. A small piece of her brain screamed at the injustice—to both of them—but she ignored it.

Drawing on an inner strength she hadn't known she possessed, she said, "Thank you. I needed this. Tonight was like the period at the end of a sentence."

"The period at the end of a sentence? What the hell are you talking about?"

"It was closure, Brawley."

"You're wrong, Maggie."

She shook her head. "No, I'm not. You and me..." She shrugged, swallowed the lump in her throat. "Well, there is no you and me."

"How can you say that? We have years of history."

"Yes, we do. Here's the thing, Brawley. History is a damn cold bed partner. And in case you've forgotten, you're the one who made us history. Me? I'd assumed we'd be present and future."

"Maggie—"

"No." She closed her eyes. "Pretend I didn't say that."

"But you did, and I can't unhear it."

"Sure you can. You've unheard lots I've said in the past."

Brawley stuffed his hands in his pockets and sighed. "Boy, you sure as hell hold a grudge. You could teach classes on it."

"Probably so. You chose your dream over me, Brawley. There was nothing I could do. No way I could change things. So maybe I needed tonight, but it won't happen again." She stumbled to her car. Fought to fit the key into the ignition.

Blinking back tears, she threw the car in reverse. Brawley stood in the beams of her headlights, starkly silhouetted against the darkness. He was angry. Very angry. She wouldn't think about it. At the end of the street, she turned south and began the long drive to Lone Tree and a future that didn't include Brawley Odell.

Time she charted a course without him.

And she would. In New York City.

How many times did you have to burn your fingers before you stepped away from the fire?

The tear that dripped from her chin went ignored.

Chapter Twelve

Maggie yawned. How could it be morning already? She'd barely slept. It had been strange coming home to an empty house last night, knowing her grandfather was on his honeymoon. Probably best she didn't dwell on that.

She threw an arm across her forehead. Yesterday had been exhausting, both physically and emotionally. But at the same time, it had been wonderful, and her grandfather had a life companion again. Dottie would take good care of him and he of her.

Last night, though, she'd screwed up badly.

Brawley, in his tailored suit, had about knocked her off her feet. A Texas cowboy from the tips of his boots to the crown of his Stetson, he cleaned up darn well.

Closing her eyes, she could still feel his skilled hands running over her body, exciting her. Could still taste him, the thrill of those lips trailing over her face, her neck. Lower. Those deep blue eyes had caressed her. His thick, dark hair had driven her wild as she'd run her fingers through it.

All these years, as much as she'd tried not to, she'd dreamed of holding him, sharing kisses with him again. Well, now she had—several times this past week. Damn if he wasn't like sugar, though. One taste and she craved another and another and another.

On an intellectual level, she understood she was being extremely unfair to him. Deep down she expected him to make amends for the past. But how could he fix something when he didn't understand how broken it truly was...and why?

She'd come so close last night to telling him about the baby. What good would that do, though? He'd be racked with guilt. For what? He couldn't change what had happened.

And at this point in her life? She had to put it behind her for good. Had to move past it. This was her time. Her chance to shoot for the stars. If that made her selfish, so be it. She'd protected Brawley from the truth all these years...and would continue to.

She tossed back the bed covers. She and Brawley had had their moment, and it was gone. Over. Last night could never, ever happen again. *Would* never happen again. That was the way it had to be.

Once she'd come to her senses last night and her brain began functioning again, she'd realized she'd miscalculated horribly. At least she'd called a halt to it before...well, before.

She'd allow herself today to lick her wounds and wallow in self-pity. One final day of mourning what could have been. When she went to bed tonight, she'd be done with it.

With the wedding over, she could concentrate on her upcoming move. She'd grab a shower, throw on her rattiest outfit, and fix herself a nice breakfast. Then she'd roll up her sleeves and pack. Time to decide what would go with her and what she'd store in the attic.

Pops and Dottie would be gone for a few days. When they returned, they planned to spend a few nights at her house. Maggie assumed they wanted to give her space. And it would give them private time to settle into their marriage. What newlyweds needed a third thumb?

They were bound to spend some time here after she left for New York. Stepping into the shower, Maggie sighed, then lathered her hair. How odd to think of another woman in Grandma Trudy's house. But time brought changes.

If Gramps could move on, so could she.

She would. She had. She'd built a great little business. Women drove a hundred miles to visit her boutique.

As she rinsed her hair, Maggie admitted the chances were good that Pops would sell this house. Women tended to nest deeper than men. Dottie would want to stay in Maverick Junction, and that was probably the smartest decision. Her place would be far easier to maintain than this big old house. The move would put Pops closer to her mom and dad, too, if he ever needed them.

Her melancholy deepened. There would be no coming home ever again. Stepping from the shower, she pressed the power button for her stereo and sang along with Lady Antebellum's newest song.

Fortified by a couple scrambled eggs and a huge glass of orange juice, she tackled her room. Knee-deep in boxes and old newspapers, she started when her phone rang. Blowing a strand of hair from her eyes, she checked the clock.

Eleven thirty. Where had the morning gone?

By the third ring, she'd unearthed her phone, hoping it was Pops.

It wasn't. It was Sophie.

"Hey, girlfriend, why don't you hop in the car and come over for lunch?"

"Thanks, but I'm good, Sophie."

"Come on. I know you. You're moping around that empty house."

Maggie laughed. "I started out that way this morning and gave myself a few minutes of pity-me. But I have so much to take care of, I couldn't wallow for long."

"What are you doing right now?"

"Packing up my personal things and trying to decide what I'll leave here and what I'll ship to New York."

"You can do that tonight. I need you to come save me."

"From what?"

"Ty's out in the barn with a sick cow."

Maggie could almost see the grimace twist Sophie's lips. City to the core, she still struggled with ranch life.

"That leaves me here with the three little ones. I could use an adult to talk to."

"Oh, you're good, Sophie Rawlins."

Her friend sighed. "Sophie Rawlins. I still find it hard to believe Ty and I are really married."

"You're happy."

"I am. Now get in the car and get over here."

"Give me about forty minutes. You don't even want to see me looking the way I do."

"Come on. You couldn't look bad if you tried."

Maggie glanced at the large mirror against the far wall. She took in her wildly curling red hair, the dust on the tip of her nose, the raggedy sweatshirt and cut-offs. "Oh, believe me, I could scare small children right now."

"I seriously doubt it." After a second, Sophie said, "That might not be a bad thing. Get over here and scare these three boys into cleaning their room."

Hanging up, Maggie took in the chaos around her. Piles covered every surface. Clothes lay heaped on her bed. Knickknacks and keepsakes peeked out of half-packed boxes. Yikes. Sophie was right, though. This mess would still be here when she got home. Unfortunately. Since no one else would see it, what difference did it make?

Even though she'd showered only a couple hours earlier, she took another quick one, swiped on some mascara, and fought her hair into submission. Digging through the mess, she uncovered a pair of denim shorts and a favorite casual, short-sleeve linen shirt.

She moved to her open window. Texas at her finest. The day was made for being outside. A break would do her good.

Hands on her hips, Maggie took one last look at the disaster she'd created, powered off her stereo, and walked out the door.

Driving through Lone Tree, she stopped at Ollie's. Packed with the after-church group, it took her a good ten minutes to make it to the counter. Everyone wanted to talk about the wedding and ask if she'd heard from Pops and Dottie.

She slid onto a stool.

"Hey, sweetheart," Ollie said. "How're you doing today?"

"Tired."

"Bet you are. That was some party yesterday."

"It was, wasn't it? I'm glad you and Judy could make it."

"Me, too. That nephew of mine comes in handy once in a while. He did an okay job running the place yesterday."

"You need to use him more often. Give you and Judy some time for yourselves."

Ollie nodded and wiped a hand on his apron. "I've been thinking about that. We've been busy, and I've been toying with the idea of hiring more help. Lots of folks coming into Lone Tree to visit the new fashion darling's shop." He winked. "They get hungry and stop in here. Judy and I can barely keep up. You've been good for the whole town, Maggie."

"I hope so."

"Oh, believe me, you have." Hands on his hips, he asked, "What can I do for you today?"

"Do you have an extra lemon meringue pie I can talk you out of? Maybe a dozen chocolate chips to go with it?"

"For you? You bet. Give me a minute." He headed to the walk-in cooler. Halfway there, one of the guys at the counter asked for a coffee refill. "Keep your britches on," he growled. "Can't you see I'm busy?"

Maggie shook her head. Oh, yeah. She'd miss this.

* * *

Armed with her goodies, she walked back to her car, a smile on her face. The grass was turning green, bluebonnets bobbed their heads along the side of the road, and the sun was shining.

Maggie put all four windows down. So it would wreck her hair. Who cared? She turned up the country-western station on her radio and let the weight slip from her shoulders as the breeze wafted over her. It wouldn't be long till they'd be sweltering in hundred-and-five-degree temperatures. In the shade.

No. She wouldn't be here. She'd be in the city. Back East.

When her shoulders tightened, she consciously relaxed them. Today, she'd spend some time with Sophie and her newly acquired sons. They could gossip their hearts out. They could talk about nothing. They could sit quietly in the sun and simply be.

Maggie started down the lane to Ty and Sophie's, then hit the brakes. Oh, those best laid plans. Brawley's black Tahoe sat in the drive. She couldn't face him today. Not after last night. Her armor wasn't in place.

Should she turn around and go home? Eat herself into a lemon meringue stupor?

Too late. She'd been spotted. Jesse hopped up and down in the front yard, and Jonah waved.

She waved back, dread crawling up her throat.

Josh ran into the house and, by the time she'd stopped her car, reappeared with Sophie in tow.

Maggie opened the car door and got out. "Here you go, guys."

She handed Jesse the bag of cookies. "You can't eat any till after lunch, though."

"Okay," Jonah said.

"What are they?" Jesse opened the bag and peered in.

Josh stuck his head closer. "I wanna see, too. Sophie, he won't let me see."

"Show him what's in there, Jesse." Sophie brushed a hand over her sleek blond hair. "Why don't you take the bag inside and set it on the table?"

"'Kay." The three took off at a run, Jesse clutching the bag of goodies.

"I see you have company." Maggie tipped her head toward Brawley's vehicle.

"Ty didn't know what to do about that sick cow, so he decided to bring in the big guns. I didn't plan this," Sophie insisted. "I had no idea he'd called Brawley when I phoned you. Honest."

Maggie said nothing.

Sophie narrowed her eyes. "What's going on? You're white as a sheet."

"It's a long story."

"And I've got plenty of time."

Maggie shrugged.

"What happened?" Sophie prodded. "I know you left with him last night, and I've got to say I was shocked. Your dad said—"

The boys came tearing out of the house, screaming like banshees. "Can we play till lunch is ready?"

"Stay close. When I call, I expect you all to come immediately and wash up. No whining."

"'Kay," Jonah said.

The other two agreed, and they were off, their now half-grown pup Trouble at their heels.

"I lost my mind," Maggie said.

Sophie's eyes narrowed. "What did you do?"

"I came this close to sleeping with Brawley." Maggie held up her thumb and forefinger, only a millimeter between them. Her lips felt stiff.

"What?" Sophie dropped onto one of the Adirondack chairs in the yard.

Maggie joined her in another. Though she hadn't intended to, she found herself confessing last night's transgressions. "We got carried away. One thing led to another, and, well, I almost caved."

"Whew."

"Yeah. Maybe I should have."

"Really?"

Maggie shook her head. "No."

"But it was good?" Sophie asked.

"It's always mind-blowing with him."

"I can—"

Sophie broke off when Jesse started screaming.

"Snake! Snake!" He ran toward the barn, while the other two stood rooted to the ground.

Sophie and Maggie both ran toward them. Ty and Brawley shot out of the barn.

The boys were in tears and nearly hysterical.

"Stay back," Ty shouted. "Boys, go to Sophie."

"But, Daddy," Jonah sobbed. "Trouble got hurted."

"I know, son. Go to Sophie," he repeated.

They did.

Brawley dashed back into the barn and grabbed a shovel. He started across the field, while Ty called Trouble to him.

"What's he doing?" Sophie, eyes wide, clutched the boys to her, shushing them.

"You might want to take the boys into the house."

"Why?"

Brawley raised the shovel, brought it down once, twice.

Maggie and Sophie winced, and the boys cried harder.

"Rattler," Brawley said, striding toward them. "Did it bite any of you?" He knelt in front of the boys.

They shook their heads, tears streaming.

"It was gonna bite Jesse," Josh said. "But Trouble growled and bit it. Then he cried 'cause the bad snake bit him back."

"Is he gonna die?" Jonah's lip trembled.

Maggie watched the overgrown pup, which had made his way to the boys and was now licking their hands. The boys wrapped their arms around him.

Ty met Sophie's eyes. Voice husky, he said, "This big, overgrown idiot of a pup saved Jesse's life."

She nodded and swallowed. "Is there anything we can do?"

Maggie looked at Brawley. "Can you help him?"

"Yeah, I can take care of this mangy pup. He's gonna be fine." His voice was gruff. "Sophie, Maggie, why don't you take the boys inside? Feed them lunch. Everything's gonna be fine, but this isn't something they need to see."

Sophie nodded.

Before they left, though, the boys surrounded Brawley, hugging his legs.

"Make him all better."

"I will." Brawley ruffled one head, then another. He knelt again to put himself on their level and hooked a finger under Trouble's collar. "You go inside with Sophie. By the time you've eaten lunch, Trouble will be fine. But I need to take care of him now. It's kind of like you guys going to the doctor."

"Is he gonna get a shot?" Jonah asked. "They hurt."

"I won't hurt him," Brawley promised.

Josh wrapped his pudgy arms around Brawley's neck and kissed him.

He returned the kiss, then gave him a man-pat on the back. Sophie started toward the house with the boys in tow.

Brawley's gaze met Maggie's, then traveled down the length of her. He whistled. "Not much of those jeans escaped, did they?"

Her mouth dropped open and, despite herself, she tugged at the fabric.

He grinned. "I like the shorts. You make them look real good."

"Now? Your head's going there now?"

He shrugged. "Works for me. You're hot as sin today, Red." He raised the back of his hand and swiped at his forehead. "You turn even a cool spring day into a real scorcher."

He scooped Trouble in his arms and headed to the barn.

Maggie watched him go. Did the cowboy ever think of anything else? she wondered. She looked at the kids racing each other to the house, then back at Brawley with an armful of dog. Yeah, he did.

Sophie must have been reading her mind because as Maggie reached her, she leaned toward her and whispered, "He's always here when we need him."

Yes, he was, Maggie thought. He'd been there with Ty when Nathan had attacked Sophie and now when the rattler threatened the boys' and Trouble's lives.

If only he'd been there for her...and their baby.

As she'd watched him with the boys, she realized what a great dad he'd have made. What a great dad he might still make—with someone else.

Chapter Thirteen

The clinic was a madhouse. Brawley rushed from exam room to exam room. He needed caffeine. No wonder Doc Gibson hadn't been able to keep up this pace.

"Phyllis, will you finish up the poodle in Room One? I've cleaned the wound on his leg and bandaged it. His shots are updated, too. I need to see him in seven days. If you could set that up—"

"Got it. Mrs. Williams called. She wants to know if we're boarding dogs. She and her husband are taking a three-day cruise and need someone to watch their dachshund."

"Nope. Call her back. Give her Dawn Marie's number. She'll take good care of Hannibal. After a couple days with her, he probably won't want to go home." Brawley rubbed the back of his neck. "You think there's a chance of talking Bobby Sue into making a fresh pot of coffee?"

"You can try. Miracles happen every day."

He rolled his eyes.

"Little Davey Iverson and his mom are in Room Three," Phyllis said. "He found a bird with a broken wing and wants to know if you can fix it."

"That Nate and Missy's son?"

"Yep. He's in first grade this year. Guess he's playing hooky today to take care of the bird."

Halfway out the door, Brawley stopped. "You're kidding. They've got a kid who's that old already?"

"Time's moving on, Doctor. You might want to think of having some little ones of your own. I saw you and Maggie dancing Saturday at Fletch and Dottie's reception. It reminded me of the two of you during high school."

"Don't hold your breath." He opened the door and stepped out. "Maggie's—"

And there she stood at the reception counter. The smile she sent him was more than a little shaky, actually touched on shy. He hadn't figured she had a timid bone in her body. The cobbler she held smelled heavenly, even over the smell of animal and disinfectant.

"For me?"

"Yes." She took a deep breath. "I wanted to thank you and thought a fresh peach cobbler might do the trick."

"Don't suppose you brought coffee?"

She shook her head.

He strode across to her and took the offered dessert. "I won't say no to this, but…I'm not quite sure what you're thanking me for. If it's for Saturday night, let me just say the pleasure was almost mine."

Intrigued, he watched the color bloom on her cheeks. Maggie Sullivan was an interesting mix of wanton sex appeal and unabashed innocence.

Her brow shot up. "If you're not careful, you might be wearing that." She nodded at the dish. "You saved Trouble's life yesterday. Those boys dote on that rascal of a pup. If he hadn't got between Jesse and that rattler, or if he'd—" She blew out a breath, unable to finish the sentence.

Tears filled her enormous green eyes.

"Hey." He set the cobbler on the counter. "Nothing happened. Jesse didn't get snake bit, and the mutt's good as new today."

"Because you were there."

He shrugged. "I drove out to Burnt Fork to check on him before I opened today."

"Early morning for you."

"Got that right." He ran a hand over his already stubble-roughened chin. "Trouble apparently felt good enough sometime during the night to eat one of Sophie's new shoes. She might not be feeling as benevolent toward him this morning as you do. The only casualty was the snake—who was probably minding his own business till three rowdy boys and their overgrown pup intruded on his territory."

Maggie grinned. "Thank you all the same."

He lowered his voice. "I thought you hated me."

"I never said that. I hate what you did, not you. And don't you dare read anything into that."

He threw back his head and laughed. "Maggie Sullivan, you're impossible."

"Good-bye, Doctor Odell. I'm leaving now."

"Thanks for the dessert, Maggie."

"You're welcome," she threw over her shoulder.

"Mags, wait." He reached out, took hold of her arm. "Are you in a hurry?"

"Not particularly. Ella's covering the store today."

"Great." He held up a finger, then stuck his head in the first exam room. "Phyllis, no one's waiting right now. Can you hold the fort while I take ten? I'll handle Davey and his bird before I go."

"You bet." She eyed the cobbler he held again. "Don't suppose this break has anything to do with the redhead who brought that in."

He tossed her a careless smile and closed the door. Then he

turned back to Maggie. "Do you mind waiting a few minutes? Davey Iverson found an injured bird this morning."

"Go. Heal. I'll be right here."

"Thanks."

He watched her walk to the waiting area, those incredible hips swaying and driving him insane. He sure wished she was wearing yesterday's short denims. There couldn't have been a half a yard of material in them. They showcased those legs of hers and made a man hungry. Made him want to slide a finger up the length of all that creamy, silky skin.

The longing was even more intense now, after their close encounter. He'd thought if he could have another taste, he'd be satiated. Instead it had been like a drop of water on the tongue of a man dying of dehydration. A single taste of what he couldn't have.

Davey's bird turned out to be a male painted bunting. "Wow, he's a real beauty, pal."

"He looks like somebody colored him."

"Yeah, you got that right."

"He's hurt." Davey got close to the cage and pointed.

"Yes, he is. We can fix him, though. Sure glad you brought him to me. You did a good job."

The boy grinned and puffed out his chest.

It didn't take long. Brawley splinted the wing and talked to Davey and his mom about the care the bird would need till it could fly again.

Brawley shook Davey's hand. "He'll be good as new in no time. Nice job, buckaroo."

"Thanks." Davey lowered his eyes and studied the floor. "Mom says I can't keep him."

"Your mom's right. He's a wild creature and needs to be free."

"Okay."

"I thought maybe next time we went to Austin we could stop at a pet store," Missy said. "Give a canary or a finch a home."

"Really?" A grin split the little boy's freckled face.

"Really."

"Oh, boy." He skipped around the room.

"Okay, settle down." His mom handed him the cage. "Here you go. You can carry this out to the car while I pay our bill."

Brawley shook his head. "No bill. No charge. This one's on the house."

"Are you sure?"

"Positive."

Davey walked out, proud as a peacock, with his wounded bird.

"Thanks again, Brawley. We're all glad you've come home."

Brawley smiled at her and watched her walk away. Not everyone was all that happy he'd returned. He leaned against the doorjamb and watched Maggie.

She stopped Davey and oohed and ahhed over the bird, listening to his plans for one of his own. Her enthusiasm was genuine. She was good with kids.

He wondered if she'd ever have any.

Right now, though, the two of them had a date—of sorts. He didn't have time to take her anywhere. Sally's would be too slow. Besides, it wouldn't be private enough. Not that they'd particularly need privacy. Still...

He considered his options. His office was out. It reeked of emotion after Saturday evening. Maybe they could take a short walk. Right now was when he missed the myriad of coffee shops he'd grown used to in Dallas.

Ducking into his office, he grabbed two sodas from his mini-fridge. Cold caffeine. A quick glance showed no patients in the waiting area. Thank God. After that flurry this morning, they could use a breather.

Maggie studied the photos he'd hung along one wall.

"Are these yours?" she asked.

He nodded.

"Seriously?"

"Seriously."

"You've captured such emotion." She stopped in front of one with a young boy kissing a large Dalmatian, then at another of a very elderly lady, her wrinkled face not totally unlike that of the pug she cradled.

"I try."

"You succeed. Did you get some this good at Pops's wedding?"

Oh, if she only knew. He thought guiltily of the ones he'd taken of her. In one, she'd been pouting and looked especially sexy. Not sure what had made him do it, he'd printed that shot and then framed the damned thing. If she wandered into his bedroom—his breath caught just thinking about that—she'd pitch one hell of a fit.

"I got some really nice ones, yeah." He held out a hand to her. "It's a gorgeous day and not too hot yet. How about a short stroll?" Looking down at her feet, he saw strappy little sandals. Dark green toenails peeked up at him.

"Those okay for walking?"

"Absolutely." She bit her lip. "We're not going to, um, rehash our, ah, last conversation, are we?"

"Why, Maggie, you sound nervous."

She frowned. "I'm not nervous."

"Of course not. You're not afraid of anything, are you?"

"You might be surprised."

"No. We don't have to talk about Saturday." He handed her a soda.

"Ahhh." She popped the top as she stepped into the sunshine. "Exactly what I needed."

Neither spoke for a couple minutes.

"You leave Wednesday?"

"Yep. Which means I have today and tomorrow to wrap things up. I'm not taking much with me. Two suitcases. That's it. If it doesn't fit in one of them, it doesn't go."

"What are you doing with the rest of your things?"

"I'd intended to leave some of my stuff in my bedroom at Pops's and stash a few boxes in the attic. But considering the recent changes, I've rethought that plan. I'll pack most of it and cart it to my parents'."

"You think your grandfather will sell his place?"

"Eventually. Dottie's going to want to stay in her home. Women get more attached to a place. It would be a good move for Pops, really. I'll worry a lot less with him here in Maverick Junction than alone at his place, miles from town. And he'll be closer to my parents."

"You think you'll like New York?" Brawley glanced at her, watched as she tipped the can back for a drink. When she flicked a drop from her lips, he bit back a groan.

"I know I will." Her eyes sparkled. "Never in my wildest dreams did I imagine this actually happening. I've been to New York twice now. Mom went with me last time. The city is energy and excitement. It's twenty-four-seven. It's—" She spread her hands.

"All the things Maverick Junction isn't."

Her smile faded. "I love Maverick Junction and Texas. I love the people here. This has been my whole life. But I need more, Brawley. So did you."

He nodded and stuffed a hand in his pocket. "Guess so." Studying her, he said, "We can't seem to get the timing right, can we?"

She didn't say anything.

After a few seconds, he asked, "What did your mom think of the city?"

Maggie sighed. "She loved the shopping, the plays, the restaurants. She didn't like the mass of people, though. Didn't like that she couldn't get in her car and simply go. If you ask her, she'll say everything is more complicated there. No stopping into the grocery store and hauling things to your car. You need bottled water? You'd better be willing to tote it back to your apartment."

"None of that bothered you?"

"To be honest, I was so busy working, it didn't even register. We stayed in a hotel and took all our meals out. Mom, however, extrapolated the myriad necessities of life and decided she couldn't live in the city."

"It's different."

"Yes. You'd know that, wouldn't you?"

He glanced at her and decided the comment wasn't snarky.

"To an extent," he answered. "Dallas isn't New York, though. Dallas/Fort Worth has less than seven million people. You take the New York, northern New Jersey, Long Island area? Almost nineteen million. Big difference."

"But you enjoyed Dallas."

"I did. Always something going on."

They both stopped, looked down Maverick Junction's one main street. Other than Sadler's Store, which was just down the road, this street comprised the town's entire business district. The post office, a florist, Mel's newspaper office, Sally's Place, and a couple other small stores. That was it.

It was what it was, and Brawley didn't regret his move.

"I can't wait." Maggie grinned.

"I can see that. Since it doesn't sound like you hit the streets sightseeing, what *did* you do while you were in New York before?"

"The first time, I met with my backer, Owen Cook." She reached, without thought, for his hand. He took it, linked their fingers.

"I was so nervous, Brawley, I thought I'd pee my pants."

He quirked a brow. "That might have been a first."

She giggled. "Don't I know it. The restaurant he took me to..." She rolled her eyes. "Incredible. I tried to talk Ollie into adding a couple of the items to his menu, but he refused. He didn't think they'd go over as well in Lone Tree."

"He was probably right," Brawley said. "How about the second trip?"

"Oh, boy, was that ever labor intensive. Poor Mom. I didn't get nearly as much time with her as either of us would have liked. I did all the prep work for my show. I chose fabrics, got the workers started on the patterns and production. My designs for my very first ever show are in place minus whatever last-minute tweaking I decide to do."

"You're happy with them?"

"I am." She smiled smugly. "I intend to knock 'em dead with my line. The pieces work. I've run them up in my workroom, fussed with them some more. Bottom line? I love every single garment." She closed her eyes. "Fingers crossed the buyers will, too."

She opened her eyes, met his. "I lay awake at night worrying, though. What if my show's a flop? What if no one buys my clothes? What if no one even comes to the showing?"

"It won't happen, Mags."

"Oh, I wish I was that certain. That confident."

"Wait a minute." He pulled back to stare into her eyes. "Aren't you the same woman who only minutes ago said you'd knock them dead?"

She put a hand to the side of her face. "I know. See what I mean? It's awful. I flip-flop back and forth, back and forth. One minute I'm on top of the world. The next I wonder why I ever thought I could do this."

"You shouldn't worry, Mags. I've seen your work. Annie walked into the Now and Then fund-raiser in Dallas wearing that dress of yours, and everyone in the room grew envious. The men because Annie was on Cash's arm and not theirs. The women because the dress was on Annie's back instead of theirs."

Maggie grinned. "Thank you for that."

"Hey, just telling it like it is." He hesitated. "So your dream's coming true."

"Finally, yes."

"You gonna be happy being a big-city career woman?"

"Why wouldn't I be?"

"No reason at all. I watched you with Ty's boys yesterday and with Davey Iverson today. You're good with kids. You've never wanted any of your own?"

Maggie reeled from the unexpected punch. Hurt, so deep-seated, so intense, tore through her. *Now. Tell him now.*

But she looked into those soulful blue eyes, and she couldn't. He didn't need to know. It was in the long-ago past and had nothing to do with now. With this sunny spring day.

So she forced a smile. "I don't know. Maybe at some point it'll be time for babies. A career and a family don't have to be mutually exclusive."

"No, they don't." He traced a pattern over her arm, sending shivers along her spine.

His innocent question had scraped the old wound raw. She couldn't stay, couldn't make small talk.

"As nice as this has been, Brawley, I need to get going. I have to drop off the first few boxes at my parents', then drive back to Lone Tree and finish packing. My guess is that by now they're wanting you back at the clinic, too. You're doing a booming business."

"I think a few of this morning's visits centered around checking out the changes I made more than making sure their dogs were taking the right vitamins."

"And a few dropped in to check out the new doctor."

He snorted.

"Hey, it's not every day a town like Maverick Junction welcomes a hot, new vet." Her cheeks burned, and she could have bitten off her tongue.

"So you think I'm hot, huh?"

"Did I say that?" She went for a teasing tone.

"In a roundabout way? Yeah, you did."

She shrugged. "I suppose someone might think that."

"But not you."

"Fishing for a compliment, Doctor Odell?" She walked to the trash receptacle outside Mel's and dropped her soda can inside.

Brawley stayed where he was, took an overhead shot with his. When it dropped in cleanly, his fist pumped the air. "Two points!"

"Men," Maggie muttered.

"What would you do without us?"

"Don't even get me started." She sent him a small smile, softening her words.

He walked her to her car. "Drive carefully. I'll see you tomorrow night at Bubba's."

Her head snapped up. "What?"

"Your dad invited me to your going-away dinner."

She said nothing.

"If you don't want me there, say the word. I won't show."

"No," she said quickly. "Everybody else is going to be there. You should, too."

"You sure?"

"Totally. See you there."

Time to escape. Keep it friendly, but get out of Dodge. Her emotions skittered all over the place.

Once that plane took off Wednesday morning, she'd be fine. Absolutely fine.

She would be.

Chapter Fourteen

Maggie felt like a dog chasing its tail. She needed, more than anything, a couple forty-eight-hour days.

At her mom and dad's, she unloaded several boxes and a suitcase full of clothes she wouldn't need. At least not right away. She and her dad stacked them in her bedroom closet.

Her mother met them at the bottom of the stairs. "Can you stay for lunch, honey?"

"Oh, Mom, I have so much to do."

"It's all ready. We promise we won't hold you up. It's just that, well, come Thursday, you won't be here. And you have to eat."

Okay, Maggie thought. Reality had finally sunk in. She'd wondered when they'd get to this. She'd actually expected it much sooner.

"Sure."

The three of them sat down to eat, and Maggie realized her mother had gone to a lot of trouble with this lunch. When she placed Maggie's favorite macaroni and cheese casserole on the table, her mouth watered. So much for losing a few pounds before she boarded that eastbound plane.

The conversation revolved around her upcoming move until her mom got too emotional. Then they switched and talked about a neighbor's herd, the prediction for this summer's weather, anything and everything except the elephant in the room. They skirted what was foremost on all of their minds.

When she finally drove away, she left a teary-eyed mom behind. This might be harder than she'd imagined. But they'd all get used to the change. Eventually. And it wasn't like she couldn't fly back anytime she wanted. She'd really only be a few hours away.

She drove back to Lone Tree and found Ella swamped. She helped with the rush of customers, then hid away in the back room to finish the month's orders.

Ella knocked on the door, then stuck her head in. "Maggie?"

"Yes?" Her eyes felt crossed from filling out too many online forms.

"I have to go. I need to pick up the kids."

"What time is it?"

"A little after five."

"You're kidding."

"Nope. Been busy back here, haven't you?"

Maggie scooped her hair off her neck. "Oh, boy, and how. Go." She shooed Ella away. "Get those kids. Kick your shoes off and relax."

Ella laughed. "I'll do that. Don't work too late." She paused. "Do you want me to put the closed sign up?"

"No, I'll get it in a few minutes."

Ella waved and left. Maggie heard the outside door shut behind her and realized this would be her last night to close up alone.

She finished the order she'd been working on, keeping an ear open for any customers who might wander in. No one came, and she found herself grateful for that.

Walking into the boutique part of the shop, she flipped the open sign to closed. She leaned against the door, her gaze moving over the space. Proud of what she'd done and feeling more than a little nostalgic, she blew out the vanilla candles she'd placed around the shop, powered off the stereo, and picked up her purse. Everything in place; everything under control.

Except her damn emotions. She'd fought back tears so many times today she was beginning to feel like the Hoover Dam. If anybody caught sight of her right now, they'd guess she'd been handed a life sentence without the possibility of parole instead of the break she'd been fighting for years to get.

She locked the door behind her.

Ollie knocked on the window across the street and waved.

She waved back and blew him a kiss.

As she slid behind the wheel of her car, she met her own eyes in the rearview mirror. "Nobody here but us girls, Maggie Emmalee. Why don't you admit it's not only the leaving that's got you tied up in knots? It's that damn cowboy come home from Dallas eating at you, too."

Brawley had picked a heck of a time to return. If he wasn't here, she swore she'd be escaping Lone Tree all grins and giggles—or at least with fewer misgivings. But he had come back, stirring up emotions she'd long held at bay. Feelings she'd thought she'd dealt with.

Obviously not.

There'd been a time when his name and hers were linked. Almost synonymous. Maggie and Brawley. Brawley and Maggie.

And that was in the past.

She stopped at the mailbox. Nothing important.

She walked into the quiet house. No one there.

This sucked.

She switched on the stereo. When Josh Turner started to sing about dancing up the stairs with his baby, she turned it off and headed for the stairs herself. Only one cure for this. A long, indulgent bath.

* * *

Maggie swiped a bubble from the end of her nose. A bath and a bottle of wine. She'd been certain the combination would smooth out the rough edges of her emotions. Would dull her hunger for Brawley.

Wrong.

She wanted him, and if she wasn't careful she'd be calling him, begging him to come to her.

Damn it!

Stretching toward the vanity, she snagged her phone. Annie and Sophie both had lives. Husbands. Too bad! She tipped her wineglass and finished it.

Before she could talk herself out of it, she texted them. Busy tonight? Need you.

She tossed the phone onto the towel heaped on the floor and refilled her glass. Resting her head against the back of the tub, she reminded herself exactly how lucky she was. She told herself how many people would sell their souls to trade places with her.

Brawley had screwed it all up by coming back to town. Damn him all to hell and back!

The ringing of the phone startled her, and her wine sloshed over the glass rim.

"Hello?"

"We'll be there in ten minutes," Sophie said.

"Ten minutes?" Maggie's head felt fuzzy. Too much wine and not enough food. "What? Is Cash flying you here in his plane? How can you get here that fast?"

"Annie and I are already in Lone Tree. We just left Ollie's."

"Ollie's?"

"Yep. Hope you're in the mood for pulled pork because we have enough to feed an army."

"Why?"

"Because we're hungry."

"No. I mean, why are you on your way?"

"We thought we'd help you pack. We intended to surprise you."

"Well, you did that."

"What do I hear?"

"Water."

"You're in the tub?"

"Yep."

"Drinking wine?"

Maggie eyed the nearly empty bottle. "Yep."

"All alone in that big old house."

"Yep. And feeling pretty maudlin."

"Throw on your pajamas, Maggie, and set the table."

She hung up, feeling better already. Her friends had been on their way even before she'd called. She grinned.

Water spilled onto the floor as she stood. Oh, well, she'd wipe it up later.

* * *

Sophie was true to her word. Within ten minutes, the house no longer felt empty. It rang with the warmth of friendship and smelled of Ollie's rich, tangy sauce. Lights blazed in the old farmhouse, and happy music played.

Halfway through her meal, Maggie blurted, "I can't believe I came so close to sleeping with him again."

Sophie set her sandwich on her plate. Annie sloshed her water and turned startled eyes to Maggie, then Sophie.

"Brawley?"

Maggie nodded.

Annie looked at Sophie. "You knew?"

Sophie nodded.

"And you didn't tell me?"

Sophie shrugged.

"I told you this would happen."

Sophie gave her a disgusted look. "Nobody likes an I-told-you-so."

Annie turned to Maggie. "I thought you two were long over."

"We are."

"Oh, honey."

A tear slid down Maggie's face. "He left me."

"He was only nineteen."

"And I was only eighteen and pregnant." Horrified, Maggie clamped a hand over her mouth. "Oh, my gosh. I didn't mean to say that. Nobody but my mom knows. You can't breathe a word to anyone."

She registered the look of shock on her friends' faces.

"He left you to have the baby alone?" Enraged, Annie said, "I hate him. What a piece of scum."

Sophie, her fairylike face red with anger, shook her fist. "I'll never speak to him again and neither will Ty."

"You guys are the best friends ever." Maggie rested her elbows on the table and dropped her head in the palms of her hands. "But I can't let either of you do that. As much as it kills me to, I have to stand up for him."

"How can you?"

"Because he didn't know."

"You didn't tell him?" Annie asked.

Maggie shook her head.

"You should have," Sophie added.

"I know."

"What did he say when he finally found out? God, I've seen Brawley's temper," Sophie said. "When he flew threw my door and saw Nathan—" She broke off. "That's neither here nor there."

She leaned toward Maggie and stared into her eyes. "Uh-oh."

"What?" Maggie drew back.

"You never told him."

"Sure she did," Annie said.

"No. She didn't. Look at her face."

"You didn't?"

Maggie shook her head.

"Oh, my God, Mags. He doesn't know?"

"No. And you can't say a word about this. Ever. Not to Ty, not to Cash. Definitely not to Brawley. It doesn't leave this room." She closed her eyes. "I can't believe I blurted it out like that. Too much wine. Speaking of, now I definitely need another glass."

She poured herself some, took Sophie's glass and filled it.

When Maggie made to pour a third glass, Annie shook her head. "None for me, thanks."

"Since when did you start turning down a perfectly fine zinfandel?"

"Since the doctor said I'm going to be a mommy."

Nonplussed, Maggie and Sophie both stared at her.

"I know. The timing totally sucks to tell you this now."

"Boy, is this a night for confessions or what?" Sophie whispered. "But don't look at me. I have nothing to confess."

Annie shot her a skeptical glance, then took Maggie's hand in hers. "I am sorry. I should have waited."

"No. On the contrary." Maggie grinned. "This is the very best news. You and Cash. Parents!" She hopped up and flung her arms around Annie. "I'm thrilled for you."

Sophie joined them and wrapped her arms around both women.

"I know technically I'll be second cousin, but can I play auntie? Please?"

Annie laughed. "You're both going to be auntie to this little one." Her hand moved to her stomach.

"How far along are you?"

"Girl or boy?"

"Whoa." Annie held up a hand. "Three months, and I have no idea. We're going to wait to find out the pink or blue. We want to be surprised."

"I have one more blessing to add to my list," Maggie said. "Looks like I'll have to come back to Maverick Junction more often than I thought."

"Yes, you will." Annie grew serious. "I have to ask, Maggie. Where is your baby? Did you put it up for adoption?"

"No."

"But—"

Sophie shot her cousin a warning look. "It's okay, Maggie. You did what was right for you at the time."

She vehemently shook her head, the wine buzzing through her. "I didn't have an abortion."

Sophie's body relaxed and, again, Maggie realized what staunch supporters she had. Sophie had been ready to back her regardless.

"I lost the baby."

"Oh, honey." Tears welled in Annie's eyes. "I'm so sorry."

"Me, too. I'd have loved him." She smiled through her own tears. "Our baby was a little boy."

"Why didn't you tell Brawley?"

She sniffed. "He made it very clear he had big plans when he dumped me. Plans that didn't include me. I didn't want someone who didn't want me. My mom was a pillar, though. I couldn't have gotten through it without her."

"Guess that's why I noticed a little animosity from your dad toward Brawley."

"Actually, he doesn't know about the baby. Mom took me to a doctor in Austin. Dad thought I had a bad case of the flu and never questioned my lying around in bed for a week."

"Good for your mom," Sophie said. "I'm so glad she stuck by you."

"I was scared to death to tell her. But, then, nature took it out of my control. When things started going wrong, I had no other option. She held me afterward, let me cry my heart out. She never once scolded me about it, and I know that must have been hard. I did, after all, get my redhead's temper from her."

"Yes," Annie said. "I've experienced her fire a couple times. It's pretty scary."

"No kidding," Maggie said. "Anyway, Dad was already furious with Brawley for leaving like he did. Why add fuel to the fire?"

"Brawley hurt his little girl. I can understand that."

"I've told him to let it go."

"But he hasn't, and neither have you."

"I don't hate Brawley. Certainly not because of the baby. That wasn't his fault." She swiped at a renegade tear. "He never knew, and that lies on my shoulders."

"Have you ever considered giving him a second chance?" Sophie asked. "I mean, I know you can never forget what happened," she added quickly. "I only meant that maybe—I don't know—that maybe the two of you could have a new relationship, a different relationship. We're all going to be together."

"No, I'm not. I won't be here. I'll be back East."

Annie and Sophie glanced at each other, then Sophie turned her attention back to Maggie. "But you'll be coming back."

"For short visits."

"But even then," Sophie persisted, "Brawley will be in town. His business is here now. It would be nice if the two of you could get along."

"We can get along." Maggie practically growled the words.

"With a whole lot of surly beneath the surface," Annie said. "Everybody deserves a second chance. That's what kept my grandfather alive."

"It worked for him. It also worked for you, and, my kindhearted Sophie, for you. So as much as it pains me to say this, stuff your second chances."

Sophie's mouth dropped open.

Before she could argue anymore, Maggie asked, "So, Mrs. Annelise Hardeman, what names are you and Daddy considering?"

Chapter Fifteen

Maggie wanted to crawl into bed and pull the covers over her head. Instead, she forced herself to finish dressing and drive to Maverick Junction for her going-away dinner.

What a whirlwind the past two days had been. All the last-minute details to handle, all the good-byes to say. Wrapping up one life before starting another.

And then last night. Argh, who said confession was good for the soul? She'd woken with one heck of a headache this morning. One she'd earned. Too much wine, too many tears.

She prayed Annie and Sophie would keep their promise to say nothing about the confidence she'd blabbed last night. All these years she'd kept her silence, had told no one, and then, just like that, she'd blurted out the biggest secret of her life.

Well, nothing to do for it now. So much of her life had revolved around Brawley Odell.

Speaking of, had he gone through this self-doubt when he'd decided to leave Dallas? Maggie had never really thought about it before. She'd assumed it had all been easy-peasy for him, but maybe not.

Had he had second thoughts? Cold feet? Did he still have misgivings? Probably not. He seemed very much at ease with his decision. Of course he'd returned home and knew exactly what he was getting into. He knew everyone.

Not so with her. She was heading off into unchartered territory, for her anyway, and leaving her little shop. Ella would take good care of it, but Maggie had worked so hard to make it a reality.

She released the breath she'd been holding. Fine. Now, she'd work every bit as hard on her new clothing line. It would soar, and she'd laugh as she thought back to tonight and her concerns.

Maggie put in her second earring and studied the effect. The emerald-cut smoky topaz earrings and ring could have been custom-made for the oatmeal-colored top. Because of the cowl collar, she decided against a necklace.

Slim, fawn-colored pants finished the outfit—along with her brown leather boots. Might as well wear them tonight. Who knew when she'd have the chance again.

Her fair skin looked paler than usual, so she added a little more blush before slicking gloss over her lips. A spritz of perfume and she was good to go.

Setting down the pretty little bottle, she took a minute to study the room. She'd moved here two months after Grandma Trudy died. Tonight she'd stay in her old room at her parents'. Since they'd be driving her to the Austin airport in the morning, it would make it easier. When she left here tonight, she wouldn't be coming back. A wave of nostalgia swept through her. Afraid she was close to hyperventilating, she forced herself to take slow, deep breaths.

Once she boarded that plane at Austin-Bergstrom International in the morning, her life would change drastically. Excitement-induced adrenaline flooded her system. Inside of a month, she'd have her first showing in New York City!

Celebrities and buyers from all over the world would attend. *Oh, please, God, let them want to buy my clothes. Please, please, please.*

These roller-coaster mood swings were wearing her out. Lightheaded, she dropped to the side of her bed. With more than a little help from Annie, her dream had come true. Now it was up to her to make Annie proud. And she would. Oh, yes.

She glanced at the bags packed and ready to carry downstairs. The two large ones held her clothes, makeup, and a few photos. The other? Her designs and personal tools. All her treasures from the little back room in the shop she'd created from nothing. She'd carry that bag with her. It would never, ever leave her sight.

Tossing her purse over her shoulder, she picked up one of the large ones and carried it downstairs. Setting her purse and bag by the door, she walked back upstairs to get the others. Her fingers trailed over the handrail.

Pops and Dottie would be at Bubba's tonight. They'd returned from their quick honeymoon for her going-away party. Tonight, though, they'd stay at Dottie's. Pops had insisted, in case she needed the extra time to get her stuff together. Considerate as always, he didn't want to be in her way.

Brawley would be at Bubba's, too. She should have realized her parents would invite him. *She* should have invited him.

She'd been hard on him Saturday evening. Unfairly so, because the fault had been as much hers as his. That old "it takes two." That darn Texas-Irish temper had reared its ugly head, and she'd said hurtful things. Words he didn't deserve. Words she couldn't take back.

And that was exactly why she'd stopped by the clinic yesterday morning. Why she'd gotten up extra early to bake him a cobbler—from scratch. Not something she did often.

Yes, she owed him a huge thanks for taking care of Trouble after the rattler. But even more, she needed to make amends. Hopefully, she'd set things right between them.

But she still hadn't come clean. He'd provided the perfect opening—and she hadn't taken it. Would she feel better if she had? She wasn't sure.

What about Brawley? He'd feel like crap if she unburdened herself. And for what? Something he'd known nothing about. Something he couldn't do anything about, then or now.

Her decision to stay quiet had been the right one.

But she hadn't stayed quiet, had she?

How many times had her mother told her something was a secret only as long as one person knew about it. The second two people knew? Forget about it.

* * *

Brawley fought with himself as he shaved. If he had any sense at all he'd either stay home or put in a few more hours at the clinic. Lots still left to do there.

But he wouldn't. He'd go wish Maggie bon voyage…and try to be happy for her.

No, he *was* happy for her.

Had he really believed he could come back to things as they'd been? Maybe it was watching Cash and Ty settle into permanent relationships that had him edgy.

Yeah, and wasn't that a bunch of bull? Hell, he wasn't the least bit interested in taking a walk down the aisle. But Maggie made him itchy. Made him want—what? Hell if he knew.

He found a clean black T-shirt in the closet. Time to do some laundry. Maybe he'd stop by and have dinner with his folks tomorrow evening. He could toss his clothes in the wash while he visited.

Sitting on the edge of the bed, he pulled on his boots, then grabbed his hat. Okay. Time to do this.

Halfway out the door, the phone rang.

Shoot!

He'd left his cell on the counter. He ran inside and grabbed it. "Yeah?"

"Hi, cutie. How're things in Maverick Junction?"

He tipped his head back in frustration and barely managed to contain the groan. "What do you want, Rachel?"

"You don't sound very happy to hear from me."

Brawley could almost see the pout. What had he seen in her? Then he rolled his eyes. Stupid question. Extremely well-endowed Dallas cheerleader. Duh. That about said it all.

Yet she'd bored him—unlike some fiery redhead here in town who surprised him at every turn. Maggie certainly didn't kowtow. She never said what she thought he wanted to hear. In fact, he suspected she sometimes disagreed simply to disagree.

"I thought you might be lonely," Rachel purred. "I could drive down, or you could come spend a few days with me in Dallas."

"Rachel, I'm pretty busy right now getting my business up and running."

"Can't somebody else take care of it for a couple days?"

"I'm the doctor. My name's on the sign out front. I have to be here."

Silence for a few heartbeats.

"Then I'll come down."

He ran a hand over the back of his neck. He could have sworn she understood they were finished. "You know, when I left Dallas…hell, weeks before I left, we talked about this."

"I know."

"Then why are you calling?"

"I thought maybe you'd changed your mind. Maybe you missed me."

He hung his head, ran a finger over one brow. Time to be brutally honest.

"No, Rachel, I haven't changed my mind. Your life is there in the city, my life is here. I never made any promises. Never hinted at more."

"Maybe—"

"No." He gentled his tone. "No maybes. We're over, sugar. Time you move on. Didn't I hear you were dating one of the tight ends?"

"It didn't work out."

"Ahhh. So I'm your rebound. Or am I a play to make him jealous?"

"Neither. It didn't click. He's not you, Brawley."

Right here was the best reason he could think of to avoid second dates and creating messy expectations.

"You have somebody new, don't you?"

"No." He thought of Maggie and decided he wasn't lying. No one would ever *have* Maggie. She lived life on her own terms.

"Rachel, I need to go. I was on my way out when you called."

"Where are you going?"

"To a private party."

"Exactly what I was hoping for, Brawley." She lowered her voice. "Just you and me."

He said nothing.

"Will you call me later?" she asked.

"No." He said it softly, hoped it helped take the bitter edge from it. "Good-bye, Rachel."

Feeling like a heel, he disconnected. He'd been upfront with her right from the get-go. Still, it didn't go down easy.

Ghosts from the past slipped inside the still-open door to taunt him. With Maggie, he'd let her believe there'd be a happily-ever-after. Hell, he'd believed it himself. Had figured it would be there waiting for him when he was ready.

He'd been wrong.

From that point on, he'd been very careful to let anyone he dated know right up front he wasn't looking for anything permanent—including Rachel.

Time to go. While he'd been on the phone, he'd seen Pops and Dottie leave. He smiled. Now there were two people who belonged together.

* * *

Bubba's was hopping for a Tuesday night. He swerved into the dusty parking lot and found an empty space at the far end. Too late for happy hour, so it must be the dinner crowd.

He spotted Maggie's car, Rita and Sean's, Ty and Sophie's truck. Pops and Dottie's. Cash and Annie's. Hail, hail, the gang's all here, he thought.

His boots sounded loud on the old wooden porch. He swung through the door, into music and laughter. A myriad of conversations rolled over him. The place was packed. The Wurlitzer jukebox pumped out a snappy tune about somebody's old red pickup, but nobody was dancing.

Cash caught sight of him and waved him over to their table. On his way there, Brawley passed their waitress.

"I'll love you eternally if you'll bring me an ice-cold Lone Star, Mitzy."

"You got it, Brawley." She threw him a wink.

When he looked back at the table, Maggie watched him out of those incredible green eyes. Her pale skin shone like alabaster in the overhead lights.

His breath caught.

New York could go either way. She'd either surpass her wildest dreams or crash and burn. The city could be dog-eat-dog, and he wasn't at all sure Maggie understood what she was getting herself into. But, she was a big girl, and he'd long ago given up any right to tell her what to do. This had to be her decision. And she'd made it—for better or worse.

He squelched the pessimist inside and plastered on his game face. Tonight was a celebration. He either joined in or turned around and left.

He was in.

He slid onto his chair as Mitzy placed a longneck bottle in front of him.

"Want a glass?"

"No, ma'am. This'll do fine." Picking it up, he took a long, slow drink, then set the beer on the table. "Evening, everybody. Y'all order yet?"

"Nope, we were waiting for you." Ty held out a platter of nachos. "Have some of these."

"Don't mind if I do." He forked a few onto one of the small plates in the center of the table and scooped up some guacamole and sour cream. "Maggie, you're looking gorgeous."

"Thank you."

"You get packed?"

"I did. I'm staying at my parents' tonight."

He nodded. Message received and understood. The lady had shut the door on any possibilities for an after-dinner rendezvous. Understandably so.

Just as Mitzy wandered over to take their orders, Doc Gibson came through the door.

Maggie waved at him. "Join us."

"You sure?"

"It's my party, and I'd love to have you with us. Unless, of course, you're meeting someone," Maggie said.

"Nope. Stopped by for some dinner."

Brawley extended his leg and pushed out the chair beside him. "Take a load off, pal."

Mitzy stood, pencil poised over her order pad.

"Sorry," Maggie said. "We're ready."

"Take everybody else's first," Doc said. "Give me a minute to look over the menu."

"Why?" Cash teased. "You have the thing memorized."

"I know, I know. But the memory's not as good as it used to be. I might see something on here I've forgotten about."

Rita chuckled. "As many times as you've eaten here?"

Their waitress made the rounds of the table and got everyone else's order. "Doc? What did you decide on? Chicken-fried steak, mashed potatoes with the gravy on the side, and a serving of grilled mushrooms?"

"I think I'll have my gravy *on* the potatoes tonight, Miss Smarty Pants." He handed her the menu as everyone laughed. "Am I really that stuck-in-the-mud?"

"Hell, no," Brawley said. "But you know a good thing when you see it." His eyes slid to Maggie.

"You're right," Doc Gibson growled. "And that's exactly why I waited till I could get you to take over for me. Had to know my patients would be in good hands."

Mitzy rolled her eyes. "And that would be my cue to go place your orders. The kitchen's a little backed-up tonight, so it might be a bit."

"It doesn't matter," Pops said. "None of us are in any hurry." He squeezed his new bride's hand.

After their waitress left, Cash scooted back his chair. "Come on, Maggie mine, let's hit the dance floor and show them how it's done."

She grinned. "Why don't we?"

Brawley envied the ease with which the two friends threw themselves into the dance, smiled when Fletch herded Dottie onto the floor. Doc Gibson asked Helen Reynolds, out to dinner with her daughter, to take a spin around the floor with him. Brawley watched in surprise. The old guy was incredibly light on his feet.

Soon, the entire table had emptied except for himself and Annie. "Come on, beautiful. Dance with me."

Hand at her back, he led her onto the floor. One song moved into another and everyone changed partners, even the newlywed Fletch and Dottie.

A third song found Maggie in his arms. And thank heavens, it was a slow one. "Thinking of You" by Dierks Bentley. Oh, yeah. He tucked her into him and dropped his chin on the top of her head.

She might be feisty as all get out, but her five-foot-eight, curvy body melted into him tonight. He held a very mellow Maggie in his arms.

"I'm gonna miss you, sweetheart."

"Brawley Odell, if what I saw yesterday is any indication, you're going to be so busy you won't know which end is up."

He chuckled. "That might be, but a fellow can only work so many hours. Then what am I gonna do?"

A hint of sadness flickered in her eyes. "I'm sure you'll manage to find someone in this town who will be more than happy to keep company with you."

He didn't answer.

The song ended, and Mitzy showed up at their table with the first of their dinners. Two by two, the couples drifted back to their seats.

Good food and good friends. The conversation flowed freely.

With a mischievous expression, Maggie leaned toward Cash and Annie. "Well?"

"Well what?" Cash asked.

"Oh, come on." Maggie swatted him.

"Ouch!"

"Aren't you going to tell everybody?"

Annie shook her head. "Tonight's your night. We'll do it another time."

Maggie's mouth dropped open. "What? And make me miss it? Bull!" She stood and tapped her water glass.

The table grew silent.

Brawley, glancing from Annie to Maggie to Cash, found himself amused at the wild-eyed glances bouncing among them.

"First and most important." Maggie took a deep breath. "I want you all to know how very much I love you."

Her lower lip trembled. Her mom and dad sat on either side of her, and she laid a hand on both their shoulders. "You've been my biggest cheerleaders. You've encouraged me and believed in me when even I didn't."

Hoots and hollers broke out.

"Don't forget about us once you hit the big time," Sophie said.

"Not a chance." Maggie grinned. "Tonight's a happy night. A time to be thankful for all we've been given. For each other. A time to celebrate life. And speaking of life, I believe Cash and Annie have an announcement to make." She gestured to them. "Your turn."

Annie blushed and Cash stuck out his chest. He stood, pulling his wife up beside him. His arm tightened around her. "You want to tell them or should I?"

"You do it."

"My Annie and I are gonna have us a baby!"

"That's why you didn't drink sangria last week," Rita shouted.

Annie nodded, her grin as wide as the Texas sky.

Cash pulled her in for a long kiss.

"And that kind of lip-locking is one of the things that no doubt led to her condition," Brawley drawled.

"You'd better believe it." Cash's eyes twinkled, and Annie delivered a playful punch to his chest.

"When?" Dottie asked.

"End of October," Annie answered.

Brawley noticed Ty had turned very quiet and sent more than

one furtive glance Sophie's way. Hmmm. Something going on there. From Ty's expression, Brawley decided that something didn't have his friend turning cartwheels.

* * *

The party finally wound down, and everyone gathered purses and doggy bags.

The girls hugged and cried. Ty and Cash each gave Maggie a long, hard hug.

Doc Gibson said, "Maggie, girl, you're gonna put this little Texas town on the map. Couldn't be prouder of you if you were my own daughter." He kissed her cheek. "You be sure to get back here to see us, you hear?"

She nodded, a renegade tear trickling down her cheek.

"Don't you be crying now, darlin'. This isn't good-bye."

"I know." She wrapped her arms around him. "I'll miss you."

"I'm gonna miss you, too." Doc cleared his throat. "And now I'd best be getting home. Got two dogs that are probably walking cross-legged about now. Been longer than I meant, and they'll be needing a trip outside."

As he walked toward the door, Brawley finagled his way toward Maggie. "How are you getting to the airport in the morning?"

"Mom and Dad are driving me."

He nodded. Then he cursed as she actually held out her hand. "What's this? A handshake? I don't think so." He snaked an arm around her waist and pulled her closer, dropped his lips on hers. He forced himself to keep it light.

When he raised his head, she said, "Good-bye, Brawley. Good luck with your clinic."

"Maggie—"

"No. Don't. I don't want to cry, and I'm awfully close. As wonderful as all this is, there's part of me that wants nothing more than to stay here and watch Annie grow big with Cash's baby, help Fletch and Dottie settle in, attend the triplets' kindergarten graduation. I'll miss all that. I'll miss everyone so much."

He took her face in his hands. Marveled again at how fragile she was. With her big personality, he sometimes forgot. "I won't lie and tell you I'm glad you're going." He shook his head. "But as much as I'd like to beg you to stay, you need to do this, Mags. You need to spread your wings. This opportunity, well, it's one you have to grab. You'll kick yourself forever if you don't."

"I know. And once I'm on that plane, I'll be fine. I'll be good. Oh, Brawley." She laid a hand on his arm, a smile blossoming. "I never in a million years thought I'd have this chance."

He kissed the tip of her nose. "You earned it, Red."

"I did."

And with that, his cocky redhead was back.

Chapter Sixteen

Her flight would board soon. It was time she headed to her gate. Laughing at Pops's joke, Maggie looked up. Over the heads of the crowd, she saw Brawley striding toward them.

Stalking would probably be more apt.

Their eyes met.

"Oh, no," she groaned.

"What's wrong?" her mom asked.

"I told him not to come."

All eyes turned to Brawley.

"If you don't want him here—" Her father stood.

"No, it's okay, Dad."

Brawley reached them, tipped his hat to the women, nodded a greeting to the men. "Morning, everybody. Mind if I steal Maggie for a couple minutes?"

"Why are you here?"

"I wanted to see you off, Mags." His eyes were bloodshot and full of pain. "Talk to me. Give me two minutes, and I'll go away."

"There's nothing to talk about."

"Like hell." He took her arm, ignored the growl that erupted from Sean Sullivan.

Maggie held out her hand. "It's okay, Dad." She shook off Brawley's grip and walked with him out of earshot of the others.

"What do you want?" she hissed.

"I want to know if there's any chance for us. I know what I said last night, and I meant every word. I don't want you not to go. That isn't what I'm suggesting. But, well, hell, after the other night, I think I have a right to know."

"After the other night? What happened the other night?"

"You slept with me."

"I did not."

"Okay, you didn't. But we were both practically naked and about as close—"

"Oh, for—" Heat raced over her face, and she broke off, staring open-mouthed at him. Arms folded over her chest, her right foot tapped furiously on the airport tile. "You should know by now close only counts in horseshoes, right? Definitely not in bed. And keep your voice down."

"Why? I'm not ashamed of anything we've done."

"Maybe I am."

"Ouch. That hurts. Cuts to the bone, in fact."

She rolled her eyes, then looked at him again. Damned if he didn't actually look hurt. His ego, no doubt. Not his feelings. He didn't have any of those. Still…

"You look like hell, Brawley. Did you get any sleep last night?"

"Very little. Come on. Talk to me, Maggie."

She stomped off across the terminal and dropped into one of the ugly, uncomfortable vinyl chairs.

He followed suit.

"Look," he said. "I'm not going to get in your way. You have to go. Have to follow your dreams. I understand that. But I want you to know that when you've seen what you need to see, done what you need to do, I'll be here for you."

"Like you were before?"

"I was young and stupid and I did you wrong. I've never denied that."

"At eighteen, I wanted you more than my next breath." She saw him wince and studied the new purple polish on her toes. "But all that's in the past. We're history, Brawley. How many times do I have to tell you that?"

"I don't believe you for a minute. See, here's the thing. You say the words, but your actions don't match. Saturday night? When we touched? Hot and explosive. If we're not made for each other, we've got a problem because I'm not sure there's anyone else for me—or for you, for that matter."

She moaned. "Don't even say that."

"I already did, and I told you before, once you hear something..."

"Right. It can't be unheard."

He took her chin between two fingers and raised her gaze to his. "I want you to think about what I've said. In the meantime, hop on that plane and put Maverick Junction, Texas, on the map. I'm proud of you. Enjoy this, sugar."

"Brawley—"

He shook his head. "You're headed for your star, and you're gonna catch it." A sad smile lifted a corner of his lips. "You have to go. Doesn't mean I can't be sorry as hell, though." He lifted her hand and brought it to his lips. "If things don't work out or you change your mind—" His voice broke. "I'll be here. Waiting for you. You can come home."

"Brawley, don't wait for me. It's no way to live. I know from personal experience. I won't be coming back."

He stared into her eyes for another few seconds. "Gotcha. One more thing before I go."

"What?

"This." Right there, in front of God, country, and her family, he thumbed back his Stetson and brought his lips to hers. He kissed her as she'd never been kissed. The emotion, raw and powerful, swept over her.

He pulled away and tucked his hands in his pockets. He nodded toward her parents, grandfather, and Dottie, then turned and walked away.

She bit her lip to keep from calling him back. He was wrong. They weren't made for each other, weren't meant to be together.

Taking a deep breath, she closed her eyes for the count of ten. Wiping damp palms on her navy pencil skirt, she jumped up and moved to where the others stood silent, watching her.

"You okay?" her dad asked.

"I'm fine." She smiled at him, then glanced at the airport clock. "Oh, you guys, I love you, but it's time to go."

She threw her arms around her mom and kissed her. She hugged Dottie, then buried her face against Pops's neck. "I'll miss you."

"I know, sweetheart, but you'll be so busy you won't have time to do more than come up for air. Call. Often. Let us know how you're doing," Pops said.

"I will, and if you newlyweds have time, maybe you can visit, use New York as a second honeymoon."

"We'll be there for your show," her grandfather said. "Wild horses couldn't keep any of us away."

Her dad threw an arm over her shoulder, drew her close, and kissed her forehead. "Keep your options open, honey. Always keep your options open. A whole new world is yours for the taking. Your mom and I are so, so proud."

"Thank you, Daddy." She hugged him tightly.

"I love you," he said simply. "If you need me, call. I'm here for you always, baby girl."

She smiled at him, waved at them all, and got in line for the metal detector. Setting her bag on the belt, she put her purse and magazine in a bin along with her shoes. She spoke to the security attendant, then stepped through the scanner, not daring a look back.

Thirty minutes later, seat belt fastened and a copy of *Vogue* in hand, the plane backed onto the tarmac, preparing for flight.

Maggie stared out the window and watched as they taxied onto the runway. She'd expected to leave Texas with a smile on her face. Instead, she was flying off to her dreams with tears in her eyes.

Damn Brawley Odell for that!

Chapter Seventeen

When the plane touched down, Maggie's heart nearly leaped from her chest. As of this moment, she officially lived in New York City! Oh, my gosh! Who'd have believed it?

Not her!

Exhausted from a nearly sleepless night in her strangely unfamiliar childhood bed, she'd slept part of the way and doodled on her sketch pad the rest of the trip. The less-than-four-hour flight had passed quickly.

Now that she was here, though, any lethargy she'd felt sloughed away. She knew the grin on her face was ridiculously huge as she gathered her belongings and headed down the narrow aisle.

The stewardess smiled at her as she stepped off the plane. "Have a good day."

"Oh, I'm going to."

No one met her plane. Zandra, her new assistant, had offered, but Maggie declined. Maybe it was pride, maybe fear. Probably a mix of both with a few other emotions stirred into the brew. Regardless of the reason, she wanted to find her own way today. She needed to. If this city held her future, would be her home, her life, she needed to learn how to navigate it.

In the taxi, she made a quick call to her mom.

"I'm here safe and sound. Let Pops and Dottie know, would you?"

They chatted another couple minutes, then she hung up and phoned Ella to check on the shop. Everything was running smoothly. Even while relief filled her, she found herself almost wishing there'd been just the tiniest snag, something that only she could fix.

Her business, her baby, didn't need her. Because she'd found an excellent employee and trained her well, Maggie told herself. Still, it was always nice to be needed.

For a fraction of a second, she actually considered calling Brawley to touch base. To hear his voice. Her finger scrolled down to his name before she caught herself. What the heck was she doing? And what had possessed her to even add his name to her contacts?

She dropped her phone into her purse and stared out the window as the taxi passed skyscraper after skyscraper. New leaves, the bright green of spring, peppered the trees along the way. A few flowering ones splashed color against the grays and browns of the buildings.

Store after store after store rushed past. The sidewalks were filled with people scurrying to work, to home, to shops. The energy fascinated her and filled her with a vitality of her own. When the driver pulled up in front of the brownstone where she'd rented an apartment, she fairly vibrated with it. Her new home.

The cabby retrieved her luggage from the trunk, and she paid him. As he drove away, she pulled out her phone and took a photo of herself in front of her stoop.

Without thought, she sent it to Brawley. U have new paint, I have a new address. ☺

Then, guiltily, she sent the picture, along with a different message, to her mom, who really should have been the first.

One bag at a time, she manhandled the luggage up the short flight of stairs to her door and dug out her key. Annie had given her an apple keychain. Symbolic.

Maggie and her dad had argued over her apartment choice. Not only would she be living solo for the first time, but she'd be doing it in a big city. One where she knew only a handful of people—and none of them well.

He'd wanted her in a building with a doorman; she'd fallen in love with a first-story flat without one. They'd compromised on a second-story sans doorman but one her mother assured him was in a safe neighborhood.

Dragging her bags upstairs, Maggie questioned her wisdom in not holding out for a ground floor. It sure would have made this part of the move easier.

But when she opened her door, any and all doubts fled. The sun poured through large windows and turned the wood floors into a river of shine. Her landlord had arranged for a cleaning crew to come in, and the place was spotless.

Best of all, there in the center of her dining room table, a beautiful bouquet of spring flowers from her family greeted her. So like them to think of that.

A note from Zandra rested beside it, explaining she'd let the florist in and had stocked the fridge with wine, some food, and a few basics in case Maggie didn't feel like going out.

She sighed and moved into the kitchen. Dark cherry cabinets, granite countertops, and stainless steel appliances. What more could a girl want? And thanks to Zandra, she had wine with which to toast her new home.

She spun in a circle, then did a little happy dance right there in the middle of the kitchen.

She spotted a container of Arabica beans by her new coffeemaker. Yes! She patted herself on the back for having chosen her assistant well, then gave Zandra a silent round of applause.

A loaf of Italian bread lay on a cutting board on the counter. When she opened the fridge, Maggie clapped her hands. This was as good as Christmas. A bottle of red, one of white, a huge bunch of grapes, cheeses, several deli containers—Wow. She'd hit the jackpot.

Zandra already deserved a raise. Spotting her favorite sparkling water, she poured a glass. Flying had dehydrated her.

She kicked off her shoes, dropped onto the white leather sofa in the living room, and sipped her water. Maybe she wouldn't go anywhere tonight. Although the flight had been fairly short, the day had been long.

Partly because they had to drive to Austin, partly from nerves, she'd been up early. She'd already had the coffee brewing and the eggs frying when her mom and dad came downstairs.

Then, of course, checking in and waiting for the flight. But the emotional toll had been the most draining. Despite the fact she wanted this desperately, when it came right down to it, it was hard to rip her roots out of the Texas soil and leave her family, her friends, her shop. And, yes, Brawley. By the time the plane had taxied from the gate, she'd felt drained.

Then they'd landed, and she'd had an incredible spurt of energy. When she'd stepped out of the cab, she'd truly believed she could take on the world.

Right now, though, instead of a stroll around the block, she'd settle for a meandering tour of her new apartment. Thank heavens it came furnished right down to silverware, linens, and coffeepot. The only thing required from her? The rent money. She had enough put away for the first few months. After that, she hoped her clothing line would cover the expenses.

Standing in the center of the room, arms wrapped around herself in glee, she thought how different this sleek, newly remodeled house was from Pops's or even her parents. It reminded her of Brawley's. Not the kitchen. He was pretty much stuck with what Dottie had there. But the furniture, the décor.

She liked it. Black and white with a pop of red in the accessories. The walls and ceilings had been painted a soft white, making them a great backdrop for the few pieces of art.

Dragging one suitcase behind her, she moved to the back, to the bedrooms and bath. The fact it had a guest room had pushed this apartment from a maybe to a definite yes. When someone came to visit, they wouldn't have to sleep on the sofa—nor would she if she gave them her bed.

The bath was sleek chrome and pristine white. The black and white floor and shower tiles added their own artistic touch, as did the black towels and the huge white vase. The total effect was something straight out of a decorator's dream.

And the bedroom. Her suitcase bumping at her heels, she stopped in the doorway and simply stared. Giving herself a quick pinch, she decided it was real. All of it.

Tonight she'd sleep in that incredible art deco bed with its plump pillows and duvet—in New York. A horn blared outside her window and another answered it. So foreign to a Maverick Junction girl. While some might find it distracting, it sounded like music to her ears.

When she woke tomorrow, she'd brew coffee in that sleek coffeemaker, eat an egg and some cheese from one of the sleek white plates, and shower in that elegant bath.

Then she'd head downstairs, hail a taxi, and make her mark in the fashion industry. What more could she possibly want?

Maybe a pet. A dog that she could walk or a cat that she wouldn't have to walk. It might be better to wait a bit on that, though, since she'd be putting in long days for quite some time. Would it be fair to an animal if she brought it home, then left it for hours and hours at a time?

Her phone pinged. An incoming message.

* * *

The instant he hit send, Brawley regretted it. He needed to let Maggie settle in and get her feet under her.

But he hadn't been able to resist. Jesse, Jonah, and Josh had been so damned earnest, and he'd caught them in an upswing, all three of them, like a trio of synchronized swimmers or dancers.

He'd stopped and had lunch on the drive home from the airport. A spur of the moment whim had him turning off onto Ty's lane. He'd used the excuse of checking up on Trouble, but, in all honesty, he'd needed to touch base with a friend. He was feeling a little raw.

Maggie had to go, deserved this chance, but that didn't make it hurt less. He hadn't made a dent in her feelings for him. He hadn't been forgiven.

Walking away this morning, knowing she'd board that plane, had been the toughest thing he'd done since he'd walked away from her all those years ago. Just like before, he'd had no choice, no options. This was her shot, and he couldn't hold her back. She'd never forgive him…or herself.

When he pulled into the drive, three swim-goggled boys and their dog greeted him. Following them to the barn, he'd watched while they pummeled a block of wood Ty'd put there. Unable to help himself, he'd snapped the picture.

Brawley stuck his phone in his hip pocket. Maggie could delete the photo if it didn't fit her new image.

"Brawley, Brawley," he chastised himself under his breath. "You've been the city dweller all these years, not her." Still…

Ty stepped out of the tack room. "Hey, Brawley. What brings you out here? Somebody have a sick horse or cow?"

"Nah. I…um…" He kicked at a clump of straw on the barn floor. "I drove over to Austin today. Thought I'd stop by and check out this mutt of yours."

"Unfortunately, the snakebite didn't seem to make him behave any better than ever," Ty said. "If he chews up another shoe, I'm afraid Sophie's gonna ban him from the house."

"Can't say I blame her. You trained all these boys not to eat shoes. Can't you train Trouble?"

"We didn't eat shoes!" Jonah giggled.

"You sure about that?" Brawley squinted at him.

"Yeah." Jesse wound himself around Brawley's leg. "Kids don't eat shoes, just dogs."

"Kids eat dogs?"

Startled, Jesse shook his head.

"You said kids don't eat shoes, just dogs."

Jesse let out an exasperated sigh.

"Just dogs eat shoes, Uncle Brawley," Josh said.

"Oh." Brawley took off his Stetson and wiped his brow. "You had me scared there for a minute." He scooped Jonah off his feet and held him upside-down. The other two stepped in to tickle their brother while he was helpless.

As he set Jonah back on his feet, he noticed Ty's frown. He gave one of the kids a tap on the butt. "Why don't you run on up to the house? Ask Sophie if she might have a cold glass of sweet tea for one of the good guys."

"For who?" Josh asked.

"For me."

"'Kay." The three tore off across the yard, Trouble yapping at their heels.

"What's wrong, Ty?"

"Sophie wants a baby."

"Doesn't surprise me. She loves those boys, but it's only natural to want one of her own."

"I'd hoped to put it off a bit."

"She doesn't want to."

"Nope. And Annie and Cash's announcement last night—Well, it didn't help matters. It turns out she already knew. But this puts some extra pressure on me."

"So go for it, pal. Give your boys a baby to boss around."

Ty let out a half-laugh. "Oh, yeah. They'd do that well."

"But?"

"Hell of a thing for a man to admit, Brawley, but I'm afraid."

"Afraid?" Then it hit him. What an idiot. Of course Ty'd be scared. He'd lost his first wife right after she'd had the boys. "It's different this time, Ty. Totally different. Sophie's healthy. There's nothing wrong with her heart."

"I know that. Here." Ty tapped a finger to his forehead. "But here?" He pounded a fist over his heart. "Scares the bejesus out of me."

"Only natural you'd feel that way."

The front door slammed, and both men watched as Sophie, wearing a short dress the color of saddle leather, stepped onto the porch.

She held up a tray. "This is as far as I go. You guys get yourselves up here."

"Yes, ma'am," Ty called out. Turning to Brawley, he said, "I couldn't stand to lose her. It would kill me."

"Understood. I think, though, what you're gonna lose is this battle." He slung an arm over his friend's shoulders. "My guess is that Sophie can talk you into just about anything."

"You've got that right, pal. She turns those big brown eyes on me, and I'm lost."

"Well, then, step up and do your duty. And while you're at it, you might as well have a little fun."

They stepped onto the porch laughing.

Sophie quirked her brow. "What's going on?"

"Not a thing." Ty leaned close and planted a whopper of a kiss on her.

"You'd think the two of you were newlyweds," Brawley muttered.

"Yes, you would, wouldn't you?" Sophie kissed Brawley's cheek.

"Kind of stingy."

"But I have sweet tea." She handed him a glass.

"So you never did say what you were doing in Austin this morning." Ty dropped onto the porch swing.

"Austin? Maggie flew out of there this morning." Sophie's eyes grew misty. "Did you take her?"

"No. Her folks did." Heat rushed over him. He felt stupid. Like a teenager caught drawing hearts around his girl's name in study hall.

"You went to see her off?" Ty asked.

Brawley nodded. "But I don't want to talk about it."

"Okay. How's business at the clinic?"

"Busy. Very busy. I honestly don't know how Doc Gibson hung on as long as he did."

"Glad he made it to Bubba's last night," Ty said.

"Me, too."

"He must be lonely all by himself in that huge house now that his wife is gone," Sophie said.

Ty's glance flew to Brawley as if to say, "See what I'm talking about? What I'd face if something happened to this woman?"

"I'm sure he is," Brawley said easily. "He and Meredith had fifty-four happy years together. He's got a lot of memories and two rambunctious dogs to keep him company."

"A shame they never had any children." Sophie took a sip of tea, her eyes meeting Ty's over the rim of the glass.

Brawley swore he could hear the groan Ty bit back. Oh, yeah, his friend would lose this battle. He might as well hoist the white flag of surrender and make the most of it.

He almost laughed, and probably would have if he didn't understand all too well that gut-wrenching fear of losing the woman you love. Ty had done that once. Now Brawley had, too. When Maggie had stepped on that plane today, she'd written the end to anything they might have had.

Hell, that wasn't true. He'd done that himself. The fire had been banked, though, not extinguished. He'd thought with enough time and patience, he could rekindle it. He'd thought wrong.

The topic of their conversation turned to the softball team Ty's boys played on, the one Ty coached.

"We could use more help if you have any free time," Ty said.

"I might consider that. I'm gonna need something to do with myself. The nights are a heck of a lot quieter here in Maverick Junction than I've been used to."

Brawley sat on the porch shooting the breeze with his friends, watching the kids roll around in the grass. He'd bet the ranch that within a year they had another to join the boys. Sophie'd get her way on this.

And Annie and Cash already had one on the way.

He finished his tea and set the glass on the pretty little tray. "Time to go." He stood. "Thanks for the refreshments, Sophie. You don't do bad for a Chicago transplant."

"Gee, thanks a lot."

"Hey, that's high praise." He thumbed back his hat. "You've got a nice place here, Ty. I think maybe it's time I bought some land. Built myself a permanent home."

Halfway down the stairs, he turned back. "You two enjoy yourselves."

"God'll get you for that," Ty said.

Brawley laughed at Sophie's quizzical expression, then high-fived each of the boys as he passed them.

As he drove away, he glanced in his rearview mirror. Ty had had it tough, no doubt about it. But now? Pretty sweet deal.

His mind caught on the idea of him and Maggie, and he wondered about the kids they might have made if things had been different.

Chapter Eighteen

Talk about smug! Maggie stood in awe of herself. She'd actually managed the subway this morning. Up at the crack of dawn, unable to sleep another minute from the excitement of waking in her own Upper East Side apartment, she'd showered, done her hair and makeup, and dressed carefully.

She'd made the slim, long-sleeve dress especially for today and hoped it hit the right note with its dark brown print paired with soft leather, high-heeled ankle boots. Authoritative, yet friendly. But not too friendly. Oh, geez. From smug to doubting Thomas in three seconds flat. That had to be some kind of a record.

No doubt Owen Cook, her angel investor, would drop by today. Annie had offered her seed money to get her line started, but Maggie'd been hesitant to mix friends and money. So when Owen, a business acquaintance of Annie's father, offered to back her, she'd jumped at it.

Owen had already invested a lot of money in her and her designs, covering the entire cost of her upcoming show. Even if he was as rich as Donald Trump, as a businessman he must have some concerns about rolling the dice on such a total unknown. He'd want to check out her new line and, when he showed up, she wanted to mirror an up-and-coming designer, not a small-town wannabe.

The fact that the show would be an off-season one raised the stakes. Made her worry no one would even attend.

As she exited the subway, she stepped to the side and let others, in their mad rush to make it to work, pass by. Then she simply stood taking in the sights. An army of taxis and cars flew by, horns honking, brakes screeching. Buses belched black smoke and stopped to disgorge passengers while others in a queue hurried to get on. Bicycles and their riders darted in and out of traffic. People of all shapes, sizes, and ages hurried past.

A pizza shop on the corner offered its fare for a dollar a slice. Starbucks, in the middle of the block, was doing a booming business, the line stretching onto the sidewalk. Vendors sold coffee and bagels from carts. And towering above it all were the buildings, magnificent towers of stone, steel, and glass.

She rubbed her hands together in glee. She was really here. And one short block away, the space where magic would happen awaited.

Another cup of coffee called to her, but, not wanting to be late, she bypassed Starbucks with a sorrowful glance through the window at the women in their chic outfits, the men in their suits and ties.

Less than twenty-four hours ago she'd been in the Austin airport, surrounded by jeans, cowboy hats, and Stetsons—men and women. What a difference a day made. If she wanted coffee in Lone Tree, she'd stop by Ollie's. Here? She had so many choices her head swam.

Would she ever get used to it? she wondered. Ever take all this for granted? She seriously hoped not.

Her feet kept moving, traveling the block to her building. Her building! Oh, gosh. Well, her space in the building, anyway. She laid a hand over her heart, felt it practically jump from her chest.

With one last swipe over the skirt of her dress, a deep breath, and a prayer, she walked through the door.

"Miss Sullivan."

Maggie grinned. The security guard in the reception area remembered her. "Hello, Orlando."

"You here to finish that new collection?"

"I sure am."

"Do you have your nametag, or should I print you a new one?"

"Oh, sorry. Yes, I have it." Belatedly, she dug through her purse till she found the tag and clipped it to the neck of her dress.

"You can go right on up."

"Thanks." She headed to the bank of elevators and pressed ten. Inside, she watched the numbers count off as the car zipped skyward.

When the doors opened, Zandra waited there for her, coffee in hand. She held the cup out to Maggie. "Here you go. Thought you might need this."

"For me?"

"You see any other big-name designer here?"

Maggie made a production of scanning the room. "I don't see *any* big-name designer. Period."

Zandra grinned and held out the coffee again. Maggie accepted it gratefully and took a sip. Oh, yes. This more than made up for the coffee she hadn't stopped to buy. At the same time, it seemed strange, awkward almost, to have someone wait on her.

"Welcome to New York, Maggie."

"Thank you, Zandra." She held up her coffee. "And I can't tell you how much I appreciate this. I've been obsessing over the second cup I didn't have. You really don't need to do this every day, though."

"Sure I do. I like you."

"Be careful. I could get used to it."

"You'd better. After your show, everybody will be scrambling for your work and your attention. Your designs are spectacular, Maggie."

"You like them?"

"Like? No. Love? Oh, yes! Wait till you see what we've done."

"I can't wait." Maggie stopped by her office to put down her purse and briefcase. "Did the red silk come in?"

"Late yesterday afternoon."

"Ooh, boy, that's cutting it close."

"Tell me about it," Zandra said. "Did you get settled in?"

"My suitcases are piled in the middle of the bedroom. That's as far as I got. I'd probably have starved if you hadn't taken pity on me and stocked my pantry and fridge. Again, I owe you a huge thanks. I can't tell you how much I appreciated it."

"I wasn't sure what you'd want, so I stuck with things I'd seen you eat when you were here before."

"Smart lady."

And drop-dead gorgeous, Maggie thought. Zandra, with her slim, six-foot body, exotic brown eyes, and long black hair, put every model Maggie had met to shame. Today she looked edgy in her black leather pants and jacket. A red top peeked from the jacket, highlighting her smooth caffé au lait skin.

They stepped into the workroom, and Maggie's heart stopped.

"I'd ask what you think, but the look on your face says it all."

Absently, Maggie set her coffee on a table. Large windows took up the better part of two walls and early morning sun spilled over swaths of fabric, patterns, and completed outfits.

Without a word, she wandered through the maze of workstations, fingering cotton, silk, and linen. She adjusted a collar, studied buttons and zippers.

This had to be nearly as exciting as giving birth, in a way. She'd created all this. Standing in the center of the room, she took it in, her smile spreading.

"I know I can't, but oh, how I want to pull out my camera or phone and take pictures." Maggie wrapped her arms around herself.

"Pretty spectacular." Zandra spoke from the doorway. "You see any problems?"

"The hem on the dark brown dress needs to be shortened. I want different buttons on the black and white blazer." Her head whirled with ideas. Alterations. Excitement. Zandra was right. The collection was pretty darn spectacular.

"All in all," Maggie said, "I'm thrilled."

A couple of the seamstresses she'd met on her last two trips wandered in, and the workday began.

* * *

Knee-deep in pleated organza, Maggie recognized the tap of Zandra's heels as she crossed the hardwood floor. Around a mouthful of straight pins, she said, "Please don't tell me we have any wrinkles in our plans."

"No wrinkles," her assistant assured her. "You have company."

"Company?" Her mind flew to Brawley. Stupid.

Owen had already been by and left a happy man. So who was here now?

From where she knelt on the floor in front of her dress form, Maggie looked up into one of the strongest faces she'd ever seen. Dark, thick brows highlighted deep-set, intense black eyes. A strong, straight nose over full lips. A heavy stubble of black over his cheeks and jaw.

She was staring but darned if she could stop.

She jabbed the pins into her wristband and stood, extending her hand. "Hi. I'm Maggie Sullivan."

He took her hand, raised it to his lips, and kissed the back of it.

"You're quite beautiful. That red hair and green eyes. A magnificent combination."

His gaze moved slowly over the curves of her body, and she felt herself flush.

Zandra cleared her throat. "Maggie, this is Jarvis Quillen. He's your photographer."

"Jarvis, it's great to finally meet you. I've heard over and over how fortunate I am you've agreed to work with me."

"How could I refuse?"

Maggie laughed. "Right. Let's see." She tapped a finger on her chin. "I'm a brand-new unknown, have no credentials, and no track record. Hmmm."

"Owen Cook never backs anything but stars. The fact he brought you to the city is enough for me." Jarvis put a hand into the pocket of his black designer jeans. "I've got a shoot this afternoon, but I wanted to stop by and meet you."

He tilted his head and narrowed his eyes. "Listen, I'd like to talk about your collection. Get an idea what you have in mind for your photos. Are you free tonight?"

"Yes, actually I am. I just arrived yesterday so my calendar is pretty open. In fact, nonexistent best describes my commitments—outside of work."

"Zandra, give Maggie directions to Gotham Bar and Grill. Why don't we meet there at, say, eight? Will that work for you?"

"Absolutely. What should I wear?"

His eyes moved over her again. "Exactly what you have on. It's perfect. One of your own?"

She nodded.

"I like it."

She watched him stride away, noticed the confidence, the self-assurance. This man had a big personality. He took up a lot of space simply by walking into a room.

Zandra started back to the office. "I'll write down the restaurant's address for you," she threw over her shoulder. "Take a cab. And Jarvis is right. Don't change. That outfit really is perfect."

She stopped.

"What?"

"He's pretty spectacular, isn't he?" Zandra asked.

The two shared a woman's smile.

"Yeah, he is that," Maggie agreed. "But tonight's strictly business."

"Tell yourself whatever works."

* * *

Brawley scratched his head. What the hell was he gonna do with this thing?

"Phyllis," he called.

She stuck her head in the door. "Yeah?"

"Know anybody looking for a dog?"

"As in to take home and keep?" She eyed the filthy animal stretched out on the exam table. "He sure has made himself at home, hasn't he?"

The dog yawned and dropped his head onto his front paws.

"I'd say so." Brawley ran a hand over his chin. "Cash's sister dropped him off while you were at the post office."

"Somebody abandoned him?"

"Seems so."

"Why didn't Babs keep him or take him out to her brother's place? I'd think Cash could always find room for a dog at the ranch."

"She wanted him checked out first."

"Nothing wrong with that one," Phyllis said, "that a good bath won't take care of. Give Cash a call yourself."

"Already did. He reminded me he's got Staubach. Says he's

enough for anyone. He doesn't want another dog, especially not a sissy one. His words."

Phyllis laughed. "What? He thinks it would emasculate him to have a fluffy little ball of fur following him around?"

Brawley took another look at the dog. "Can't say I'd argue with that. Cash's real concern is that he'd get in the barn and end up under one of the horse's hooves. Or spook one of them and both dog and horse would get hurt. Can't blame him. I sure as hell would never own a dog like this."

The dog in question took that moment to crawl to the table's edge and lick Brawley's hand.

"Not gonna work, boy. Not enough sugar-coating in the world."

The dog stared up at him with huge brown eyes.

"He loves you already," his assistant said.

"Bull. He thinks I'm an easy mark." He turned back to the dog. "I'm not."

The dog licked him again, his stubby tail wagging.

"Call Dawn Marie. Maybe she'll take him or know somebody who's looking for one."

"She was my first call. I tried to guilt her into taking him, but no go."

"Good luck, Doc." Phyllis started to close the door.

"I'll have to put him to sleep."

His assistant slapped a hand on the door and held it open. "You wouldn't."

"I can't keep every animal that gets dragged in here."

"No, I guess you can't. But last time I counted, you had exactly zero pets of your own."

"And that's the way it has to be right now. I'm renting."

"So? Didn't you talk Sophie into keeping Lilybelle? Seems to me she was renting the very same apartment you're in." Phyllis narrowed her eyes. "Call Dottie. She'll tell you to bring him home."

"No. No way. If I get a dog, it's gonna be a man's dog, not this six-inch-tall, five-pound runt."

The dog whined.

"Oh, see?" Phyllis walked back into the room and ran a hand over the dog's head. "Did he hurt your feelings? Mean old Doctor Odell. You're a good boy, aren't you?"

The little tail wagged so hard the ball of fur almost vibrated off the table.

"He's an ankle-biter," Brawley groused.

"A Yorkie," she corrected. "Don't see many of them here in Maverick Junction. They're more of a city dog."

"Yeah, they're good for apartments."

"There you go. Isn't that what I just said?"

He rolled his eyes. "Don't you have something you need to do?"

"Yes, and I was doing it until my boss called me in here to look at this sweet thing."

The sweet thing yapped and blinked, tail still going a mile a minute.

The door swung shut behind her, and Brawley leaned against the exam table. "What are we gonna do with you, huh? Maybe I'll call Dawn and see if she'll at least give you a bath and a new haircut. But, I promise, Boy Scouts' honor, no bows or ribbons. We guys have to stick together. Once we get you cleaned up, people will fall over each other to take you home." He scratched the dog's head. "Yes, they will."

* * *

Maggie groaned when she caught sight of the clock. Too late to run home and change so she would, indeed, be wearing what she had on. Thank God she'd chosen a day-to-evening dress this morning. She trusted Zandra's word that it would be fine, but a shower would have been nice.

Needing a little time alone with her collection, she'd sent Zandra and the other workers home an hour ago. She freshened up her makeup, then spied a bolt of blue fabric. Exactly what the doctor ordered.

Crossing to it, she cut off a length, then sat down at one of the sewing machines and whipped up a scarf. It added a little extra pizzazz to her outfit.

She turned off the lights, but, instead of leaving, she moved to the large windows. Incredible. Not quite dark, streetlights were just flickering to life. Some windows in the buildings around her still glowed with lights, people working late like herself. Others were dark.

But down below, traffic streamed by in a steady pace. Stoplights shone red and green, making her think of Christmas. If possible, the street was even busier than when she'd arrived this morning.

She swiveled on her heel. Dress forms scattered around the room sported her creations. Some had been finished, some nearly, others in the midst of major reconstruction. Every single one carried a Maggie label. Had she ever been this excited? This terrified?

And she'd be late if she didn't leave right this minute. She grabbed her purse and briefcase, then set the security system.

When she stepped outside the building, the chill in the air surprised her and made her glad her dress had sleeves. A taxi barreled down the street toward her. She held up her hand, and it actually stopped. Grinning, she hopped into the back seat and gave the driver the restaurant's address.

Her phone pinged. Uh-oh. Had Jarvis canceled?

She brought up the message. It was from Brawley.

Want a dog?

Nope.

The next message was a photo. He's been abandoned.

She smiled at the little dog in the big man's arms. He looks good right where he is.

You'd love him.

He was right. She would. And hadn't she been thinking a pet would be good company?

He's in TX, I'm in NY.

I'll hand-deliver.

Her breath caught. Would he actually come to New York?

She gave herself a mental head slap. Nope. Not going there. The old "Fool me once, shame on you. Fool me twice, shame on me" ran through her head. She was nobody's fool.

2 busy for a pet, she typed.

Brawley's next message hit hard. Four simple words.

Can we be friends?

She closed her eyes. There'd been a time when that was a given. They'd been so close, known each other's thoughts without any need for words.

She texted him back.

Don't think so.

She hit send and experienced a jolt of pain. Without giving herself time for second thoughts, she tucked her phone in the side pocket of her purse. If he answered, she'd ignore it.

Tonight she was taking one more step toward the beginning of her new life.

* * *

It had been one hell of a day.

Sprawled across his bed, Brawley dug his phone out of his pocket and stared again at Maggie's message. She was a tough one to figure out. This—so cold. Yet the night of her grandfather's wedding she'd been almost too hot to touch. That dance they'd shared in the front yard had been a little slice of heaven. She'd let down her guard. Forgotten to be all bristly and standoffish.

What was she doing tonight?

It didn't really matter, did it? He scrolled through his texts and found the picture of her outside her new brownstone. Sighing, he turned off the phone and tossed it onto the bed beside him.

He rolled over and caught sight of the picture he'd taken at the wedding. Maggie, her head thrown back in laughter. Those green eyes shining with happiness.

Grabbing it, he turned it facedown. He didn't want to look at it anymore. Jamming a pillow under his head, he curled into it and fell asleep fully dressed, the stupid little dog curled up beside him, snoring.

Chapter Nineteen

Standing in front of Gotham's bathroom mirror, Maggie chewed herself out. She should never have come out with Jarvis. Huge mistake. When he'd asked her, though, she'd jumped at the chance. He would be the photographer for her new line. The stronger their connection, the better his work. Right?

She worried her bottom lip. It would have been unprofessional not to have come.

How could she figure out the correct etiquette in these situations? In Maverick Junction, she understood the rules. Knew how the game was played. But here? A fish out of water.

While a part of her found it unbelievably thrilling to sit in this elegant restaurant across the table from a veritable stranger who looked like something straight out of a girl's bad boy fantasies, she also found it unsettling.

They'd discussed work, her upcoming show, and his ideas about the photography side of it. She'd shared her plans for the future, and he'd told her about his own. His struggle to get where he was.

And right now, he had to be wondering if she'd dropped off the face of the earth. Hands wrapped around the edge of the sink,

Maggie leaned closer to the mirror and stared into her own eyes, reminded herself this was exactly what she'd worked so hard to achieve. She was suffering a case of adult homesickness tonight. Period.

Reaching into her purse, she pulled out her lipstick and flicked it across her lips. So why did she wish it was Brawley waiting for her?

Damn! Why couldn't he have waited another couple months to return home? She'd have been gone and wouldn't have missed what she'd never had. Except she *had* had him. Once upon a time, long, long ago.

She shook her head.

She had an exciting new life. And part of that newness sat at a white-cloth-covered table twiddling his thumbs waiting for her. She exhaled sharply. Everything would be fine. Better than fine.

A smile on her face, she left her temporary refuge.

Jarvis stood as she approached, an expression of relief on his handsome face. "You're incredibly beautiful, Maggie." He held her chair for her. "I'd love to shoot you sometime."

Her smile broadened. "I'm assuming that's with a camera."

"Of course."

"Back in Texas, when you talk about shooting something... Well, enough said, huh?"

Rather than answer, he took her hand in his and kissed the back of it. "Would you like dessert? Another coffee?"

She patted her tummy. "No, thanks." She took in the ambience. "This was wonderful, Jarvis. Back in my small hometown, we have two restaurants, three if you count Ollie's in Lone Tree. Believe me, they're nothing like this."

"Would I like it there?"

She tilted her head, gave it some thought. "You know, I think you might—for a short time. Then you'd miss the cosmopolitan scene. Maverick Junction is really in the boonies."

"And you love it, don't you?"

"Yes. I do. But this?" She held out a hand. "I love this, too. I confess it's going to take a while to get used to all the people, the noise, the nonstop of it all."

"Do you miss your family?"

"I'd be a liar if I said no. My parents, my grandfather, my friends. Yes, I miss them. But it's only been a day since I left. I don't have my sea legs under me yet." She smiled. "Besides, they're all flying in for my show."

"Really?"

She nodded. "You can meet them then. And my friends Annelise and Sophie have both agreed to walk the runway for me."

"Annelise." Jarvis's forehead creased in thought. "Is that Annelise Montjoy?"

"Hardeman now, but yes. She started this whole crazy ride when she wore one of my designs to a fund-raiser in Dallas."

"An incredible gown."

"You saw it?"

"The world saw it, Maggie, and was brought to its knees."

She blushed. "I think that's a total exaggeration, but thank you."

Jarvis shook his head. "It's not. Those pictures popped up and had everybody asking the same question. Who is Maggie Sullivan, and how can I get my hands on her and her designs?"

She laughed. Jarvis was easy to talk to.

"Besides family and friends, anything else you miss back home?"

She frowned. "Anything else?"

He chuckled. "My attempt at subtle. I'll go for blunt. Do you have a guy back home? Someone waiting for you?"

"Duh." She raised a hand to her forehead and rolled her eyes. "Sorry. I don't get out much."

She shook her head and another wave of melancholy washed over her. "No. No one at home." Her heart pinched as she remembered Brawley's parting kiss.

"Good to know. But I have to wonder then, what the hell is wrong with the men in Maverick Junction?"

"Excuse me?"

"Why aren't they swarming around you? Are they all blind?"

She grinned. "Hardly. I've been pretty busy."

"Still. It makes no sense to me that a woman like you doesn't have half a dozen men chasing her."

The waiter returned with Jarvis's credit card. He signed the charge slip and slid his AmEx into his wallet.

"Ready?"

"Yes. Thanks for dinner."

"You're very welcome."

He stood, then came around the table to slide her chair back for her. He took her hand as they walked together from the restaurant.

After they hailed a taxi, she slid across the seat, and Jarvis got in, moving across till their hips touched. Resting his arm on the back of the seat, he gave the driver her address.

As they pulled away from the curb, he wrapped an arm tightly around her, and Maggie found herself uneasy again. She wasn't sophisticated enough for this man.

Yet she felt totally at ease with Brawley. She had no problem telling him exactly how she felt, good or bad. And Brawley could match this urbanite step for step in social graces. In Dallas, he'd mixed very easily with the city's elite.

Still, he was Brawley.

Jarvis broke into her thoughts. "I had a nice time tonight."

"Me, too."

Both remained quiet as the taxi fought its way through the still-heavy traffic, wending street by street to her new apartment. Before

Maggie realized exactly where they were, the cab pulled over to the curb.

"We're here already?"

Jarvis nodded and asked the cabbie to wait. Opening the door, he got out, then reached in to help her.

Maggie's tongue shot out to lick suddenly dry lips. She had no idea what to expect. Stupid. Jarvis was a colleague, someone she worked with. Tonight had been business.

She turned to him. "Thanks so—"

His lips came down on hers.

Surprised, Maggie opened her mouth to protest. Jarvis took advantage and slid his tongue inside.

Her mind reeled. Jarvis's kiss was pleasant. Very skilled.

And she felt nothing. His kiss didn't set her on fire the way Brawley's did. She didn't find herself wanting more. Wanting to tear this man's clothes off and take.

Jarvis lifted his head and studied her. "Should I apologize?"

"What? No! Of course not. It's just—I didn't expect that."

"Really? I'd think that even in Maverick Junction, Texas, a nice meal out, a beautiful woman, a red-blooded man, the moonlight—" He pointed to where it peeped out behind a cloud. "Seems to me the evening would end like this or with the woman asking that man in for a cocktail or another cup of coffee."

He trailed off, and Maggie knew exactly what he hoped for. She might be small-town, but she doubted even in the city every first date ended up with a roll in the hay or the boudoir as the case might be.

Was Jarvis taking advantage of her vulnerability, or was he truly interested? She couldn't tell and that bothered her.

If Brawley was here, he'd punch the guy's lights out for even suggesting it. But then she wouldn't be with Jarvis if Brawley was here, would she?

And she'd done it again. She had to quit inserting Brawley into every situation.

"Jarvis," she started, aware she needed to tread lightly. They'd be working closely on this upcoming show. "Right now isn't a good time. I think, at least until the show is over, we need to shy away from any personal relationship and keep things on a professional level."

"Nothing says we can't do both."

"I'd prefer we didn't."

An uneasy silence ensued.

Finally, he nodded. "Okay. I won't push. But when we put the show to bed, I intend to do the same to you."

Oh, geez. Her breath caught. She couldn't think of a thing to say.

He laughed softly. "I believe I've shocked you, Maggie Sullivan. We're not through, you and I. We could be very good together."

Looking over his shoulder at the taxi, he said, "Run on in. I'll stay until I hear the lock snap into place." He kissed her lightly on the cheek. "Go on now." His voice deepened. "Pleasant dreams."

Like a cowardly lion, she did exactly that. She hurried up the stairs, gave him one quick wave, and ducked inside, throwing the lock behind her.

Upstairs, she let herself into her apartment, then simply collapsed against the door and closed her eyes. She stood there a good five minutes, trying to decide exactly what had happened.

Kicking off her shoes, she dropped her purse onto a chair and flopped down on the sofa. She wouldn't have gone to bed with him tonight under any circumstances. She wasn't into sleeping around. Never had been.

The apartment was too quiet. She turned on the stereo system and fussed with it till she found a country station. Dierks Bentley.

"Thinking of You." The same song she and Brawley had danced to at Bubba's.

She grabbed a pillow off the sofa and threw it across the room. "Damn it, damn it, damn it!" She had to exorcise the man from her mind. He didn't belong there. He'd left her without any warning. Left her pregnant and hurting. Scared and heartbroken.

And now he was screwing this up, too!

Well, damned if she'd let him. No siree.

Time to go to bed. Tomorrow would be another long, busy day. As she started down the hallway, she heard her phone signal an incoming message. Digging it from her purse, she saw it was from none other than Brawley.

Fine. Nothing said she had to read it. She'd hit delete and it would be gone. Just like that. Her traitorous finger, though, opened the message.

Settling in okay?

Not as well as I should be, she wanted to scream, because you're haunting me. Instead she typed, Does it really matter?

His answer came quickly. Of course.

Shouldn't u b asleep?

Can't. Took a late nap. Wide-awake now.

What do u want, Brawley?

I'd start with being your friend again.

Don't think that's possible.

A long distance friendship, Red. What can it hurt?

She sat cross-legged on the bed, chewing her bottom lip to a bloody pulp. It can't hurt a thing, she typed. Because I have no feelings for u.

Yes, u do, came his response. U don't like me. Negative, true, but a feeling nonetheless.

Good night, Brawley.

She closed her phone and slid out of bed. Fifteen minutes later, face scrubbed, teeth brushed, and wearing her favorite pajamas, she turned out the light. Willed sleep to come. Refused to acknowledge the tear that slipped down her cheek and onto her pillow as the moon shone through her window, the same moon that shone on him in Texas.

Chapter Twenty

Maggie had worked harder than she'd ever worked in her life, her first full week in New York extremely productive. At this point, the list of to-dos had whittled down to finish work on her garments, last-minute decisions about presentation. And those things she had to do herself. It seemed strange today with only Zandra and herself at the studio.

She'd sewed, ripped, and sewed some more until she swore her fingers bled. But when she'd locked up tonight, she'd been pleased. It was good.

Opening the door to her apartment, she sighed and almost cried when she stepped out of the shoes she'd loved only this morning. Right now, she didn't care if she ever saw them again.

She'd had the forethought to turn on a lamp before she'd left that morning, and now, in the twilight, its soft glow bathed the living room. Its warmth welcomed her home.

After the steady stream of phone calls, the chatter of delivery boys, and the constant traffic and sirens, the apartment was blessedly silent except for the quiet humming of the refrigerator. It almost made her ears hurt.

She needed to eat, but she needed to sit down even more badly. Sliding onto the sofa, she propped her feet on the coffee table and rested her head on the back of the couch. She'd give herself ten minutes, then she'd get up, wash off her makeup, and start dinner.

The ping of her phone woke her.

She sat up, looked around, and wondered for two brief seconds where she was. The twilight outside her windows had faded to full-fledged black—or as close to black as the city got. A quick glance at the wall clock told her the ten-minute sit-down had turned into almost an hour's nap.

Running her fingers through her hair, yawning hugely, she grabbed her phone. Brawley.

Phone in hand, she headed for the kitchen and food. What had he sent her now? The photo of Jesse, Jonah, and Josh in those outrageous swim goggles, goofy smiles on their faces, had her laughing out loud. And the one of the sweet little dog. Ohhh. She'd loved to cover him in smooches and prayed Brawley found a good home for him.

In the next second, her refrigerator door hanging open, homesickness hit, far worse than the one summer she'd gone to camp. She'd fought with her parents for three years to go. They'd finally given in, but once she'd arrived, she'd wanted nothing more than to be home. If her folks were surprised when she didn't bring up camp the following summer, they never said a word.

And now? She was a big girl with a job to do. The homesickness would pass.

She opened her text. No message. Just a photo of her and her parents at the wedding. Exactly what she needed.

Tomorrow, she'd get a copy made and set it by her bed.

Why was Brawley being so nice?

* * *

By Friday, Maggie needed a dose of normality and escaped for a quick lunch. She ate a hot dog from one of the street vendors as she walked the crowded streets. Eighty degrees and sunny. She felt like a kid playing hooky—which only added that touch of the forbidden to her enjoyment.

On the way back to the workroom, she spied the ugliest stuffed dog she'd ever seen in her life in a store window. She swore the manufacturer had used Staubach, Cash's lovable, but horrendously ugly mutt, for the model. His and Annie's baby absolutely had to have it for the nursery. She ducked inside the shop.

But if she sent a gift to Annie and Cash's unborn baby, shouldn't she send a package to Ty and Sophie's boys? Aunts, even honorary ones, couldn't play favorites. So she stole another thirty minutes to scour the shops for just the right thing. She finally found it. Pint-size New York firefighter helmets. The boys could wear them with the goggles when they did construction work. She'd have Zander pack them up today—along with the little Yorkie figurine she'd bought for Brawley.

Annie had told her he still had the dog and that, even though he complained about it constantly, the Yorkie went to work with him and followed him everywhere.

What she wouldn't give to see that!

* * *

Brawley swerved into Sadler's Store. Cash and Ty were coming over tonight for a card game, so he'd need to stock up on some cold ones.

He cracked his window for the dog. "Stay put, and keep quiet."

The dog plopped his butt on the seat and gave Brawley a soulful look.

"Cut it out. You can't go with me."

Brawley closed the door and started across the lot. A former teacher, long retired, stood beside her car with a full shopping cart.

"How about I load that for you, Mrs. Sandburg?"

"Why, Brawley Odell, I'd appreciate that. How are your mother and father?"

"They're great, ma'am."

"And the clinic? I hear you've really spiffed up the place."

"Doc had a good business, but I figured it might be time for a few changes."

She patted his cheek. "Doc did a fine job with the animals. Last time I was in there, though, just before Bootsie passed, the place looked ready to cave in."

Brawley chuckled. "Hopefully that's not the case anymore."

"You hear from Maggie?"

Zing. The woman always did have a habit of tossing you a question you couldn't answer. Math, language arts, or relationships. She had it covered.

"I've had a couple e-mails. She's doing well and working hard."

"Humph. That doesn't sound very personal."

A blush, damn it, heated his face.

"Maggie and I are old friends, Mrs. Sandburg."

She gave his shoulder a nudge. "Go on now. You expect me to buy that? I used to see the two of you walking along Main Street or after the high school football game. I've got eyes, boy, and there was a whole lot more than friendship between you."

Brawley remembered all that, too. "That was a long time ago."

"Understood. But when I heard you planned to move back, I'd hoped there might still be a spark there. She's not involved with anybody, you know. Got a notion she's been waiting for you."

"No, ma'am." And that hurt more than he cared to think about. He set the last bag in her trunk and closed it. "There you go. You drive carefully."

"I always do. Thank you, Brawley."

"You're very welcome." He opened her door for her, then tipped his hat and moved into the store, a far cry from the fancy deli he'd shopped at in Dallas. And a lot more interesting.

Sadler's sold everything from nuts to bolts to Stetsons and sirloin steak. If you needed it, you'd find it here—or a damned good substitute.

He made a face at the stuffed buffalo inside the door and gave his nose a minute to adjust to the mixed scent of leather and produce.

Grabbing a cart, he headed to the cooler. On the way, he passed the chips and threw in a bag. At the freezer section, he tossed in a couple pizzas. Two six-packs from the cooler joined them. Never knew if somebody else might show up, and it sure wouldn't do to run out of beer.

His basket much fuller than he'd intended, he wheeled it into Missy Iverson's checkout lane.

"How's that bunting's wing doing, Missy?"

"Almost healed. Davey and a couple of his friends are planning a bon voyage party for Tweety next week."

"That's kids for you."

"Yeah." She held up crossed fingers. "I'm praying none of the neighborhood cats crash the party."

He grimaced. "That would be bad."

He emptied his cart's contents onto the conveyer belt. While Missy rang him up, his eye caught on one of the tabloids. Bored, he grabbed the scandal sheet off the rack and idly flipped through it.

What the hell?

He checked the cover, saw yesterday's date. Some of the blood returned to his brain. Maggie worked fast.

He wanted to toss the sorry excuse for a news magazine to the floor and stomp on it. Instead, he added it to his groceries.

"You want that?" Missy looked surprised.

"Thought I'd, ah, put it in the waiting room. Give my patients' owners something to read."

"Yeah, a lot of people like these things. Can't believe they actually think the dribble in them is true."

"You got that right."

Woodenly, he paid for his groceries, picked up the bags and the beer, and left.

Once inside his SUV, he fed Marvin a couple doggie biscuits, then pulled out the magazine and flipped to page five. There, at the bottom, was a color image of Maggie and some smarmy guy, glasses of champagne in hand, toasting each other.

And she was smiling at him. Smiling at the jerk the way Brawley wanted her to smile at him. The difference between them? Real estate. The jerk apparently lived in New York while he lived in Maverick Junction.

He squinted at the photo. What was Maggie thinking? The guy was a mess. His hair stuck out all over the place—and he'd no doubt worked hard to get it like that. He had a major case of five o'clock shadow. Again, no doubt deliberate. And an earring, for God's sake. A mammoth diamond earring. Probably fake.

How had she hooked up with him so fast? Didn't she know it could be dangerous to pick up guys in the city? Hell, anywhere for that matter. Look what had happened to Sophie.

He tore his eyes off the picture long enough to read the small paragraph beneath it.

Maggie Sullivan, up-and-coming fashion designer, is seen celebrating her new clothing line with go-to photographer Jarvis Quillen.

So she'd met him at work. Okay. He breathed easier. She should be safe.

She'd met him at work! Shit! That meant they had shared interests, would spend a lot of time together.

The guy looked like one of those bad boys girls swooned over. Brawley squinted at the grainy snapshot. From what he could tell, old Jarvis even dressed in the stereotypical bad-boy black leather. Brawley wondered if he'd arranged with one of his photographer friends to get *caught* on film. The picture looked posed.

Jarvis Quillen? What the hell kind of name was that? A made-up one he'd bet. The guy's real name was probably something very uncool. Maybe Seymour Smith or Norbert Jones.

He leaned up on his left hip and pulled his phone from his right back pocket. Jabbing much harder than necessary, he typed a quick message. How's Jarvis?

Before he could hit send, though, he came to his senses and deleted the snippy words. His stomach growled. If he hurried, he'd have time for a quick snack before the guys showed up. He'd eaten lunch on the run today, between patients, and he'd passed hungry an hour ago.

* * *

Brawley had barely cleaned up after his PB&J when he heard the truck pull in.

Ty and Cash came up the stairs together, Staubach at their heels. Ty had apparently left Trouble at home again. Hearing the door open, the Yorkie came tearing out of Brawley's bedroom. Seeing the big dog in his kitchen, he hit the brakes and skidded halfway across the flooring.

Brawley glanced at Cash.

"They'll be fine," his friend assured. "Staubach's an old hand at this."

"You name him yet?" Ty asked.

"Marvin."

"Marvin?"

"Yeah. Got a problem with that?"

"None at all."

"Doesn't mean I'm keeping him."

Cash looked at Ty. "Bet you twenty."

"No way. I'm using my money to take yours tonight in poker."

"You guys are butts," Brawley growled.

"Probably. Welcome to the dog owners club." Cash patted his friend on the back. "Always figured you for a hunting dog. Something a little more masculine."

"In his heart, Marvin's a killer."

"Right."

A little sniffing and circling, a few small yips from the Yorkie, and the dogs accepted each other. Staubach roamed the kitchen, accepted the piece of cheese Brawley offered, then curled up on the living room rug, tail thumping a wild beat on the floor. Brawley wondered if Dottie and Fletch could hear it downstairs.

Not to be outdone, Marvin sat on his rear, patiently waiting for a handout.

"Go away," Brawley said.

"You started it," Cash said. "You can't play favorites. Give him a piece."

Brawley tossed the dog some cheese, and it disappeared immediately. When Marvin turned his big brown eyes back to him, Brawley shook his head. "No more. Go lay down."

With a sigh, the little dog wandered off to the living room and dropped down beside Staubach.

"You get any bites on the ad you ran with Mel?"

"Not a one," Brawley answered. "Either nobody's reading the paper or no one wants a new dog. Least not like him." He tipped his head toward Marvin. "People in Texas like things big."

The other two nodded.

"What are Sophie and Annie doing tonight?"

"They decided it would be a good movie night. They're setting the boys up with a Disney film in the den, and the two of them have big plans for some new chick flick," Ty said. "I swear they have enough food to feed an army."

"I've got pizza. Some cheese, chips, and beer."

"What more could any man want?" Cash asked. He sat down at the table and started shuffling the deck of cards Brawley handed him. "Open me one of those beers, why don't you?"

Brawley popped the top on three of them, then set the oven to preheat. Staubach watched everything with one eye. "That dog doesn't miss a thing, does he?"

"Nope." Cash dealt five cards to each of them.

Ty picked up his, studied them, and took a sip of beer. Then he pushed a few of his chips to the center of the table. Brawley eyed them and met his bet. Cash followed suit.

"Remember the time you lifted the bottle of Jim Beam from your dad and I borrowed a pack of Camels from mine?"

Ty groaned. "I don't think I've ever been so sick in my life."

"Yeah, you tossed your cookies all over the back seat of my dad's Buick. He grounded me for a week and made me clean up the mess."

Ty laughed. "If I remember right, you tossed a few of your own cookies doing it."

"Damn straight. Recycled Jim Beam is rank."

Cash picked up the deck. "How many?"

Ty tossed two cards onto the table. "A pair."

Cash dealt him two. "Brawley?"

He discarded three, and Cash gave him a trio. After another look at his own, he replaced two.

"How about the time Maggie followed us to the pond behind

your grandpa's, Cash?" Ty grinned. "You threw that snake in the water with her."

"I think that's why she learned to shoot. Always figured she'd plug me with the first bullet, the snake with the second. As it was, she gave me one hell of a shiner."

Ty nodded. "That girl turned into a monster when she got mad."

"Still does," Brawley said.

"You should know."

"Yeah, yeah, yeah."

A knock sounded at the door, and the guys looked at each other.

"You invite anybody else?"

"Nope."

Another knock at the door had Brawley tossing his cards on the table. When he scraped back his chair, Staubach leaped to his feet, wanting to be part of the welcoming committee. Marvin yipped and darted across the room to join them.

"What am I? The zoo keeper?"

Brawley had hung a blind over the door's window to give himself some privacy, but it kept him from seeing who was outside.

"I'm gonna grab another beer," Ty said.

"Get one for me, too," Cash said.

"Make it three. Then toss that pizza in the oven." Brawley threw open the door, then simply stood there, hand on the knob.

"Are you going to invite me in?"

Behind him, he could feel Ty and Cash studying the new arrival. Staubach licked their guest's hand, and she drew back, a look of disgust on her face.

Cash snapped his fingers and pointed at the floor. Both dogs reluctantly lay down.

"Rachel." Brawley blinked, but couldn't for the life of him think what to say. She'd called. He'd told her not to come.

Then he spotted her overnight case.

Oh, boy. This was so not happening.

Ty closed the fridge door and cleared his throat. "We can go, bro, if you want—"

"No. The lady's not staying."

Rachel made a small indignant squeak. "I drove all the way from Dallas."

"And I'm sure your car will make the drive back just fine."

Cash stood. "Maybe this is a conversation you should have in private."

"I know you," Rachel said. "We met at the Then and Now fundraiser."

"Yes, we did."

"You were with Annelise Montjoy."

"Annelise Hardeman now."

"I know." She glowed. "I saw your wedding pictures in all the magazines."

Cash's face took on a pained expression. Brawley knew he had yet to get comfortable with his wife's celebrity status.

Brawley threw his pal a heated look. "You and Ty stay right where you are." He turned back to his uninvited guest. "Let's take this outside."

She pouted but stepped back.

Joining her on the landing, he closed the door behind him. He could only imagine the conversation between his friends inside.

"I miss you." She stepped closer and laid a hand on his chest.

"Oh, God." He ran his fingers through his hair. He hated this. Why did women have to push? When a relationship ended, it ended.

Then he thought of Maggie. Was that how she felt about him? That he was trying to breathe life into a dead affair?

That was different. Their relationship hadn't actually ended.

"Brawley?"

He snapped back to the present problem. Damn, dressed in white leggings and a skinny little top, Rachel looked good. A man would have to be dead not to notice her. But she had no depth. She'd never be Maggie.

"Why are you here?"

"I told you. I miss you." Her hand ran up the front of his shirt. "I called."

"Yes, you did, and I told you not to come. We're done, Rachel. I'm sorry." He laid a hand on her shoulder and was shocked to see tears.

Real? he wondered. Or good acting?

"You mean that, don't you?"

"Yes."

"Can I spend the night with you?"

He shook his head.

She reached up, traced a finger along his ear.

Brawley jerked his head away. "Stop that."

"You can't really expect me to drive all the way back to Dallas tonight." Temper replaced her tears.

He sighed and raked his hair again. No, he couldn't send her down the road. Not this late. But by damn, she wasn't sleeping here. Glancing down the stairs, he made up his mind. As much as he hated to do it, he couldn't think of any other solution. "Come with me."

He picked up her case and headed down the steps. "My landlady has an extra room. I'm sure she won't mind if you use it tonight."

"Your landlady?"

"You met her in Dallas."

"The older woman with Annie?"

"Yep."

"But—"

Pops answered the quick rap on Dottie's door. "Hey, Brawley. I almost talked Dottie into letting me join you upstairs tonight."

"You're more than welcome. I told you that."

"Yeah, I know, but *we've* decided to watch one of her favorite movies. *Doctor Zhivago*." He rolled his eyes, then caught sight of Rachel, who'd made her way slowly down the stairs and now stood behind Brawley. "Who's this?"

Dottie peeked around the living room doorway. "Hey, Brawley." Then she saw Rachel. "Oh, I thought tonight was poker night with the boys."

"It is." He shifted, scuffed his foot on her welcome mat. "Dottie, this is Rachel Morgan. You met her in Dallas."

"Oh, yes." Dottie smiled. "Come in, Rachel. Brawley, what's wrong with you keeping her standing outside?" She tucked her arm through her husband's. "Rachel, have you met Fletch?"

Looking more than a little stunned, Rachel shook her head.

Fletch held out a hand. "Fletcher Sullivan. Come on in. Both of you."

Rachel shook his hand. "Nice to meet you."

"I have a huge favor to ask," Brawley said.

"Wait." Rachel turned to him and whispered, "I can get a hotel room. I don't want to bother them."

"No rooms for a long way, Rach. I think this is your best bet for tonight." He raised his voice. "Dottie, Fletch, do you think you could put Rachel up for tonight?"

Dottie blinked, and Fletch's eyes narrowed.

"Certainly," Dottie said. "The spare room's all freshened up. I did it right after the kids left, when we came back from Austin."

"Personally, I'd be glad to have her." Fletch met Brawley's gaze. "Seeing how you've only got one bed upstairs and all. Pretty hard to have overnight company, right, boy?"

Brawley stared Maggie's grandpa down. "Message received loud and clear, and you're right. A hundred percent."

"Well, then, Fletch, why don't you take the girl's suitcase back to the extra room?" Dottie nudged her husband.

"Yep."

"Have you had dinner?" Dottie asked.

"Yes. Yes, I have."

Dottie tipped her head at Brawley. "When you're done saying whatever it is needs said, you come on into the living room, Rachel. We've got cookies and coffee to go with our movie." With that she drifted into the front room.

"Good night, Rachel. Have a safe trip back." He opened the door and stepped outside.

"Wait." She followed him out. "I'm sorry, Brawley. I didn't come to cause you any problems. I think you underestimate yourself. You're a good person, and I'm not sure I appreciated you enough." She laid a hand on his cheek. "There's more to me than my role as a Dallas Cowboy cheerleader."

"I know that."

"Do you?" Her eyes searched his face. "I wonder. I'm not sure I ever really showed you the real me. I was too busy being the sexy, empty-headed cheerleader I thought you wanted." She stepped back into the house. Putting a hand on the door, she started to close it. "I wish you well."

He stared at the closed door, then watched through the window as she joined Dottie and Fletch in the living room. And he felt like a heel. He just couldn't seem to get it right.

* * *

"You're sure you don't want to come to Maggie's show?" Cash asked.

Brawley sighed. "We've been through this before."

"Doc will take care of the clinic."

"Have you been talking to him?"

"What? No! But I'm sure he wouldn't mind." Cash ran a hand over his chin.

"I'm sure he wouldn't, either. He's offered a dozen times this past week," Brawley admitted.

"You need to think about it," Ty said.

"I have."

He walked outside with his friends and stood at the end of the drive as they headed home to their wives. He thought about Rachel tucked away in Dottie's spare room. All in all, that had turned out better than it should have. He'd expected Rachel to make more of a fuss. Maybe he *had* underestimated her. She wasn't for him, though, and he wasn't for her. He'd never make her happy, not in the long run.

While he climbed the stairs, he resolved to make a change. He'd been on idle way too many years, and it was past time to take charge of his life. If he wanted Maggie in it—and he did—he'd better man up and do what needed to be done.

Back inside, he locked the door behind him in case Rachel decided to pay a late-night visit. He tossed beer bottles into the recycling bin, broke down the pizza boxes and added those, then mopped up the crumbs and water rings from the table. He dumped the dirty plates and silverware into the dishwasher. Marvin trotted right along beside him, his nails clicking on the aged linoleum.

Finished with his tidying, he picked up the remote and turned the TV station to ESPN. Two sportscasters argued over the value of pinch hitters.

The overhead kitchen light glared in his eyes, and he flipped it off. A lamp beside the sofa shed a soft glow over the small apartment. Flopping onto the leather sofa, he jammed a throw pillow under his head, then covered his face with his hand.

The sofa cushion sagged as Marvin hopped up beside him. He reached down and rubbed the dog's head.

What the hell was he going to do?

Cash's question had started the debate raging in his head again.

When everybody else flew off to New York to support Maggie at her showing could he really sit at home twiddling his thumbs?

Forget that!

He reached for his laptop, but his eyes caught on the clock. Oops. Way too late to mess with this. Besides, he couldn't simply show up there, could he?

He'd already eaten more than a fair share of crow. He'd apologized, tried to explain. But would Maggie have any of it? Oh, no. She wouldn't listen. Wouldn't believe. And damned if he intended to crawl again. He needed to think about this.

Time to go to bed. He had to work tomorrow.

He toed off his boots and stripped off his socks. Walking barefoot into the bedroom, he dropped his clothes inside the door. Jeans, shirt, boxers—all of it—landed in a heap on the hardwood floor.

Sliding beneath the sheets, still rumpled from last night, he stared up at the ceiling. Sleep refused to come. Marvin, curled up beside him, didn't have the same problem. He started snoring inside two minutes.

Slowly, a plan formed in Brawley's mind. A way to save face. Throwing back the bedclothes, he jumped up, grabbed his boxers from the pile, and stepped into them.

In the living room, he turned on his laptop. Somewhere in that huge city, there had to be a veterinary conference he could attend. Animal doctors came together all the time to discuss the latest treatment and medicines. It was simply a matter of finding it and registering.

Voila. The answer to his problem.

Chapter Twenty-One

On her hands and knees adjusting a hem, Maggie heard the door slap open. When she turned, Sophie and Annie stood just inside the room, a look of awe on their faces.

"Hey!" Maggie scrambled to her feet. "I'm so glad you're here! How was the flight?"

"Great!"

She opened her arms, and the three of them met in the middle of the room for a huge hug. All of them talking at once, she showed them around, pointing out features of the outfits arranged on dress forms.

"Which is mine?" Sophie asked.

"Over here." Maggie led them to a slim, floor-length gown in black charmeuse. Swirly black lace over a nude, barely there fabric formed the top.

Sophie stared at it, then at Maggie. "I can actually wear this?"

"You'd better wear it. I made it specifically to your measurements."

"Oh, Ty's going to want me so bad when he sees me in this," she sang.

"I think that's a pretty accurate prediction, although my guess is he'd want you even dressed in a feed sack. We'll try this on and see if I need to make any nips or tucks."

Sophie clapped her hands. "I feel like a kid on the last day of school."

Then Maggie glanced at Annie, her eyes taking in subtle changes. "We may need to make a few adjustments to the fit on yours, Mama-in-waiting."

Annie beamed and patted her still flat tummy. "I'm so glad the doctor gave me permission to fly. I'd have died if I couldn't be here."

"Me, too. Without friends..." Maggie shook her head. "Nothing's quite as sweet."

She walked them over to a black two-piece outfit. The knit top zipped halfway down the front and had bat sleeves. Maggie had paired it with a very short, slim skirt.

"This one's yours, Annie. The top has a blousy fit. It should be perfect for you."

"Oooh, I like this." Annie ran a hand over the shoulders and down the sleeves. "I think I'll let Cash buy it for me." She grinned.

"And I'd be eternally grateful. That way I'll have at least one sale."

"Maggie." Sophie draped an arm over her shoulder. "You're not seriously worried, are you?"

"Yes, I am. Owen has invested a lot of money in all this." She waved a hand around the room. "I'm praying he didn't misplace his trust."

"No way. They're going to love you." Annie pulled out her phone.

"You can't take any pictures," Maggie said quickly.

"No, I know. I'm texting a few friends to tell them how wonderful your collection is and that I can't wait to see them at the show tomorrow. They'll tell a few friends who will tell a few friends. Can't hurt to salt the place, right?"

"You're good."

"I've spent too many years with Dad and Grandpa to let this kind of opportunity pass." Glancing around, Annie said, "I'm starving. Feeding two, you know. Can you take time for lunch?"

"I can't, but there's a great little restaurant two doors down. Why don't you go have lunch, bring something back for me, and we'll do your fittings?"

"Sounds good."

"Don't eat too much. Remember, you have to fit into these outfits tomorrow."

Annie waved over her shoulder. "We'll skip dessert."

"Speak for yourself," Sophie said.

* * *

Maggie put a hand on her back and stretched into it. It had been a long day. But she was ready. Every single outfit had been completed and accessorized. A lot of designers seemed to thrive on last-minute drama. Not her.

She'd insisted Annie and Sophie go back to her apartment earlier with orders for Annie to nap. She'd been looking rather peaked by the time they'd finished her fitting.

Having already sent everyone including Zandra home, Maggie shut off the lights and locked up. After months, heck, years of preparing for this, now, on the eve of her first showing, it all seemed surreal.

Rather than take the subway, she decided to splurge on a taxi. It wasn't every day she finished putting final touches on her very own runway show.

When she reached her apartment, she smiled at the lights on in the windows. Her friends waited inside for her.

She flew up the stairs with renewed vigor. Opening the door, she called, "Hello. Anybody home?"

Annie peeked around the kitchen counter. "Hey, Maggie. This place is wonderful."

"It is, isn't it?" She dropped her keys and purse on the little stand inside the door.

Sophie came down the hall, a towel wrapped around her. "I already took my shower, so the bath is open."

Maggie dropped into a chair. "Good. I might stand under the water for the rest of the evening. I'm beat." She reached down and pulled off her shoes. "Oh, my feet love me right now."

Sophie and Annie glanced at each other.

Maggie caught it. "What?"

"We thought you might be in this shape when you hit the door," Annie said.

Sophie nodded.

"And?" Maggie prompted.

Sophie took a peek at the wall clock. "You have about twenty minutes for that shower. I noticed a comfy, terry cloth robe hanging on the back of the bathroom door. If you want, you can wear that to dinner."

"My robe?" Maggie's forehead creased in a frown. "That's pretty casual even for Maverick Junction. I'm not sure I'd get away with it here in the city."

"Not out and around maybe," Annie said. "But you certainly can here in your own home."

"I intend to wear my pj's," Sophie said.

"And I'm changing into mine," Annie added. "As soon as the food comes. Somebody has to be decent to answer the door."

"What are you talking about? Who's coming?"

"The delivery boy with all things decadent from my favorite restaurant."

"You ordered in?"

"I did."

"Oh, Annie, I do love you."

Maggie hadn't realized how badly she'd missed this.

The food came ten minutes after her shower, and they ate in the living room, talking a mile a minute about Maverick Junction, her show, the coming baby, books they'd read, and movies they'd watched. About everything and nothing.

A church bell tower down the street chimed eleven times.

"Can it be that late?" Maggie checked the wall clock.

"We're running on Central time, so according to our internal clock it's only ten," Annie said. "Between the trip and this little one, though, I'm bushed."

"You slept almost the whole way here," Sophie said.

Annie's brows rose. "I'm surprised you noticed. We barely had our seat belts fastened before you, the nervous flier, fell asleep."

"Guilty as charged. I had a good reason, though. Jesse caught some kind of virus at school and spent most of the night in the bathroom throwing up. My guess is the other two will be at it tonight, although when I checked in, Ty said so far, so good."

"Who are the boys staying with when he flies out?"

"His mom and dad. They'll have their hands full if the upchucking starts while they're with them. Babs wanted them for a little auntie time, but she has to run to Austin tomorrow. She'll be on standby after she gets home if Gram and Grampa need her." Sophie threw Annie an evil grin. "You have no idea what you're in for, cuz."

"That may be," Annie said. "However, I'm only going to experience everything times one, not times three."

"There is that."

Maggie yawned and stretched. "I hate to be a party pooper, girls, but I need to find my bed. I've been working my butt off, and tomorrow promises to be a long day."

She pointed at them. "And you. I've told everyone I have the two most beautiful women in the world modeling for me, so we can't have any red eyes from lack of sleep."

Sophie picked up their glasses and walked to the kitchen with them. "Good night, then, Cinderella. Sleep well."

"You have everything you need?" Maggie asked.

"Yes, we do."

"I hate having you sleep on the couch, Sophie."

"It's a comfortable sofa, and I'll be fine. Go to bed."

"Okay, okay." Maggie hugged her friends. "I can't even begin to tell you how glad I am that you're here. You're exactly what the doctor ordered."

As she closed her bedroom door, she heard Annie and Sophie talking and smiled. The apartment had been too quiet. She liked it like this, full of friends and laughter.

She brushed her teeth and slid into bed. Her phone chirped, and she reached across the nightstand to check the text.

How's it going? Ready for your big day?

Brawley was thinking about her.

Maggie quickly typed an answer. I hope so. Sophie and Annie arrived today.

Company's always fun.

Got that right, she typed. Hear you had company, too.

No response. Maybe she shouldn't have taunted him with that, but darn it, the idea of Rachel showing up at his door raised her hackles.

It shouldn't. Brawley deserved a life. A wife and children. Regardless of whether she'd stayed in Maverick Junction or moved here, the cowboy would never be hers. Sooner or later, he was bound to find someone, but she didn't want it to be Rachel.

Her phone chirped again, and she grabbed it.

Rachel slept in Dottie's extra room. Didn't speak to her more than a couple minutes.

He sounded impatient. Good. Of course, she'd already known Rachel hadn't stayed with him, but still…

Wasn't talking that had me worried.

The instant she sent it, she groaned. That had been a mistake. She'd told him she didn't care. And she didn't. But he might get the wrong idea from that message.

She quickly typed another.

Love life a little bumpy?

His response was almost immediate.

Never loved her, Mags. You're the only woman I ever said those words to.

Oh, God. The phone nearly slid from her boneless fingers. Before she could respond, another message blipped onto her screen.

Cat got your tongue, Red?

She silenced the phone and pulled the covers over her head.

Chapter Twenty-Two

The morning sun had barely peeked between the two buildings across the street when Maggie padded into the bath. So much rode on today.

Please, please let the show be a success, she prayed. If it flopped, she'd never get another chance. Never be able to hold up her head.

If it was a success…She shook her head. She couldn't go there. Not yet. Didn't want to jinx it.

She took a quick shower, did her makeup carefully, and fixed her hair in a messy twist. When she opened her closet door, she didn't even try to curb her heartfelt sigh. The outfit she'd wear today hung front and center. She'd designed it with as much care as she'd put into any the models would wear.

The slim black pants and hunter green and black printed tunic top fit her perfectly. A short leather jacket with zippers galore finished it off. Oh, and the boots. They were almost orgasmic. The outfit was a mix of edgy and professional. It shouted successful and chic. She loved it.

For right now, though, she threw on a pair of jeans and a tee. She still had far too much to do. She'd take the outfit with her and change at the studio.

Sophie roused enough to give Maggie a sleepy smile as she tiptoed past, boots in hand.

"You leaving?" she asked.

"In a few minutes. Will it bother you if I make a cup of coffee?"

"Not at all." Sophie rubbed her eyes. "You have no idea what mornings are like back home. This is heaven." She nestled down into her pillow and fell instantly asleep again.

Any other morning, Maggie might have envied her, but not this morning.

Flying high on adrenaline, she impatiently watched the coffee gurgle into her cup. She slathered a piece of toast with peanut butter, grabbed her coffee, and rushed out the door. A taxi, like a hungry shark on the lookout for prey, cruised slowly along the street, and she flagged it down.

Even though she'd checked and double-checked everything before she'd left her studio yesterday, she needed to be there when the movers loaded the racks of clothing into the van for their trip to the show venue.

Zandra arrived ten minutes after she did.

"Did you eat this morning?" she asked Maggie.

"Toast and coffee."

"You need protein."

"I put half a jar of peanut butter on my toast."

Zandra slid her sunglasses down her nose and looked at Maggie over the top of them. "I seriously doubt that."

"Okay. I might have overstated, but I did cover it with PB."

Rather than bothering to answer, Zandra punched in a number on her cell and ordered two full breakfasts from the corner deli. "We can eat while we wait for the transport guys."

"I'd argue, but I've got an idea this will be our last chance at food for quite a while."

"You are so right, Kemosabe." She frowned. "What did the Lone Ranger call Tonto? If you're Kemosabe, who am I?"

Maggie laughed. "I have no idea. But honestly, Zandra? I don't care what you call yourself. You're a gift from heaven. I couldn't have pulled this off without you."

"Oh, I think you'd have done fine."

A knock sounded at the door before Jeb from the deli stuck his head inside. "Got a couple breakfasts here. Anybody hungry?"

"Starving," Zandra said.

Maggie pulled some bills from her top drawer and handed them to Jeb. "Here you go." She took the bag from him.

"Break a leg today, Ms. Sullivan."

"Thanks."

They sat cross-legged on the floor in the middle of the studio and ate. Maggie realized that, despite her toast, she was ravenous. After last night's dinner, she hadn't thought she'd ever eat again. Annie had ordered enough food for an army. Half of it was stacked in plastic in her fridge.

The door popped open again, and a flash went off.

Startled, Maggie dropped her fork, then laughed. "Jarvis. Good morning."

"It is that." He hadn't shaved, and his clothes looked thrown together carelessly. Maggie was certain, though, he'd chosen each piece carefully to gain exactly that effect. As a photographer, he knew better than anyone that this business was all about image.

"Thought I'd take a few shots of you doing last-minute prep on the collection."

"Instead you caught me stuffing my face. Hungry?" she asked.

He dropped to the floor, picked up one of the plastic forks, and took a bite of her scrambled eggs. "Not bad. But I'm not all that hungry. Not for breakfast."

The look he sent her told her exactly what he craved.

Zandra shot to her feet. "I think this is where I exit left and find something in the office to keep me occupied."

"No." Maggie stood. "I need you right here to help with the loading. The men will be here any minute."

Jarvis shrugged. "Nothing ventured…" He wandered to the racks. "Looks like everything's under control."

"I sure hope so."

"Come stand by the window. I want a couple shots with the buildings behind you, the racks of clothes in front of you."

She rolled her eyes.

"It's all part of the game, Maggie."

"I know." Sitting on the window ledge, she sent him a megawatt smile.

Jarvis blew out his breath. "Don't understand how any man still breathing can resist that."

His camera clicked, once, twice, three times.

* * *

Two hours later, Maggie stood looking over the venue. The pristine white tent in Bryant Park symbolized her dream come true. Rather than wait for September Fashion Week, she and Owen had opted for an off-season showing. In just under four hours, the first model would walk down that runway wearing one of Maggie's designs.

Right now, though, not another soul was here.

Annie and Sophie, along with Zandra, understanding her need to enjoy this moment alone, would arrive shortly. The movers had finished, and her outfits hung on covered racks. She'd actually ridden in the truck with the guys to oversee the transfer.

Right now, though, at this moment in time, it was only her, a dream, and row upon row of empty chairs. She tried to envision the room full of people and worried again that no one would show up for an unknown's premier.

Overhead, chandeliers sparkled. The stage crew would be here any minute to do their job with lighting and backdrop, and the florists would show up to handle that part of the staging.

Slowly, she walked to the runway, ran a finger along the edge of it. Had Valentino, Versace, or Carolina Herrera ever been this nervous? Doubted their vision? Not that she considered herself in their league. But then, *they* hadn't been in their league, either, when they first started out, had they?

She made her way around the stage to the back. The dressing area, the makeup section, the cubbies for the hairstylists. Unable to resist, she stepped through the opening and took a walk down the runway—with attitude. At the end, she stopped, pivoted, and bowed. Then, laughing out loud, she sauntered back and slipped through the curtain.

God, she loved this!

With any luck, she'd be back for a repeat performance next year and the year after that. She prayed she never took it for granted. Never lost this magical feeling.

For the actual show, there'd be lights and music. More magic.

Last night with Annie and Sophie had been wonderful. Had grounded her. Today, her mom and dad, Pops and Dottie, Cash and Ty would all be here to share her special day. Initially they'd considered flying in early, then decided to wait. Last night had been girls' night. Today, they'd meet her at the show, then they'd all go to dinner.

If some small part of her cried foul because Brawley would be missing, she shushed it. After all, she'd made it more than clear she didn't want him to attend. She'd been celebrating without him for years.

Not true, the devil on her left shoulder chided.

And darned if her right-shoulder angel, the one who should be on her side, didn't nod in agreement. *He's always come when it's important. He's been around for every big day of your life.*

Well, too bad. He wouldn't be here today, and that was that.

Security had been stationed out front, both to ensure her designs remained secret till the unveiling and for crowd control. Attendees had to be vetted. Since they had a limited number of seats, it was crucial they accommodate invited guests and photographers before admitting the public.

Again, Maggie smiled. She could only hope that would be a problem!

A florist burst through the door holding a fragrant bouquet of white and purple lilacs. "For you, Ms. Sullivan."

"Thank you!" She took the vase and inhaled deeply. Was there anything that smelled better? She read the card and smiled. Brawley had sent her flowers. He would be part of today. She wanted to cry. She missed him, damn it.

One by one, and in small groups, workers, models, and stylists trickled in, and Maggie set the flowers on one of the workstations. Pushing Brawley farther to the back of her mind, she wished she had handcuffs and duct tape to keep him there.

She peeked at each outfit again, checking for the hundredth time that everything was exactly right.

At their stations, hairdressers and makeup artists set out the tools of their trade. Zandra zipped around the room, lending a hand wherever needed. Sophie and Annie, after a quick sniff of lilac, sat down in a couple of the makeup chairs.

Once the show started, this area would turn to chaos regardless of her planning. She understood that. But the whole show had to be choreographed to the second. Inside twenty minutes, the backstage team would send all her models down the runway. She couldn't afford to screw up.

Not wanting to be thought of as a one-note designer, but understanding the risk, she'd included a little of everything in today's show. A belted thigh-length hooded leather jacket over a silk top and black leggings. A camel-brown leather skirt and a cashmere top. A woolen jacket paired with a skirt in alternating corduroy and leather panels. Tights and cowboy boots would finish that outfit, a nod to her Texas roots.

Along with the casual, she'd created office and evening wear. She'd added chunky jewelry and big bags. There was nothing shy about her collection.

The last rack held the real showstoppers. Two wedding gowns. One an A-line flow of champagne-colored velvet, the other a white silk chiffon strapless dress with a deep front slit and lots of layers. They couldn't be more different—and she loved them both.

She'd hesitated to include them, then figured what the heck. After Annie's wedding, a lot of brides had tapped her to create their gowns. Why not go for it? It was a part of the business she adored, designing a dress for the most memorable day of a woman's life.

While the last of the models drifted in, Maggie and her assistants busily steamed dresses, slacks, and tops. The noise escalated. She closed her eyes and took two seconds to envision the earlier quiet, the peace that reigned when she'd first entered, and tried to match that with the present madhouse.

She couldn't and grinned. She loved it.

Chapter Twenty-Three

If Lady Luck hung with him, he might make it. Thankful he hadn't checked any baggage, Brawley swung the strap of his carry-on over his shoulder and headed for outside.

New York air, heavy with late spring heat, smog, and noise, hit him the second he stepped through the doors. And this was the world Maggie chose—just as he'd picked Dallas.

Hadn't he always missed Maverick Junction, though? The longing to return had grown every time he'd visited. Each time he and Maggie bumped into each other.

Hailing a taxi, he told the driver to take him to Tiffany's. Before he went to his hotel to change, he had some shopping to do.

* * *

An hour and a half later, arms folded over his chest, Brawley leaned against a tent pole. It had been almost a month since he'd seen Maggie, and this first sight was as sweet as honey drizzled over one of his mama's warm, homemade biscuits. God, he'd missed this woman.

Totally in her element, Maggie looked absolutely stunning in a black leather jacket and boots, slim pants, and a dark green and black top. With her wild red curls somewhat tamed into submission in a sexy twist, she was a vision. Surrounded by high-paid fashion models, she outshone them all.

He watched her sew on a loose button, find a missing shoe, and handle a hairdo problem without missing a beat.

One of the models approached her. "Don't you think this dress would have been better in a brighter fabric? Red maybe?"

For the briefest second, Maggie's eyes flashed. Then a thin veneer of cool professionalism covered her redhead's fiery temper. "No, I don't."

With that she walked away, leaving the pouting diva behind.

When she stopped beside a vase of flowers, he recognized them for the ones he'd sent, and his heart staggered into a crazy Texas two-step. She traced a leaf and leaned in to smell the lilacs, her lips curving in a smile.

Good. She was thinking about him.

With one heavy-lidded glance her way, he touched the box in his pocket and slipped from the doorway. He'd stepped back here to wish her luck. It didn't look like she would need it. From what he'd seen, Maggie Sullivan should be all the rage come tomorrow morning. New York's newest darling.

She wouldn't be coming home.

He pulled out the ticket Rita had palmed him and tracked down his seat. Scanning the crowd, he recognized a lot of celebrities. Owen Cook had done his job, got the right group here. And Maggie would wow them with her work.

He took his seat in the nick of time. The curtain parted, and the first model stepped out to wild applause. One after another, they paraded down the runway in Maggie's designs. The show eclipsed anything she might have wished for. He caught a glimpse of her as she peeked through a crack in the curtains and knew she had to be over the moon.

Every single piece was enthusiastically received.

When Sophie glided down the aisle in her black, floor-length gown, the crowd went crazy. Beside him, Ty beamed with pride. Then Annelise Montjoy Hardeman, the darling of the press, stepped onto the runway in a short two-piece outfit. It was insane, and Brawley's chest swelled with pride right along with Cash's.

Maggie had outdone herself.

When the models lined up for their last walk down the runway, Brawley breathed a sigh of relief. Not a single glitch.

The last disappeared, and Maggie stepped out. If she was nervous, if her stomach was doing some major cartwheels, it didn't show on her face.

She sent the crowd a dazzling smile, and Brawley figured every male in the place instantly fell in love. How could they help it?

The blinding smile in place, she looked out over the crowd as cameras flashed. How many times had she pinched herself? he wondered.

He knew the exact moment she saw him. A few feet down the walk, she missed a step, her mouth opening slightly. He sat immobile beside her parents, Pops, Dottie, Ty, and Cash. Brawley grinned at her, giving her a thumbs-up, and recognized the quick start of happiness in her eyes. She winked.

Her father and grandfather both looked proud enough to blow a gasket. Her mom blew her a kiss, and she blew one back. One last wave to the audience, one last bow, and she disappeared behind the curtain.

The applause died down and, while the crowd milled, her family made their way backstage. That's when Brawley saw him. The man in the tabloid photo. He looked like a mussed bed—or like he'd just crawled out of one. It better not have been Maggie's.

The creep put his arms around her and gave her a very unprofessional, non-brotherly kiss. A muscle in Brawley's jaw jumped.

This wasn't the Maggie he'd grown up with, the one he'd played cops and robbers with. The one he'd slept with. This Maggie, the one kissing the unmade bed, was a mature woman. Determined. Insightful.

She'd see through this jerk who had his hands all over her. The same one she'd had dinner with—at least once.

What did she see when she looked at *him*? Brawley wondered. Another jerk? One who'd been too stupid to realize how deeply she loved him? One who'd been careless with that love?

Before he hurt her again, he'd do well to sort out his feelings for this older, wiser Maggie. Curiosity? Nostalgia? Love? Sweat popped out on his forehead.

Maybe tonight wasn't the right time for this soul searching. It could wait until tomorrow.

* * *

"Boy, Brawley. Once again I'm amazed at how well you clean up." Maggie ran a hand over the collar of another of his impeccable dark suits. Irresistibly handsome in jeans and a T-shirt, he was mouth-wateringly devastating in formal dress.

"You look incredible, Mags." He took her hands. "You've lost weight."

"It's been a busy month."

"Today was a huge success."

"You think?" Uncertainty still nagged at her.

"I know."

She grinned, then looked down. "What? No boots?"

"Not today. I've gone city."

She laughed, but she missed her cowboy. *Her* cowboy? No. *The* cowboy. She missed the cowboy in him. She touched a hand to his face and realized she rarely saw him without at least a couple days' stubble. Today, he was clean-shaven. Gorgeous, but still dark and dangerous.

A little territorial, though. She hadn't missed the scowls flying between him and Jarvis and hated that it gave her just the tiniest thrill of satisfaction. Could Brawley be jealous?

Jarvis disappeared backstage to speak to one of the makeup artists.

"What's up with him?" Brawley did a head-jerk in the direction the photographer had gone.

"He's my photographer and a friend."

"Friend, my ass."

"He is attractive, isn't he?"

"Wouldn't know," Brawley growled. "He's not my type."

"He's not mine, either."

"Sure wouldn't have guessed that from the picture in one of those tabloids they carry in Sadler's."

"You saw that?" Zandra had told her about the picture.

"Yeah."

"Why, Brawley Odell, I had no idea you read that kind of trash."

"I don't. Missy took forever to ring up my poker night groceries. Out of boredom, I picked one up, and there you were, all cozied up with your *friend*. A friend who wants to get you in bed."

His words, soft, silky fire, burned through her.

"That's nonsense," she bit back even as her mind flashed back to the kiss she and Jarvis had shared outside her apartment. His warning.

Brawley shook his head. "Afraid not. I've been watching him watching you. He hasn't had you yet. He's too hungry. But he wants you, darlin'. Bad."

"Well, he can't have me."

Brawley smiled. "You hold on to that thought." He dug into his jacket pocket and came out with the little blue Tiffany bag. "The package is kind of crushed, but that won't change what's inside."

He handed it to her.

Reaching into the bag, she came out with the jeweler's box. Her eyes went wide. "Brawley—"

He held her gaze. "Go ahead. Open it."

"But—" Her tongue flicked out, slicked across her lower lip. She looked at the box as if it would bite.

"Oh, for—" The first lick of temper flared in his eyes. "It's not a ring if that's what has you looking like you're about to pass out. It's a gift to celebrate today, that's all. Something to add to the charm bracelet I gave you when you turned sixteen—if you still have it."

"I do. It's one of the things I brought to New York with me." She brushed at a strand of hair that had fallen into her eyes. Opening the box, she smiled. "Oh, Brawley. It's perfect." She lifted the charm, a tiny pair of silver scissors. "I love it."

Not stopping to think, she threw her arms around him. "Thank you," she whispered.

Brawley closed his eyes and held her tight. Just for a minute. This one moment when she'd forgotten to be angry and hugged him the way she used to.

When he opened his eyes, he caught Annie's. She gave him a big thumbs-up. He smiled. Maybe he did have somebody on his team after all.

When Maggie stepped back, he kissed her cheek. "Congratulations. You're a huge success, Red. I'm proud of you."

He was. So damned proud and happy, even though he knew in his heart her success spelled the end for any hope he still held.

* * *

They all went out to dinner. Jarvis, Zandra, and Owen joined her family and friends.

Owen insisted the night was his treat. He raised his glass. "To the first of many, many successful shows for Ms. Maggie Sullivan."

Everyone clinked glasses and echoed the sentiment.

"Thank you, Owen," Maggie said. "And to all of you. Every one of you had a part in this day." Tears threatened, and she blinked them away. She held up her own glass. "To quote the Bard, 'My heart is ever at your service.'"

She caught Brawley's eyes and looked away quickly.

"Okay, let's eat," Cash said. "I'm starved. Lunch was a lifetime ago."

"Amen to that," Ty agreed.

Over caviar, champagne, and the best steaks Maggie had ever tasted, they shared stories of the day.

With Jarvis on one side and Brawley on the other, she felt a little like the 38th parallel between North and South Korea. Between their jabs at each other and the fact her phone never stopped ringing, Maggie had a hard time following the conversation at the table.

Her phone rang again. It was Doc Gibson.

"How did your show go, Maggie?"

"It was beyond anything I could have hoped for. Let me put you on speakerphone."

Everyone chatted for a few minutes.

"When are you coming home?" he asked.

"I don't know. I'll probably be back in a month or so to check on things at the shop."

"You be sure to save some time for me. Maybe lunch at Sally's?"

"It's a date." She laughed, and they said their good-byes.

No sooner had she hung up than the phone rang again.

"Hey, Mel," she answered.

"How's it going, dollface?"

"Great!"

"Don't suppose there's any chance of snagging some photos and an exclusive interview to run in tomorrow's edition is there? I stayed late, just in case. The fourth estate never sleeps, you know."

She chuckled. "So ask away, pal. You've been granted that exclusive. Jarvis is here, but I doubt he'll share any of his photos."

Beside her, Jarvis shook his head. "I can't. I'm under contract."

"That's what I thought," she mouthed.

"Who's Jarvis?" Mel asked.

"He's my photographer. I've been working with him on the collection, and he covered the show."

"I have pictures." Brawley glared around her at Jarvis. "Lots of them. Tell Mel I'll download several and send them to him when I get back to the hotel."

And I'll bet they're great, Maggie thought. *Artistic*. He had an eye for exactly the right moment, the right shot, the right angle.

"Did you hear that, Mel?"

"I did. Tell him not to forget." He paused. "I thought he said he wasn't going."

"Yes, that's what we all thought." She eyed Brawley who was now ignoring her. "Turns out he had a convention in New York this week."

"*Hmmm*. Pretty convenient." Laughter laced his words.

"Yes, wasn't it?"

They talked for a couple more minutes and he asked some questions for his interview. "I'll let you go, Maggie. I know you're busy. Congratulations. Maverick Junction is proud of you."

"Thanks, Mel." She pressed the off button and turned to Brawley. "He told you not to forget those photos."

"I won't." He scooped up a forkful of baked potato. "Eat. Your food's getting cold."

* * *

Dinner ended, and Zandra and Owen caught cabs. Jarvis made noises about sharing a private celebration with Maggie, but she cried off, claiming exhaustion.

The tension between him and Brawley had grown palpable, testosterone and animosity oozing from both. When Jarvis hailed a taxi, she stood at the curb, relief flooding her as it pulled away.

Her mom and dad had an early flight and wanted to get to bed. Ty and Sophie had rented a car and intended to steal three days in the Poconos for the honeymoon they hadn't quite managed between kids and work. Annie and Cash planned to drive to Boston for a quick visit with her family before going back home.

Dottie and Pops? She couldn't quite believe it, but they were flying south—to Disney World. They'd both wanted to visit there forever and were finally going to do it. Maggie was glad.

As happy as she'd been to see them all, it broke her heart to say good-bye to everyone. Hugs, kisses, and tears made the rounds.

"Thank you, Daddy, for coming all this way for me."

"It's not every day our little girl makes history." Her dad's arms, warm and reassuring, enveloped her. "How could we not share it with you?"

She hugged him back. "I love you."

She stood on the sidewalk outside the restaurant waving as her friends and family climbed into cabs and headed to their hotels.

And then it was just her and Brawley.

The night echoed around them. Taxis, horns, and sirens. Neon signs. Jostling people. A full moon directly above the spire of the Empire State Building.

"Brawley—"

"Maggie—"

They laughed.

"Go ahead. Ladies first."

"I really am glad you came today. Thank you for that and the lilacs and for my little scissors." She patted her purse where she'd tucked the charm safely away.

"You're welcome. For everything."

He reached for her hand, and she took his, aware of the energy radiating off him. His warmth seeped through her. This man did things to her insides that no one else ever had.

"Here's the thing, Mags. I'm wondering if you and I could hang up the gloves for a day."

"But—"

"Today was good."

Confused, she said, "Yes, it was."

"I'd like to spend a day as *unguarded* friends. Friends who don't have to weigh everything they say before they say it for fear of offending, of stepping on toes." He tipped his head and studied her.

"We've been doing that a long time, haven't we?"

"Yes, ma'am. And I generally end up having my head bitten off and handed to me on a silver platter."

"Have I really been that bad?"

"You've had your moments."

She laughed. "Yes, I guess I have." She laced their fingers.

"I'm thinking I could skip my conference tomorrow."

Her brow arched. "Like you did today?"

He chuckled and raised her hand to his lips.

She wondered if real women actually swooned. At this moment, she considered it a strong possibility.

"Yeah, like I did today. I'll skip my conference *another* day. Let's do New York, Maggie. Let's play tourist. The two of us. We can ride one of those double-decker buses, take the ferry to Staten Island, climb the Statue of Liberty, and eat pizza in Times Square. Let's do it all."

After a stunned heartbeat, she said, "I'd like that. I never did get my play day. Not even when Mom was here. Zandra and I already decided we'd indulge ourselves. Take a day off to chill, then hit it hard again."

Without warning, he kissed her, long and deep.

Rattled, she fought for equilibrium. "Um, will you, ah, pick me up?"

"Yep."

"Bring food... and coffee."

He nodded, then hailed a cab for her. When it pulled to the curb, he opened her door, helped her in, then walked off down the street, whistling.

Maggie waved as they passed him.

She had a date tomorrow. With her urban cowboy.

Chapter Twenty-Four

True to his word, Brawley showed up at her door the next morning with coffee and a bag of fresh bagels. Dressed in jeans, a crisp blue shirt with cuffs rolled up to show off his strong forearms, and his signature dark glasses, he made her awfully glad she was the one seeing the town with him today.

He could have commanded a fortune as a male model.

He held up the bag. "You have a toaster, don't you?"

"I sure do."

She led him inside.

He let out a slow whistle. "This is nice, Red. Really nice."

"I love it. My first place."

He moved around her apartment, taking in the layout and décor. Stepping to the sofa table, he studied the photos she'd arranged there.

He picked up one of him and her with Ty's boys. "When was this?"

She felt foolish and wished she'd put it away before he came. "Sophie took it. The day Trouble got into, well, trouble…with the rattler."

"That could have turned out badly. We got lucky." He set it down. "This is your first home alone, isn't it?" he said. "You've been with your folks or Pops."

"Pathetic, huh?"

"No. Unselfish. I understand why you went to Lone Tree instead of moving out on your own. You're a good person, Maggie Sullivan."

Heat flared over her face. "Don't paint any halos on me."

"Oh, no!" He laughed. "I'd never do that. You're far from angelic."

She punched both him and the button on the toaster.

They sat in her tiny kitchen and ate breakfast, talked about their agenda for the day. Brawley cleaned up while she fetched her purse and shoes.

She'd decided on black capris and a black-and-white geometric top. If they intended to crawl all over the city, dark seemed her best option.

"Ready?" he asked.

"Yes."

"Then let's get this show on the road."

An hour later, hands raised overhead, the wind blowing her hair, Maggie enjoyed the sights from the top of a double-decker sightseeing bus. She couldn't remember the last time she'd felt so carefree. Beside her, Brawley grinned, whipped out a camera, and took a picture of her.

She groaned. "Lose that thing."

"No way. I'm a tourist."

She snorted.

True to his word, Brawley bought tickets for the ferry to Liberty Island and climbed all three hundred fifty-four steps with her.

"Bet you're glad you wore sneakers today, huh?" He glanced down at her feet. "Sure do love those legs in heels, though."

"So not practical for today."

They stood side-by-side taking in the view from inside Lady Liberty. When his arm slid around her waist and he drew her close, she laid her head on his shoulder, breathing deeply. He smelled so good. So Brawley.

"I like the easy way you slide between mile-high stilettos and cowboy boots, Red. It keeps things interesting. I'm never sure which woman is going to show up."

"I hadn't thought about it."

"I have." They stood another moment, enjoying the closeness. His lips close to her ear, he asked, "Ready to head down?"

She nodded.

On the ferry, headed back to the mainland, Brawley leaned against the rail and watched as the colossal statue grew smaller. "Three-hundred-and-fifty copper pieces shipped in two-hundred-and-fourteen crates. Now that's what I'd call some assembly required. A parent's Christmas Eve nightmare."

"And batteries not included." Maggie grinned. "You know what surprised me most? That the copper surface is only two pennies thick. That's pretty amazing."

"Yet there she stands, guarding our harbor." He laid a hand on his stomach. "I'm hungry. Time for lunch."

They took a cab to Times Square to find Brawley's pizza.

* * *

She fed him a piece of pepperoni from hers. When his lips closed over her fingers, she caught her breath. "Brawley—"

"Maggie?"

Clearing her throat, she started to remind him they were friends today. Period. But the words stuck, wouldn't pop free. She shook her head.

"Forget what you were going to say?"

"Something like that."

He hand fed her a bite of his sausage pizza. "Having fun?"

"I am, yes. I'm having a great time." She planted her elbows on the table and rested her chin in her hands. "Is there anywhere you're not at home, Brawley?"

His forehead creased. "That's a strange question."

Carelessly, she shrugged one shoulder. "You always seem so at ease. So comfortable with who you are."

He smiled. "I'm happiest when I'm riding a horse in the Texas hills. I'm probably most at home in the clinic working with my animals. But, yeah, I'm okay with all this, too. I like cities and what they have to offer. I enjoyed my time in Dallas."

"You looked good yesterday."

"So did you." His voice deepened. "What do you say we grab a couple tickets for one of the off-Broadway shows?"

They did. They laughed, she cried, and when it was over, Brawley saw her home, then, after a *very* friendly kiss, he left to go back to his hotel.

* * *

She stood in the center of the sidewalk and watched his taxi weave through the traffic. Today had been wonderful. She'd rediscovered the Brawley she'd grown up with, an older, easier version of the boy she'd fallen in love with. She missed him already, and wasn't that a kick in the pants?

Heading inside, she told herself to get used to it. This was her new reality. It included more perks than she deserved, but it didn't include Brawley.

Well, she'd take a shower, change into her pajamas, and get a good night's sleep. Tomorrow would be busy. She hoped. Owen had texted her several times during the day, and sales appeared to be through the roof.

She'd just turned on the shower when her phone pinged. She opened Brawley's text.

My last night in NYC, Mags. Flying out in the morning. Miss me?

She did. Her fingers flew over the keys.

Dinner at 8. My place. Unless you have other plans.

She hit send and waited. Nothing. No response.

Disappointed, knowing it was for the best, she took a quick shower, then sat down at her computer. She scanned the orders flooding in. Owen was right. The collection was a hit. Bigger than she'd ever imagined.

Yet her heart was heavy. How pathetic!

Her phone beeped.

Missed your message earlier. Am I still welcome?

You bet.

She raced into the kitchen. What would she feed him? She opened one of the containers of leftovers from the other night and sniffed it. Probably not.

A mad dash to the corner deli netted everything she needed.

* * *

Brawley showed up right at eight.

"Hungry?" she asked when he walked in.

"Yeah. But not for food." He leaned in, kissed her neck. "Maggie, sweetheart, I need you."

"Dinner can wait." She moved into his arms, met his lips.

They fell onto the sofa, a tangle of arms and legs.

Panting, laughing, she pulled back. "I have a bed."

"How far away is it?" he breathed.

By the time they made it to her room, Brawley had both their shirts unbuttoned. He picked her up and gently placed her on the bed, then knelt and very slowly removed her shoes. His hand ran over each foot, a finger gliding over the arch, making her moan. His lips followed, and she thought she'd die.

Oh, he'd been good in high school. But since then? He'd undoubtedly earned a doctorate in the art of lovemaking.

One side of his mouth kicked up in a wicked grin. "Margaret Emmalee Sullivan, I want you to the point of aching. I want you in every way possible."

He lowered himself to her, melding his body lengthwise to hers, pressing her into the bed. His hand slid between their bodies and peeled her top from her, his knuckles grazing her breasts.

And then he kissed her. Kissed her till she was drowning in it.

She met him and demanded more.

"It's been so long, Mags." He breathed the words into her ear.

"I know."

He laced their fingers, stretching their arms overhead, exposing her body to him. His breathing ragged, he said, "Now."

Maggie nearly cried when he entered her, when they became one again after all the years. Then she simply quit thinking and welcomed Brawley home.

* * *

Spent, they lay together amidst the rumpled bedding.

"I don't think I can move," he finally said.

"Me, either. My bones have melted."

"That good, huh?"

"Don't start crowing."

"Wouldn't think of it." He patted her bare bottom and rested his chin on the top of her head. "God, you smell good."

"I'd like to return that compliment."

"No, you don't. Men aren't supposed to smell good. We're supposed to smell manly. Like rawhide. Like—"

"Like you've been working out in the sun all day? That's good, too," she snuggled into him. "I have to ask. Did you make a stop at Arnold's before you left Maverick Junction?"

She felt the soundless laughter travel through his body.

"For condoms?"

She nodded.

"I haven't bought them there in the last ten years or so."

"How many boys do you think have visited that gas station before date night?" Maggie asked.

"More than you want to know." He nuzzled the side of her neck. "I have another in my wallet. Want to take it for a ride?"

"Oh, yes. Please."

Maggie had never had any man focus on her the way Brawley did, as though *her* pleasure, not his, was the ultimate goal. Yet a tiny doubt niggled at the back of her mind. No matter how hard she pushed, it wouldn't go away.

"Brawley, what's going on here? Between us."

"What do you mean?"

She tried to slide away, to put a little distance between them, but he threw an arm around her waist and drew her back. The feel of him against her did crazy things to her, but she fought to stay focused.

"Tell me this isn't some kind of game for you. Some bet you've made with yourself." He stiffened beside her, but she continued. "It's been a long time since we were together like this. A lot of years have passed. Why now?"

"You wouldn't give me the time of day before, Maggie. If you recall, I've tried. More than once. It was you who held back."

She wanted to argue that, but honesty wouldn't let her. He had indeed held out the olive branch before, and she'd taken her clippers to it. Still…

"How many serious relationships have you had?" she asked.

"Besides you?"

"Besides me."

"None."

Skeptical, she asked, "How many women have you given a drawer in your house? A key."

"None."

"Really?" She turned her head to study him, realized that put their lips too close together. She moved slightly to stare up at the ceiling.

"How about you?" His breath tickled her ear.

"It hasn't fit. I've lived with either my parents or Pops. No overnighters at my place." She shrugged. "I've had a couple flings. You'd know all about those."

"So we're both virgins."

"Virgins?" She almost choked on the word. "After what we just did? I don't think—"

"Virgins when it comes to serious."

"To living with someone, yes."

"I was your serious, wasn't I?" he asked.

Reluctantly she nodded. "My one and only. So what? We both win a blue ribbon?"

"Ohh, a little prickly."

"No, I'm just—I don't want to get hurt again."

"Understood."

After a minute, she said, "You know, when you came into the shop screaming at me—"

"Shouting."

"What?"

"Men don't scream. We shout."

She rolled her eyes heavenward. "Grant me patience."

He chuckled.

"So," she started again. "When you came into my boutique *shouting* at me, I was furious."

"You wouldn't talk to me. Wouldn't communicate. It had been way too long."

"Well, that sure woke me up. It gave my customers plenty to talk about, too."

"I am sorry about that, but I probably wouldn't do it any differently even if I could. I was pissed that you hadn't shared your big news with me."

They lay together in the darkened apartment, listening to the night sounds.

"I really do have to go back tomorrow, Mags." Brawley brushed aside a strand of hair and kissed her neck. "Doc Gibson and Phyllis are taking care of things at the clinic, and my mom and dad are babysitting Marvin."

"I still cannot believe you named that dog Marvin."

"It's a good name."

"If you say so."

"Actually, I named him after Lee Marvin."

When she stared blankly at him, he said, "You know. The actor. Now talk about a manly man. Marvin played Kid Shelleen, a legendary gunfighter in *Cat Ballou, and* Tim Strawn, the hired killer Kid's supposed to off. Double role. The hero and the villain both. It won him the Academy Award for best actor."

"*Cat Ballou*?"

"Yeah. 1965. I love that movie."

"You're weird, Brawley." She sighed. "I'm sorry you have to go, but I understand."

"And I know you have to stay."

She nodded and stretched. "So tell me again about this conference you flew here to attend. The one you skipped out on to come to my showing…and play tourist."

The streetlight outside her window slanted its muted glow across the bed, and she saw color wash over his face. "There wasn't any conference was there?"

"Yes, actually there was."

"Did you register? Pay to attend?"

"Yes."

"Did you go to any of it?"

He shook his head.

"Why?"

"You promise not to tell anybody?"

She sent him a quizzical look.

He put a hand to his ear. "I can't hear you."

"Okay, okay. I promise."

"The conference was on panda bears."

She blinked. "Excuse me?"

Voice gruff, he said, "You heard me."

"Panda bears?"

"It was the only one I could find in the city this week."

"But that makes no sense, Brawley."

"Sure it does." He tugged her close and nibbled at her neck. "You told me I couldn't come."

"I didn't say—Ohhh, Brawley. I can't think when you do that." She ran her fingers through his hair, drew him closer still.

"Good. I don't want you to think. Just feel." He kissed her forehead, the tip of her nose. "You're beautiful, Maggie."

"You're not so hard on the eyes, either." She ran her tongue over his bottom lip.

"Be quiet, Maggie."

"Okay." And she let him pull her under, to a place where only the touch of his hands, his lips, the scent of him existed.

She gave herself up to him, thought she'd die for wanting more. The first time had been hard and fast, the second more leisurely. This time, Brawley more than took his time. He drove her crazy with his slow caresses and long, drawn-out kisses.

* * *

His arms wrapped around Maggie, Brawley pressed his face into her hair and breathed in her unique scent. He ran a hand along her waist, down her hip, her leg. The woman was smooth as silk, soft as dandelion fluff.

"What are you thinking about?" she asked.

"You," he whispered. "And how incredibly lucky I am to be here with you." He felt her smile in the dark. "How about you?"

"My thoughts are running along that same track." She turned in his arms, molded her body to his, and buried her face in his chest. She kissed the spot over his heart. "I've missed you."

"Oh, Mags." A finger beneath her chin, he lifted her face to his, took her mouth. Fire raged again, and he was lost.

When they finally surfaced, voice ragged, he said, "I might have a coronary here." He put a hand to his chest. "You do things to me. Things I can't even begin to describe."

She snuggled in with a sexy little purr.

"What's going on with Ty and Sophie? Things seemed a little, I don't know, strained between them," she said.

"Sophie wants to have a baby."

Maggie went quiet on him. He pulled back and rose on one elbow, tried to read her face in the moonlight that filtered through the partially opened blinds.

"Maggie?"

"Hmmm?"

"What's wrong?"

"Nothing," she said quickly. "Absolutely nothing. Of course she wants a baby of her own."

"That's what I told Ty."

"He has a problem with it?" She sounded surprised.

"He's scared—and you didn't hear that from me."

"Scared?" Maggie frowned. "Why on earth—" She stopped. "Oh, my God, of course he is. He's afraid he'll lose her like he did Julia."

"Yep."

"Sophie's not Julia."

"No, she's not."

"Julia had a heart problem long before her pregnancy."

"I reminded Ty of that, but I don't think logic figures into this. For him, it's a deep-down emotional trigger. Any man would worry about the woman he loved. But with Ty, he's lost his first love. He's afraid to risk his second."

Maggie stirred beside him, swiped the hair from her face.

"Would you worry about me?" she asked.

"Darlin', I'd worry myself sick."

She went still.

"What?"

He saw her eyes close.

"Hey, don't worry. I dressed for the occasion tonight, remember? Every time. We didn't make a baby."

"Not tonight."

Her words were so quiet he wasn't sure he'd heard her correctly.

"Excuse me?"

She lay absolutely still. "Not tonight. We didn't make a baby tonight."

He jerked up and snapped on the bedside lamp.

She blinked and brought up a hand to shield her eyes. Her face had gone ghostly white.

"What are you saying, Maggie?"

She pulled the sheet around herself, but he saw the rise and fall of her breasts as she breathed deeply.

Focusing on a spot on the ceiling rather than look at him, she said, "When you came home at the end of your fall term—" She stopped.

"Spit it out, Maggie."

"We took your dad's truck out for a moonlight ride."

"I remember."

"Do you remember the blanket you spread in the back? What we did on it?"

He pulled her hand away from her face. "Look at me, Maggie."

She cut her eyes to his, then averted them again. "You only had one condom with you. We made love twice."

His stomach dropped. "What are you saying?"

She laughed, but there was no humor in it. "Come on, Brawley. You're a big boy. You know what I'm saying."

"You got pregnant?"

She nodded.

"You carried my baby and didn't tell me?"

"I lost your baby." Hot tears burned in the eyes she turned to him.

Anger or grief, he wondered. "You lost it?"

She nodded. "At the end of my first trimester."

"And you didn't tell me."

"Why should I? It wouldn't have changed anything. You'd already decided I had no place in your life."

His head spun, trying to make sense out of what she said. Furious, he reached out to take her hand, but she jerked it away.

"When you say you lost the baby, do you mean miscarried or aborted?"

"You can ask me that?" She sat up and slid across the bed, as far away as she could get. "I'm sorry, Brawley. I think it's time for you to leave."

"No."

"No?"

"No. The question's justified, Maggie. You're pregnant with my baby and don't think to tell me till now? Jesus. How did you think I'd react?"

"Exactly like you are."

"I could have been a daddy."

A single tear rolled down her cheek.

"Ah, damn, Red. Don't cry." He leaned across, wiped the tear away with his thumb. Cursed when she flinched. "I need to know the answer to my question, though. I think I deserve that much."

She sniffled. "Yes, I guess you do." Her eyes met his. "Do you really believe I could have aborted your baby? I loved you."

"Maggie—"

"I miscarried."

When he reached for her, she drew farther away.

"Don't touch me, Brawley. Not now."

"Okay." A muscle worked in his jaw. He supposed he should take the high road here, tell her it didn't matter. But it did. "Why didn't you tell me?" he whispered.

"What?" She turned hurt eyes on him. "I should have called you after you dumped me? And say what? Hey, Brawley, I know you don't want anything to do with me, and that's okay, but I thought you should know I'm pregnant."

"If you'd told me, I wouldn't have."

"Wouldn't have what? Dumped me? Too late. You already did."

"I'd have done the right thing, Mags. God, you should have known that."

"I didn't want you under those circumstances."

Ouch. Her words hurt. Hurt more because he understood. He'd picked a hell of a time to cut the strings. It didn't much matter that he'd done it as much to make sure he didn't hold her back as for himself.

"Still, you should have told me. You shouldn't have had to go through that alone."

"I didn't. Mom was there for me."

He grimaced. "I'm surprised your dad didn't drive to Dallas and take me out."

Maggie smiled lopsidedly. "He probably would have—if I'd told him. I didn't. He still doesn't know. When things fell apart, I went to my mom. She drove me to a clinic in Austin."

At Pops's wedding, Rita, big-hearted Rita, had asked if he still loved her daughter. He was surprised she hadn't hired a hit man instead.

"I owe her. Big time," he said.

"Yes, you do. So do I. She was my rock."

"What can I do?"

"Nothing." Wrapping a sheet around herself, Maggie stood. "It's probably best if you leave now."

His chest ached. "I don't want to. We need to talk."

She shook her head. "We really don't have anything to talk about. It's all in the past, Brawley, and as nice as today was, as this was—" She gestured toward the bed, toward him, "We both know it won't work long-term."

Plucking at the sheet, she said, "For what it's worth, I didn't intend to tell you. Tonight or ever. I figured why dump a load of guilt on you for something you can't change." She hesitated. "I'm going to take a shower. When I come out, I'll expect you to be gone."

"So I'm dismissed." His jaw set in a hard line.

"That's a little dramatic, but, yeah."

"Just like that."

"Just like that," she said.

"You're not the Maggie I used to know."

She tipped her head and regarded him. "I'm not so sure you ever did really know me, Brawley."

"Don't be stupid. We grew up together."

"Yes, we did. And then we grew apart." As regal as any queen who ever lived, she turned her back and walked away from him.

The moonlight highlighted her back and turned it into shimmery alabaster, her red tangle of curls into every man's dreams.

Finally he understood his sin. What he'd done that could not be forgiven. He'd left her—eighteen, pregnant, and alone. God, no wonder she'd kept him at a distance all these years. He'd screwed up, and it was so much worse than he'd ever imagined.

He'd watched Jarvis touch her, kiss her yesterday, and it had been enough to drive him crazy. How had Maggie felt about all the women he'd dated over the years? Did she still harbor any of the feelings she'd once had for him? Or had he ruined that, killed those feelings forever when he'd walked away all those years ago? When he hadn't been there for her—and their baby.

After tonight, he'd have thought he could answer that question. He couldn't. He was more confused now than ever.

Together, he and Maggie had created a baby. An innocent little life. A lost life. He mourned for the child he'd never known about, would never know.

When the shower turned on, he reached for his clothes, dressed slowly, then stole out of the apartment like a thief.

Only it was Maggie who was the thief. She'd stolen his heart—and refused to return it, teasing and tantalizing him with a glimpse of what could be before snatching it away again.

Chapter Twenty-Five

Overhead, seagulls circled, cawed, then swooped down to scavenge their breakfast. A breeze off the ocean tossed Maggie's hair, and she brushed it back. Her coffee had cooled. She broke what was left of her bagel into small pieces, throwing them into the air and watching as each was snapped up by a dive-bombing seabird.

The sun warmed her skin but nothing could warm her inside. It had been a week since she'd sent Brawley away. She hadn't handled that well. All this time she'd held her silence. Then, at the worst possible moment, her secret had spilled, catching him totally off guard.

She hadn't heard a word from him since she'd left him there in her bed. He must hate her. Laying a hand on her flat stomach, she mourned again the loss of his child. A child he'd known nothing about until seven days ago.

Plucking her phone from her purse, she dialed her grandfather. She missed him, his wisdom. When he answered, his voice gruff-sounding, she missed him even more.

"Hey, Pops, how are the newlyweds?"

"Can't speak for the other half, but this half's doing well."

"Have fun at Disney World?"

He laughed. "We had a great time. Dottie could wallpaper a room with all the pictures she took. How about you? How's the city treating you today?"

"I'm at South Street Seaport drinking my morning coffee. Listen." She held up her phone, sharing the sounds of the birds and a boat's whistle.

"Hear that?" she asked.

"Sure do. Quite a difference from Lone Tree, Texas, huh?"

"And some. You and Dottie are at your place now?"

He hesitated. "Yeah. We're, ah, going through some things."

"You're moving." Her voice sounded flat.

"We are, darlin'. Even if we could keep them up, we don't need two houses. Dottie's offered to sell her place and move in here, but I can tell her heart's not in it."

"I can't say I blame her. Her gardens—she's spent a lot of hours creating that oasis."

"It's a pretty little place."

"It is, and you'll be happy there, Pops."

"I'm glad you called, honey. I've held off talking to a Realtor. Wanted to ask you first."

"Me? It's your house."

"I know that." His old voice took on a deeper timbre. "But your grandma and I always figured we'd leave the old homestead to you. To do whatever you wanted with it. Now, well, I kind of feel like I'm selling your birthright."

"Nonsense. It's yours. I'm in New York. If you and Dottie want to sell the house, then that's what you should do."

"You're staying there then?"

"I am." If she suffered a little melancholy at the words, she tamped it down. "How's everyone doing?"

"Your mom and dad both miss you, but otherwise they're fine.

Your mom's actually bullied Sean into taking a country-line-dancing class."

"I know. Can you believe it? I talked to them on the way here this morning."

He harrumphed. "Saw Ty and Sophie and the boys last night. They sure do make a nice family."

"They do. The boys Skyped me yesterday to show me Trouble's new trick. They're growing like weeds."

"So's Annie with that new little one she's carrying."

"Really? I talked with her last night, and she didn't say anything about it." A pang of regret stabbed her. She wanted to watch Annie grow big with her friend's baby. She'd never had the chance to do that with Brawley's, never felt their baby quicken.

"So let me make sure I've got this right," Pops said. "In the last twenty-four hours, you've talked to Sophie and the boys, to Annie, and to your mom and dad. That means your earlier question about everyone was either rhetorical or you're taking an around-the-barn route to asking about Brawley."

She closed her eyes and said nothing. The old man was too perceptive by far.

"He's good," her grandfather said. "That what you wanted to know?"

She expelled the breath she'd been holding. "We had a fight before he left."

"Nothing new about that. The two of you have been bickering for over a decade now."

"We have not."

His chuckle drifted over the line. "Girl, this is me you're talking to. You and Brawley rile each other without even trying. I know he hurt you. Hurt you bad. And I'd like to take him over my knee for that. But don't you think it's time you pulled out that thorn and let the wound heal?"

"I'm not sure I can, Pops. It's a pretty big thorn and buried deep."

"Then go in for surgery. But get it done and put it away."

In the background, she heard Dottie.

"Listen, Pops, you're busy, and I have to get to work."

"Okay, but you think about what I said."

"Will do. Love you."

"Love you, too. Dottie sends her love."

"Tell her it's more than reciprocated."

"That's a mighty big word."

She laughed and hung up. Tossing her now very cold coffee into a nearby trash bin, she stood and brushed a couple stray crumbs from her dress.

Facing the river, she let the breeze flow over her, wishing it could blow away the hurt. She'd put it away—or nearly had—for all these years. Brawley's move back to town had irritated old wounds. Sleeping with him had been a huge mistake. Rather than healing, it had ripped those wounds wide open.

Her phone rang. Brawley? *Don't be an idiot.* Pops? Maybe he'd remembered something he'd wanted to tell her. She glanced at the caller ID and frowned. She didn't recognize it.

"Hello?"

"Maggie? It's Jarvis."

Disappointment raced through her, but she tamped it down. "Hi. The photos you took are beyond amazing. I can't thank you enough."

"Sure you can. Have dinner with me tonight."

"Tonight?"

"Do you have other plans?"

"No, I don't." She chewed her lip. She liked Jarvis, found him sophisticated, different from anyone she'd ever dated. But she couldn't see any future for them.

Whoa. Dinner, Maggie. That's all he was proposing. A meal together. She'd had a good time with him before. If she intended to live here, wasn't it time to start that life? How better than dinner with Jarvis?

"I'd love to."

* * *

Jarvis took her to a small outside café. They ate pasta, drank wine, and talked. The food was some of the best she'd ever eaten, the evening warm, the stars brilliant. One hour turned to two, edged toward three.

Over coffee and a shared piece of cheesecake, he mentioned a friend was playing sax at a club across town. "Do you want to stop by? Listen to a set?"

"Sure, why not?"

The club, in the basement of an old bank, turned out to be quintessential New York. Posters and graffiti covered the walls, and smoke hung in the air.

The quartet had a sound that wrapped itself around you and held on. At the break, Jarvis wandered to the front to speak to his friend. He waved her over and introduced her.

"I could listen to you all night long," Maggie said. "The saxophone is one of the most romantic instruments ever made…and you really make it sing."

They talked for a few more minutes.

"You ready to go?" Jarvis asked.

Maggie nodded.

The evening air felt fresh and cool after being inside.

He insisted on seeing her home. When the taxi pulled up in front of her house, he asked the driver to wait.

At the base of her stairs, he said, "I had a wonderful time tonight."

She smiled at him. "I did, too. Thank you. I was feeling a little homesick, and this evening was exactly what the doctor ordered."

He looked at her, his dark eyes hooded. "You could ask me in. I can pay the cab and get another later. Or in the morning."

Maggie's heart raced. Before she could tell him no, his arm circled her waist and he pulled her to him, his lips covering hers.

This second time was no different from the first. She still felt nothing. This gorgeous man wanted her. That was more than evident as he held her close, but she couldn't respond.

He drew away. "No?"

She shook her head.

"Is it the cowboy?"

"No."

He laid a hand on the side of her face. "You sure? He's definitely got a thing for you."

She almost snorted, caught herself in time. "You are so wrong."

Now, his lips tilted in the faintest smile. "You're kidding me, right? I honestly thought he might tear my head off at your runway show when he caught me kissing you. If looks could kill, I'd be six feet under now."

"We had a thing. In high school. It's long over."

"Then maybe we should give this another shot."

He bent his head, but she reached out, rested a hand on his chest. "It's been a long day, Jarvis."

He nodded. "Good enough." After a quick kiss on the cheek, he said, "Go on. Scoot inside then. Like before, I'll wait till I hear you lock up."

She felt like a heel. He was a good man. "Thank you, both for the wonderful evening and for understanding."

She hurried up the stairs and inserted her key in the lock.

"I think I understand far more than you do," he said.

Maggie stepped inside, and Jarvis walked to the taxi. She watched the taillights as they disappeared into the traffic, then laid her head on the door frame.

She needed a hobby. Something that required a great deal of concentration. For tonight, she'd try a bath and a good book. Maybe a complicated whodunit.

Problem was she already knew whodunit.

The long, tall Texas cowboy.

Chapter Twenty-Six

The warm weather invigorated Maggie. The tree in front of her brownstone sported leaves, and flowers bloomed in a window box next door. Energy flowed, and people walked faster, smiled more.

She missed the big sky in Texas, though. The stars at night, competing with the city's lights, didn't shine quite as brightly. The moon didn't seem as large hanging over a skyscraper as when it hung over the Texas prairie.

There were moments when she found herself at a loss. So at home as Maggie Sullivan in Maverick Junction, she wondered about the New York Maggie Sullivan. Who was she?

She checked her watch. Since she didn't need to be at the studio for another hour, she had plenty of time to stop at the neighborhood Starbucks. She could use a good cup of coffee.

The line was short this morning. Coffee in hand, she actually found a table and sat down. From her vantage point, she people-watched.

A mother came in with her two daughters. The girls perched on stools at the counter and devoured sweet rolls. Mom, standing behind them in six-inch heels, looked as though no carb would ever dare venture near her Marilyn Monroe–red lips. She wore a size two black pencil skirt and a phenomenal white silk blouse. Her Gucci purse made Maggie's mouth water.

At a corner table, another woman took a mirror from one of her four bags and quickly applied her makeup. There'd been a time Maggie would have thought four bags overkill. Not anymore. She'd quickly learned that when she left the house, she had to carry with her everything she'd need for the day and into the evening. No running back home to change or pick up something she'd forgotten.

Smartphones, tablets, iPods. Everybody in the coffee shop was plugged in. She'd heard horror stories about the city. How you had to keep everything close. Watch your purse with an eagle eye. Yet, even here, there were neighborhoods. People called each other by name. They left purses and laptops at their seats and stepped outside for a cigarette or to the counter for a refill. It was comfortable and accepting.

And it made her homesick for Ollie and Sally and Bubba. For Rhonda at her beauty shop and Mel at the newspaper.

Even though she'd talked to Pops a couple days before, she needed to hear his voice again. He'd be up and around. A couple minutes with him would settle her restlessness. Taking a tentative sip of coffee, she found her phone in her massive purse.

"Maggie?"

"Hey, Pops."

"You okay?"

"Absolutely. I'm on my way to work and decided to give you a quick call."

"You in a taxi?"

"No, actually I'm sitting in Starbucks. Are you in Lone Tree or Maverick Junction?"

"We're at Dottie's."

"You know, sooner or later, you're going to have to quit thinking of the house as hers. You're a couple now."

They talked about everything and nothing. Maggie heard about Dottie's newest cookie recipe, last night's T-ball game where they'd rooted on Ty's boys, and Jessie's double.

"Ollie told me his business has dropped off since you left. He's not getting as many out-of-towners."

"I'm sorry about that."

"Not a thing you can do about it. I miss you, girl."

"I'd be a third thumb, Pops. You've got a new bride."

"The boy's keeping busy at the clinic."

Maggie didn't need to ask who the boy was. "I'm sure he is."

"He's taking most of his meals out. Dottie's had him to dinner a couple nights, but he usually doesn't leave once he's home. Don't think he's sleeping well."

"How would you know that?"

"I hear him wandering around at night. He's got a chair on the upstairs landing and sits out there sometimes. My guess is he misses you as much as you miss him."

"I don't miss him."

"Yeah, yeah, yeah. Don't try to bluff your grandpa. I've been playing poker a heck of a lot longer than you've been drawing breath."

She sighed. "I have to go, Pops. I don't want to be late."

"Okay, sweetheart. Love you."

"Love you, too." The man read her like a book.

She decided to take her coffee with her. Swinging out the door, she walked down the street. As she passed one building, the fire escape caught her attention, and she smiled. If she'd had an umbrella, she'd have been tempted to hook the handle over the bottom rung and pull it down like Edward in *Pretty Woman*. She loved that movie, loved that he'd come to his senses and gone after the woman he wanted.

She imagined Brawley in that limo, flowers in hand, music playing. A horn honked, startling her out of her reverie.

Flagging down a taxi, she gave him her work address. The light turned green, and the cabbie took off so fast her head snapped back. She missed her car, missed driving off to wherever, whenever.

But the clothes, the fashion, the endless choices of shops and restaurants? She loved it. Loved the freedom she had here. Everything had a trade-off, though. Everything came with a price.

She'd heard Owen on the phone the other day talking about his new designer, the fiery redhead with the Texas twang. She smiled. She was that.

* * *

Brawley checked his watch again. Five minutes later than the last time and still no Doc Gibson. It wasn't like him to be late. He took out his phone and hit redial. It rang six times and went to voicemail.

"Hey, Doc. Me again wondering where you got off to. I'm at the café. Did you forget our lunch date?" He hung up and slipped the phone back into his shirt pocket.

"Want another refill on your tea, Brawley?"

"No, thanks, Sally. My teeth are practically floating now."

"You gonna order some lunch or wait a little longer?"

"What have you got that you can fix me up with fast? Something to go."

"Chicken salad or egg salad sandwiches are quick."

"Egg salad."

"Anything with it?"

"Why don't you toss in a bag of chips? And bring me a Styrofoam cup for this, please." He held up his tea.

"Gotcha."

Brawley toyed with his key ring while he waited. Worry niggled at him. Doc Gibson had called last evening and asked if he wanted to meet for lunch today. Brawley had jiggled a few appointments around to make it work.

Retirement was still new to Doc, and Brawley figured it would take a bit for him to settle into it. He'd stopped by the clinic every day this week, visiting with the staff, talking to the patients, even handling an appointment here and there.

Today's lunch had been his suggestion, and it wasn't like him not to keep an appointment.

"Here you go." Sally slid two containers on the table. "Catch me for it next time you're in. I know you're impatient to get going. I added a second sandwich in case Doc's involved in something out at his place and hasn't eaten yet. No charge on that one."

"Thanks, Sally, but I'm gonna tell Doc he owes you for both. The man stood me up." Brawley picked up the food, gave her a quick peck on the cheek, and headed out the door.

On the way to Doc's small farm, Brawley gave Phyllis a quick call at the office and explained the situation.

"I've got things here," she said. "Go check on the old guy. We'll all feel better if you do."

"I won't be any longer than I need to be." Brawley hit end and cranked up Miranda's new CD. The woman had attitude. She reminded him a whole lot of Maggie. Feisty as all get out.

Starving and driving one-handed, he ripped into his sandwich. Breakfast had been too little and too long ago.

Swinging into the long, unpaved driveway, he braked when Doc's bluetick hounds rushed to meet his SUV, tongues lolling. He turned off the engine and hopped out, rubbing both dogs' ears at the same time when they greeted him, their feet braced on his legs.

Doc's old Chevy truck sat in front of the dilapidated garage. Brawley's uneasiness grew. Doc seldom left the dogs outside unattended for long. Too many times, they'd caught a scent and took off into the surrounding hills chasing their quarry.

"Hey, boys, what are you doing out here, huh? Where's Doc?" He patted their backs and started up the walk. Raising his voice, he called, "Doc? You outside?"

When he got no answer, he walked around back, the dogs at his heels. "Doc?"

He stepped onto the porch and knocked. When there was no answer, he turned the knob and the door swung open. The dogs tried to rush past him, but he held them back by placing his booted foot in front of them.

"Stay outside for another minute, boys. I'll come back out for you."

The house was quiet. Still.

As he started down the hall, he saw one bare foot. "Oh, shit!"

He ran the rest of the way to the kitchen, then stopped in the doorway. Doc lay on the floor, his arms outstretched, one leg bent beneath him. A mug had shattered and pieces scattered across the old linoleum. Coffee pooled on the floor and soaked into his shirt.

"Doc." Brawley knelt on the floor, felt for a pulse even knowing there'd be none. "Oh, God, Doc."

Brawley's breath caught in his throat.

Still on his knees, Brawley looked around the room, then back at his friend. From the amount of rigor, Brawley guesstimated he'd been dead about six hours. Doc must have let Holmes and Watson out for their early morning potty break, then come inside for his first cup of coffee.

Brawley hoped he'd at least gotten that first taste. Doc loved his caffeine. He brushed away a tear he hadn't realized he'd shed.

"Please, God, let him have gone quickly. Painlessly," Brawley prayed. Hot tears filled his eyes. He was too late. Not a thing he could do.

The egg sandwich he'd eaten roiled in his stomach, and Brawley thought he might be sick. Fighting nausea, he sat on the floor beside his good friend.

Outside the front door, the dogs whined, and Brawley thanked God he hadn't let them inside. How many times had Doc come into town, the two blueticks riding in the cab of his truck, to buy them all an ice cream? Never again.

Sorrow swamped him.

"I'm gonna miss you, Doc." He swiped at his eyes, at his nose. There were things that needed done. He should probably call Howard, the county coroner.

Instead, his finger hit the instant dial for Maggie. He had to talk to her. After that, he'd be able to deal with the rest.

Zandra, Maggie's efficient, nerveless assistant answered.

"I'm sorry," he said. "I thought I was calling Maggie's personal line."

"You did. Ms. Sullivan is busy right now and can't come to the phone. If I could take a message—"

"I don't friggin' care if she's halfway up a pole flying the Lone Star flag, I—" The fight drained out of him. In a quiet voice, he said, "I need to talk to her."

"I don't interrupt her unless it's life and death. Not when she's designing."

Brawley laid his warm hand on Doc's cold one. He swallowed hard and let out a shaky breath. "Then you're gonna want to interrupt her."

Her heard Zandra's sharp intake. "Did someone—"

"Yeah."

"I'm sorry. I'll put her right on."

The room was so quiet, he heard her footsteps as she took the phone to wherever Maggie was hard at work. For one fleeting second, he wondered if he should hang up. Not drop this heartache on her.

No. She'd find out anyway. He'd tell her and maybe find a little solace in the sound of her voice.

* * *

Hunched over her sketch pad and lost in thought, Maggie was vaguely aware of her phone ringing. She ignored it, heard Zandra pick it up.

The dress she worked on needed something more. Maybe different shoulders or a longer sleeve. Fiddling with it, she heard Zandra's heels on the old oak floor. Maggie looked up when her assistant knocked on the doorjamb.

"I hate to bother you when you're working, but you have a call I think you need to take."

The expression on Zandra's face warned Maggie this wouldn't be good news.

"Who is it?"

"Brawley."

On rubbery legs, she stood and reached for the phone. The door closed behind Zandra. She took a deep breath. "Brawley? Is Pops okay?" The question gushed from her.

"Yeah."

Something was wrong, though. She heard it in his voice, in the tone of that single word.

"Brawley?"

"I'm here."

"Where exactly is here?"

"At Doc Gibson's. He—" Brawley's voice broke.

"He isn't okay, is he?" It was more a statement than a question.

"No. Oh, Mags, he's dead. He was supposed to meet me at Sally's for lunch. He didn't come, and I couldn't get him on the phone. I drove out here—"

"Is anyone there with you?"

"Just Doc."

She could hear the tears in his voice, along with a touch of anger. "Did you call an ambulance?"

"No. He doesn't need an ambulance. There's nothing anyone can do for him."

"You're absolutely sure he's—you know."

"Yes. I'm a doctor, Maggie."

"Okay." She hesitated. "Do you want me to call the police for you? The coroner?"

"No, I'll call Howard. I need a minute first. I needed to hear your voice."

Her insides tumbled, and she hated every single mile between them. She needed to be there with him. "You shouldn't be alone right now."

"It's the way it is."

She could practically hear his shrug.

"Doc was alone when it happened."

"Brawley, that wasn't your fault. You had no way of knowing. I'll be there as soon as I can."

"No, Maggie. That's not why I called. To be honest, I'm not really sure why I did."

"Because you know I care."

"Time was it was a lot more than that."

"Yes, time was."

They talked quietly for a few more minutes.

"I have to go now, Red. It's time to notify Howard. Time he gets out here."

"Are you going to be okay?"

"Sure." And he disconnected.

Maggie stared at the phone for all of two seconds before she punched in Cash's number.

He answered on the second ring. "Hey, sweetheart. What's up in the city?"

"Are you busy?"

"No." His tone turned serious. "You okay?"

"Not really, but nothing's wrong here. Doc died this morning."

"Son-of-a— How do you know?"

"Brawley called. He found him. He drove out to Doc's when he didn't show up for a lunch they'd planned."

"Oh, damn!"

"Cash, if there's any way you can swing it, he needs you. Right away. He's at Doc's alone with him."

"Why didn't he call me?"

"Male pride? I don't know. I do know Brawley isn't in a good place right now. He's calling the coroner, but he needs somebody there with him, Cash."

"Yeah, he does. Doc was like a second father to him."

"I don't know when the next flight leaves, but if I can get a seat on it, I'm on my way home. I'll get out of here somehow or another today. Somebody should be there with Brawley now, though, not in five or six hours. Not tomorrow."

"I'm hopping in my truck even as we speak. Thanks for calling me, hon. I appreciate it."

"I love you, Cash."

"Love you, too."

She hung up. Throwing her door open, she called out, "Zandra?"

"Yes?"

"I hate to ask you to do this, but could you make a flight reservation for me? The earliest one you can find."

"Already on it." She held up her laptop.

"Thanks!"

"Are you okay?" Zandra gave her a careful look.

"An old friend died. Doc Gibson."

"Ah, he called while we were at dinner celebrating your showing."

Maggie nodded. "He owned the animal clinic Brawley took over."

"They were close?"

"Very. Brawley's the one who found him."

Zandra grimaced. "That's a tough one."

"Yes."

"You never did tell me, even after repeated questions and nagging, what's between you and Brawley. It's impossible to miss the vibes. You love him, don't you?"

Maggie's chin came up. "Loved. Past tense. A long, long time ago."

"Hmmm. Not sure I believe that, but whatever you say." She bent over her keyboard. "I'll let you know when I have something nailed down."

"Okay. In the meantime, I'll take care of what absolutely needs done here."

"Leave me a list. I can handle most of it," Zandra mumbled absently.

Maggie zipped around making phone calls and putting the finishing touches on a couple projects. Much easier to keep busy than to dwell on what Brawley was going through right now.

Doc had had a good life, but still—He should have had more time to enjoy his retirement.

She started when Zandra put an arm around her.

"There isn't anything here that I can't take care of or that can't wait." She handed Maggie a torn-out notebook page. "Your flight number and times. You have just enough time to run home and grab an overnighter. I'm sure you have plenty of clothes in Maverick Junction or at your shop there."

Maggie nodded, choked up again.

"Go. Brawley's a good man, Maggie, and despite what you claim, he's still in love with you. Right now your place is with him, not here."

"I called Owen and explained everything to him."

"And he told you to get out of here and get back to Maverick Junction, didn't he?" Zandra asked.

Maggie nodded and hugged her. Picking up her purse and briefcase, she started for the door. "You're sure?"

"I'm positive."

From the taxi, she called her mom.

"Pops called me," her mom said. "I'm sorry, honey. He told me Brawley was the one who found Doc."

"Yes. My plane leaves in about two hours. Can you pick me up?"

"In Austin?"

"Yes." She gave her the flight number and arrival time.

"Daddy and I will be there. Do you need us to bring anything along?"

"Nope. Just you." She started to cry. All afternoon, through the call with Brawley and afterward, she'd held back her tears. Now, with her mom, she could let go.

"Have a safe flight, baby. We'll see you in a few hours."

Chapter Twenty-Seven

The setting sun painted the sky in vibrant streaks of pink and orange as her plane touched down. Staring out the window, Maggie wondered where Doc was right now. She didn't believe life ended when the last breath left the body.

Was he up there in those picture-postcard clouds? If so, she wished he'd help Brawley. It tore her up to think of his suffering, the sorrow that had seeped through the phone lines.

Gathering up her purse and bag, she walked out into the concourse and made her way to the luggage area. And there stood her mom, arms outstretched to comfort her. Maggie almost fell into her embrace.

Her dad came up behind her to take her bag. "I'm sorry, honey. Sorry as hell. Brawley and I haven't seen eye to eye for some time now, but it's a hard thing he did today."

The evening sky had deepened by the time they reached her dad's Buick. They stopped once for coffee and a bathroom break. After a short discussion about what had happened that day, her mom and dad kept the conversation light.

Still, the drive seemed endless to Maggie. By the time they passed the Maverick Junction city limit's sign, the night was pitch-black.

Her mom half-turned in the seat. "Will you stay with us tonight? Pops's house is closed up right now. They're at Dottie's."

Maggie pushed her hair away from her face. "I don't know. To be perfectly honest, I hadn't even thought about it." Her mind tussled with the question. "Would you drive by Brawley's, Dad? I want to see if he's home."

"Sure."

When they turned onto the street, they saw lights on in the downstairs, but all the upstairs windows were dark. Brawley's SUV was parked at a slant in the driveway, though.

"Pull in, Dad."

He did, and she hopped out. Leaning in, she grabbed her purse and bag.

"What are you doing?" her mom asked.

She closed the back door and crouched so she could see into the car. "I came home for Brawley. Because he called. Because he needs me."

"What makes you think he's up there?" her dad asked. "Doesn't look like there's a soul home."

"His SUV's here."

"He might be with Cash or Ty, honey. Or maybe he's at the clinic. I'm sure with everything that happened today he missed a lot of appointments and has things to take care of."

"You're right. About all of it. If he isn't here, I'll visit with Dottie and Pops for a while. One of them can drive me home, or I'll call you and you can come for me." Belatedly, she added, "If that's okay."

"Of course it is," her dad answered. "If he's not here, he might not return anytime soon, honey."

"Understood."

"I don't want you hurt again."

"I know." She blinked back her tears.

Dottie came to the kitchen window and peeked out as her dad backed down the drive. Seeing Maggie, she waved. Maggie waved back, but walked past, slowly heading up the stairs.

Fletch stepped out. "Maggie!"

"Hey, Pops." She stopped on the third step and waited till he came to her.

He squeezed her so hard she could barely breathe. "Geez, it's good to see you, girl. Sorry it has to be under these circumstances, though."

She nodded and hugged back. "Is Brawley home?"

"Yeah, the boy's up there. He's hurting." Fletch hugged her again. "He could use a friend right about now."

Barking sounded behind her, and Maggie turned. "What's that?"

"Holmes and Watson."

"Doc's hounds."

"Yeah." Pops scratched his head, the gray hair a little thinner than she'd remembered. "They, ah, needed somewhere to go. Doc was a good friend. Least Dottie and I can do is give his dogs a home."

In the moonlight, she saw a sheen of tears in her grandfather's eyes. "So many people loved him, Pops."

"Yep." He clapped her on the arm. "Go on up. See if you can help the kid."

She nodded and picked up her carry-on.

"Want me to tote that up for you?"

"No. I'm good."

Not a single light was on. Still she pounded on the door. Nothing. She pounded again.

"Go away."

Her gut instinct had been right. Like a hurt animal, he'd crawled away to hide.

Not going to happen. She pounded hard enough that her hand would be bruised in the morning.

"Go away!"

"You open this damn door, Brawley Odell, or I swear I'll go down and get Dottie's key. You know her as well as I do. No way she'll stay downstairs. She'll come up with me, and then instead of one, you'll have two—"

He jerked open the door. "Maggie, leave. I don't want you here." His body swayed unsteadily.

Her chin went up. "If you didn't want me here, you shouldn't have called." Her nose wrinkled. "Geez, you're a mess. This place smells worse than Bubba's on Sunday morning."

She pushed past him, dropping her overnighter on the kitchen counter.

He raked a hand through his hair and swore ripely when she turned on the overhead light.

Covering his eyes with one hand, he said, "Maggie, I swear if you don't—"

"Huh-uh. You already swore. Quite nicely, too." She tapped a finger to his lips. "You kiss your mama with the same mouth those words passed through? Huh?"

His eyes were bloodshot, his clothes rumpled, his beard heavy. She couldn't decide if the eyes were the result of tears or the empty beer bottles strew on the floor and coffee table.

She almost hoped it was the beer. Her stomach twisted at the thought of him sitting up here all alone in the dark crying for a lost friend.

A yapping machine started up in the bedroom, then shot across the floor at her.

She knelt to scoop up the tiny fur ball. "Well, hello. Aren't you the cutest little thing?" Brows quirked, she turned to Brawley. "Marvin?"

"Yeah, the worthless mutt."

She covered the dog's ears. "He doesn't mean it. He loves you."

Brawley muttered what he thought about that while the dog slathered Maggie's face with kisses. She chuckled. "At least somebody's glad to see me."

"What the hell are you doing here, Maggie? Why'd you come? You're a busy woman."

"A friend called. A friend who's had the worst kind of day. I'm never too busy for a friend." She set the dog on the floor and moved to Brawley. He stood unmoving, watching her through slitted eyes.

"A friend?"

"Yes."

Ignoring the back-off warnings, she simply stepped into him and wrapped her arms around his waist. "Words are totally inadequate. I'm so sorry, Brawley. I know how much you loved Doc."

His chin trembled, but he said nothing.

"You can't hold it in. It'll eat you alive."

When his eyes filled with tears, he dropped his head, buried his face in her hair.

"What happened?"

"Howard said it was a massive coronary. Hard and fast. He doubts Doc had time to know what hit him. He was standing with his morning coffee one second and gone the next."

"So he didn't suffer."

She felt his head shake.

"I fed Holmes and Watson, then sat on the floor with Doc until Howard came. I waited till they—" His breath caught. "Till they took him away. Cash came. He waited with me. Thanks for calling him."

She nodded.

"Your grandfather has a scanner and heard the call-out. He came, too. Got there way faster than Howard. He waited with Cash and me, Maggie. Just waited with me."

She knew he was fighting back tears. Knew how hard the telling was. How important it was. So she didn't interrupt.

"Fletch took the dogs with him. He said he and Dottie would be glad to take care of them for his old pal and fishing buddy."

A low keening sound deep inside Brawley worked its way out. The floodgates opened, and his tears started.

She said nothing, simply held him.

Finally, embarrassed, he pulled away, rubbing his hands down his face. "Sorry. Shit, I'm so sorry. I'm okay now. That was the beer talking, making me all sloppy."

"Bull. That was your heart breaking, Brawley, and it's nothing to be ashamed of. It proves you're human—like the rest of us."

His brow jerked up.

"Have you eaten?"

He blinked at the smooth segue. "I'm not hungry."

"I'll assume that means no. Good."

He frowned.

"I've had a long day, and I'm starving. Besides, it'll give me a chance to cook for you."

He snorted. "Right. Our own Julia Child."

"Hey! I might not be Julia Child, but I can cook. In fact, I'm a darn good cook."

"When I look at you, sugar, domestic goddess and chef are the very last two labels that come to mind."

"Really?"

"Yeah, really."

"So what does come to mind?"

"You fishing?"

"Maybe."

"Here's the thing about that, darlin'. You never can tell what you might snag on the end of that hook."

She looked him straight in the eye. "I'll risk it."

"Okay, don't say I didn't warn you. And, remember, you asked for it."

"Oh, geez. Maybe I don't want to know."

"Nope. Too late." He narrowed his eyes and studied her. "Sensual. A little bit of a wild child." He held up a hand and ticked them off on his fingers. "Creative. Sexy-as-hell. Bright. Fun. Tenacious as all get-out. Those are a few that come to mind. But cook? Nope."

She chuckled.

"What? No comment?"

"None that I can think of right now. Go take a shower, Brawley. You need one. By the time you're done, dinner will be ready."

"Good luck with that. Have you taken a look in my fridge?"

"Not yet. Should I be scared?"

"Yes, be afraid. Be very afraid." With that, he headed off for the bathroom. "By the way," he tossed over his shoulder, "I don't have a shower. Just this great big old claw-foot tub."

"That should do the trick. Don't drown yourself while you're in there."

"Hah-hah." Unbuttoning his shirt, he came back to stand in the doorway. "Don't suppose you'd care to join me?"

"Not tonight. I have KP duty."

"One call for take-out pizza, and I could relieve you of that."

She shook her head.

"See? Tenacious."

She laughed and faced the fridge, prepared for a full-on battle.

When Brawley returned, his hair wet but combed, he'd shaved and pulled on a clean shirt and pants. His feet were bare. He studied the table, then looked toward his fridge. "You found all this in there?"

"I cheated. Either your mom or Babs has been taking pity on you. You actually have a pretty well-stocked freezer."

"Yeah, they both drop off casseroles once in a while. Annie and Sophie do, too."

"Not bad. So why aren't you eating the food instead of stockpiling it?"

He shrugged. "I forget it's in there. By the time I leave the clinic, it's late. I stop by the café and Sally feeds me. No dishes to wash that way, either."

"Well, sit down. I think you'll like this. Homemade chicken pot pie. Comfort food."

He pulled out a chair and dropped into it. "Smells good."

"It does that." She scooped him up a serving and set it in front of him. He looked exhausted and totally wrung out.

As they ate, she wished she had some kind of magic wand to wave over him to take away the pain. But she didn't. Time would help, but nothing would ever completely erase it.

He cleaned his plate, but she doubted he'd tasted a thing.

She yawned. Her body clock was on Eastern time.

"Time for bed, Brawley."

"Oh, yeah?" He tried for cocky, but it fell short.

"Yes."

"I'm tired, Maggie. So tired." He rubbed his eyes, then met hers. "In the morning I have to go to the funeral home. Make arrangements."

"I'll go with you."

His eyes, so sad, so sorrowful, stared into hers. "You're a good woman, Maggie Sullivan." With that, he headed into the bedroom, Marvin trailing behind.

Scowling at the dog, Brawley scooped him up one-handed and dumped him in the center of the bed. "Spent a fortune on a fancy little bed for him, but the damned thing won't sleep in it. I've tried shutting him out, but he yaps and yaps till I let him in with me."

He unsnapped his jeans. "It's not right. I'd thought about a dog, but he was gonna be big. Masculine. Something useful. One that could hunt ducks or rabbits maybe. Instead, I'm stuck with Marvin here."

Kicking off his pants, tossing his shirt to the floor, Brawley flopped onto the bed, sprawled on top of the covers.

Maggie walked into the room. "Move."

"What?"

"You need to turn back the covers and crawl between the sheets. You'll sleep better."

He slid to the far side, and she pulled back the spread and top sheet. Grunting, he rolled over.

When she leaned in to cover him, he caught her hand. "I don't want you to go."

"I won't."

Wordlessly, she stripped down to her T-shirt and panties and slid in beside him. He wrapped himself around her and laid his head on her chest.

"Did you feel like this when our baby died?"

His question, so softly spoken, nearly took her down for the count.

"Maggie?"

"Yes. Yes, Brawley, I did."

"Oh, God, Mags, I'm so sorry." His hand tightened at her hip.

"I am, too."

A sob tore through him.

She ran her fingers through his hair and murmured words of comfort as they mourned both the loss of a friend and their baby. Brawley's tears soaked into her shirt.

She'd never seen this Brawley. This vulnerable Brawley. He'd never shown her this side of himself, not even in their most intimate moments. This Brawley crawled beneath her skin and left her almost as defenseless as him.

Lying in the dark beside him, listening to him grieve, another sound intruded. A quiet sound. A warning sound. The crumbling of the immunity she'd built up against him in self-protection.

Was there a booster shot—or an antibody? With a sinking heart, she accepted that she probably wouldn't avail herself of it even if it existed.

Sometime after the midnight hour, she fell into an exhausted, troubled sleep.

Chapter Twenty-Eight

Since neither had thought to close the shades, early morning sunlight danced through the window and bounced over the bed. Brawley simply burrowed beneath his pillow.

Marvin, sensing his person was awake, crawled across Maggie and snuggled up on top of Brawley's pillow.

"What the hell are you doing?" he mumbled. "Bet I can sell you to some truck driver heading back East. You want to take a ride, Marvin?"

Maggie fought to contain her laughter. The dog, head resting on his front paws, wagged his tail. She wished she had a camera.

"Grouchy in the morning, huh?"

"Not always."

"You know, you might want to rethink that Great Dane."

"No kidding." Brawley reached up and moved the dog down beside him. Then he tossed the pillow aside. Hair tousled, he rolled to his side to face her. "Morning, Maggie. You naked?"

She laughed out loud. "And he's back."

"Yeah." He ran a hand over his stubble-covered chin. "Thanks for staying with me." A blush started dead-center of his chest and crept up his neck and face. "I, ah, would have been okay, but the company helped."

No doubt embarrassed, he was throwing a wall between them.

"Look, Maggie, about last night." He focused on a spot on the far wall, his eyes no longer meeting hers. "I don't know what to say. I apologize for everything that went down. And for dragging you away from New York and your work. I shouldn't have done that. Too many beers."

"You know," she said, "I could simply tell you it didn't matter. That it was okay. Or maybe I could say it was time to come home for a visit anyway. That I needed to check in on the shop. See how Ella's doing. But I'm not going to."

Confusion raced over his face, and his eyes drifted to hers.

"You hadn't had a beer or anything else to drink when you called me, Brawley. You can't blame it on alcohol."

A trace of anger darkened his eyes. "Fine. You're right. What do you want me to say?"

"I don't know. That's something you have to figure out for yourself."

"Nothing more I *have* to say."

Brawley threw back the covers. The grief would return, but for now it had been pushed aside by temper. Ordinarily that would have been okay. But right now? She didn't want to fight with him nor did she want him rehashing last night and beating himself up over what had happened. Time the conversation took a detour.

"Nice ass," she purred.

His head turned. "Oh, yeah?"

"You could model with that butt."

"Seen a lot of them, huh?"

"I've viewed my share, and yours ranks right up there at the top."

He gave a half-laugh. "Maggie, I don't think if we both live to be a hundred, I'll ever figure you out."

"That's the plan." She started to get up, then stopped, her mouth dropping. "What's this?"

"Oh, shit!"

"Brawley?" She picked up the framed photo of herself at Pops's wedding.

"Don't suppose you could just forget you saw that?"

"No, I don't suppose I can."

He scratched his bare chest, then reached for his jeans.

She read indecision in his expression and knew he was toying with possible answers. Trying to come up with something she'd buy. "I want the truth."

"The truth?" Pants on and zipped, button still undone, he faced her squarely.

Staring at those rock-hard abs, that amazing six-pack, she almost forgot the question.

"I've been handing you the truth ever since I came back to Maverick Junction. You're not hearing it."

"That's bull."

"No, it's not," he said quietly. "I hated the lack of anonymity here in a small town. Everybody knows your business before you do. You can't so much as sneeze without somebody hearing you and taking out an ad in the *Maverick Junction Daily* to spread the word. So I moved to Dallas after I finished school, in search of my dream and a little elbow room."

He leaned down, rested his hands flat on the bed, and stuck his face close to hers. "Problem was my dream wasn't there. I had to come back here, home to Maverick Junction, to find it."

"I understand that," Maggie said. "And I've been living here in this small town wanting out to find my own dream. In the city."

"Did you find it, Mags?"

"Yes."

"You sure about that?"

Now it was her turn to look away. "Yes."

"Not certain I believe you."

She gasped. "Are you calling me a liar?"

"No, ma'am. I wouldn't do that."

"But you're thinking it."

"I'm thinking I'm hungry."

She glared at him, then decided that, for now, she'd let him off the hook. But they'd get back to this discussion. "I'm hungry, too. But I cooked last night. I'm not cooking again this morning."

"You thawed out a casserole."

Her brow rose. "Your point?"

When he said nothing, she nodded. "That's what I thought. Put on a shirt and take me to Sally's."

"I need to go to the funeral home."

"I know." Her heart ached for him, and she took his hand. "After we've eaten and you've flushed the rest of the alcohol out of your system with several cups of coffee, we'll go together."

"You don't need to do that, Red."

"You're right. I don't. But I'm going to—unless you really don't want me along."

"I'd be grateful to have you there."

"Then grab a shirt, cowboy, and make it quick." She set the picture on the nightstand. That discussion would wait. Kneeling down, she unzipped her suitcase. "And you're paying."

He laughed. "Honey, I've been paying for years."

Chapter Twenty-Nine

Dread filled Maggie. She hated funerals.

Two days had passed since she and Brawley sat in Harlan Buchanan's office and picked out Doc's coffin. Between them, they'd taken care of the myriad details of funeral planning, from writing the obituary to which song would be sung first. They'd decided to hold the service at Doc's church rather than at Buchanan's Funeral Home.

She hadn't seen or talked to Brawley since.

When she walked into the small chapel with her mom and dad, she spotted Brawley up front with his parents. His head was dipped as if in prayer.

Doc's death had shaken his world. The two had spent a lot of time together tending the animals they both loved. Doc Gibson had mentored Brawley, had given him a place to develop and grow. And now he was gone.

The world had lost a good man.

Brawley had lost a wonderful friend and teacher.

She couldn't bring herself to look at the casket. She and Doc had planned to have lunch together on her first trip back home.

He wanted to hear all about her life in the city. Instead of Sally's, though, she'd come to the church to visit. To say good-bye.

Maggie understood funerals were a necessary part of the grieving process. They were for the living, the ones left behind, not the one who had moved on. Still, she hated them. With a passion.

Even with the air conditioner running full tilt, the interior of the chapel had already grown hot and close, the scent of flowers nearly overwhelming. She couldn't remember ever seeing so many baskets and arrangements. Apparently, the good people of Maverick Junction had paid no heed to the notice about sending donations to the National Humane Society instead of flowers.

Darn shame they didn't have a humane society here in town. They sure could use one. Both Marvin and Sophie's cat Lilybelle had been darned lucky to find a good home.

Someone bumped into her.

"I'm sorry." She stepped off to the side. More and more people entered the sanctuary. Doc Gibson might not have had any blood relatives left, but a lot of people loved and respected him. He'd be missed.

"We'll sit back here," her mom said.

"That's fine. I need to check on Brawley."

Her mother nodded. "He's going to need a friend."

Maggie walked down the aisle and slid into the bench behind him. Wordlessly, she laid a hand on his shoulder.

His hand came up to rest over hers, but he didn't turn. He sat stoically, facing front.

Annie and Cash came in, followed by Ty, Sophie, and the three boys. They sat on either side of Maggie. Each leaned forward and whispered to Brawley. He answered but never turned. Maggie's heart ached for him.

The small church filled to overflowing. Ranchers and their families from this and several adjoining counties had come to bid Doc Gibson a final farewell.

The preacher stepped to the altar, and the service began. Maggie listened to those who came forward to speak. So many, like her grandfather, were getting on in age.

Her eyes roved about the church. Who would be next? Which of these friends or family members wouldn't be here next time she flew home for a visit?

She cast a glance at Annie and Cash. They held hands. Annie already sported a tiny baby bump, and Maggie wouldn't be here to watch it grow. Jesse, Josh, and Jonah graduated from kindergarten in a couple weeks. She'd miss the ceremony, miss celebrating with them.

Her eyes misted, not only for Doc Gibson this time. She'd reached for the brass ring and actually caught the damned thing. Now what did she do with it?

* * *

Yesterday's funeral had taken on the feel of a bad dream. She'd practically sleepwalked through the day, afraid to fully accept that Doc was truly gone. She'd miss him.

Brawley would be lost without him.

So antsy she could have crawled out of her skin, Maggie found herself torn between her dreams and new life in New York and her friends and family, her shop, her always and forever life here in Maverick Junction.

She might not know what she'd do tomorrow, but today? She'd spend it at her shop greeting customers and piddling around in her back room. It was something she needed to do every once in a while.

She could fly in once every month or two and spend a few days looking over the stock and ordering new. Going over the books. Modifying and adapting to changes. It would let her keep in touch with both her business and her family and friends.

Pops and Dottie were happy, but neither one was a spring chicken. She missed Pops horribly. Doc's passing reminded her how quickly a loved one could leave. Without warning or time to say good-bye.

She probably needed her grandfather far more than he needed her. Especially now he had a new bride. The thought made her smile. She still couldn't get over that.

And their family had expanded by two since they'd adopted Doc Gibson's dogs. With Marvin upstairs that made three canines in the house. Who'd have thought? Dottie, it seemed, had a knack for taking in strays—of both the two- and four-legged variety.

First on today's must-do list? A stop at Ollie's for an iced coffee. The month and a half she'd been gone had been enough for the summer heat to sink her claws into Texas. It was beautiful now and not supposed to climb higher than eighty today. By tomorrow, they could be at ninety and sweltering.

As she pulled in behind her shop, she rolled up her windows. Next month would make a year since Annie'd ridden her Harley into Maverick Junction. What a difference that year had made. For all of them. When Annie and Cash got married, Sophie had come for the wedding and, basically, stayed. She'd fallen in love with Ty and his three boys. Pops and Dottie had hooked up. No doubt about it. Cupid had been working overtime. Everybody in the county seemed to be seeing red hearts and flowers.

Not all the changes were in the romance department. Brawley had come back to town, and now they'd lost Doc Gibson. She'd moved to New York City and had her first runway show. Make that *successful* runway show!

And now, here she was back home. Temporarily. She'd catch a flight back on Sunday. But for now, she'd enjoy the rest of her time here.

She grinned as she crossed the street to Ollie's.

The skirt of her pale green sundress fluttered around her legs as a breeze whipped up. She glanced up at the sky and saw clouds building to the west. Looked like they might get some rain a little later. They could use it.

She pushed through the café door, a small whirlwind whipping in behind her. Ollie looked up from the counter he wiped down.

"Hey! Look who's here. A big city, high-fashion designer in our humble diner."

"Go on," Maggie said.

Judy set down the platter of eggs and ham, refilled her customer's coffee cup, then hurried over to give Maggie a hug. "How long you here for?"

"This week."

"Shame 'bout Doc, huh?"

"Yes." Her heart hurt. "It is."

"Good thing Brawley decided to come back when he did or the ranchers around here would be up…ah, a nasty creek."

"They would indeed."

* * *

Before she left Ollie's, she ordered a cranberry-orange muffin and a glass of sweet iced tea for Ella. If history meant anything, she hadn't taken time to eat breakfast.

Plastic cup and Styrofoam container in hand, Maggie stood outside Ollie's and studied her shop. It looked good. She'd missed it. Missed coming here every morning, missed her routine.

New York was exciting, she reminded herself. Full of energy and wonderful people. Something different every day. It held everything she'd ever wanted. It did. It really did, her mind insisted. Her damned heart, though, still dragged its feet, mumbling it wasn't so sure.

"Maggie!" Ella, a necklace in one hand, flew across the room to her the second the door opened. "Oh, it's so good to see you. I'm sorry about Doc."

They hugged, and Maggie handed her breakfast. "Sit. Eat. And tell me all."

Ella laughed and dropped into a chair. She took a bite of the muffin. "*Mmmm*. Good. Where do I begin?"

Maggie sipped her iced coffee and soaked up the details of what had happened in the shop, with Ella's kids, and the latest gossip winging around Lone Tree.

"Most of the talk lately has been about you." Ella popped the last bite of muffin in her mouth. "Everybody's so proud. Mel ran a great story. Brawley took the pictures?"

She nodded.

"I thought he wasn't going."

"So did I. He handed us all a tale about a conference he had in New York."

"But?"

"Oh, the conference existed, and he did register for it. But he never attended a single day, and I don't think he ever intended to. My opinion? He went to support me."

Her heart did a little flip-flop. She was having the damnedest time trying to hold on to any leftover mad.

"He's a good man, Maggie."

"Yes, he is."

"I don't know what happened between you and it's really none of my business, but sometimes people make mistakes." Eyeing Maggie over her cup, she added, "And sometimes they deserve forgiveness."

They sat quietly. Casey James's "Crying on a Suitcase" played over the sound system. The words arrowed straight to her already abused heart.

When she'd left, Brawley had dropped everything to drive to

Austin to see her off. Then he'd flown to New York to be with her the day of her show. Her fingers moved to her bracelet, ran over the charm he'd given her that night. He'd always been there, cheering her on and supporting her.

Except the day their baby died.

He'd been nowhere around that day.

But then he hadn't known. Guilt assailed her. If the shoe was on the other foot, how would she have reacted when she'd found out about it?

She'd have been mad. No. Mad was too small a word. She'd have been livid. And he was—at first. Then his concern was for her. Sorrow at what she'd gone through. Regret he *hadn't* been there for her.

She let out a deep breath and said a quick prayer of thanks when the door opened and one of her Austin customers walked in.

"Laura!"

"Maggie? What are you doing here? I thought you'd be hobnobbing with the elite."

She laughed. "Unfortunately, I'm a working girl regardless of where I lay my head at night." Then she sobered. "A friend passed away. I came home for the funeral."

The two talked as Ella showed Laura their new stock. When she finally left, loaded down with purchases, Maggie said, "Is it okay if I sneak away to the back room? I've got a couple ideas I'd like to get on paper."

"You're the boss." Ella waved a hand toward her hidey-hole. "Your room's been sad without you. Go. Have fun. Create."

"Thanks." She slipped off and closed her door. The room welcomed her, and she spent the first few minutes simply savoring the feel of it. She'd missed this. Missed her private spot. As great as her new studio was, she was rarely alone.

Perched on her stool, she pulled a drawing pad toward her and sketched quickly, the ideas scrambling to get out.

Time ceased to exist.

Every once in a while, she became aware of customers coming and going, heard snippets of conversation, but she quickly blocked them out.

Ella. What a gem. How lucky she'd been to find her.

The bell over the door chimed again. From the backroom, Maggie heard Ella's cheerful greeting followed by a deeper, masculine voice. Brawley. Asking for her.

Her stomach plunged to her toes. She could hide out in here. Pretend she didn't know he'd come.

Yeah, like he'd simply turn around and leave.

Girding her loins, so to speak, she decided she'd go to him rather than cowering in her hideaway. She caught a glimpse of herself as she passed the large mirror propped against the wall. If she stopped to run a hand over her hair or fuss with the skirt on her dress, it had nothing to do with the man outside the door. It was simply a professional woman who wanted to look her best for her customers.

She snorted. Who the heck did she think she was kidding?

Opening the door, she stepped out. "Hey, Brawley. Thought I heard you out here."

He hung up the lacey blouse he'd been toying with. "Hey, yourself, gorgeous."

"Don't you have work to do?"

"Yep, and I'm doing it. Ray Barrett called this morning. He's got a ranch on the outskirts of Lone Tree and had a sick horse. Been there for hours. Now, I'm finished, so I stopped by to ask if you'd have dinner with me."

"Tonight?"

"Tonight."

Maggie blinked and glanced at Ella.

"We're almost out of bags," Ella said. "I'll get some more from the stockroom." She disappeared, leaving Maggie alone with Brawley.

"Well?" he asked.

"I can't."

"Sure you can." He nudged his hat back from his forehead, then tucked his thumbs in his jeans pockets. "You afraid of me, Red?"

"Absolutely not." Her chin rose. "I'm not afraid of anything."

"Good. Glad we got that out of the way. Have dinner with me."

Silence settled over the shop. She stared over Brawley's shoulder toward the street, praying she'd spy a customer or two headed her way.

The street and sidewalks remained empty.

"Brawley, I have so much on my mind right now. So do you. This isn't the best time for us to try to start anything again."

"No, it probably isn't, but I think we already have. To be honest, I don't know if the time will ever be right, Mags, so maybe we need to grab what we've got. We're both here. Right now."

"But not for long."

"No, not for long. Would it really be so terrible to grab today, to take advantage of what we have for as long as we have it?"

"And not think about tomorrow?"

"And not think about tomorrow."

"See, Brawley, that's where you and I differ. I can't operate that way. Tomorrow is always on my mind."

"Actually, you might be surprised just how often I do think about tomorrow—with you."

Oh, God. She couldn't speak. It was as if she'd taken a punch to the stomach.

"What? No smartass comeback, Red?"

She'd come back for him, hadn't she? To help him through this. "All right."

"All right? All right what?" His expression grew wary.

"I'll have dinner with you."

"Just like that?"

"Just like that."

"How about I pick you up?"

"Fine." She toyed with her necklace. "Where are we going?"

"It's a surprise. Dress casually. Jeans."

"Okay."

He waved and moved to the door. Hand on the knob, he said, "I'll be by at six. You're still at your folks?"

She nodded.

Without giving her a chance to say another word, he was out the door.

Ella stepped from the back room, a handful of bags tucked under her arm.

"Boy, don't you have good timing," Maggie said.

"I don't know what you mean."

"And you can say that with a straight face." Maggie grinned. "You're a pro."

"I've got two kids. It's a skill you have to learn." Ella studied Maggie. "Brawley's a good man."

Maggie bit her lip. "Yes, he is. But I can't afford to lose sight of my goals."

"I don't think you need to worry about that. Be sure, though, to stay flexible."

"Stay flexible? Would that be the same as keeping my options open?"

"Yes, I suppose it would. Why?"

Maggie shook her head. "My dad handed me that same piece of advice before I left for New York."

"He's a wise man." Ella stepped behind the counter to restock the bags.

"Not sure where you're going to put those," Maggie muttered, "since I know you already stashed a new supply there this morning."

The door opened. Spotting Maggie, her customers started talking at once, congratulating her and wanting to know if she had any of her new designs to show them.

* * *

As promised, Brawley showed up at six, right on the dot. From her parents' living room window, she watched him walk toward the house. Jeans, white with wear, hugged his lower body. A navy blue T-shirt highlighted his muscular torso and made her mouth water. Black boots, cowboy hat, and dark glasses finished a look certain to make any woman's heart do a happy dance.

Dressed in an old pair of jeans, a short-sleeve dark green T-shirt, and a pair of kick-around boots, she hurried out to meet him. No sense him and her dad getting into it.

Opening her arms wide, she asked, "This okay?"

"You look beautiful, Red." He tugged at her ponytail. "A man could get lost in that body."

Heat rushed through her as she remembered him doing exactly that in her New York apartment. She slid on a pair of oversized sunglasses as much in defense against Brawley as protection from the low sun.

He opened the door and helped her in.

"Still not telling me where we're going?"

"Not yet."

"Hey, Marvin." She leaned over the seat to rub the puppy's head. "How are you, boy?"

His entire body shook in ecstasy.

"Don't get him too excited. He'll pee all over the seat."

Maggie laughed and turned around to hook her seat belt.

A country song played on his radio as they turned onto the highway. She lowered her window and rested an arm on it. Brawley did the same.

"The fresh air feels so good," she said. "It seems I've been cooped up forever."

About two miles outside of town, Brawley turned onto a small back road. Maggie narrowed her eyes. "This goes back by the lake."

"Yes, it does."

Rounding a curve, the lake came into view. A small hill led down to it. Brawley cut his wheels and started through the grass.

She let out a small squeak and gripped the door. "There's no road here!"

"No kidding, Sherlock."

He drove straight to the lake's edge. A carpet of Texas wildflowers spread out around them. Mature live oaks clumped together near the lake and reflected in the water.

Without a word, she opened her door and got out. "Brawley, it's beautiful."

He came to stand behind her, and she felt his heat. Then he put an arm around her waist and pulled her against him. Her breathing quickened.

Laying his head against hers, he said, "I love it here."

A bird chirped high in one of the trees and was answered from a nearby oak. Marvin yapped from the car.

"Guess I'd better let the mutt out. He sure can't handle it by himself. Another reason a man should have a real dog."

"Marvin's real."

"Yeah, a real pain in the butt."

"Thou dost protest too much, methinks."

Brawley grunted. "You and your Shakespeare." But he moved to the car to lift down the dog. Marvin scooted off through the flowers and, sticking his nose in one, started sneezing.

"Why'd you bring me here?"

"Beautiful lady. Beautiful scenery. I thought we could eat by the water." He walked to the back of the SUV and grabbed a blanket and a picnic basket.

"I hope you brought lots of food because I'm ravenous."

He chuckled. "That's one of the things I like about you, Mags. Some women won't eat around a man. Not you. You like your food, and you're not shy about it. It makes eating with you fun."

"Well, let's get the fun started. What's in that basket, Little Red Riding Hood? Or are you the Big, Bad Wolf?"

"I'll let you decide." He opened the lid and pulled out a bone. Tossing it to Marvin, he said, "That might keep him busy for a few minutes."

"It's bigger than him."

"Everything's bigger than him," Brawley muttered. Next, he took out two plates, already made up. "If you're expecting caviar and champagne, I'm afraid you're gonna be disappointed. We have buffalo chicken wraps and tomato-basil pasta along with a bottle of sparkling water."

"That sounds perfect. I'm too hungry for caviar."

"I figured you'd say that." He held up a bag of Dottie's cookies. "And these for dessert."

He handed her a napkin.

"Cloth?"

"Yep. Only the best for you." His hand dipped into the basket again, and he handed her a single yellow rose. "It made me think of you."

She took it, their fingers touching. "Oh, Brawley. What am I supposed to do with you?"

His lips curved in a slow, sexy smile. "I've got a couple ideas."

"I'll bet you do." She laid the rose on the blanket beside her and uncovered her plate.

The water lapped on shore, the birds sang, and Marvin gnawed on his bone. Maggie hadn't been this much at peace in months.

Both of them tucked into their food.

"I've been thinking," Brawley said.

"That could be dangerous."

"Hah-hah. Seriously, Maverick Junction doesn't have any kind of animal shelter."

"I know." Marvin crawled onto her lap, and she ran her hands over him, driving him into a frenzy of pleasure. "This little guy really lucked out."

Brawley shook his head. "He's not staying. I'm a temporary landing pad until we find him a home."

"You are such a liar. Wild horses couldn't drag this guy from you, and you know it."

He grinned. "Marvin does tend to get under your skin. Guess he's okay. For a runt."

"It's in the breeding, Doctor Odell."

"Speaking of…" He rolled toward her, placed his hand behind her neck, and pulled her in to him.

The first touch of his lips was electric. She moaned and slid her body closer still. Marvin, squashed between them, wiggled out and climbed over Brawley to find a safer spot for his post-dinner nap.

Brawley whispered, "Maggie, I want you."

"Nothing has changed. All the problems we had before are still problems."

"Is it the camera guy?"

"Jarvis?" She frowned. "No! It's you. It's me. It's the fact we live fifteen hundred miles apart."

"And the fact I acted like an ass when I was nineteen years old."

"That, too."

He dropped onto his back on the blanket. "I don't know how else to tell you I'm sorry. To show you I mean it. I'd give anything to be able to go back and handle things differently. If I'd known, had any idea—"

"I know that, Brawley. I believe you."

He raised his head to stare at her. "Does that mean you've forgiven me?"

She let out a long sigh. "I think so."

"You think so? You don't know?"

"It's complicated."

"Tell me about it." His head thunked back to the ground. Then he reached for her hand and squeezed it. "I'm sorry about our baby, Mags. So sorry I wasn't there for you. That's a regret I'll take to my grave."

When she said nothing, he cut his eyes to where she lay beside him. "Oh, Maggie, don't cry. Please don't cry." He thumbed away the tears that trickled down her cheeks.

"Did I tell you our baby was a little boy?"

"Oh, God." He shook his head. "No."

One single word, but in it Maggie heard a world of pain. Of suffering.

"I would have loved our baby." His voice cracked. "A little boy. A little girl. It would have made no difference."

Her throat so tight she doubted she could speak, she simply ran her thumb along the back of his hand.

Twilight deepened around them as they lay side by side, holding hands. Marvin snored, and the cicadas began their nightly serenade. The moon began its slow climb into the evening sky.

"You said earlier you were thinking about something. I assume you wanted to run an idea by me." Maggie spoke softly.

"Yeah, I did." He licked his lips. "It's about an animal shelter. We've got all of Annie's leftovers from the apartment in storage. Ty said he and Sophie have a bunch of junk they'd like to get rid of. So do Cash and Annie, Rosie and Hank, Dottie and Fletch. My mom and dad said they'd do some cleaning out, too."

"And?"

"One man's trash—"

"Is another man's treasure," she finished.

"Yep. So I'm thinking we should hold a town yard sale. With the money we raise, we can start The Doc Gibson Animal Shelter. I found the perfect building for it, and I think we can get volunteers to run it."

Maggie came up on one elbow. "I'm sure Sally and Ollie would both run a booth to sell drinks and food."

He nodded. "I've already talked to Mel. He'll do the publicity for free."

"I can put signs up in Lone Tree," Maggie said. "I get customers from all over. I'm sure some of them would donate even if they can't participate."

"I think we can do it." His eyes met hers. "What do you say?"

"Yes, we can."

"Does that bleed over into us, Mags? Can we possibly do it, too? Somehow mend this gigantic rift?"

"We can work on it." She leaned over and kissed him.

He pulled her down on top of him, and she sighed at the feel of that hot, hard body beneath her.

"When are you leaving again?"

"I'm supposed to fly out Sunday morning."

"Supposed to?"

She nodded. "I can't believe I'm saying this, but to be honest, I'm having second thoughts."

"About what?"

"Living full-time in New York." She sighed. "God's honest truth, it feels so good to get back in my jeans."

His hand slid lower, worked its way beneath her waistband. "There was a time you wanted to get into my jeans, too."

"Don't flatter yourself, Brawley. I was a naïve young girl and didn't know better."

"What about our night in New York?"

She kissed him lightly. "That would have been an adult woman who probably *ought* to have known better but decided to go for it anyway."

"I applaud your decision."

"I'll bet you do. The thing is I love the city and all it has to offer. I really do. But this is home."

"Yes, it is." His lips found hers. "Kiss me, Maggie."

And then she was lost in him. In his kisses, in his embrace. Celebrated that he undressed her slowly, relishing her the way he would an unexpected gift.

She undid his buttons, slid his shirt from him. A warm breeze wafted over them, caressing their bare skin.

He trailed kisses over her face, down her neck, over her body. Then she simply gave in to the pleasure that was Brawley, said a prayer of thanks when he cried out her name.

After, lying in Brawley's arms, her head on his chest, Maggie heard his heart thumping as wildly as her own. She shivered, and he pulled the edges of the blanket around them, held her tighter.

She smiled. Had she ever had such romance as he'd shown her today? When they'd made love, he'd savored her. Every inch of her. He'd made her feel as though she was the only woman in the world. The only woman he'd ever been with. The only man she'd ever been with.

With his kisses, his caresses, his demands, he'd erased their past. Electrified the present. Promised a future.

Exactly when she couldn't say, but she'd made her decision. She wouldn't be going back to New York. Not full time.

The city would be there next month, next year.

She could design here and travel back and forth when it was necessary. Tomorrow, she'd call Zandra.

That brass ring? Maybe it was right here in Maverick Junction.

Chapter Thirty

Dreams didn't always equal reality.

Maggie had read enough biographies to understand life inside a house didn't always match what someone looking through a window saw.

Rock stars, princesses—their lives weren't always what they seemed. She only had to look as far as her friend. Annelise Montjoy Hardeman appeared to have had the perfect life before she met Cash. Not so.

Time to take the first step. Grabbing her phone and her courage, she dialed her grandfather before she could change her mind.

"Pops, I have a question, and you have to promise to be honest with me."

"Okay," he answered slowly.

"It's all right," she assured him. "This won't hurt."

"Good."

"What are your short-term plans for your house?"

"The house?"

"Yes, Pops. The house."

"Why?"

She took a deep breath and plunged in. "I'd like to stay there. For a while. Not permanently. I know you want to sell it, but—"

"Honey, of course you can stay there. What about New York, though?" Pops sounded confused. "Wasn't this just a quick trip home for Doc's funeral?"

"Yes, it was. I like New York, but I can do my designing from here and go to the city when I need to for business. Nothing says I have to live there."

"I see."

She laughed. "No, you don't. I'm not sure I do entirely. I'll fill you in on everything later. Before I did anything drastic, though, I wanted to make sure I had a place to stay."

"Your parents would love to have you with them."

"I need to be on my own, Pops."

"Figured you'd say that. The house is yours as long as you want. Love you, honey."

"Love you, too." She hung up and dialed Zandra.

With any luck, her assistant could put her in touch with a Realtor to sublet her apartment.

When Zandra answered, Maggie spent some time catching up with everything that had happened since she'd left, the orders that continued to pour in, and her plans for the next line.

"Jarvis called."

Maggie grimaced. "He did?"

"Uh-huh. I told him about your friend. That you'd gone home for the funeral."

"Thank you, Zandra."

"He might call, so I thought I'd give you a heads-up. If I'm reading things right, you've got your eye elsewhere."

Maggie made a small sound of agreement. "And that brings me to the real reason for this phone call."

She steadied herself. She shouldn't be so nervous about this. She was, after all, her own boss. She made her own decisions.

Right. And this decision could bring about the collapse of everything she'd worked for. How would Owen feel about her staying in Texas?

Did it matter?

Yes. He'd provided her a huge break. Instead of starting at the bottom of the ladder, Owen had made the climb much less steep. If she did this, would he think her unappreciative and withdraw his support?

The show had been uber-successful, but that guaranteed nothing.

So which could she live without? Career or family?

Oh, boy. She hoped it wouldn't come down to that, that she wouldn't have to make a choice. She could do it all. She knew she could.

"What do you know about subletting apartments?"

After a few seconds of silence, Zandra answered. "Quite a lot, actually. I'm subletting right now—and hunting for a new place. My lease is up at the end of the month."

"Seriously?"

"Yes, and places are hard to find. Why?"

Now or never. Maggie leaped off the cliff. "Because I don't want to live in New York year-round."

Silence met her words.

"Zandra?"

"I thought you liked it here."

"I do."

"But you're happier in Texas."

"Yes, I am. That doesn't mean I'm giving up designing," she said quickly. "I can design here and fly to New York for the work-ups and shows."

"Are you sure about this?"

"Oh, boy." She huffed out a breath. "I think so."

"You think, or you know?"

"I know."

"It's a big step, Maggie. Have you talked to Owen?"

"No. Not yet. He's my next call." When she didn't get any response, she asked, "Zandra? Are you still there?"

"Just thinking, weighing things. I doubt Owen will have a problem with this. He wants your creativity, your fantastic designs, regardless of where you put them together."

"I sure hope you're right." She nibbled her lip. "What's your best suggestion for handling the apartment?"

"I'll take over the lease. When you come into the city, you can stay with me. In the extra bedroom."

"Really?"

"I love that apartment. It's a win-win."

"Tell me about it." She hesitated. "Are you sure about this?"

"Probably more than you are. I'll let you play with the whole idea a bit more before we make a final decision."

The memory of Brawley at the lake the night before ambushed her. Brawley holding her in New York while she cried for their baby. Brawley mourning his friend.

He'd been more than clear that he wanted her. The question was for how long. Did he want her for a night or two, a month, or forever? Did *she* want *him* forever?

Absolutely. She always had and always would. He'd crushed her before, ground her heart beneath his boot heel. But it hadn't been intentional. Careless? Totally. Immature? Without a doubt. And a long time ago.

He was right about that. He was no longer the boy who had done that. He was a man, a man who kept his word. Who took his responsibilities to heart. She could only hope he'd taken her to heart, also.

Time would tell.

She wanted to give it a shot. To do that, she needed to be where he was. The chance of a future with Brawley was worth what she might be giving up.

"I don't need to think about it anymore, Zandra. I'm sure."

"Then I'll contact the landlord and get the paperwork started."

"I'll fly back for a week or so to wrap things up from the showing."

"Yes, you will. Should I expect you Sunday?"

Torn between her work in New York and her desire to help out with the fund-raiser, she made a decision. "No, I'm taking an extra week."

When she hung up, she called Owen. Zandra had been absolutely right. Owen didn't care if she designed in Timbuktu as long as she came to New York when necessary.

Ending the call, Maggie flopped onto her bed, grinning like a Cheshire cat. She felt good. Better than she had in a long time.

* * *

The fund-raiser came together quickly, and the entire town of Maverick Junction and most of Lone Tree turned out for it. Adults and kids alike manned the tables.

By late afternoon, though, the heat hit hard, and Brawley decided to roll up the carpet. He and Cash dragged the few things that hadn't sold to two tables and posted a big "FREE" sign. Inside half an hour, nothing remained.

Brawley grinned as he watched Henrietta Greene tote away the ugliest table lamp he'd ever seen. The turquoise base was topped with a red and purple shade.

He shivered. "Can you believe she actually wants that?"

"Maybe she's planning on some target practice tomorrow," Ty said.

"Frankly, I don't care what she does with it. Saves me having to pitch it in the Dumpster." They took down the empty tables and stowed them in the back of Cash's pickup. "We did well here today." He high-fived his friends.

"We did," Cash said. "You've got enough to open the shelter. Sure is nice of Arnold to donate the building behind his gas station."

"Yep." Ty stretched his arms overhead and yawned. "What now?"

"Now, we relax." Brawley tipped his head in the direction of the piled wood. "Time to light our bonfire. Might be hot, but you can't do this right without one. I think we should stretch this thing right on into the night. Maybe somebody—"

He trailed off, his eyes straying to the three women who walked toward them. "Now isn't that the prettiest sight you've ever seen?"

"Yeah. It is." Ty reached out his hand and caught Sophie's, pulling her to him. They kissed. "Where are the kids?"

"Talking Sally out of an ice cream cone. Babs is with them."

"I'd ask where our kid is," Cash said with a grin, "but you've got that covered." He kissed Annie and rested a hand over her baby bump.

Brawley crooked a finger at Maggie. "Why don't you come on over here and give me a smooch? I think I deserve it after today."

"Why, Brawley Odell, I do believe we agree on something."

Before he could respond, she planted a doozy of a kiss on him. He growled and wrapped an arm around her waist.

When she drew back, her lips were red and swollen, her chest rising and falling as she fought for breath.

Cash laughed. "Get a room."

Annie punched her husband's arm. "What are you? Twelve?"

The triplets came running up to them, Cash's sister and her two in tow.

"I don't know about anybody else, but I'm famished." Ty rubbed his stomach.

"Help is on the way. Let's get the fire started first."

Grumbling about having to wait, Ty followed Cash and Brawley.

Brawley stopped to look over his shoulder. "You're not going anywhere, are you, Red?"

"Nope."

He winked at her and caught up with the others.

By the time they had the wood stacked, a crowd had gathered. A cheer went up as flames shot into the air. Lawn chairs and blankets magically appeared as people settled in. Mr. Sadler showed up with all the fixings for hot dogs, bags of chips, and marshmallows to roast. Bubba's delivered a keg of beer and enough soda for an army. Dottie set up a battered card table and charged a dollar for the impromptu barbecue.

"Come on," she nagged her neighbor. "It's for a good cause."

Brawley noticed that very few one-dollar bills crossed her palm. Most of the townspeople handed her fives and tens for their Saturday-night dinner.

He stepped to the food table, prepared to plate hot dogs for the throng, but his mom pushed him out of the way. "Dad and I have this covered."

She tipped her head toward Sadler's parking lot, which had become a makeshift dance floor. Someone had set up a stereo system.

Brawley caught sight of Maggie dancing to an old Merle Haggard song with little Josh.

His mother followed his gaze. "She's good with kids. She should have some of her own."

He closed his eyes to hide the pain. His mom would see it and recognize it. He'd never been able to hide anything from her. Maggie should, indeed, have children of her own. *His* child.

Would their little boy have had Maggie's red hair, her green eyes? Or maybe his dark hair with those incredible blue eyes. Without thinking, his hand moved to his chest to rub the spot over his heart.

"Go to her," his mom said. "Time the two of you healed the hurt."

His gaze whipped back to her. Did she know?

"Go," she repeated, giving him a little shove.

"Okay." He laughed. "Sure you can handle this?"

"We handled you, didn't we?" his dad said. "After that, everything else is a cakewalk."

"I wasn't that bad."

"No, you weren't. You're a good son. Now listen to your mother and get out of here. The girl's waiting for you."

Sure enough, when he looked at Maggie again, she was watching him. Without another word, he moved to her, cut in on Josh, and drew in the scent of her, the feel of her. Thank God for slow songs. Dancing with Maggie was the next best thing to making love.

He didn't get to keep her to himself long, though. Seemed everybody was glad to have her home and wanted to congratulate her on her success. Hands jammed into his jeans pockets, he stood off to the side drinking it in, so damn proud of her he thought his heart would burst.

Finally, she broke free and stumbled toward him. "I'm exhausted, and my feet are screaming at me to take a load off."

"I've got just the thing." Brawley went to his Tahoe and came back with the old red-and-black-checked blanket they'd used for their picnic at the lake. He spread it over the grass.

He bowed low, removed his cowboy hat, and placed it over his heart. Taking her hand, he helped her down.

"Cowboy chivalry at its finest."

The moon rose in the sky, and, gradually, people headed to their trucks and cars. Things wound down quickly. Ty and Sophie said good night and bundled their boys off. Cash and Annie stopped by to tell them they were leaving.

Mr. Sadler pulled the plug on the music and locked up.

Finally, they were alone under the stars. The bonfire crackled and sparks flew into the night sky. The temperature had dropped, and a slight breeze lifted strands of Maggie's hair as they sat hip to hip on the blanket.

"When I heard you were leaving for New York, my stomach took a nosedive," Brawley said. "Selfishly, I wanted you here when I came back."

"That's not selfish."

"Yes, it is. I left for college and stayed away."

She nodded. "I never expected that. You hurt me, Brawley."

"I did, and it was the biggest misstep of my life." He took a deep breath. "You told me earlier I'd have to decide for myself what I needed to say. You were right. I'm not sure, though, if I can put my feelings into words."

"Try."

He rubbed a thumb over the back of her hand. "Growing up, I felt like my whole life had been planned for me. By others."

"And I was doing the same thing. Assuming we'd get married, have kids—"

"I let you believe that, Maggie, because I wanted it, too. But then I got a taste of the rest of the world, of the possibilities, and I couldn't give it up. Not for anything or anybody. I needed to find myself."

"I can understand that."

"Yeah, I think you can. You needed to find yourself, too. It's why you went to New York. We're kindred spirits, Red. Too bad that's what's been keeping us apart."

He took her hand. "We wouldn't have lasted, Maggie, if we'd married way back then. Both of us would have given up our dream. A year, two at the most, and we'd have ruined what we had."

"So you did it sooner."

"No! Yes. I guess." He raked fingers through his hair. "I figured without me in the picture, you'd go off to that fancy design school you'd been yammering about."

"Yammering?"

"Don't nitpick. Pops offered to send you. To pay the freight."

"I stayed here. At first because I thought you might come back. Then Grandma got sick, and Pops needed help. After she passed, well, I like it here. I worked hard and opened my shop. I was happy. It was what I wanted."

"I see that now. You belonged here, not in some big city. And before you go getting your back up, that's not a bad thing. I'm not slamming you. I'm complimenting you. You knew, even then, where you belonged, where your heart was. It took me years to come back to mine."

Tears threatened, and she blinked them away.

"What do you want now, Maggie? From life."

She wanted to say, "You, just you." But she bit the words back, figuring that wasn't what he'd want to hear. Instead, she said, "Let's talk about you. What do you want?"

"Me?"

"Do you still feel penned in by the small town atmosphere? The lack of fancy restaurants and shops? The lack of privacy?"

"No, I don't. That piece of land I showed you out by the lake?"

"A slice of heaven."

"I bought it."

She drew back. "You did? Oh, Brawley, that's fantastic!"

"I hoped you'd feel that way because I intend to build a house on it. You asked me what I want. That's it. I want to wake up every day for the rest of my life right there."

"That would be wonderful."

"Yes, it would." He took her hand. "The thing is, Maggie, I need someone to share it. I need you. I want you there beside me every morning."

"You do?"

"I do."

A nervous half-laugh escaped her. "That sounds like a proposal."

"Yes, it does, doesn't it?" He kissed her fingertips.

Maggie could barely catch her breath. He had to feel her heart racing; he could probably hear it.

Right there in the middle of town, beside the flickering bonfire, Brawley dropped to one knee. "Maggie Sullivan, I love you. You're my first love and my last love. How about you design another wedding gown? For yourself this time. For our wedding. Will you put me out of my misery and marry me?"

"Oh." She raised a hand to her mouth. "Are you serious?"

"For Pete's sake, Red, I'm down on my knee. I'm asking you to marry me. I understand you need to go back to New York. We'll work it out. I don't expect you to give that up."

She shook her head. "You were right, Brawley, when you said I'm not a big city girl. I've already decided to stay right here. I'll fly back East on an as-needed basis. I'm Texas through and through."

"When did you decide that?"

"Last week."

A lopsided grin curved his lips. "I have this, too." From his back pocket, he withdrew a jeweler's box and flipped it open.

Light from the bonfire caught on the magnificent emerald, flanked on either side by a diamond.

"Brawley. I don't know what to say."

"Say yes."

"Yes! Yes, yes, yes." She flung her arms around his neck and kissed him.

He drew her close. When they finally parted, he whispered, "If you don't like the emerald, we can exchange it for a diamond. I saw this, though, and..." He shrugged. "The fiery green made me think of you."

"I love it." She held out her hand.

As he slid the ring on her finger, she said, "I love you, Brawley Odell."

"That's the best news I've ever heard, Red, 'cause I've tried and tried, but I just can't stop lovin' you."

Grandma Trudy's Chocolate Pie Recipe

This pie combines the flavors of chocolate, marshmallow, and malt, and doesn't require baking. What could be better? This is a great make-ahead dessert.

- 2 cups miniature marshmallows
- ½ cup semisweet chocolate pieces
- ½ cup milk
- ¼ tsp salt
- 1 cup whipping cream
- ¼ cup chocolate malted milk powder
- 1 tsp vanilla
- 1 9-inch prepared chocolate graham cracker crust
- Chocolate shavings or chopped pecans for decorating (optional)

Combine marshmallows, chocolate chips, milk, and salt in a microwave-safe bowl. Set the microwave to medium and melt, stirring occasionally. Do not let the ingredients boil. Cool until slightly thickened.

In a mixing bowl, combine whipping cream, malted milk powder, and vanilla. Beat until very thick. Fold in the chocolate-marshmallow mixture.

Spoon this filling into the chocolate graham cracker crust, and chill at least three hours before serving.

If desired, decorate the top of the pie with chocolate shavings or chopped pecans.

Not ready to leave Maverick Junction?

See the next page for an excerpt from

Somebody Like You

Chapter One

You've got to be kidding me."

Annelise Montjoy motored her Harley along what appeared to be the town's main street. This was Maverick Junction?

A blue Cadillac, surely old enough to be in a museum, was parked nose-in to the curb. An incredibly ugly dog sat in the front seat.

Thank God, this, the final destination of her cross-country trip from Boston, was temporary. It looked like the kind of place you ran *away* from, not toward. If luck was on her side, she'd be out of here in a couple of weeks at the most.

And then a store door opened and her breath caught. *Go, Texas!* Look at that cowboy. So different from any of the men in her life. So...intriguing. She slowed to nearly a standstill and watched as he swiped an arm across his forehead, then dumped a grocery bag in the back seat of the old Caddy.

Cracking open a bottle of water, he turned his head in her direction. Her breath hitched as his gaze ran lazily over her, her bike. Then he snagged a Styrofoam cup from inside his car and filled it before setting it on the blistering pavement for the dog waiting patiently beside him.

Leaning against the faded fender, he thumbed back his battered Stetson and chugged the rest of the water. Twisting the cap back on, he tossed the bottle into the recycling bin beside the grocer's door.

Annelise pulled her bike into a parking space across the street, deliberately turning her back on the stranger. While his clothes might have been stereotypical cowboy—worn jeans, a faded T-shirt, cowboy boots, and hat—he took everything from simmer to boiling point. The jeans hugged long legs, while the shirt stretched taut across his muscled chest. There was something very alluring about him and that surprised her. He wasn't the kind of man she was usually drawn to.

He shouldn't appeal to her.

He did.

Not so much as a breeze stirred. The flag on the post office hung limp, and the cheerful red, white, and blue balloons someone had hung outside a beauty salon drooped listlessly.

Unable to stop herself, she peeked in the bike's rearview mirror. Cowboy was bent over, talking to the dog. Quite a view, but she wasn't here to admire a fine jean-clad butt. She needed something cold to drink and something light to eat. Then she'd go in search of Dottie Willis and the apartment she'd rented over the Internet. Maverick Junction, Texas. Annelise wished she was driving through, wished she could view it as simply a spot on the map where she'd stopped for lunch one summer day.

Well, she'd just have to work fast.

But before she'd even taken two steps, her cell rang. She checked caller ID, blew out a huge sigh, and dutifully answered.

"Annelise, where are you? When are you coming home?" Her mother's voice sounded strained.

"Don't worry, Mom. Are you and Dad okay?"

"We're fine."

"Grandpa?"

"He's had a good day. A good week, actually." Her mother hesitated. "He misses you."

"I miss him, too."

"Then come home."

"I can't."

"You're being selfish."

"No, I'm not. I'm trying to help while the rest of you stand by and do nothing."

"We're respecting Vincent's wishes."

Her grandfather, her strong, always in control grandfather, had been diagnosed with acute myeloid leukemia. After aggressive treatment by the country's best doctors, Vincent Montjoy was in remission. But the prognosis wasn't good. Her grandfather needed a bone marrow transplant, and none of the family matched.

And then, Annelise's whole world had flipped upside down—again. There was hope. It turned out he might have a half sister. One who could carry the life-saving marrow match. One he'd adamantly forbidden anyone to track down.

Well, she would.

And that's why she was in Maverick Junction, Texas. Why she'd ridden her Harley here from Boston.

Her first stop had been at a sorority sister's whose husband was a whiz with both computers and genealogy. If anyone could ferret out the information she needed, it would be him. By the time she'd left the next morning, Ron had already been knee-deep in research for her.

But she hadn't taken into account the physical toll of riding the heavy motorcycle a couple thousand miles. By the time she'd been on the bike for an eight-hour stretch, her butt and legs ached. Sharing the highway with semis, hour after hour, alone, was no picnic.

"Annelise Elizabeth Katherine Montjoy, you *will* get on a plane today and come home. We'll arrange transport for that motorcycle of yours."

"Mom—"

"Not another word, honey. Tell me where you are, and I'll phone you back once your travel arrangements are made. Silas will pick you up at the airport."

"No."

Her mother sighed. "You're sure you're safe? Nobody—"

"I'm fine, Mother. Believe me. I'm right where I need to be." With that, she hung up.

Guilt nagged at her. When you had as much money as her family, the threat of kidnapping always hung over you. For as long as she could remember, she'd had her own bodyguards. Which equaled no privacy. Two muscle-bound men tagging along had turned more than one date into a fiasco.

But she couldn't let her parents or her grandfather worry. She'd call her cousin. Later. Right now, she was thirsty. She headed for the café.

* * *

Seated toward the back of Sally's Place, Annelise heard the door open and close. The bell overhead jingled as outside heat rushed in. Without even looking, she knew who'd blown in with it. Well, he was no concern of hers. In all fairness, she doubted there was anywhere else to eat lunch in this one-pony town.

Annelise went back to studying the menu. Chili, country-fried steak, burritos, enchiladas, and just about anything that could be deep-fried.

A pair of dusty boots stopped at her table. She lifted her head and looked straight into the greenest eyes she'd ever seen. For an instant, all sense left her; speech deserted her.

"Seems there're no tables left," Cowboy said. "Mind if I sit with you?" Without waiting for an answer, he pulled out a chair.

She blinked, sanity returning. Her gaze swept the wealth of unoccupied tables. "No empty tables?"

"Well—" He held out his hands, palms up.

Up close, Cowboy was wicked handsome. If she wasn't dead set on settling in today so she could head over to Lone Tree tomorrow— "Actually, I'm afraid I do mind."

He cocked his head, tipped back his cowboy hat. "Not very neighborly."

"Good thing I'm not your neighbor, then."

"Ouch." He grimaced. "I don't bite, and I've had all my shots."

Sadly, she shook her head. "I suppose someone told you that line was cute."

"Nope." He looked at the chair, then back at her.

"I don't mean to be rude, but I have a lot on my mind, and I really don't want company."

"Okay, let's head at it from a different direction. I do. Need company, that is. I've been out on the ranch with nothing but surly bulls and even meaner cowhands for way too long. Sure would be a pleasure to sit across from you for a few minutes. I won't hold you up. Honest. When you're ready to go, you go."

Her mouth dropped open. "Are all Texans this persistent?"

He narrowed his eyes in consideration. "We might be. Guess that's why we lost so many good men at the Alamo. Texans hate to throw in the towel. Never can tell when things might start going your way."

Despite herself, Annelise laughed. She hadn't expected such a rough-and-tumble-looking cowboy to be so optimistic.

The owner chose that moment to wander over. "Hey, Cash, ain't seen you in a while."

"Been busy breaking in a couple new horses and doing some branding. So, how's my favorite gal, Sally?"

"My feet hurt, and my cook's throwin' a tantrum. Other than that, all's good." Sally pushed at frizzy blond hair and snapped her gum. "How 'bout you?"

"Can't complain. Tell you what I'd love right now, though. A tall glass of your sweet tea. Lots of ice." He dropped into the chair beside her.

Annelise gaped at him. Cowboy was one smooth operator.

"Comin' right up. How 'bout you, sweetheart? You want some tea?"

"Yes. That would be wonderful. Unsweetened, please. And I'd prefer to drink it without company." She shot Cash a get-lost look. He simply smiled back.

Sally's gaze shifted between the two of them. When Cash made no move to change tables, she asked, "Need a minute to look at the menu?"

"No. I'd like your house salad with vinaigrette dressing on the side."

"That's gonna be your lunch?" Cash scowled. "That's all you're getting?"

Annelise sat up straighter. "I hate to be rude, but I have a lot to do today. I came in for lunch. Not company."

"Understood."

Still, he didn't move.

What was with him? So much for Texans being gentlemen. Anger, an emotion she rarely allowed herself, lapped at her. Mentally counting to ten, she turned her attention to Sally. "Just the salad, please."

"That's not enough," Cash said.

"Who are you? The lunch patrol?"

"You'd dang well be eating better if I was. I'd order a nice steak, some hand-cut fries, and a big old piece of Ms. Sally's apple pie à la mode for you."

"For lunch?"

"Darn tootin."

"I'll stick with my salad, thanks."

When their waitress headed off, Cash said, "You're sure more hospitable with her than you are with me."

She shrugged. "Like I said, you can move to another table if you'd like."

His gaze traveled past her, and he stood suddenly. "Excuse me."

More than a little disappointed, she turned in her chair and watched him cross the room, his stride easy. Despite what she'd said, a traitorous part of her had actually hoped he'd stay.

He walked over to where an older woman struggled to slide her chair from the table. Giving her a quick kiss on the cheek, he reached out to her. "Can I help?"

With a sigh, the woman laid a shaky hand in his. "This getting old isn't for sissies." Standing, she said, "You're a good boy, Cash Hardeman. But that doesn't mean I've forgotten about the snake you and Brawley Odell put in my desk."

He picked up her purse and carried it with him as he walked her slowly toward the door. "You've got a memory like an elephant, Mrs. Sandburg."

"And don't you forget it." At the door, she called out, "Sally, I left the check on the table. That pie of yours was as good as ever."

"See you next week," Sally answered.

"You bet." She patted Cash's cheek. "I can manage from here. Tell your mother hello for me when she and your dad get home."

"Will do." He waited till she started down the walk and then returned to Annelise's table.

Something about the easy candidness of this Texas cowboy tugged at her. His kindness touched her heart. But she needed to stay focused on the reason she'd come.

"So." He reached for the tea Sally slid him and took a long drink of the cool, soothing liquid. Setting it down, he asked, "Where were we?"

She raised her chin a notch. "I'd just told you that you could move if you didn't like my company."

"Right." He grinned. "I like it fine, thanks. You have a name?"

"Yes. I do."

"Ah." He nodded. "But you're not willing to share." He shot out a hand toward her. "I'm Cash. Cash Hardeman."

"I heard." She hesitated, then sighed and extended her own hand. "Hello, Cash. I'm Annelise."

"Nice to meet you, Annelise. You just get that bike?" He nodded toward the street. "Must've paid through the teeth for it."

"My guilty pleasure." She smiled. The bike represented her first rebellion—her first step toward independence. "I've had it for almost a year now. Some friends wanted to do the fall leaf tour on motorcycles. One of them took me to a Hanniford grocery store parking lot after hours and taught me how to ride. Then he helped me pick out a bike. My father about had a conniption."

Cash laughed. "I can imagine."

"Why?"

"Big bike for a wom—anybody to handle."

"Oh, good save." She laughed and shook her head. "You're fast."

"You'd better believe it." He studied her a minute. "The fall leaf tour? So you're from New England, Annelise?"

Her eyes shuttered. She'd screwed up. "No. I was there visiting." She almost choked on the lie, but she had no choice. His expression said he wasn't buying it. Well, too bad. Once she left this café, she'd never see Cash Hardeman again. A chance meeting. That's all this was. It made no difference whether or not he believed her.

"You ride a lot?" he asked.

"Unfortunately, no. I took the bike out for two weekends last fall and it's been parked ever since. Till this trip."

"Too bad." He swiped at the water ring on the table.

Her eyes widened. Through the front window, she watched the cowboy's mud-brown dog sail through the air and scramble into the old car.

"Cash?"

"Hmmm?"

She pointed toward the window. "That big, hairy dog of yours just executed the best impersonation of Superman I've ever witnessed."

"Huh?"

"The animal may or may not be able to leap tall buildings, but he sure managed to clear the door of that big old monstrosity you're driving. Right now, he's working his way through the groceries in the back seat."

"Oh, brother!" Cash jumped up and ran outside to salvage what he could.

She watched him go and stabbed a forkful of lettuce, wishing the salad would morph into that juicy steak he'd suggested. Oh, well, she sighed. Some things weren't meant to be.

* * *

Two steps out the door, the heat sucker-punched Cash. And instead of sitting inside drinking iced tea with Ms. Ride-into-town-on-a-Harley, he was heading out to deal with his scoundrel of a dog.

"Staubach! What in the hell am I supposed to tell Rosie about her groceries, huh? Shame on you!" he scolded.

And shame on me, he thought, *for leaving the dog alone.* Still…Annelise was some looker. All that black hair and those intense, ice-blue eyes. And the body. Whoa, boy!

Okay, she was about as friendly as a mama bear with week-old cubs. But if they'd been able to finish their lunch together, he might have been able to change that.

She hadn't given him a last name. What was that beautiful thing hiding? Or, maybe, she really, truly hadn't wanted to sit with him. Didn't want to exchange names.

Her voice held a hint of an accent. New England definitely, despite what she'd said. Maybe Boston? Well, whatever. The voice was hot. Silk. And though she had started off sounding totally teed off, he'd heard amusement and a sense of humor creep in.

He tossed the now nearly empty sack of groceries into the trunk. When he looked up, he saw Annelise at the counter, paying for her lunch. Might as well run the ad over to Mel in time for tomorrow's edition. Looked like he'd struck out with the tempting Ms. Cool Eyes. Time to pack up his bat and ball. Game over.

No doubt she planned to hop on that hog and ride out of Maverick Junction without a backward glance. Too bad. He'd have liked more time with her. Time to dig a little deeper. Unless he was mistaken, and he rarely was, there was more to Annelise than met the eye. She might ride a Harley and wear leather, but everything else about her screamed class and money, pampering and top-notch schooling.

Her hands were manicured to within an inch of their lives. The diamonds that winked at her ears could feed a small third-world country. Yeah, the lady had been indulged.

Maybe he had been, too, but to a far lesser degree.

His gaze landed on the Caddy, and he ran a hand over the hood. God, he loved this thing. He had a lot to thank the old man for. And one very good reason—no, make that two—for being royally irritated with his grandpa. But he wasn't about to travel that road right now.

Reaching under the front seat, he found the folder with the newspaper ad he'd put together last night. Time to hire some help. As much as the old guy would fight him about it, Hank, whom he'd more or less inherited from Gramps along with the Caddy, couldn't handle the responsibility of the barn area alone anymore.

"Come on, Staubach." The dog's ears perked up, and he came to heel. Cash took another look at the dusty black-and-chrome Harley, and his stomach knotted in lust. Both the bike and its rider were double-take worthy.

Black bike, black helmet, black shades, black leathers and shirt. One cool lady. One heck of an attitude.

And that mouth. Oh, yeah. He'd give up a Monday-night football game or two for a taste of that.

See the next page for an excerpt from

Nearest Thing to Heaven

Chapter One

Not fair!"

Forehead pressed against the icy windowpane, Sophie stared out at the gray Chicago skyline. The mere thought of hopping on a plane made her palms damp.

And now this weather.

Sighing, she sipped from her mug of cocoa and fingered the amethyst in her pocket.

Mother Nature, who'd either gotten up on the wrong side of the bed or suffered from a major case of PMS, was throwing herself one monstrous, rip-roaring tantrum. During the course of a single hour, the sun had disappeared and left behind a low, ominous cloud cover. The temperature had dropped almost twenty degrees.

A mix of snow and rain spit against the glass. Even tucked away in her fourth-story apartment, Sophie swore she could hear the slush on the sidewalks contracting and solidifying to ice. Her taxi ride to O'Hare would be a slip-sliding, horn-honking nightmare.

Only mid-November and already the temperature had dipped below freezing. Dirty snow and boot-soaking slush blanketed the sidewalks. Frigid gusts of wind, intent on seek-and-destroy missions, whipped off Lake Michigan and zeroed in on pedestrians unlucky enough to be out and about.

But by tomorrow, none of this would matter. This afternoon, nerves or not, Sophie fully intended to be on a flight headed to Texas, sipping a glass of wine, and eating the last of her carefully hoarded birthday stash of Godiva.

Breathing deeply, she turned her back on the ugly outdoor scene. Enya's ethereal voice poured from her stereo and relaxed her... until she glanced at the clock. Shoot! Where had the morning gone?

Her suitcase—her still-empty suitcase—lay open, dead-center on her bed.

With this weather, she'd need an extra half-hour to make it to the airport. Checking the time again, she slapped her forehead, upset with herself. She'd procrastinated—again. Now? She had ten minutes. Ten lousy minutes to pack. Adrenaline surged through her. Being on that plane when it took off wasn't optional. She had a wedding to attend. Thank God it wasn't hers.

What should she pack for Maverick Junction, Texas? She'd only been there once before. She'd flown in with her aunt and uncle who'd hoped to talk some sense into her cousin. Turned out they didn't need to. Annelise's cross-country trip on her Harley had already accomplished that. They'd stayed all of one afternoon.

But that was then, and this was now. In a panic, Sophie studied her closet's contents, an eccentric mix of vintage pieces and quirky thrift store finds. Last time, like an idiot, she'd taken white silk to wear to a Fourth of July barbecue at the Hardeman ranch.

The memory brought to mind a handsome cowboy whose kid had dumped his cherry soda in her lap... and the way said cowboy had tried to wipe it clean. Whew! Maybe she should stick her head out the window and cool off.

Ty Rawlins. So hot she could almost forget he cowboyed for a living. The man was something else. Yeah, and wasn't that the truth?

How about starting with the fact he had three-year-old triplets? No, they'd turned four in August, hadn't they? Annelise had mentioned a birthday party.

Three, four. Made no difference. Anyway you cut it, it still added up to three little boys. And didn't that cool a gal off faster than any Chicago winter. Yikes. She loved kids. Loved spending time with them. But a mother? She didn't see herself in that role. Didn't know if she had enough to give a child.

Toss in the fact that Ty was a widower, to boot. Talk about baggage. *Three* little ones? And a dad who'd lost the woman he loved? She'd have to be insane to jump into that mess.

Insane? Her? No. Behind on her work deadline? Definitely.

And if she didn't meet it, she'd also find herself behind on her mortgage—and out on her butt on that ice-covered sidewalk.

All that had to wait, though, because this weekend her cousin, her BFF, was tying the knot. Annelise, who'd grown up in the lap of luxury, was marrying a cowboy. An honest to God cowboy. Sophie still couldn't quite wrap her head around that.

And now she had six minutes. Sophie grabbed clothes and stuffed them willy-nilly into her bag. She opened drawers and pawed through them, pulling out everything she might need and dumping it in her suitcase. She added her iPod to her carry-on along with her pouch of crystals.

Her bedroom looked like a hurricane had roared through. Her fingers itched to set it to rights, but there simply wasn't time.

Or was leaving it like this tempting fate? Her fingers found the amethyst in her pocket, stroked its smooth surface. No time. She had to go.

Satisfied she'd done all she could, she slung her carry-on over her shoulder, zipped her large suitcase, and, with one last look around, rolled it out to the living room. She had one hand on the doorknob when her phone rang.

Without thought, she answered—and instantly regretted it.

Nathan.

"Hey, beautiful," he said. "What are you up to?"

Her stomach dropped, and she leaned against the jamb. "Actually, you just caught me. I'm heading out the door as we speak. I'll be away for a few days."

"Business?"

"No."

"Want company?"

A low-grade headache instantly took root. Her neck and shoulder muscles tightened, and she wet her lips. "No, I don't."

She hated that he forced her to walk so close to rude.

"Where are you going?"

"Out of town."

Uncomfortable silence fell between them.

"You won't even tell me where you're going?" Petulance seeped into his voice.

She closed her eyes and breathed deeply. "Nathan, we've had this talk before."

"What talk?"

Okay, now he was being deliberately obtuse. "Look, I have a plane to catch."

"What talk, Sophie?" His voice lost the wheedling tone and took on a harder, demanding quality.

"This isn't a good time—"

"It's the perfect time."

"Okay." Resolve squared her shoulders. "We decided this wasn't going to work. That we both needed to move on with our lives. Separately."

"*You* decided."

Her pulse kicked up a notch. She hated confrontation, but she couldn't give in on this.

"Fine." Her carry-on slid off her shoulder, and she hitched it back up. "You're right. *I* decided."

"I figured by now you'd have changed your mind."

Oh, boy. This had been hard the first time—and the second and third times. She didn't want to rehash it. Why couldn't he simply accept they were done?

Actually, they'd never really started. Nathan Richards. Good-looking, successful, and, at first blush, personable. They'd dated a couple times and had fun. Then he became possessive. Very possessive. He started showing up at her door. At the grocer's. At the theater.

Truth? He spooked her.

"I haven't changed my mind. I'm not *going* to change my mind. Good-bye, Nathan." She hung up and stared at the ceiling. She'd been foolish to get involved with him, but smart to end things.

Her plants. In her hurry, she'd nearly forgotten about them. Dropping her bag to the floor, she moved to the window. Scooping up pots of herbs and lavender, she walked across the hall to her neighbor's.

Dee was at work, so Sophie set the plants in the hallway outside her door. Rushing back into her apartment, she scrawled a quick note.

Take care of my babies for me, Dee? Thanks so much! You're a doll!

Love, S.

She propped the card against the pale blue pot of English lavender. Okay. That was taken care of. Her plants wouldn't wither and die while she played bridesmaid.

The heat kicked on, reminding her to adjust the thermostat before she left. This summer had been a scorcher, and she'd practically lived on Lake Michigan in her little sailboat. But winter had come roaring in early, teeth bared. Only a few weeks into colder weather, and she was tired of it already.

This wedding might be exactly what the doctor ordered. Time and space should cool Nathan's heels while sunshine and warm weather cured her sudden lack of creativity.

Speaking of... She slid her laptop into its case in the happy event her muse stirred. Even with all the pre-wedding madness, she should be able to sneak in a few minutes of work time.

If she planned to catch that flight, there was no more time to fuss. Sophie turned off the lights, locked her door, and headed for the elevator. Unconsciously, her hand slipped into her pocket to touch the amethyst again.

As she let herself out of the building, she glanced cautiously up and down the street. She wouldn't have put it past Nathan to have called from right here on her doorstep.

Not a soul in sight.

About the Author

Lynnette Austin grew up in Pennsylvania's Allegheny Mountains and moved to upstate New York, then to the Rockies in Wyoming. Presently she and her husband divide their time between southwest Florida's beaches and Georgia's Blue Ridge Mountains. She has a master's in educational leadership and taught middle school language arts before leaving to write full-time. Her books have been finalists in Romance Writers of America's national Golden Heart contest, PASIC's Book of Your Heart contest, and Georgia Romance Writers' Maggie contest. *Somebody Like You* is the first in her Maverick Junction series, followed by *Nearest Thing to Heaven* and *Can't Stop Lovin' You*. Her other books, written as Lynnette Hallberg, include *Enchanted Evening, Moonlight, Motorcycles, and Bad Boys, Chantilly Lace and a Pretty Face, Night Shadows*, and *Just a Little White Lie*. Lynnette loves to read, write, and lose herself in her characters' world. She also enjoys traveling—always on the lookout for new characters or a new story. Visit Lynnette at www.authorlynnetteaustin.com.